JENNY PATTRICK is a writer and former jeweller whose eight previously published novels, including *The Denniston Rose*, its sequel *Heart of Coal*, the Whanganui novel *Landings*, and *Inheritance*, set in Samoa, have all been number-one bestsellers in New Zealand. In 2009 she received the New Zealand Post Mansfield Fellowship. In 2011 she and husband, musician Laughton Pattrick, published the children's book and CD of songs, *The Very Important Godwit*.

JENNY PATTRICK

LEAP OF FAITH

BLACK
SWAN

BLACK SWAN

UK | USA | Canada | Ireland | Australia
India | New Zealand | South Africa | China

Black Swan is an imprint of the Penguin Random House group of companies, whose addresses can be
found at global.penguinrandomhouse.com.

Penguin
Random House
New Zealand

First published by Penguin Random House New Zealand, 2017

10 9 8 7 6 5 4 3 2 1

Text © Jenny Pattrick, 2017

Cover design by Kate Barraclough © Penguin Random House New Zealand
Text design by Emma Jakicevich © Penguin Random House New Zealand
Cover images by Denys C Whyte (train over Makatote viaduct) and Parker Deen/istock (boy)
Back cover image: Camp life in the New Zealand bush: Alexander Turnbull Library, Ref C-065-006
Prepress by Image Centre Group
Printed and bound in Australia by Griffin Press,
an Accredited ISO AS/NZs 14001 Environmental management systems printer

A catalogue record for this book is available from the National Library of New Zealand.

ISBN 978-0-14-377091-6
eISBN 978-0-14-377092-3

penguin.co.nz

For my publisher, Harriet Allan,
who has overseen every one of my nine novels
with exceptional skill and grace.

Volcanic Plateau 1908

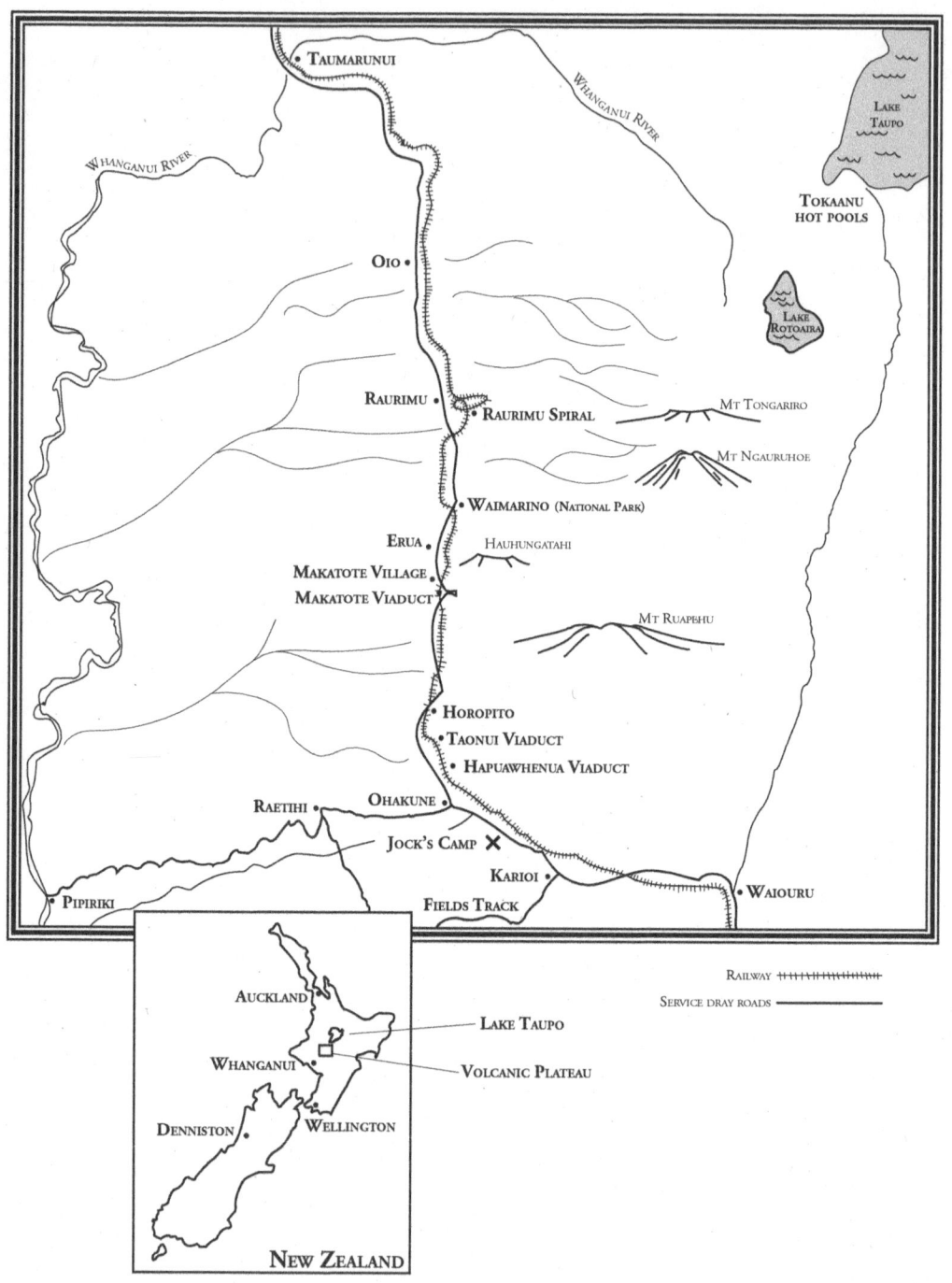

OBSESSIONS

In 1987 we walked from The Junction at Ohakune, across the road bridge, under the railway line and along a dirt road north. There was a new attraction at the old Hapuawhenua viaduct. It was, in fact, AJ Hackett's first installation of a bungy jump — an experimental and controversial enterprise at the time. The electrification of the Main Trunk Line had allowed for speedier trains; the curve on the wonderful Hapuawhenua viaduct was too tight for such speed, so a new viaduct had been built further down the valley. Hackett's bungy jump off the old viaduct was drawing crowds of spectators and a handful of foolhardy jumpers.

The new viaduct was — still is — beautiful. A simple and elegant concrete curve set on six slender concrete pillars; a lovely contrast to the equally magnificent but more delicate tracery of the old steel Hapuawhenua. We walked down into the gully under the towering pillars and sat on sun-warmed rocks, overlooking the river. High above, a tiny figure hesitated on some kind of plank jutting from the steelwork of the old railway bridge. Then he fell.

Silently. We held our breaths as the rope followed him down, snaking and loose at first and then, at last, taking the falling man's weight. His head almost touched the bright, rock-studded water. We rose in alarm. Then the rope recoiled, hurling him upwards again, and down, up and down, like a rag doll, until that poor fellow finally came to rest, upside-down, ankles tightly bound, high above ground. Still he made no sound. We were the ones shouting.

Some kind of mechanism above lowered him slowly. The attendants by the river captured the rope and took him in their arms, righted his body and set him free.

Then the man shouted. A long, high scream — was it joy or relief? Pain, even? He set off running up the scree towards us, and paused, panting, as we clapped him. That unforgettable face! Eyes staring madly, stretched grin, head shaking a little. The dark hairs on the nape of his neck stood out stiffly. The picture of a man possessed. It seemed more than a simple adrenalin kick. He frightened me.

'I have to do it again,' he shouted, 'I have to!' And ran on up.

I took the photos to show my grandmother. She studied them closely: the modern bridge and then the old iron one: she had lived in the work camp when it was being built. Her crabbed old finger traced the figure of the man standing high against the sky, ready to jump. She dropped the photo and growled. There was no other word for that sound — an angry animal growl.

'That wicked, wicked man.'

She was remembering another time, a different man. I knew the story. She had told it many times — as a warning to her children and grandchildren. Perhaps that was why the fervour in the bungy man's eyes had frightened me.

Years later, long after my grandmother had died, we returned from visiting friends, driving from the north on the Waimarino plain towards the Makatote gully, one of my favourite pieces of road in all New Zealand. I stopped the car just before the road plunges down and got out, promising to be quick. A muddy track led through a patch of dark bush then out into lumpy scrubland. I scoured the scene, clumping over tussock, stumbling through mud puddles. Not a sign. Not one scrap of evidence. Once, a huge workshop had stood here, filled with machinery, electric hoists, steel drills, great girders and an army of workers. There had to be some relic. I scuffed the ground, hoping for a discarded rivet, a length of cable. Nothing. How was it possible? As if that miraculous engineering feat, the Makatote viaduct — longer and higher, even, than beautiful Hapuawhenua — had risen by the wave of some magician's wand.

We drove on down into the gully. That north side is dank, often icy, ferns dripping off the sheer walls. If there's no traffic — there was none that day — we often stop on the bridge to look down in wonder at the deep slot that the river has carved. Bush scrabbles over rocks right to the water's edge, boulders flung from the volcano in past times churn the water into bright spray. The mountain, Ruapehu, is framed in the V of the valley (I like to think that word derives from the shape of its initial). We drove on, up out of the gully. I turned into the lookout carpark and switched off the engine. Mark sighed but said nothing.

There stood the great Makatote viaduct, tallest of them all, the fine steel latticework still — more than a hundred years later — bringing trains safely over that terrifying gap, a straight line through empty air from ridge to ridge across the gully. That day, half of the ironwork was encased in scaffolding, which in turn was encased in grey plastic, trussed like a giant parcel. The other half was finished — the steel girders glistening handsomely in the afternoon sun. An army of men had worked on it for a year already, grinding off the old lead-based paint, bagging and carting away every last flake lest the endangered blue ducks and native fish below became poisoned; knocking out old rivets and screwing in new bolts, painting and repainting and topcoating — dark red paint like the original. A loving and careful reconditioning of a beautiful old lady.

Mark shifted in his seat. 'Time to move on?'

'Wait just a moment.' I wanted to watch the men silhouetted against the sky as they walked off the job, most carrying equipment — tools, sacks, machinery perhaps, you couldn't tell at that distance. They walked carefully along planks laid on the trusses just below the railway tracks. One by one they crossed, step after step, over the abyss. Were they afraid? Was that journey commonplace to them — or thrilling? I wanted to know.

'You're thinking about your grandmother. Her brother and his mates who painted it the first time.'

I was. My great-uncle had clambered up those girders — no scaffolding, no protective shield, no safety harness. How did they survive? Some didn't.

'Listen. This is the third time you've had me stuck here while you stared. You have become as obsessed as she was.'

'My grandmother obsessed? She was the one sane soul in all that mad fervour. She and her friend Rose, though Rose's sanity had, by all accounts, its own brand of madness. But that driven engineer; the temperance woman; the strange preacher. Gran saw clearly when others were swept along.'

'Isn't it time you wrote it then? Her story? Get it out of your system? You've been fiddling with it for years.'

'Yes.' I'd said it before. Difficult to tell it though, to get it right.

I should start with Billy.

AUTUMN 1907

Billy Cameron sets out for Makatote

A Sunday in May 1907 Billy Cameron, fourteen years old, his spirits as lively as the fiery red of his hair, set out through the bush towards Andersons' Workshop at Makatote. He went with his parents' somewhat anxious blessing and his brother Freeman's curse.

'It should be me going!' Freeman had raged, 'He's stealing *my* dream! What can Billy manage at the Workshop that I would not do ten times better?'

Jock tried to calm his son with reasoned argument. Freeman was stronger and bigger and was needed in the work gang. Billy had not the muscles yet for cutting away hillsides. The Andersons were hiring all sorts, and no doubt Billy's work would be menial — sweeping the factory floor maybe — nothing that Freeman would enjoy; nothing that would pay as well as the co-op gang.

None of these arguments placated the fuming Freeman, who had his heart set on working with machines; becoming an engineer, maybe. He turned his back as the rest of the family gathered to farewell Billy. His mother wrapped a hunk of bread and some bacon and a screw of tea, rolled the food in a square of oilcloth and shoved it inside Billy's bedroll. Goodness knows if even that would keep it dry. Sarah smiled at her youngest son who stood there jiggling with impatience to be off.

'Try and make a proper go of it, Billy love, none of your silly nonsense, mind. Time to earn your keep like a sensible lad.' She was worried though. Billy's head was off in some other world half the time.

His sister, Maggie, who did housework four miles up the road, had good advice. 'When you get to Ohakune, look for an engineer. They head out on horseback most days to inspect the workings. You might hitch a ride. Peter Keller, he's a nice man.' She grinned. Maggie was sweet on engineer Keller, without much hope that the busy man would ever notice her.

Billy nodded, suddenly overwhelmed by the farewells. He shook hands with his older brother Dirk and his father, gave his mother a quick hug, shouted some sort of garbled goodbye to Freeman who still sulked inside the tent, and set out into the rain.

The track through the towering bush was well enough formed, though muddy. In a year or two the railway would come along this line, but first it was a matter of digging away cuttings and filling gullies. And building great viaducts. Billy's heart lifted at the thought of that mighty work — bridging the deep gullies that the rivers from the mountain had cut in this wild land. He imagined — well, he found it hard to imagine *how* the viaducts were built. Soon he would know. He tramped on, skirting the deep and mud-filled ruts, hoping the rain might stop before nightfall.

Next morning, having sheltered under a lean-to at Ohakune and scrounged a hot drink from a worker up early and brewing at the entrance of his tent, Billy presented himself at the engineers' quarters. Sure enough, someone was heading north (not Mr Keller) who, laughing at the boy's cheeky plea, agreed to take him up the track a few miles. So all morning he rode piggyback, chattering and asking questions about the great viaducts that were being built. When the engineer reached his destination — a hillside half cut away by a formation gang — Billy hopped down, said his thanks and set out readily enough. From there on it was Shanks's pony and a solitary lunch under a huge sheltering beech tree. But Billy was resourceful and used to the life. He whistled as he swung along the rough service road. He wanted to arrive at Makatote in the morning, so as light began to fade he paid for a bite of food and a place to sleep in a loggers' tent. The loggers had not seen the Workshop but had heard tales of its size and grandeur. They had noticed three travellers passing through a day earlier in search of work there. Hundreds were employed, it was rumoured, paid a wage and given lodging. But pay was better in the Government co-ops.

'I know that,' said Billy, always ready to chatter. 'My da's a gang foreman back there a while. Jock Cameron. You know him?'

They did not. Must be a thousand men in the gangs at present and more employed daily. Billy rattled on in the face of their indifference. He wanted to build bridges and learn a proper trade and travel to other towns. Explore unknown mountains. Maybe become a surveyor's chainman. The loggers yawned and fell asleep.

But when Billy finally made it down into the devastation of the Makatote gully and back up the other side to where the Workshop stood against the sky, when he stood in that huge entrance and looked in, he could find no words. For minutes he stood on trembling skinny legs, mouth agape and eyes staring. Towering raw tree-trunks marched in two rows down each side of the building, holding up an iron roof. Even taller trunks supported the ridge. Men shouted and hurried, dragging long lengths of timber; great hoists groaned their way across the lofty spaces above, transporting girders. Everywhere there was the sound of hammering, of sledgehammers striking on metal. The noise took his breath away. For a while Billy's strong spirit failed him. This was too loud, too grand after the silence of the bush camp. He would never belong here. He turned and walked outside and away until the racket became bearable.

'Hey! You, boy!' On the edge of the great open yard, a dark-skinned fellow was sitting on a fallen log under a tree, grinning. 'Come on over!' He patted the log. 'Pretty damn noisy, eh?'

Billy nodded.

'Don't worry. You get used to it. You looking for work?'

'I thought so, but . . . I'm not sure.'

'Mr Pascoe, he's the boss. He wants every hand he can find. A good boss.'

Billy sat. His legs were still trembling, exhaustion or shock or both. He hid his shaking hands between his knees and tried a smile. 'Billy Cameron.'

The dark boy extended his hand. 'Ruri Rokipoto. I come from downriver. Papatupu. Where you from?'

'From a work camp the other side of Ohakune. Before that my dad hewed coal in the South Island. Before that Scotland.'

Billy was curious. He had known one or two natives working on the railway, but Ruri seemed more open, easier in his way of speaking. 'Do you work for Mr Pascoe?'

'Of course. Everyone does. He's in charge of it all. One day I'll be a big boss like him,' Ruri grinned, 'but maybe I'll take longer to get there. That boss fellow is only twenty-five. Bright man, eh?' He broke off a piece of the food he was chewing at and offered it. 'Hungry?'

Billy had seen smoked eel before but never eaten it. The meat was dark and tough and full of bones but delicious. He began to feel more like himself. 'So you don't mind that racket all day?'

Ruri laughed. 'I couldn't stand one minute of it. I work down in the gully. Plenty of work down there. Except not for the last week. We're waiting for cement to come through from the north, but this rain—' he wagged an admonitory finger at the sky — 'is holding up everything. The boss says we'll find our own cement from clay upriver if the supply doesn't make it soon. He's already made electricity from the river. Nothing stops Mr Pascoe, not even Tawhiri.'

'Who's he?'

'Tawhirimatea, god of rain. And wind, and thunder and storm. Seems like he's decided to throw all his bag of tricks at us this last year. My mother says he's angry over the railroad.'

'Do you think so, too?'

Ruri shrugged. 'Maybe. Maybe not. I think Mr Pascoe is strong enough to deal with him.' He winked. 'But I don't tell my mother that!'

A clap of thunder wiped the grin off both boys' faces. Ruri rolled his dark eyes. 'Aue! My big mouth.' He pointed to a clearing beyond the Workshop where a man holding an umbrella over his head was peering into the rain. 'That's the boss. Come on. I'll introduce you.'

The two boys dashed through the rain, laughing now that the thunder had grumbled away into the distance.

George Pascoe looked sternly at the two lads. 'Ruri, have you nothing better to do today than chatter to strangers?'

Ruri hung his head and shrugged, all his earlier confidence gone. Billy, on the other hand, was excited to be in the presence of the man in charge of all this. He stood as tall as he could manage against the wind and rain.

'Sir, I am Billy Cameron, come looking for work. Ruri here was helping me.'

For a moment Mr Pascoe said nothing. Billy could feel those sharp eyes scrutinising him from head to toe. 'You've come here on foot?'

'From the south, sir, four miles south of Ohakune. My dad—'

'I don't need the whole history, lad. How old are you?'

'Fourteen, sir, but I'm tougher than I look and used to rough work, and—'

The boss seemed distracted. He kept staring down the muddy road that cut through a wasteland of felled branches, stacked logs and timber. 'We can't take you on just now. Maybe in a week we'll try you out. Ruri, show him where the pay clerk's office is. Get him signed up on provision.'

'Sure, boss.'

'Is there room in your tent?'

Ruri looked doubtful. 'Not really, boss. Five already.'

Mr Pascoe frowned. 'Five? Who assigned you?'

Ruri looked at the ground. 'Not sure, boss.'

'I think you *are* sure. Tell Mr Fellows I said you and this lad were to have a tent between you. The next two lads to arrive can share with you. Understood?'

Billy piped up, excited now. 'I can set up a tent pretty smart, Mr Pascoe, you can leave it to me. I know how to—' He swallowed. How many times had his mam warned him to keep quiet at these times — that bosses don't take kindly to chatterboxes?

Ruri was still hesitant. He looked at his boss from under his eyebrows and made a writing gesture.

George Pascoe sighed, still peering into the rain, but he took out notebook and pencil and scrawled some words. 'I see, Ruri;

best make it official, eh? They giving you a bit of a run around?'

Ruri shrugged but took the paper. Mr Pascoe patted his shoulder. 'Never mind, boy, keep your head down. Work hard and you'll survive.' But then, before the boys could move away, the boss gave a great shout and slapped a hand around each curly head. 'Here come the Clarkin Brothers! Look, boys, look! Billy Cameron, you can start work tomorrow!'

Out of the mist and rain five huge horses, hitched three and two, plodded steadily towards them. They hauled a great wagon heaped high and tarpaulin-covered. Behind that came another load, and in the distance another dark shape toiling up the slope.

'Magnificent beasts, magnificent,' breathed Mr Pascoe. 'They could challenge Atlas himself. There'll be three tons on that wagon. Four maybe. Here is our cement, boys — please God, still dry — and our drilling machines and a new load of steel, if I am not mistaken. Well, boys! We are in business!'

The bogus evangelist

Sarah Cameron wiped damp hair from her eyes and looked again. Something strange about the man riding out of the bush from the south. She emptied the bucket over the moss where it might not add to the mud surrounding the tent and went inside to bang it down under the leak again. Back at the door, she realised what was out of kilter with the man: he was riding a thoroughbred! His mount, slick with rain and muddy to its hocks, picked its way slowly on delicate legs, tossing its head and shying when tree branches slapped. What was the point of bringing a thoroughbred into this wilderness? You could get a wage and fodder for a working half-draught like Jock's, or a full draught that her eldest had saved for and now owned outright, hiring it to the Public Works. She sighed. This poor wet fool would want hospitality, no doubt, and what had she to share? She went inside, hoping he would ride on.

'Glory, glory!' sang the man, outside the tent door now and obviously in no mind to move on. 'Glory to God in the highest!' His voice, high and lilting, reminded her of sunshine, of pleasant times in a warm climate. 'Good morning, Mrs Cameron! May I dismount?' He waited on his nervous, handsome bay until she returned to the opening.

'Have we met?' She stood there, one hand on the rough wood of the doorway, hoping to block this strange fellow from entering.

He laughed, and raised his sodden hat, revealing unusually long hair the colour of a rising moon. 'Have we met now? In this world, not to my knowledge, madam. In a previous — who knows?' Then, noticing perhaps her lack of enthusiasm, 'I met your good husband down the track away. He said you would have something for a traveller to eat if he was civil about his greeting.'

'Jock said that?' Sarah eyed him coolly. 'My husband said I would give you a meal?'

He cleared his throat and shrugged; shook the water off his hat.

'Sir, you look well enough fed, and we are scraping the bottom of the barrel until the bullocky makes it through. In this place we earn what we eat.'

The man laughed again. He dismounted quickly, gracefully, swung the reins over a branch, bowed slightly. 'You have caught me out in a lie, Mrs Cameron. I apologise. He said no such thing. My name is Gabriel Locke. May I at least come in out of the wet for a moment or two?'

Sarah removed her hand from the doorpost and stepped back inside. Gabriel Locke was a tall man, a little older than her boys but not yet thirty, at a guess. His yellow hair could have been a child's, but his face was long and his bright blue eyes set deep under fine, fair eyebrows. His woollen coat, sodden and sporting twigs and leaves from his ride, was nevertheless well cut: out of place in this rough work camp where everyone wore sacking or oilskins against the weather. He looked quickly around the tent, nodded as he noted the wooden floor, the iron fireplace and chimney, the glowing fire. Then walked over to stand, dripping, in its warmth.

'Thank you. You have a fine little home in this wilderness. Better than most I've seen in the camps.'

'Well you've not seen many, then. None of us would survive a winter here on the Plateau without a decent fire or planks to keep us from sinking into the mud.'

'Indeed, indeed. Would a cup of tea be too much to ask? Only if you have to spare.'

Sarah gave in. Gabriel Locke seemed pleasant enough though somewhat odd. And it was rare to have a man to talk to during the day. 'I have no milk. If you'll take it black, there is sugar.'

'Ah, Mrs Cameron, you are a saint in heaven. May I sit?' He sat anyway, humming a little tune and smiling at her. 'Praise the Lord for your kindness.'

Because there were three working men in the family, Public Works had supplied them with two large tents, which Jock had laced together to form a 'T'. Now from the inner room came a persistent coughing. Sarah set the kettle back on the fire. 'You'll have to excuse me for a moment.' She dipped a cupful of hot water and carried it in to Maggie, who sat on her stretcher, clutching her throat.

'It's sore.' Maggie's face was flushed, her red curls plastered to her forehead.

'I know it is, hen; try not to cough. Here, sip on this.'

'Who's that you're talking to?'

Sarah suspected that her curious daughter had forced herself into a spasm. 'Just a rider on his way to the depot. He'll be gone soon.'

'The way he talks — is he religious?'

Gabriel had come to the opening — a liberty in Sarah's opinion — and laughed. 'Well, young miss, I am indeed a man of

God. Well guessed. I am Preacher Gabriel Locke. May the good Lord bless you.'

He came forward and laid a long-fingered hand on Maggie's brow. Sarah wanted to snatch it away. What effrontery! As if he belonged.

Gabriel prayed in a light singsong, asking the Lord to heal the girl, to send His ministering angels to protect her against the bitter weather and so on and so forth. Sarah finally moved his hand and administered a sip of hot water. 'Thank you, Mr Locke, that will do,' she said firmly. 'My daughter needs to sleep. It's only a bit of a chest.'

His polite nod of acquiescence irritated her. Nothing seemed to unsettle the man. Sarah led him back to the fire and poured tea. She no longer felt ready for a chat. 'You'll need to report to one of the engineers at Ohakune. Mr Grice perhaps. He deals with placements. A couple of the co-op groups are in need of a man. It will take you a good half-hour's riding from here.'

'Well now, I see you would like to be rid of me. And so I will take my leave. But, Mrs Cameron, I build healthy souls, not railways and bridges. I am not after manual work.' He spread his fine white hands. 'As you can see. These are not made for grasping a pick and shovel.'

Sarah was puzzled. 'We have no church in these parts yet. The priest comes up from Pipiriki now and then. A few months ago the Anglicans sent a vicar to baptise and bury. What denomination would you be?'

'Why, I have my own preaching which needs no church, madam. It is sad news indeed that there is no church hereabouts. I am needed then. There will be brothers and sisters who are missing the word of the Lord. I have a mind to head on further to Andersons' Workshop at Makatote. They say there's a goodly number of souls there. And decent accommodation.' He stood, put down his tin cup and shook her hand. 'You have been very kind, Mrs Cameron, and I have stretched your patience, I see. Forgive me.'

His genuine smile and gentle manner charmed Sarah out of her mood. 'I am a practical woman, Mr Locke, with little time for prayers and such.'

'You possess a soul nevertheless, and I will pray for you and your daughter.'

A gust of wind shook the tent; raindrops fell down the chimney to hiss on the fire. Sarah bent to poke it into more vigorous life. 'I fear you will find many like me over at the Workshop. There is a great push on to complete the railway and little time for fancy words.'

This seemed at last to dent his good humour. He looked at her without expression. 'We will see, then. I generally succeed. Good day.'

At the door he paused and seemed lost in thought for a moment.

Sarah waited. What now?

Gabriel Locke sighed. His quiet words were silky. 'Mrs Cameron, when I administer the laying-on of hands, when my prayers are answered and the ailment is cured, it is customary for a grateful parent or patient to offer a coin or two.'

Sarah stared at the man.

'How else,' said Gabriel Locke, 'does a preacher survive in this world?' There was an edge to his voice now.

From the back room came another burst of coughing.

'Good day to you,' said Sarah firmly. 'A cup of tea for a prayer is good payment in my book. And she is not cured, as you may hear.'

The preacher, unsmiling, raised his hat and left.

Sarah turned to find Maggie standing watching at the door. Her cough, resounding a moment ago, seemed to have quietened. Sarah laughed at her. 'Well, miss, that cough was well timed. Did you hear the man? He asked for payment!'

Maggie grinned. 'My cough was better anyway. He did nothing to help it.'

'Don't think I didn't notice. Do you think I was harsh, hen? Not giving him a penny? He was nice enough. Kind, do you think?'

'I do not. Look at the way he treated his horse. Left it in the rain with no cover. Rode away without a pat or a kind word. I don't like him at all. Can I go back to work tomorrow?'

Sarah put an arm around her daughter's sturdy shoulders. 'We'll see. Maybe if the rain stops.'

Maggie, who didn't take kindly to staying indoors, threw her hands in the air. 'I'll *never* get back to work if we wait for the rain!'

An hour later Rusty, the half-draught, plodded into the little clearing pulling his burden of muddy workers. Already seven men had jumped off when their tents were reached. Now it was only Jock and his two sons, Dirk and Freeman, on the cart, back from a hard day's work at the cutting.

Jock, foreman of the co-op gang, was exhausted. Working in the rain with shovels, picks, horses and carts to cut a channel through a hillside half a mile south of the camp was no easy task. Underground in the mines had at least been dry. The cutting they were assigned was huge — both long and deep. Sometimes Jock felt that their picks and shovels were not equal to the task; that they'd never bring the level low enough for the bloody railway gradient. One in fifty. Even a powerful steam engine couldn't cope with steep inclines. Yesterday when engineer Keller came to measure, he said they still had forty feet to go. Forty grinding bloody feet through hard rock and solid papa! The tree-felling gangs were way ahead of them now, and the platelayers were complaining about being held up. Ninety miles of wilderness and broken terrain before the railheads finally joined. Tough work, and no fun in this wretched weather.

But today Jock's muddy face managed a grin. 'Good news!' he shouted as he unhitched Rusty. 'The bullock train has made it up from the river. The Works cart will bring food supplies through tomorrow, they say.' He patted Rusty's muddy coat. 'And the pay clerk's on his way. Put the kettle on for him, Sarah. Got to keep Mr Stone happy!' He led the big horse around to the slab lean-to behind the tent and rubbed him down with a bunch of ferns. 'There, my Rusty, there, good old fellow, you've earned your rest, by God you have today.' He filled a nosebag with the last of the oats and hitched it over Rusty's ears. He turned to his son. 'Come on, Dirk, Mother's waiting.'

But quiet Dirk was still lavishing attention on his horse Snow, brushing his wet coat, tying a canvas blanket over his shoulders. Animals came first with Dirk. Besides, Snow could pull two tons of rock and soil and was already learning from Rusty the trick of nudging the loaded cart down to the spillway. Snow was a clever worker in Dirk's eyes — and a useful earner; he was paid almost as much as a man for a day's work.

Jock shook his head to see Dirk take from his pocket a lump of bread to feed to his pig-dog. 'That should have been your lunch, son. You can't keep up this kind of work on an empty stomach.'

Dirk shrugged. 'It's only a scrap. Skipper's hungry, too.'

Jock, too tired to argue, squelched over to the tent door. He hung his oilskin on a nail and slapped at his muddy boots with a fresh bunch of fern.

'Lord, Sarah, wouldn't you think the sun might recognise the needy wee souls down here and show us a hint of things to come? Just a hint?' He dipped water from the brimming rain barrel, sluicing arms and hands and face before he entered.

Freeman had already washed and was sat at the rough plank table. Sarah slapped at his hand, which had strayed towards the hunks of bread. 'Wait for your da, you big lump, where's your manners?' But she smiled as she spoke. Lanky, good-natured Freeman had his mind set on other work. Engineering most likely — like young Billy, who had started at the Workshop last week. As soon as Jock could recruit another gang member, Freeman would be off to join his brother. Freeman was by nature a builder, not a hewer like his older brother and Da. He had fashioned the iron chimney, and loved to beat out the treacle tins to make cups and bowls and dippers.

He grinned back at his mother, drumming his fingers on the planks. 'We can eat up then, tonight? Finish off that bit of bacon if the supply's coming through? I'm famished, Mam.'

'You'll wait all the same.'

Freeman, seventeen and ginger-headed like his sister, sat on his hands and laughed. 'Hey, Mam, did that weird fellow come through? On the thoroughbred?'

'He did.'

'Was he singing holy songs?'

'I wouldn't know what he was singing. But he took it into his head to cure our Maggie of her poor chest.'

'The devil he did! Is she cured?'

Maggie appeared in the opening to the back room. 'I am

cured by my own self and Mam's soup. His hands were cold and slimy.'

'Well,' said Sarah, pleased to have most of her family safely through the day's work and home, 'his name is Gabriel Locke and he's off to save the souls of the men at Andersons' Workshop.'

Jock sat heavily, his face lined with exhaustion. 'This railroad brings all sorts, God knows, but I doubt Mr Locke will find converts. Our imp Billy will laugh him out of town, for one. '

Maggie and Freeman raised their eyebrows at that. Billy would believe any story if you told it with a straight face. They'd both tried it on. But their da looked too tired for an argument.

'Shall I bring you a tot, Da? There's enough for at least two.' Maggie loved her father and knew how quickly his colour returned after a draught of bootleg.

'Hush your mouth, hen,' said Sarah laughing at her cheeky daughter. 'The pay clerk will be here any minute.'

Jock put out his hand to ruffle Maggie's red curls. 'Mr Stone knows all about the bootleg. They all do, the bosses, and turn a blind eye. They know they get better work from us if we have our little sup.'

Maggie warmed a tin mug on the griddle and brought him his tot. 'Mrs Grice up at the village would never turn a blind eye, Da. She'd have you frying in the fires of damnation if she as much as smelled what's in this mug.'

'Well, Mrs Fancy Grice is not in charge, and for all her ferreting and threatening she has no idea where we get the stuff. You make sure you hold your tongue on that score, missy, when you're doing her scrubbing and what-not.'

Maggie laughed. 'I'm all innocence up there, Da. Don't you know she thinks me the sweetest little maid and feeds me pieces of her horrible cakes.'

Their laughter was interrupted by the sound of men outside. Sarah went to the door. Mr Stone sat there astride his big horse, his Winchester tucked into the dry of his coat but ready enough for any trouble. His broad-brimmed hat cascaded water down his back. 'I won't stop, Mrs Cameron,' he called, 'we're both dripping wet. We'll head straight on and get these precious bags inside. I'll see you no doubt tomorrow.'

His mounted escort, Sergeant Baker, nodded, tipped his hat and they both moved on.

Jock drained his mug and, in good spirits again, called for another. 'We'll see them alright. And claim our bonus. Lord what a temptation to be carrying all those sovereigns — thousands, must be, with the workforce on the line. Mr Stone's horse is a champion to carry that weight through the mud. Will you come up with us then, Maggie? Back to work?'

The driven railroad boss

When Jock had finally worked his way to the head of the queue, Paymaster Stone glanced up at him.

'Foreman Jock Cameron?'

Jock nodded.

'Engineer said you'd not reached your quota.'

Jock took breath to argue, but the paymaster held up his hand. 'But it is recognised that the weather played a big part in that. Mr Keller says you are to be paid the bonus.' He counted out sovereigns and shillings from the neat piles on his desk. Sergeant Baker, his beefy arms crossed over his broad chest, watched. But there was never any trouble. The men were keen to take their pay and head to the co-op shop.

'That's six pounds three shillings plus bonus of twelve and sixpence,' said Stone. 'Foreman's pay. Next?'

Freeman stepped up. His pay was a quarter of his dad's — two shillings and tenpence ha'penny a day, and only threepence more than Maggie earned as a maid, but together the family earned good money. Sarah would let Freeman spend threepence of his pay on something he wanted; the rest went into the family biscuit tin.

Later Dirk and Freeman, loading flour and bacon, a wonderful sack of potatoes and cabbages, tea and sugar onto the cart, saw their father approach Mr Furkert with some determination as he came out of his office. Freeman left his older brother to finish the loading and ran to hear what might be said; he hoped he might be the subject.

'A word, sir, if you please.' Jock was never fazed by rank or privilege: if he had something to say he'd say it straight out. Down in the mines he had earned a reputation as a unionist.

Mr Furkert paused, managing to indicate in the way he turned that he was a busy man and that this had better be brief. 'Your name?'

'Jock Cameron, foreman of the formation co-op on the Karioi to Ohakune section.' He motioned towards his sons. My boys Dirk and Freeman, also in the co-op.'

Mr Furkert shook Jock's hand. 'I remember now. You were a miner?'

'I was. A hewer and then an underviewer on Denniston. I was recruited from there. Thought I might try hewing above ground for a change.'

'Do you regret it?'

Jock shrugged. 'This weather has been a trial, Mr Furkert. It was always dry in the mines. But no. I enjoy the co-op life.'

'Your business with me?'

'Dynamite, sir. It is not well controlled. Many of our co-ops are using it. The men are carrying it inside their jackets. That is dangerous practice, sir, which I do not allow.'

Mr Furkert frowned. 'I should think not. Are the explosives overseers allowing this?'

'They turn a blind eye. They measure it out and see the men walk away with dynamite under their coat or in their pocket. If the stuff is too cold the charge will not go off.'

'And if it is warm and the man stumbles—'

'Exactly, sir. And we lose our bonus if we do not follow suit.'

'Your solution?'

'Warmed, jacketed containers to carry the explosives.'

Mr Furkert sighed. 'Well. Thank you Mr Cameron. I'll see what can be done.'

Freeman tugged at his dad's arm. 'Dad! Ask him.'

'One thing at a time, son,' said Jock, ruffling his son's hair. 'Safety first.'

But Mr Furkert had another matter on his mind. 'Cameron, in the next months there will be a big push to finish this railroad. I need more men. More engineers. Are there others on Denniston willing to come up, do you think?'

Jock considered this. 'I can think of a few. There's a bright young engineer I know. Pegged out the railway from mines to bins.' He chuckled, thinking of something private. 'He might come.'

'Good man. Come up to my office. Give my clerk some names.'

'Dad!' pleaded Freeman.

Dirk, who had joined the group, shoved an elbow in his ribs. 'Leave it, Free. Da needs you on the cutting. Think about Da for a change.'

This was a long speech for Dirk. Freeman looked at him in surprise — by which time the busy Mr Furkert was already off on another errand.

The crusading prohibitionist

Up at the engineers' quarters, Maggie giggled as she flung water at the wooden floor and scrubbed away. Mrs Grice was on her hobby-horse again. This time it was Gabriel Locke who received the harangue. The preacher, feet up against the stove, looked the picture of a settled man. It seemed he had the knack of worming his way into any situation.

'I hope you are not a drinking man, Mr Locke?'

'I am not, madam.'

Mrs Grice managed a prim smile. She tucked a fading lock back under her morning cap and poured a cup of tea for this suitable visitor. 'I have a difficult task ahead of me here, Mr Locke, very arduous.'

Gabriel nodded and sipped, rocking back a little on his chair. He noticed Maggie and tipped her a secret wink. 'Arduous, Mrs Grice?'

'You should know that this entire area — from Taihape to . . . well, some town far to the north — is dry.'

The preacher raised an eyebrow to the drizzle outside. 'Dry, Mrs Grice?'

Maggie scrubbed harder to hide her giggles.

'Dry, in the sense that no liquor in any shape or form may be sold here. Not one drop! Apart from weak hop beer and I would ban that, Mr Locke, if I had the power. The native leaders have requested this entire area be dry. The Government has decreed it, yet nothing is done to prevent the shocking lawlessness that goes on under our noses. Our very noses, Mr Locke!'

Gabriel gestured towards a flagon of liquor on the sideboard for anyone to see. 'Shocking, yes, I do see—'

Mrs Grice reddened. 'If I had my way that flagon would not be here. Mr Grice of course never touches a drop. But the other engineers . . . They obtain it legally, yes, bought in Taihape and carried up here, but what kind of example does that set the men? They see the engineers partaking and so they are led astray.' Mrs Grice heaved her large frame off her chair. 'Do you belong to the Alliance?'

'Ahh . . . I'm not sure—'

'For the Abolition of Liquor in this country.' Mrs Grice thrust a pamphlet into his hands. 'If you are not a drinking man then you must join us, Mr Locke. We are winning the battle! At the election last year three new areas were won over: Invercargill, Oamaru, Grey Lynn. Thirty-eight liquor licences lost. A glorious victory. I need recruits here in the King Country, Mr Locke. This, the very first area to become dry. There is backsliding. There are bootleggers. There are the droppers who creep in at night and supply the camps.' Mrs Grice paused to take breath; pressed a hand to her heaving bosom. Tears brightened her eyes.

Maggie stopped scrubbing. Such fervour, over a drink or two. Her dad was no drunkard; nor were any of the men in their co-op.

They just liked a drop in the evening to give them heart for the next day. She wanted to argue, but bit her tongue. She needed the job.

Gabriel Locke, attentive in the face of such an onslaught, put down his cup and stood. 'Well, Mrs Grice, I will pray for your cause, and will consider a sermon on the subject. God bless you and your work.' He turned to go.

Mrs Grice put out a hand to stay him. 'Oh, but Mr Locke, you have only just arrived. A kindred spirit in this wilderness—' She stood close to him, pink-faced and simpering in a way that Maggie found uncomfortable.

Mr Locke held her hand earnestly. And for too long.

'Perhaps, Mrs Grice,' he murmured, 'another wedge of your excellent cake to sustain me on my way?'

Mrs Grice hurried to cut and wrap cake, then added a precious apple from the engineer's bowl. An unwarranted liberty in Maggie's eyes.

'The Lord bless you, dear Mrs Grice.' The preacher pressed her hand again, bestowed a twinkling smile and left.

'Oh what a lovely man,' breathed Mrs Grice to no one in particular.

Mrs Grice, indisposed it seemed after such an emotional morning, took her midday meal in her quarters. Maggie carried her plate over to the rough hut where the Grices slept, then ran back to the main dining room. She loved to hear the engineers talk. Mr Grice was older but most of them were young men, lively and ready for any adventure.

Mr Keller was in especially good spirits. He poured a good measure of whisky. 'I have learned a new dance,' he said. 'The foxtrot. It's all the rage down at Raetihi and there is to be an evening next week where we are all invited.' He snatched up a chair and guided it tenderly among the laughing men, chanting 'Step, step, quick-quick step.' Seeing Maggie with the dish of potatoes, he shouted, 'Come on, miss, and I'll teach you!' But she wouldn't, not with all of them looking at her.

Mr Furkert came in and stood watching. The hilarity subsided. The new boss didn't have the easy way of his predecessor; even on a Saturday Mr Furkert expected his engineers to be focused on the job.

Maggie dumped the dish of potatoes on the table and went back for the cabbage. She kept her head down as she passed Mr Furkert. She'd left her hated apron back in the kitchen and he noticed every little detail. When she came back he was addressing the men with almost as much fervour as Mrs Grice had attached to the liquor problem. His blue eyes shone as he rolled out a map, clearing dishes and knives with little regard for who might be using them.

'Now,' he said in high good humour, 'we have been set a challenge. A wager which I intend to win. The Minister wants to bring most of Parliament and several other guests by train from Wellington to Auckland in August 1908. He doubts it can be done. I say it can. He says we will have to bridge the gap between railheads with coaches. I say there are not enough coaches to do the trick. He says, Well, then we will have to go via New Plymouth and then by sea. I say, No, Minister, we will have the Main Trunk completed.' He studied the faces of his startled engineers, then continued.

'So. We will recruit more men and more engineers. On Monday we will make a reconnaissance. We will travel the distance north and south to measure what needs to be done. Every cutting and every yard of fill to be completed will be measured. I want all of you with me. Have your horses ready. Bring the plans and your tools. Your chainmen, too. We will show those politicians the true mettle of hardworking men.'

Peter Keller, chief engineer for this section, spoke up. 'Sir, what about the viaducts? We have no control over them now they have been let out to contract.'

Mr Furkert's good humour was in no way dented. 'Leave that to me, Peter. I am in charge of the whole project and will see that the Andersons and their men keep up with us. The viaducts will be built in time. I have George Pascoe's word on it.'

Peter Keller raised an eyebrow at that. George Pascoe, in charge of the Workshop at Makatote, was a young man, inexperienced for such a mammoth task. Everyone had been surprised that the Andersons would put such a young fellow in overall charge.

Maggie, clearing the dishes, thought of Billy; he would be working, she supposed, at the Workshop now. They'd heard no word, but he hadn't returned, so presumably this George Pascoe had found work for him. She missed her lively younger brother and wished now that she'd asked that preacher to take a message to him.

Gabriel Locke arrives at Makatote

By the time Gabriel Locke arrived at Makatote, Billy considered himself an old hand. He and Ruri were at work in the gully that day — a pair of happy larrikins in charge of keeping the water running down the flume and the boxes of stone moving along on top. A marvellous smart invention, according to the boys. One of Andersons' engineers had designed it back in Christchurch, and as soon as enough bush had been cleared George Pascoe himself oversaw the construction. A wooden flume had been built to bring river water from half a mile upriver down to where the viaduct would be built. A torrent erupted from the flume, gushing down over a man-made waterfall and into a generating chamber. 'There's your electricity,' Mr Pascoe had said. 'Now let's bring the rock down, too.' He had his men build a wooden railway on top of the flume, so that the same structure could bring rolling boxes of rock, hewn from a good patch of volcanic material upriver, down to a stone-crusher, run by modern electricity. The land itself provided the stone for the foundations and the power to crush the stone. All that was needed was cement from up north and a pair of likely lads to run up and down all day giving a jammed box a shove or a blockage in the flume a quick clear. The boys were as proud of the mechanism as if they'd designed it themselves. They had to be nimble, mind. Occasionally a box, not filled properly, would unbalance and tip over, spilling its load and threatening young limbs.

Billy saw the preacher first. He and Ruri were throwing stones into the river during a quiet spell when Billy heard a scrabbling above and looked up to see a horse and rider making heavy work of descending the valley. Felled logs and loose rock had turned the once beautiful slopes into a steep and slippery test of strength for man or beast. The rider cursed, unwisely beating his mount, for with only one hand on the reins he soon slid over the horse's handsome neck to tumble close to where the boys stood laughing.

'You have the wrong horse,' said Billy. 'He won't do for these parts.'

'I have been told that more times than I wish to hear,' said the man sourly.

Ruri, who possessed kinder manners, helped the rider up and dusted him off. He pointed towards the mountain. 'It's best to go deeper into the valley and then come up the other side; more gentle, sir. There's a good track. You have missed it.'

The man nodded without further speech and set out, picking his way carefully and leading his mount in the direction Ruri had indicated.

The boys thought no more about him. Of much greater excitement, a little later, was the sight of the sun, which broke through the day's usual overcast. At last colour returned to the world. The mountain appeared for the first time in months, white and majestic at the head of the valley. Woodpigeons erupted from what was left of the bush, flying from ridge to ridge flashing their blue-green wings. The men down at the crusher raised their fists and cheered as if their favourite boxer had just won.

'Ha!' said Ruri. 'Tawhiri's decided to move on.' He raised one hand in a salute, fingers vibrating lightly. 'Best keep on the good side, eh!'

Later that evening, back at the little settlement, they found the traveller's horse tethered outside their tent and the fellow ensconced within.

'Come in, come in, boys,' sang Gabriel Locke. He was lounging on a third stretcher, and welcomed them as if this was his tent and they were new arrivals. The hand that beckoned them held a steaming mug of tea; the other fed a hunk of bread into his grinning mouth.

'So, the Lord and I have brought the sunshine and the men are grateful. I am to stay a while.' His blue eyes twinkled at them. 'Your boss is a wise man.'

They soon learned what had happened. Gabriel Locke had ridden into the work camp opposite the Workshop with one fist held high, a finger pointing to the heavens. His big horse, tightly reined, pranced and snorted. 'Let there be sunshine!' shouted the preacher. A small crowd of men playing two-up outside the pay clerk's hut looked around in surprise at this unusual entry. 'The Lord has promised to come to our aid,' Gabriel continued in ringing tones. 'He sends me to tell you that the weather will break and the sun will shine upon us!'

At that very moment the sun did indeed break through, eerily striking the group of men then spreading through the camp and across to the Workshop. 'Praise the Lord!' sang the preacher, leaping from his horse to kneel in the mud, head bowed. 'Your servant thanks Thee, as do all these men gathered before Thee!'

Some men walked away in embarrassment; a few openly mocked. But several younger, more impressionable lads went to shake Gabriel's hand and congratulate him, half laughing, half in awe. They stumped into the office and demanded that this man, who had brought good luck, be given lodging and food. The boss, not superstitious himself but sensing the mood of his men, shrugged and agreed.

'A sensible decision,' said Gabriel, winking.

Ruri screwed up his eyes and looked away, but Billy grinned and returned the wink. 'I would like to learn that trick, sir. Did you have a good view as you came up the valley so you could time your entrance well?'

Gabriel put down his mug, his face grave. He reached out to seize the boy's wrist tightly. Too tightly. 'Young lad, that was no trick. The Lord spoke to me. I am a true man of God and you would do well to remember that.' Billy, startled, would have wrenched his arm free, but it was suddenly released; the preacher's good humour reappeared as quickly as it had disappeared. 'Now, let us introduce ourselves, for I feel we are to be good friends.'

Billy's rather guarded opinion of Mr Locke changed after he heard him preach the next Sunday. Most of the construction workers were seated in the large dining hall, breakfast being a more leisurely event on a Sunday. Gabriel Locke rose from his seat and jumped up onto one of the long trestle tables. He began to sing, arms outstretched, eyes gazing up at the rough plank ceiling.

'Praise the Lord!' he sang in his peculiarly sweet, high voice. 'For He has given us food and good company and a day of rest. Hallelujah!' The preacher's golden hair, brushed smooth, hung to his shoulders, lit by a single shaft of sunlight that slanted through a high window.

The men grew silent. The preacher spoke briefly then, addressing them all — capturing their attention easily — his voice lower, more familiar now, friendly. He invited them to come to a short service in this very room in an hour's time. 'I hear it is many months since a man of the cloth came into these parts. Whatever your religious persuasion you are welcome. I promise to bring you peace. We will pray together and receive the blessing of the Lord.'

The men pushed back their benches, cleared their throats, looked in other directions. Hard to give up time on your day off. One wit shouted, 'Look at that yaller hair! It's Goldilocks!' That brought on a murmur of uneasy laughter. No one was quite sure what to make of this strange fellow who might or might not have brought with him this spell of fine weather. They headed outside, jingling their pennies, eager to bet at their two-up school. But an hour later, with no other entertainment on offer, there was a goodly crowd back in the hall willing to hear the preacher out. Billy was among them. Ruri, carrying a slingshot of his own making, had disappeared into the bush, promising to bring back a fat pigeon for their tea.

Goldie — for from that day on the name stuck — began with a familiar hymn, then spoke about the love of Jesus, the blessing that came from confessing sin, the joy of righteousness. None of this was much different from what the occasional visiting priests said, but the manner of speaking was vastly different. Goldie joked, asked questions, drew responses from usually surly fellows, gave personal advice that often displayed a startling private knowledge of the worker in question. Addressing Billy, he asked after his sister Maggie; she had been sick, said Goldie, but was now cured. Billy listened, his mouth agape. The preacher then asked Billy to pass around the plate. The boy was eager to help, and passed with a will. Grinning with pleasure, he came forward as he'd seen in church back home, and offered up for blessing a goodly enough collection of coins — mostly pennies but a sprinkling of silver, too.

'The Lord has bestowed on me the hands of a healer,' said the preacher quietly after a last hymn. '"Let all men come unto me," said the Lord Jesus. And so that healing power will flow through me. Bring me your troubles and your ailments and I will lay on my hands.'

He waited. The men, many of them embarrassed now, got up to leave. One thin fellow limped up to Goldie, grinning sheepishly, but with hope all the same. He pointed to his left leg. Goldie seated him, laid the man's hands on his head. Prayed silently. He moved his hands slowly over the man's shoulders, his torso and down to the leg. Several of the congregation stopped to watch. Billy stepped closer, fascinated. The thin man closed his eyes; seemed to fall asleep. Goldie murmured to him and then, taking his hand, raised him to his feet, made the sign of the cross above him and sent him away. The man walked several steps without a limp, then turned to come back and shake the preacher's hand. He took from his pocket a shilling and offered it.

'Praise the Lord!' sang Gabriel Locke, triumph in his voice.

Billy Cameron was hooked.

SCOBIES

My grandmother was known for her 'opinions'. She loved to tell stories of the old days, but was often harsh in her judgments. Perhaps it was the Scottish blood. More likely just her nature. 'That wretched fellow!' she might say, slamming a hand on her bedside table; or 'What a fool, who on earth would vote for such an idiot/believe in that nonsense/put a man like that in charge!' But when she talked of Rose, her voice would soften; we watched for the little shake of her head, the small sigh — almost of wonder. Rose never received any jot of Gran's famous vitriol. Gran was rather in awe of her famous friend and proud to know her, though they lived a good distance apart. They kept in touch by letter, and once Gran took us three grandkids to meet her. It must have been important to Gran: she paid for the fares across in the ferry to Christchurch and then the train to Westport and the bus up to Denniston. This was before they closed the Incline. I must have been about ten.

At first we were surprised. After all that we'd heard about the famous coal towns on the Hill, there were hardly any houses, just a handful dotted here and there. But the Incline was roaring away, wagons rising and descending out of the mist. That was a sight.

'She doesn't like to be called Mrs Scobie,' said Gran as we walked along the road to her house on the edge of the plateau. 'She won't mind if you just address her as Rose.'

This seemed shocking to us. 'What about Aunty Rose?' I asked.

Gran considered. 'You could try. She'll soon let you know if she doesn't approve.'

Gran's friend was waiting at the door. She was tall — much taller than Gran — and straight as a die although she must have been about seventy. And quite apart from her height she was noticeable. Her long woollen dress was bright red; a purple scarf, wound twice around her neck, trailed down her back, the tassels whipping in the wind. Pinned to her shock of grey hair was a glowing silk rose, scarlet and green and somehow strange in that spartan landscape.

'Maggie!' she called, all smiles, 'Maggie, you rogue, what have you brought to lighten my day? Come in, come in!'

In we trooped, marvelling at the paintings — some of them by her — the glass ornaments, the coloured rugs. It was as if Gran's friend was beating back the bleak weather and stark rocks outside with floods of colour. And then the views from her big front windows! You could be on a ship — a very tall one — with the sea breaking on the shore far below and the horizon rising, it seemed, almost to meet you. Rose (we never needed to try Aunty, she and Gran did all the talking) gave us cake and scones and raspberry drink and a chocolate bar each. The two old women laughed and held hands like a young couple. We'd never seen Gran so animated, so pink-cheeked.

'Did your gran tell you how we met?' Rose asked, settling the flower more firmly in her hair.

We nodded shyly. Yes, we had heard the famous story of the Makatote viaduct and the railway.

Rose didn't seem so interested in that story. 'Ah, but before that I taught your gran here on the Hill. Did she not say? She was a pupil at Denniston School. Little Maggie Cameron. And her brothers.'

Gran was silent at the mention of brothers. Rose patted Gran's hand. 'Well. The railroad. I'm glad you have told them. It's a lesson needs drumming in.' Her eyes were a pure sky blue and fierce when she turned her gaze on us. 'Do you know that song *The Silver Swan*? A favourite of mine.'

We didn't.

She sang, her voice as pure as a young girl's: *More geese than swans now live, more fools than wise; more fools than wise.* She sighed. 'How true. Listen, children, to what your Gran tells you. Now, I think we should come and inspect *my* railway.'

———

I am finding it difficult to bring Brennan and Rose Scobie into this narrative. In my grandmother's telling she never placed much emphasis on their part in the final drama. But my great-uncle's side of the story gave the Scobies a much stronger role. He would talk about that time reluctantly, in a low, hesitant voice, answering my questions in single syllables. Not surprisingly, I suppose.

The Scobies. I must include them.

WINTER 1907

Two letters for Brennan Scobie

Brennan's horse plodded slowly up the winding road to Denniston. Plenty of time to ponder these two offers of work — or, more precisely, to work out how to broach the subject with Rose. He was excited by the prospect. She would not be. These past months working in Westport had not been easy. His work in the office was dull. The ride up to Denniston took too long: several days a week he was forced to find lodgings in town and he hated (and feared) leaving Rose to care for the children alone. Her teaching and her other interests in the mining business were her life-blood. She had been better with the children recently, but there were times in the past . . . Yet the prospect of Brennan's mother returning to care for the children would not be welcome — to either woman.

He reined in at the last bend to let Moses blow. There above he could see part of Rose's famous house, built to her own design, standing alone on the very edge of the plateau. Its windows flashed gold in the setting sun. Soon they would be dark. He imagined the children's welcome, their weekend together; Rose's arms around him. She, at least, had been happy recently. To Brennan that was a blessing worth the drudgery of his present work. Still, this offer — should he simply forget it?

It was Rose who brought up the subject. When the excited children were finally coaxed to sleep and their own dinner finished, Rose came over to the window where he stood gazing at the blackness outside. She linked her arm in his, drew him over to the settee. 'Something's on your mind, my dear. Spit it out. I'm not in a mood to bite you.'

Brennan scratched an ear. 'I'm not so sure.' He took out the two letters; handed them to her without a word. Rose carried them to the table; smoothed them out under the lamp and stood there reading. Brennan watched, loving the long curve of her back, the soft lights in her hair; fearing her reaction.

She returned to the settee. 'I think the Andersons' offer is more interesting,' she said, 'though Furkert's has merits. Which do you favour?'

Brennan burst out laughing. He gathered Rose into his arms and kissed her. 'Oh, Rose, my Rose! You are endlessly surprising. I was fearing an explosion.'

Rose disentangled herself. 'Yes, but which? I would rather go to Makatote.'

Brennan could not believe his ears. 'You would come?'

She nodded slowly. 'I know what you are thinking. That I cannot stay well if I leave Denniston. But I'm much better now, Bren, and it would only be for a year, maybe two. Besides, I am very interested in the Andersons' methods. I hear the viaduct they plan at Makatote will be a challenge even for those clever brothers. Also there is the Spiral — an engineering miracle, if they can complete it.'

Brennan shook his head in wonder. 'How do you know of the

Andersons, for heaven's sake? And the Spiral?'

'I can read, my dear; I follow the newspapers and journals. We may yet need the Andersons' bridge-building expertise up here on the Hill. And I have heard that they are building a little settlement in the bush there. The Makatote offer includes a small cottage if you bring a family. The Ohakune position doesn't mention accommodation.'

Brennan whooped with joy. He grabbed his trumpet from the corner and would have played a fanfare if Rose had not dived on him. 'Don't you dare, you wretched man. Have you forgotten the children?'

Brennan had. He put the instrument down with exaggerated care, whirled his wife silently around the room and whispered in her ear, 'Makatote it is, my lovely darling.'

Black ice

The Scobies would have been at Makatote a month when the first man fell. Billy and Ruri, working the ropes, saw it from below; Rose, walking alone in the chilly morning, from above. She had left the children in the warmth of the cookhouse with Mrs Bright ('just for half an hour?') and stood at the lip of the gully, looking down. Most of the foundations were finished now and the shorter piers were rising, girder by girder, rivet by rivet, the delicate crisscrossing pattern a fascination to Rose. Hard to believe that such an open structure would soon hold up a heavy engine and a rake of carriages filled with travellers or goods. From above the workers looked like stick figures.

Rose grasped a branch and leaned forward to clear her view. She could now see the great cable that bridged the gully directly above where the viaduct would go. The winch — 'Blondin' the men called it, after the famous tightrope walker — was grinding its way out along the cable, out into space; a girder, freshly drilled and shaped in the Workshop, swinging below it. A man standing nonchalantly on the highest strut of the pier made hand signals. The column began to descend. Long ropes were attached to it, stretching out, down to the gully to men — were they men? Rose couldn't see among all the wasteland of broken trees and piled rocks.

Two of the ropemen were, in fact, Billy and Ruri. They watched for hand signals from Jack Tar on the top of the unfinished pier. Other men — one-time sailors, like Jack — scrambled up to join him. Billy was in awe of their prowess and wanted to learn that skill. It seemed that their feet could stick to the girders, no matter what angle they might be set at.

Down came the steel column, the pulley on the Blondin screaming. Jack signalled; Ruri held his rope firm while Billy scrambled to the left and pulled on his rope. The girder swung a little, then too far. Jack Tar's curse could be heard all down the valley. The ropemen on the other side of the gully corrected the swing and with a clunk the girder fitted. Jack's hand now indicated to hold steady while the first rivets were inserted. These were temporary pegs. The riveters would move up soon with their little furnace and their bucket of hot rivets.

It was at that moment — concentration was relaxed, perhaps — that Jack reached out to ram in the last peg and lost his footing. Billy and Ruri heard the shout; they looked up to see Jack Tar falling, arms flailing, thirty feet down onto the concrete foundation block. Jack Tar! The surest, the steadiest of all of them.

Rose, leaning too far, almost lost her own footing. Breathing heavily, heart pounding, she scrabbled back up to firmer ground. Seeing the man fall she had guessed (correctly, as it turned out) the reason for the fall: black ice. Jack's hand or foot had slipped on that invisible and deadly coating. The men knew about the ice, knew to chip it off or, more likely, just to take extra care. The riggers scorned any form of harness — it slowed them down too much. But they were usually miraculously sure-footed. Rose watched as workers ran to help the stricken man. Then she turned and hurried to the cookhouse. She could help prepare for a body or, please God, an injury. She wondered if anyone had thought to keep a stretcher down in the gully.

Jack was not dead: one leg was badly broken, perhaps some ribs busted; there was a gash on his head. Thank goodness the pier was only one thirty-foot column high.

'Dear God, dear God!' shouted one older fellow, holding Jack's head tenderly, 'Are you with us, man? Give us a word!'

Jack's eyes rolled. He could say nothing.

The riggers and ropemen stood watching, at a loss what to do; Jack was usually the one with the orders. But quiet Ruri was already making a stretcher. He had found two matching staves. Quickly he sliced off a long section of his rope and, motioning Billy to help, wove it back and forth, in and out, cleverly making a bed. One of the riggers gave the lads a pat on the back. 'Good boys. We'll take him up now.'

Billy, ashamed of his tears, his quavering voice, said, 'Take him up to the preacher. He's a healer. He'll make him whole again.'

The rigger snorted. 'Take more than mumbo jumbo to heal poor Jack, lad.'

'No, but it's true! I've seen him heal. Take him to Goldie!'

The men lifted the stretcher and set off up the wretched lumpy slope as carefully as they might — easier said than done — Jack moaning at every jolting step.

Billy and Ruri followed behind. Ruri put his arm around his friend's shoulder. 'That preacher, don't put too much hope in him. Jack'll die, I reckon.'

'But —' Billy dashed away his silly tears — 'he does heal! I saw it! They got to try!'

'It was a trick. I seen that sort before. Don't believe it, Billy.'

Billy pushed off Ruri's arm. 'You just don't like him, that he's my friend. He's going to teach me. I bet you anything he can heal Jack.'

Ruri shrugged and laughed. 'Boy, you got it bad. Wake up Billy. Look around. This is the real world we're living in, not some fairy tale.'

But Billy walked on ahead, frowning. He didn't want to hear.

Rose cleared one of the cookhouse tables and laid on it a pair of towels: the best she could do.

Mrs Bright had boiling water ready. 'Wouldn't you know it,' she said sourly, 'our famous healer has disappeared just when he's needed.'

The boss had told Goldie that if he wanted to stay and be fed he must work like all the rest. Preaching on Sunday didn't count. So the preacher now fed the three cookhouse fires and Mrs Bright's great stove, a task that he found well beneath his dignity. But in this emergency, when plenty of boiling water would be needed, he was gone.

'Bring in a pile of the driest wood you can find, plenty of it,' Rose had said. 'There's a badly injured man on the way.'

Goldie had looked at her for a moment, his pale eyes expressionless, then left. Not a sign since.

'Jack Tar!' said Rose when she learned the injured man's name. 'We could not be further from the sea.'

'Many of the riggers are sailors.' Mrs Bright was rummaging in the medical cupboard for splints and brandy. 'Now that the big sailing ships are being laid off, here's a job worthy of their talents.'

She looked at their meagre preparations. 'There's no doctor for miles, let alone a hospital. We'll have to do what we can, poor sod.'

Jack was unconscious when they brought him in. George Pascoe himself arrived, panting; news had spread quickly. But he was rendered silent at the sight of the damage. The jagged bone of Jack's leg protruded through the skin; the man's breathing was shallow; the strips of shirt tied around his head were soaked in blood. Jack moaned. He was alive at least.

Rose thrust a bottle and spoon into a rigger's hand. 'Spoon brandy into him. Little by little. All of it if he can keep it down.' She turned to Pascoe. 'We can't set that bone. I think the leg will have to go.'

A voice behind her shouted, 'Send for Mr Locke! Quickly! Where is he?'

Rose was surprised to see Billy. 'Billy Cameron? Is that you grown a foot taller? I would recognise that shock of red hair any day!'

Billy's anxious face broke into a grin. 'Mrs Scobie!' But the urgency of the moment left no time for greetings. 'Mrs Scobie, send for the preacher!'

George Pascoe pushed the boy roughly out of the way. 'Find him yourself, lad; he's not here and not needed.'

'But . . .' cried Billy, dancing from one foot to the other, 'but he could—' No one was paying him attention. He dashed from the room. His friend must be close by. Here was a chance to prove his healing powers; to confound his many doubters. 'Gabriel! Mr Locke!' He ran for the woodpile: Goldie would be there.

In the cookhouse a rigger came forward. 'I can cut the limb off if you have a saw, sir. I've done it before.'

George Pascoe hesitated. 'Could we get him to Taumarunui?

Or Raetihi?' But they all knew they could not; nor was there a hospital at either place.

Mrs Bright had already thought that her butcher's hacksaw might be needed: she had it sterilising in a pot of boiling water. Then Rose, cleaning the wound on Jack's head, saw that it was too late. She touched Mrs Bright's sleeve, shaking her head. The unconscious man's breath faltered and stopped. Jack Tar was dead.

'Dear God, dear God!' wept his old mate, clasping the dead man's hand. 'And we are as far away from the sea as can be, in this cursed place. God rest ye, Jack Tar.' He turned to George Pascoe, anger and blame in that look. 'It were black ice on the steel. You cannot see it. We should not be on the piers in this weather.'

Pascoe patted the man's arm, but the rigger turned away. All the men walked out, muttering, leaving the women to tend to the body.

When Jack Tar was laid out in his tent and ready for burial, Ruri crept in quietly and laid a bunch of leaves at his feet. In his own tongue he said some words of farewell. Rose, walking back to her own cottage, heard the chant and stopped to listen: it was a comforting sound. She resolved to talk to this lad who was often the butt of jokes or worse. The only native in the settlement. She was curious about his family; wondered how he came to be working here.

'Where were you? I looked everywhere!' Billy was desperate for an explanation. Ruri, now lying on his stretcher and feigning sleep, had assured him that the preacher had run away, fearing to be shown up. Billy's eyes pleaded for reassurance. 'You could have saved him and then everyone would know!'

Gabriel Locke, his hair wet, his coat muddy, shook his head sadly. 'Ah Billy, it was not to be. We cannot always know what path we must take. The voice of the Lord called me into the wilderness. I have been praying. There is an important task for me here, but alas, saving Jack Tar was not in my calling. The ways of the Lord are not always clear to us.'

'But you could have saved him, couldn't you? Ruri said—'

Gabriel Locke laid a warm hand on Billy's flaming hair. 'Take no heed of what doubters say, Billy. We know the truth.' He yawned, then smiled at the anxious boy. 'Our time will come, Billy, believe me. Our time will come.'

The Scobies were well settled in a rough plank cottage in the crowded Makatote settlement: two rooms, tiny windows, a privvy ten chilly yards away out the back. Towering trees pressed in on the buildings and tents. There were no streets. Makeshift dwellings had been erected in a hurry and faced whichever way the hastily cleared land might suggest. It was piercingly cold, being winter on the high Plateau, but the Scobies were used to that. The children ran wild, making forts among the felled logs and branches, searching for crawlies in the clear stream that ran out of the bush, carrying with it that fresh scent of earth and fern, before hurtling down to the river below.

Rose was useful in the cookhouse, and had agreed to help teach at the little school in the settlement one day a week, but her fascination was in the Workshop and the construction: that massive undertaking to erect such a huge viaduct here, far from civilised amenities. She wanted to study the whole process; would like to be one of the workers, but even she was forced to accept that this would not be allowed.

'Why don't we hire someone to watch the children?' said Brennan, anxious that Rose might lose heart if she was not free. 'Then you can go down to the gully; talk to the men; make your drawings.'

So when Rose found her former pupil Billy in the workforce, she was quick to give Brennan's suggestion an airing. Billy had loved his teacher on Denniston — who hadn't? — and was pleased to chat when she invited him inside.

'The rest of your family?' asked Rose. 'I've not seen them here. What about Maggie, and the boys?'

Billy told her about his dad being recruited from Denniston; how the older boys were already grown men in a formation gang fifteen miles south. How Freeman longed to come to the Workshop but must stay in the gang until a replacement was found.

'And Maggie?'

'She's maid-of-all-work for the engineers at Ohakune, but she doesn't like it much. Da says we all have to earn our way, but she won't stay longer than she has to.'

'Do you think she might agree to come here if I offered her more?'

Billy's freckled face split into the widest grin Rose could imagine. 'Course she would, Mrs Scobie! I'd give a week's wage to see Maggie again, I would that. Da and Mam wouldn't mind.' Though he was not sure about that. He looked at her hopefully. 'I don't suppose you know anyone wanting a navvy? Then Freeman could come too!' Rose had been famous on Denniston for making anything happen.

'Let's settle for Maggie first, shall we?' said Rose.

A nursemaid, a chainman
and two new recruits

After two months working on the steelwork at Makatote, Brennan received a visit from Mr Furkert. It seemed he was to be 'seconded' to Public Works. Though Brennan would remain based at Makatote he would, in fact, report to Mr Furkert. There had been some 'discussion' between the two bosses — Pascoe and Furkert — over who most needed an engineer. The older man won, as he mostly did. It was agreed that Brennan would design and peg the approaches to the viaduct when the time came, but meanwhile he would oversee the formation of a coach road between Ohakune and the northern railhead. The Minister needed to see progress, and demonstrate that some return was being made on the vast Government investment. The idea was that passengers could make a three-day trip from Wellington to Auckland by taking a coach trip between the two railheads.

Brennan couldn't see it. 'The railhead is not to Ohakune yet.'

Furkert grunted, 'That's my worry. I have a deviation planned.

The earthworks south of Ohakune will take another' — oddly, he consulted his pocket watch — 'six months and five days. Meantime we'll construct a temporary deviation around the unfinished cutting.'

Brennan thought this a strange waste of manpower, but held his tongue. He looked down at the wasteland of the Makatote gully. 'Can we expect a coachful of passengers and luggage to make it down to the bridge and back up? That is a steep climb, sir, and often icy.'

'That's your task, Mr Scobie. Peg it out. And the bridge will need strengthening. Do you have a chainman?'

Brennan remembered Rose's account of the Cameron boy who wanted to be an engineer. 'No, sir, but I could train one up. I have someone in mind — one of the Cameron boys — if you can spare him from a formation gang.'

Furkert shook his head. 'He's needed.' He turned to go. Always in a hurry was Mr Furkert. But then a thought struck him. 'I have two new recruits just arrived. Fresh off the boat. I'll put them with Jock Cameron's gang — if he'll have them. He's a tough taskmaster, Jock. Then you may have your chainman.'

First Brennan delivered the invitation to Maggie. She was on her knees in the engineers' bunkhouse, cursing the mud; the inevitability of its return as soon as the engineers came home from the field. Indeed, here was a fresh set of muddy boots in front of her eyes. She looked up to see a new fellow, a dark-haired nuggety man; black smiling eyes over a strong beard. Something familiar about him.

'Maggie Cameron?' Brennan offered a helping hand, but she jumped up of her own accord.

'I am, sir.' Maggie, always ready for a chat, was particularly pleased to be interrupted today. Mrs Grice, who considered herself to be overseer of Maggie's tasks, had ridiculous expectations of what could be achieved in the way of cleanliness. Ohakune was no more than a work camp in the bush. 'Are you new here?'

Brennan remembered this lively, quick-witted girl, one of Rose's favourite pupils. 'I've grown a beard since you last saw me. Brennan Scobie from Denniston.'

'Oh Lord, yes! Now I see it.' Maggie's eyes widened. 'Don't tell me Mrs Scobie is with you.'

'She is and that is why I'm here.' Brennan told her of Rose's idea — that Maggie might come and live with them and look after the children, Con and Alice. 'Maybe a little housework, too, but Rose says there's not much point keeping a house clean in this wilderness.'

Maggie laughed. 'Oho! A woman after my own thoughts. But here's the thing. I've not looked after little ones before. Also—' She looked down at her roughened hands.

'Rose believes you would be good at it. Shall I put in a word here?' Brennan liked the easy way she stood talking. The light in her blue eyes, the wisps of gingery hair escaping from her scarf. He could see she was tempted by the idea.

Maggie tossed her head. 'Oh, I can walk away from this. It's my mam I'm thinking about. And Da.'

'Well, I have another matter to discuss with your father. And business here with Mr Furkert. What say we go back to your camp together when your work and mine is done?'

Hope and doubt shadowed Maggie's face, but finally a wicked grin broke through. 'Mrs Grice will not be pleased. Feckin' bloody mud!'

Brennan laughed out loud. 'I will come for you, Maggie Cameron. We'll ride together.'

It turned out there were four of them heading down to the work camp at the end of the day: Brennan driving a borrowed cart, Maggie sitting beside him and two new recruits in the back with their belongings and a tent. The pair of them — young lads — chatted at a rate of knots, laughing and carrying on, taking no notice of the grand trees crowding in or occasional glimpses of the mountain.

Brennan winked at Maggie. 'They'll soon sober up after a day's work on the gang.'

Maggie nodded. She'd seen others arrive, cheerful, ready with opinions, looking for adventure, who, after a week of work, turned surly or querulous. Usually these were new recruits from England; those born here, like the men on Jock's gang — West Coasters all — understood hard work.

But her mind was on other concerns: would her parents give permission?

The men were not back from work when the cart drew up. Sarah was alone in the tent, stirring a pot over the fire. She came to the door, startled to see such a party arriving at tea time. She stood there, arm on the doorpost — barring entry, it would seem — and frowned at her daughter.

'What's this you've brought, Maggie?'

Maggie wished her mother could be more welcoming. It was always this way when strangers arrived. Her mother worried too much, feared being labelled a poor hostess. Yet everyone in the camps understood that feeding a family was hard when you only had an open fire; strangers must arrive with their own provisions.

Brennan jumped down, handed the reins to one of the

new recruits with instructions to unload, then turned to Sarah. 'Mrs Cameron! I remember you well from up on Denniston. Brennan Scobie, the engineer who laid out the new rope-road. What a pleasure to meet you again.' He held out a bulging sack. 'Here is a piece of bush pork, cooked and ready to eat, and a loaf of bread. May we share it with you?' He waved a hand at the two recruits. 'These two are looking for work in your husband's gang, but we'll discuss this later. May we come in?' He laid the sack on the ground and offered his hand. Sarah, charmed by this bushy-bearded man and eager to make up for her sour greeting, wiped her hands on her apron, shook hands and invited them all in.

'I remember your wife, of course, the teacher. You were often away, I think?'

Brennan nodded. Maggie was interested to see that he didn't want to follow that line of conversation. He bent his head to slicing pork and bread, while her mother added flour to the stew to bulk it out a little.

While they waited for the gang to return and the recruits searched for a place to erect their tent, Brennan brought up the possibility of new employment for Maggie. He described the settlement at Makatote, the proper plank cottage where Maggie would live, no need to walk three miles to work each day, the good nature (a slight exaggeration in Alice's case) of the two children.

Maggie watched her mother take it all in; knew what she was thinking. With Maggie gone she would be alone, the only woman in the camp.

'But, Mam, I'm already often away. You know how I sometimes sleep up at Ohakune. It would not be that different.' Maggie touched her mother's rough hand. 'I'd like to go, Mam. And I could keep an eye on Billy. He'll be missing us.'

Brennan smiled. 'I know Rose would be pleased. She has a

high opinion of your daughter, Mrs Cameron; a clever girl, she says . . . young woman, I should say.'

Sarah sighed; stroked her daughter's bright curls. 'Well, we'll see what your da says. I dare say I can manage without you.' She turned to Brennan. 'It will not be for ever. When this railway is complete we'll all be moving on, I expect.'

Their conversation was interrupted by a great commotion. Jock Cameron and his sons arrived with their two horses and the cart, and as they were seeing to the beasts the two recruits burst into the tent, giggling and swearing. Their laughter, though, was laced with fear or anxiety.

'We can't make the bloody tents stand. There's no bleedin' poles. What are we to do?'

Brennan took each by an elbow and steered them into a corner, frowning. 'Settle down, lads. There's a lady here. In these parts you cut your own poles. And your foreman has arrived back home. If he doesn't take to you, you're on your way. It's his co-op.'

'But it's dark out there. The tents are no good—'

Jock came inside, his head and hands dripping from his wash, his face thunderous. 'What's all this circus, Mother? What kind of welcome is this to a tired working man?'

The recruits shut up smartly enough and stood in the shadows where Brennan had placed them. Maggie skipped up to her da with a mugful of bootleg and kissed him. 'Sit down, Da, have your tea first. Mr Scobie has brought wild pork and fresh bread.'

Jock shot Brennan an alarmed look. He remembered this engineer from the Hill, but what was his attitude to illicit drink? Brennan laughed and produced from his pocket a bottle. 'No need for bootleg tonight, Jock Cameron, here is engineers' whisky from Taihape. My mother is a famous prohibitionist, but thankfully she is many miles distant. Will you join me?'

That put matters on a more cheerful footing. Dirk and Freeman stumped in exhausted and sat at the table. The recruits stood, silent and hopeful. Jock ignored them, too tired to puzzle over their presence. Sarah took them each a wedge of bread and meat, which they ate standing — there was no room at the table, nor extra seating.

Finally, when Jock was onto his second measure of good whisky, Maggie could hold back no longer. 'Da, Mrs Scobie is over at Makatote and has asked if I might care for her children!'

Jock frowned, but said nothing.

'It'd be more pay than at Ohakune.'

Jock sighed. 'You don't care to live here with your own family, hen?'

'Oh, Da, of course I do! But I dislike the work at the engineers' quarters, and Mrs Grice is a right pill to work for. Mrs Scobie is a teacher. I might better myself there.'

Jock took another sip. Cocked an eye at Brennan, who gave a quick nod. 'We'll discuss terms later, Mr Scobie. Now—' he turned at last to the recruits — 'I suppose I can guess what this is about?'

Freeman sat up straight, not daring to speak but his eyes alight. He looked from his dad to the men while they were introduced: brothers Alec and Arthur Hope from Birmingham. Jock called each one up; turned over their palms to examine for calluses, felt their muscles. He shrugged.

'Not much sign of hard labour here, lads.'

Alec, the older of the two, was quick to answer. 'Nay, sir, we're used to it. But the months on the boat . . . We'll harden up soon enough.'

'Miners?'

'Nay sir, roadmen. We can handle a shovel and pick.'

'We are miners all in this co-op. You will need to keep up with us if you want to share the bonus.'

'The boss explained, sir. He said yours was one of the best gangs. Said it was up to you, yay or nay, to have us.'

Freeman held his breath. Jock pulled at his lip, eyed the boys again. 'We'll try you then. Be ready for work at dawn.' He turned away. 'Now I'm off to my bed. You'd be advised to do same.'

'Da!' Freeman could contain himself no longer. 'Da, you said—'

Jock slammed his mug down on the table, his face red with the liquor and a deep anger. 'Enough, son. I've had enough for this night. Did you nae hear me say I was off to bed? You, too, son.'

He stomped away into the inner room, pulling the flap down. They could hear him stumbling and cursing. 'Mother, will you come and set up this fecking bed!'

Arthur gripped Brennan's arm. 'What are we to do?' he whispered. 'Our bleeding tent won't stand. We are not unpacked.' He looked around at the amused Camerons. 'It's not blimmin' funny.'

Dirk laughed. 'Don't mind Da, he's just tired, is all. Doss down in the corner there. You have to cut your own poles from the bush, didn't they tell you? I'll show you tomorrow.'

Meanwhile Brennan talked quietly to Freeman, explaining about the position as cadet chainman. 'I'll ride back to headquarters now but leave the cart here. I think your father understands what is involved. You and Maggie have your things packed. I'll be back at first light and explain to Jock. But truth is you're old enough to decide for yourself.'

Freeman, torn between excitement and fear, nodded. They could hear Sarah calming her husband. The crashing subsided; soon he would be snoring.

Maggie came to hold Freeman's hand. They clung together, wanting to leap and shout, but mindful of the need to keep silent. 'We can go together!' whispered Maggie. 'There'll be three of us at Makatote!'

As the recruits tiptoed in with their bedrolls, Sarah emerged from the back room. She touched Freeman's shoulder and spoke quietly. 'You should go, son. Your da might take it hard, but go all the same. It's time.' She wiped a tired hand across her eyes. 'I'll miss you both sorely. But you're grown now.'

Maggie, tears in her eyes, hugged Sarah. 'Thanks, Mam.'

Brennan walked out to his horse. For once it was a starry night, no breath of wind. He gave his mount her head and they plodded through the dark. A kiwi called nearby — a wild wailing cry that was answered more distantly. A morepork began its evening hooting. The bush was coming alive. But Brennan rocked, half asleep, and pleased. Rose would be pleased too.

Blisters and blood

Mr Furkert had asked Brennan to check on the big cutting since he was heading that way to pick up the Cameron boy. (Brennan had not mentioned Maggie.)

'It's a major obstruction,' said Furkert, 'and a major gully to be filled north of it. I've two gangs on it now. Do we need a third, is what I want to know. At any rate I'm putting another gang on the deviation. I want the railhead to Ohakune early next year.'

While Maggie and Freeman loaded their meagre possessions onto the cart and said their farewells to their mother, Brennan rode down to the cutting. He whistled when he saw the hill towering above, dwarfing the men working on it. Now he understood why Furkert planned a temporary deviation. It would take months to cut through to the planned gradient. Already the gangs had driven a small tunnel through the hill at the correct level for the railroad. Jock's gang, working on the north side of the hill, had drilled a shaft down to the tunnel and were now enlarging the hole shovel by shovelful, sending the rocks and earth down this chute to a pair of carts waiting in the tunnel below. Thus gravity did some of the hard work.

Brennan watched Dirk emerge from the tunnel, leading Snow. The big draught horse leaned against his harness, snorting with the effort. The cart ran along makeshift wooden rails towards the spillway, which would in time fill the gully ahead. At the spillway Snow turned the cart, then waited while Dirk removed the pins from the tailgate. He then unhitched Snow and turned him to face the cart. On his master's order, Snow leaned his leather breastplate against the cart and shoved. The cart moved slowly, then more quickly; it came to a stop when it hit the trip and over went the load, spilling out rubble and big rocks, rattling down into the valley. Without being told, Snow turned and backed into the traces again, ready for the trip back to where a second cart was already almost full.

Brennan walked into the tunnel and looked up through the chute. It was much wider at the top. Jock waved briefly but went on shovelling, a deceptively easy rhythm, sending the material down in a steady slide to the waiting cart. Soon the men would break through to join their earlier work around the entrance. Far away to the south he could just see the other gang toiling away over a second chute. But there were many months of work ahead, many tons of spoil to be shifted before the cutting was open, the battens cut to an even backward slope, all neat and ready for the platelayers.

Arthur Hope sat on a rock at the entrance, his face screwed up. He held out his bleeding and blistered hands. 'Look at them,' he moaned. 'Would you have a rag on you?'

Brennan dug in his bag and produced a pair of leather gloves. 'You'll need more than a rag until you toughen up. What about your brother?'

Arthur hung his head. 'To be honest, sir, he's the one done roadwork. I never. I worked as a clerk.' He breathed in sharply as he drew on the gloves, then stood. 'Don't tell the boss, eh? I'll get by in the end. Alec wants to keep us together. We ain't got no one else this side of the world.'

Brennan nodded.

'Ta for these. I can't pay you except with thanks.' He shook his hands as if to free them from the pain and picked up his shovel.

Brennan took some measurements, wrote in his notebook and turned back to his horse. He had some doubts about this co-op system. With a boss like Furkert driving them, and a tough foreman like Jock eager to earn a big bonus, the likelihood of accidents must be increased.

Sly grog

Mrs Amelia Grice drew up her bosom, which she kept tightly laced inside stays even here in the bush. 'You have no right to hive off without notice! No right to *leave* at all.'

Maggie stood tall in front of her, not at all ashamed of enjoying the moment. 'Our arrangement was simply that, Mrs Grice; there is no paper or such signed by you or the pay clerk. I am free to go — and I will. My father will collect my dues on pay day. I hope you can find someone as willing and hardworking as me.' This was said straight-faced. They both knew there was no other woman willing or free to do the work.

Maggie turned towards the cart where Brennan and Freeman were waiting. Mrs Grice followed, her long skirts, which she refused to trim, dragging in the mud, her face purple with exertion or rage or both. 'Maggie Cameron, come back here! I have important work to do and cannot be left without a maid.' She laid a hand on the trace as Maggie climbed aboard. 'Sir, whoever you are, it is quite unconscionable that you should carry off my maid-of-all-work from under my very nose!'

Brennan leaned down and shook her hand, an action which removed her grip on the trace. 'Delighted to meet you, Mrs Grice. I am Brennan Scobie, engineer at Makatote. I met your good husband last night. I'm afraid Miss Cameron here prefers to work for my wife. It is her right.'

Mrs Grice drew breath to argue further but then paused. 'Scobie? Are you from the West Coast?'

'I am.'

'Then perhaps your mother is Mrs Mary Scobie, the famous prohibitionist?'

Brennan cleared his throat; turned to his horse, which was unfortunately at that moment otherwise engaged.

Mrs Grice latched onto the trace again. 'But, Mr Scobie, you will understand my predicament. There is serious illegal trading in this area. The consumption of sly grog among the workers is increasing by the day. I am close to discovering the source. How can I pursue my calling if I am forced to serve the engineers and clean their quarters? You of all people, son of the famous—'

But the horse, having finished its business, was ready to move. The cart, laden with supplies for several work camps on the road north, moved slowly away out of earshot — a laughing Freeman sitting atop the pile, and Maggie with Brennan up front.

Mrs Grice beat her fists against her sides to see them go. The whole world, it seemed (except of course her husband and that nice preacher), was against the cause. How could they ignore this source of evil — spirituous liquor — which ruined working men, harmed children and left wives beaten or worse? Her own father had died a drunkard; had fallen intoxicated, in broad daylight, into Wellington harbour. A shameful and mortifying spectacle, reported in the local newspaper. Her mother, born into a respected family back in the Home Country but now left alone with two small children, was forced to clean other people's homes to support them. The shame and the drudgery drove her mother to drink, and eventually to an early death. Amelia, only seventeen at the time, had found comfort and strength in the temperance movement. But here, now, in this wilderness of towering trees, of the overwhelming predominance of men, of their careless flouting of the law — where was her support? Amelia sorely missed the meetings, the songs and speeches, the righteous company of kind and like-minded women. How could Mr Furkert, that otherwise upright man, turn a blind eye to the sly-grog trade that infested the camps? Quite apart from the evil effects, this was against the law! She could only suppose that his all-consuming zeal to complete the railway left him no time to address this other matter. She paused in her slow walk back as a new thought struck her. Perhaps Mr Furkert recognised her own fervour and was leaving the task to her? Was he setting her a challenge? A daunting one, goodness knows, but one she must somehow rise to.

Amelia Grice straightened her back, quickened her pace. More serious planning was needed. Calmer now, she marched into her cabin. She looked at the muddy patterns her skirts were leaving on the floor. She took out scissors and carefully cut a good foot off the hem. Some standards would have to be sacrificed, but the battle must continue. 'There will be arrests made, mark my words,' she muttered. 'Those who supply the poor, vulnerable and lonely men in the camps will be brought to justice.'

Feeling better, she ate a quick breakfast and made plans. She had heard whispers of a sly-grog shop some miles south at Karioi: perhaps the headquarters of the illicit distribution was centred there. It would be her mission to travel to Karioi and expose the operation. Looking down at her cut skirts she remembered her old uniform. Of course! This was the moment to bring it out again. She would pack a bag and head for Karioi, wearing her Women's Khaki Corps uniform. Those miscreants were in for a shock.

During the Second Boer War, which had come to its inconclusive end five years back, Amelia Grice had been a 'sergeant' in that fervent band of women known as the 'Wellington Amazons'. She and her fellow stalwarts, who preferred their self-appointed title 'Ladies' Rifle Corps', donned khaki uniforms and, shouldering dummy rifles, marched the streets in formation, their bandoliers of imitation bullets correctly displayed, military hats firmly in place. They were popular. They urged menfolk to enlist, and they raised money to help supply those recruits. Townsfolk cheered and filled their buckets with coins as they marched through the town. Amelia Grice's proudest moment had been marching shoulder to shoulder with Miss Elizabeth Seddon, the Premier's daughter, at Government House. There had been a special fête, organised by Lady Douglas herself to raise money for the troops. The cream of Wellington society was there, applauding as the Wellington Amazons marched and wheeled and presented arms. Oh, it had been a wonderful occasion! Amelia so missed that heady time when she and her Wellington friends became the inspiration for a nationwide movement.

She took her beloved khaki uniform from its tissue and stroked the fitted jacket with its row of brass buttons. The slim skirt, a good foot off the ground for smart marching, would still fit her. Carefully she pinned up one side of the hat brim and attached the feather cockade: a little crushed but still jaunty. Should she wear the bandolier and carry the rifle? Yes! This was a battle just as important. She wondered if other women from the Khaki Corps might at this very moment be pressing their uniforms into prohibitionist service. More than likely.

Two days later she slung her bag into the little dog cart, hitched up Molly and set out south for Karioi, sitting proudly upright. I must be a fearsome sight, she thought, with my bandolier and rifle. Let the sly-groggers beware.

By the time she had passed through three work camps, the word was running ahead of her. Children in a small Maori kainga, camped on the outskirts of Karioi station, noticed her progress and laughed. But one old kuia knew of this engineer's wife and her purpose. 'E moko, run down the back track and warn your aunty,' she said to her grandson. 'Tell her the liquor lady is on the warpath.'

As light faded, Amelia Grice headed out of the bush and into cultivated land. Here were Maori vegetable gardens. Sheep and horses grazed. In the distance the houses and whares of Karioi could be seen, the tall roof of Cox's boarding house above the rest. She decided to head there and make a discreet enquiry or two. In this relatively civilised settlement there would surely be kindred spirits.

Mr Cox himself made her welcome. It had been a quiet week; no coach parties through on their way to the hot pools at Tokaanu, and now that the Ministry had shifted railway headquarters to Ohakune much of the supply traffic came up through Raetihi from the riverboats. Business was slow.

'In the distance I took you for the paymaster,' he laughed, 'that uniform and the rifle. But now I see it is you, Mrs Grice. I remember the old Khaki Corps. No sense letting a well-made uniform go to waste, eh? Come in, come in. Mrs Cox will have a hot meal for you in no time.'

Amelia was disquieted to be recognised. She had hoped to arrive incognito. She gave her host a quick salute and then turned her attention to a group of men seated at the large table by the window. They were all studiously eating, their eyes on their plates in a rather suspicious manner. She wandered towards them, her manner deliberately unconcerned. What were they drinking? Mrs Grice had a famous nose for sniffing out liquor.

'Good evening, gentlemen. I am Mrs Grice from Ohakune, here to purchase supplies for the railway engineers. May I join your table?' A rhetorical question since there was only one table in the room, but politeness dictated.

One of the men indicated a spare seat. The others went on eating. They appeared to be drinking tea. She engaged them in what she hoped was innocent conversation — the weather, the price of wool (they were wool-washers working down at the river) — then turned to the problem of food supply in these distant parts. The men answered as briefly as possible; two of them, grinning rather rudely, kept glancing at her firearm.

'No need for alarm,' she said, 'It is in fact a dummy. But you could never tell it from the real thing!'

'Aye, I could,' said the rude fellow. 'It has no hammer. So is the uniform a dummy, too?'

The others guffawed, which alarmed Mrs Grice. Had the uniform perhaps been a mistake? She had supposed everyone would recognise and respect the Khaki Corps.

'Take no notice of these rough fellows,' said Mr Cox, arriving with her meal. 'Now what will you have to drink with that?'

Mrs Grice gave him a coy look. 'What is on offer?'

'Tea, Mrs Cox's lemonade or water. You know the rules out here.'

She inhaled. Her nose twitched. 'Do I detect liquor?'

One of the wool-washers slid his eyes towards her and surreptitiously placed a hand over his mug, but Mr Cox was quick to reply. 'Our friend here, Simon, has brought his own alcoholic beverage in from Taihape. That is perfectly allowable. He might be persuaded to offer you a drop — free, of course — if you have need.'

'Tea would be sufficient tonight, thank you all the same,' said Mrs Grice calmly. Best not to show her hand yet. But her pulse quickened. She felt in her bones that this wool-washer would not have travelled to Taihape for liquor. Somewhere here she would find the sly-grog supplier.

A Chinaman is erected

For once there was a break in the weather. Jock decided this day would be the one to erect the Chinaman. The whole gang would be needed for this. He called the new recruits, Alec and Arthur, down from the dray where they sat huddled together in the frosty air. He indicated a pile of logs stacked at the entrance to the cutting.

'Watch the other lads and follow. We need to shift these logs up the slope and jam them in tightly to make our Chinaman.'

'Our what?' Alec and Arthur giggled, jabbing each other in the ribs. 'Going to trap a Chow then, are we?'

Jock sighed. The boys were bone ignorant, and together hardly worth a single one of his other workers. If they didn't buck up they'd have to go. It wasn't fair on the rest of the co-op. He shouldn't have let Freeman go.

'Just watch and learn, boys. I want this built before lunch.'

Dirk, always ready to move the work forward, silently steered the new recruits towards a pile of logs. Jock nodded his approval.

The new lads were as different from his stocky, silent son as chalk from cheese. If anyone could make decent formation workers out of Alec and Arthur, it would be Dirk.

The sides of the cutting were wide now. The dirt and stones dislodged by the gang's shovels would fall short of the waiting drays if they were not guided down by the log construction — Jock himself had no idea why it was called a Chinaman. One by one they raised the logs, wedging them side by side until they spanned the gap between the walls of the cutting. The lattice they built left a hole in the middle. Now, when they sent the rubble down it would bounce over the bridge of logs and fall through the hole into the waiting dray below.

Alec and Arthur struggled to keep up, and they found the big logs too heavy to manage on their own. All morning they were cruelly teased. Once or twice Jock and Dirk had to intervene when a fight threatened to break out. But by lunch the thing was built and the back-breaking work of widening the gap shovelful by shovelful continued.

Jock grunted with satisfaction as he worked. One day trains would roar through this cutting. Passengers would look out at the towering walls and give no thought to Jock and his men who had cut and shaped the walls with nothing but shovels and picks. He levered out a boulder. At least they were not working in hard rock. The volcanic soil had big boulders embedded in it but with care they could be rolled down to land heavily in the dray.

Alec and Arthur were levering away at a large one when it popped out too quickly for them to control and bounced down to the Chinaman. One of the gang, Dusty, working a little to the side of the boys, was clipped on the leg. He lost his balance and rolled down the slope, narrowly missing being crushed by the boulder. Dusty's language was more than ripe. A nasty gash below his knee bled into his boot, he had knocked his head on the logs of the Chinaman and he was bruised all over.

'You shout a warning when a rock's coming down!' raged Jock at the recruits, who stood up on the embankment in silence. An embarrassed grin threatened to break out on Arthur's face. 'And it's no laughing matter, you fool. Get down here where you can do no more damage! I'll dock you a day's wages for that.'

'That's not fair.' Alec was always the one to stand up for them both. 'We didn't bleeding know you had to shout.'

'Dear God, what is that brain in your little head for? A pair of idiots.'

The rest of the gang muttered while Jock wrapped a cloth around the gash. Dusty shook his fist at the lads. His look promised trouble.

Alec dug his brother in the ribs. 'This ain't going to work,' he whispered. 'Tonight I reckon we scarper.'

Arthur winked. 'Too right. Bloody boss.'

'Keep your head down, Art, and show willing. It's not for long.'

Seeing Dirk was watching him, Alec apologised to the hurt man and set to guiding the spoil into the Chinaman, earning plenty of retaliatory knocks himself.

A nose for liquor

In the morning, after a fine breakfast of eggs, bacon and freshly baked bread (how it raised one's spirits to be out of the bush in the open air with several properly built houses in sight!) Amelia Grice strolled around the town, glad of her warm uniform in the brisk air. The bandolier of bullets and the rifle she left in her room. No point in forewarning the enemy!

She stopped outside the little Native School, pleased to hear them singing very prettily one of her favourite hymns — *What a Friend we have in Jesus* — and then decided to visit the general store and Post Office. There must be someone in this fine little settlement who would have information for her. Here she was in luck. Behind the counter, knitting, was a bespectacled lady who welcomed her in. They exchanged names in a very civilised manner.

'I have heard of you, Mrs Grice,' said Miss Evans, folding up her knitting. She offered Amelia her pick from a jar of boiled sweets. 'You are the temperance lady from Ohakune. I also belong to the Alliance, though we have little to battle for here, as you know. The whole area is dry, thank the good Lord.'

Mrs Grice frowned. 'Is there not drunkenness here? Are families not suffering through liquor? In the work camps illegal liquor is readily available.'

Miss Evans lowered her voice. 'Indeed, Mrs Grice, but I would lose business if I complained. Look there.' She pulled back the curtain of her side window. A man could be seen leaving a small shack, half-plank half-tent, a few paces away. 'Mr Price sells cordials and tobacco and will give a rough shave for a penny. But—' here she lowered her voice even further — 'it is his strong hop beer that the men come for.'

'Ahh,' breathed Mrs Grice, 'hop beer. It is strong, you say?'

'Well above three per cent. Not that I have partaken, of course,' she hastened to add. 'I have seen men drunk after one bottle.'

'Outrageous!'

'And he brews it in that very tent, under the nose of the authorities. But I dare not complain, Mrs Grice. Dare not.'

'Though I, Miss Evans, have nothing to lose,' said Amelia Grice grimly.

Their conversation came to a halt as Mrs Cox, her apron still floury from the morning's baking, came in for the boarding-house mail: two letters and a parcel of condiments from Napier. Mrs Cox eyed the two women sharply but said nothing. Her husband had no problem with his guests bringing their own liquor, nor did he ask questions concerning where the drink was obtained. Mr Cox enjoyed a drop himself of an evening.

'Now,' whispered Miss Evans when the lady had left with her parcel, 'I think you will find the source of your bootleg trade down by the river.' She indicated the direction. 'The native store beyond the wool-washing. There is a great coming and going there on certain evenings. I watch it from my cottage. But they are rough men, Mrs Grice. Half-caste. I would fear for my life if they knew the complaint came from me.'

Amelia Grice fingered the buttons of her jacket; set her cockaded hat straight and rose. 'I understand your predicament, but it is our duty to act,' she said. 'Think of the lives we will improve, the families we can save.' She promised to keep Miss Evans's name out of any complaint she made, purchased two yards of green ribbon and a box of handkerchiefs for Mr Grice and left, full of hope.

Down by the river she was halted by a sea of snowy wool, laid out in the sun to dry. There seemed to be no path through it to the native store, which was a simple rough-planked whare close to the water's edge. She stood watching the activity as men and women, native and white, scoured the wool in the water and then laid it out to dry. A friendly native woman explained that the distance to market was so great and so difficult — across the island by packhorse to Napier — that it was best to reduce the weight by removing whatever they could — oil, sticks, dung — before they baled it.

'And what is all that activity down there?' asked Mrs Grice, pointing to the whare and feigning only a casual interest.

'Oh, not much happening,' said the woman, scrubbing away. 'Maybe catching eels. That people catch eels to smoke. Very good.'

Short of hiring a canoe to take her down, Amelia could see no way of reaching the whare. In any case, if the fellows were rough she would be wise to take the policeman with her. She left the spread of drying wool and walked back to the tiny police hut, hoping that an officer might be present. This was awkward. She respected Miss Evans's wish to remain anonymous, but she herself was more than happy to claim an arrest in her own name. If she loitered too long at the police station this might send an alarm to the bootleggers.

She decided the best plan would be to make an official complaint in writing. Back at the boarding house she laid out her request in clear terms that even the simplest police sergeant could not mistake.

> *Sir,*
> *I wish to lay two formal complaints thus:*
> *1. Against Mr Price whom I ~~understand~~* (she crossed out understand — it might implicate Miss Evans — and wrote) *believe to be selling over-proof hop beer illegally from his cordial and tobacco store in Karioi.*
>
> *2. The Native store by the Tokiahuru stream is reputed to be supplying sly grog to the bush camps. You would be well advised to conduct a surprise search of those premises.*
> *Signed*
> *A Concerned Prohibitionist*

After some internal debate, she added:
Mrs J J Grice, Ohakune

Through the door of the kitchen, Mrs Cox watched the uniformed guest busily writing. 'Look at that busybody,' she said to her husband who was taking his morning tea at the kitchen table. 'She'll be writing to the police, I'd lay threepence on it.'

Mr Cox agreed. 'She's been sniffing round all morning. But she'll be too late. Look down there.'

His wife went to the window and looked over the sea of white wool to the native store. Three men stood in the river and seemed to be busily hauling up their long eel baskets. Mrs Cox chuckled. 'No flies on those fellas. Someone's tipped them off. They're burying their grog in the river mud, inside those eel baskets, any fool can see that.'

'Not Mrs Grice, she can't. And Sergeant Baker, if he comes round today, which I doubt, will not look in the river. He has more than enough to do, the territory he has to cover.'

'Escorting the paymaster as well.' Mrs Cox tut-tutted to see Mrs Grice cross to the police station and slip the note under the door. 'But poor Sergeant Baker will have to act if it's a complaint.'

'Sergeant Baker enjoys his drop. He won't be in too much of a hurry.' Mr Cox stood. 'Thank you, Mother, a lovely scone. Now I'll hitch Mrs Grice's horse to help her on her way.'

Sarah Cameron saw the dog cart rattling its way up the track in the rain. By the time she had seen who it was, and regretted calling out, it was too late. Mrs Grice had reined in and was stepping down. The military attire was rather smart, thought Sarah, but what on earth was the purpose? Could Mrs Grice have some role in the constabulary? She dodged quickly inside and hid the liquor jar in the food locker.

'Will you have a cup of tea?' she asked the sodden woman.

Mrs Grice nodded. She looked around the tent, a strange light in her eye. 'This is where my maid-of-all-work, Maggie, lives?'

'Lived,' said her mother and sighed. 'They all leave the nest; it's to be expected, but I miss her.'

Mrs Grice, who at forty-two had no children and now did not expect any, had no answer to this. She sat shivering in her wet clothes, watching as Sarah poured tea.

'Mrs Grice,' said Sarah, 'you have come up from Karioi?'

'I have, and a more unpleasant journey I hope never to make again. Wet every step of the way.'

'Did you happen to see two lads on foot and laden?'

Mrs Grice thought. 'I did not, though my head was down with the rain driving.'

Sarah paced the tent. 'I am that mad I could spit. My husband had two new recruits in his co-op and they have disappeared, along with a Ministry of Works tent, a shovel that was lent to them, a side of bacon and my fresh loaf, the wretches.'

'Dear me.' Mrs Grice sipped her tea. 'Oh dear.' The hand holding the cup trembled. 'I hear Paymaster Stone and Sergeant Baker are due shortly. What if the boys attempt to hold them up? I would not care to get caught in a shoot-out. Perhaps I should stay here until—'

But Sarah was laughing. 'You need have no fear, Mrs Grice. Those poor idiots would not have the courage to face Stone and Baker. The paymaster is legendary. Two years he's been bringing in the pay, his saddlebags loaded, but not once has he been robbed. An attempt last year ended in ignominy for the miscreant; he was forced to walk ahead of the paymaster, a bullet through his hand, jeered and spat at by every co-op gang they passed, all the way to the lock-up. Since then no one would dare.'

Mrs Grice set down her cup. 'Nevertheless, perhaps I will wait for an escort.'

'Well, you are too late on that score, they have already ridden through. But it's Jock's gang I worry about. The co-op is two short now and Jock is being pressed to finish the cutting. It is more than he can manage, poor soul. Mr Furkert expects too much.' Sarah knew she was running on, knew this woman's husband was an engineer under Mr Furkert, but her anxiety loosened her tongue. 'Does your husband not find it hard, working for such a driven man?'

Amelia Grice nodded. 'Well, there have been moments. Mr Furkert has his little ways. Fussy, I might dare to say, but he is usually right and the Government values him.' She warmed her frozen hands at the fire. 'I expect some say that I myself drive too hard, in my own way.'

'Prohibition?' Sarah forced herself not to glance at the food locker.

Mrs Grice looked up eagerly. 'You have heard of my efforts? Are you a member of our band, then?'

'No, I am not,' said Sarah firmly. 'Perhaps in the cities there is hardship and poverty due to drunkenness, but I have not experienced it. I see no harm in a drink now and then.'

Mrs Grice held up a warning finger. 'Thin end of the wedge, Mrs Cameron, thin end. No doubt of it.'

Sarah's patience deserted her. She was tired of this pompous woman. 'You would deny a hardworking man, at the end of a long day's work, the simple comfort of a tot of whisky? A man driven beyond exhaustion by some engineer's desire to win a bet? Shame, Mrs Grice, your views are too black and white.'

Mrs Grice stood. 'And yours are ignorant. There is great hardship in the world that can be laid directly at the door of liquor.'

'You will find no hardship in this household. We are an upright and loving family.'

'Do I take that to mean, Mrs Cameron, that there is illegal liquor in this household?'

Sarah stood too. She removed the mug of tea from her guest's hand and put it down on the table before her anger drove her to throw it in her face. 'Whatever we keep in this household is no business of yours, Mrs Grice. I must ask you to leave now.'

Mrs Grice gathered her damp coat about her and made for the door. Her manner was not at all cowed; triumphant, rather. 'I think you will find that from now on the supply of liquor to these camps will cease. I am aware of the source and I have taken steps.'

Sarah shut the door firmly behind the departing woman. That last remark had her worried, though. These days Jock would hardly manage without his evening tot.

The dummy rifle

Mrs Grice was perhaps two miles short of Ohakune when two lads stepped out of the bush and hailed her. She was startled. They hadn't been walking ahead of her and there was no side track. But there they were, one each side of her horse. The taller one put a hand to Molly's bridle and the placid horse was happy enough to stop.

'Sorry to be a nuisance,' said this fellow with a grin, anything but sorry, 'but we have urgent need of your horse.' He nodded to the other boy and they both began unbuckling the traces.

Amelia Grice remembered about the co-op workers who had absconded with various items not their own. These would be those boys. For a moment she feared they might attack her, but when she saw how they fumbled with the buckles, how their fingers shook, she decided on action. Her dummy rifle lay at her feet. She felt for it, raised it slowly to her shoulder and said, in a voice that was not quite steady, 'Hands up, boys. Leave my horse alone.'

The fellows jumped to see the rifle. 'Hey, missus, no need for that,' said the leader of the two.

Amelia thought he might be signalling to the other lad; feared they might be about to jump her. She waved the rifle back and forth, pointing to one then the other. 'I want you to walk slowly up ahead of me. I know who you are. The authorities will be pleased to see you, no doubt.' She sat up straight, enjoying herself now.

All the bravado seemed to go out of the lads. They looked at each other, then back at the gun. 'Have a heart, Missus,' said the small one. 'We don't want no trouble. What say you just go on your way and leave us?'

'Do up my traces,' ordered Amelia Grice, 'and no funny business. This is loaded.' She waved it back and forth as the lads rebuckled the traces. Their eyes were shifting this way and that; she could see they were hoping to make a run for it. 'Now out in front, slowly. Walk ahead.'

This was the real thing! A true capture. Wouldn't Mr Grice be proud when she brought in the two runaways! Mr Furkert himself would no doubt have a word of praise.

Suddenly the boys bent down and sprinted for the bush at the side of the road. Mrs Grice clutched the rifle and, to her astonishment, it discharged. The taller of the two lads fell without a sound, his head shattered. The other boy screamed. He looked at his brother, then at the woman who sat there frozen, the gun still pointed in his direction.

'Don't, don't shoot! Please!'

Mrs Grice lowered the gun. The boy ran into the bush. She looked at the other one lying on the road. He was certainly dead. She examined the rifle. It was certainly real. Not a dummy. Her fingers shook. For several minutes she sat there. Then she turned back to look into the dog cart. There was her dummy rifle and bandolier, just where she had laid them that morning. This rifle — the real one — she remembered now, picking up from beside the boarding house door as she left. It would be Mr Cox's or a hunter's. A dreadful mistake.

For several more minutes she sat, unable to decide what to do. Then, raising her arm clad in its brave khaki uniform, she tossed the real firearm deep into the bush. Whimpering quietly she flicked the reins and clucked to Molly. The horse moved on, skirting the body on the road and headed back home to Ohakune.

Perhaps no one need know.

When the cart was out of sight, Arthur Hope emerged from the bush. He bent to his brother's body, cried out to see the ruined head, one eye missing. Tears streamed down his face. Fearful, stumbling through the mud, he dragged the body out of sight into the bush. Then, unable to see for tears, he searched among the ferns until he found the rifle. He sat in the damp undergrowth beside his brother. What now? He had no idea. Alec was the one who made the plans.

A police report

In the privacy of her bedroom, Mrs Grice unfolded the official letter with shaking fingers. The envelope was stamped 'New Zealand Police'.

Dear Madam,
In response to your complaint:
1. Mr Price, when approached by myself, admitted to selling over-proof hop beer. Before he could be officially charged, however, he has disappeared, no doubt taken his business elsewhere. Karioi has subsequently lost its only supplier of cordials and tobacco and its only barber, a matter that has upset many in the town.
2. The native store was searched by myself. No evidence of liquor of any sort was found.
3. Several Karioi townsfolk have assumed Miss Evans, our postmistress and general storekeeper, was the source of the complaint and have unfortunately made her life a misery.

She has taken ill. I have therefore felt it reasonable to make known the author of the complaint, viz yourself.
4. I do not intend to take the matter of Mr Price nor the native store any further.
Sergeant S Baker, Waimarino Police

A week ago Mrs Grice would have taken umbrage at the rude tone of the letter; might have complained to his superior and demanded her complaints be pursued further. Today she sat on her bed, staring at the words. A tear rolled down her cheek. She had acted only out of the highest principles. Fighting for prohibition was important, a noble cause. Yet what had she achieved by her trip to Karioi? The hop beer. Yes, a small victory perhaps, though the officer suggested that the business would only have shifted elsewhere. Oh! She crumpled the letter, the tears running freely now. It was too hard, fighting for the cause in such an isolated place. She needed the strength of other prohibitionists. The support of the sisterhood. Perhaps some leader could be persuaded to visit? A rally? But no. She didn't have the stomach for it at the moment. She stared out of the little window at the great trees, the grey sky, the mud.

The 'accident' on the return trip she tried to forget. Perhaps it was a dream? The body had not been reported. But the image of the terrified boy, the other's shattered head, would float up uninvited. Every time an inspector returned from that direction she feared to hear that the body had been discovered. Could they trace the gun to her? Would Mr Cox report the loss? And the other boy! He had seen it all. Of course he was a runaway himself and a thief. Perhaps he would disappear. But what if he came forward and accused her? The questions churned and churned: an insistent little railway thundering around and around until she could hear no sound of normal life. It had been an accident, an accident, of course it had. But then, they would ask, why hadn't she reported it? What could she answer? She was afraid of their laughter; that was the truth of it. They would have thought her a fool in her uniform with her silly wooden gun. She *was* a fool. Worse.

Outside, a bullock train plodded slowly into the settlement. Amelia Grice watched dully as men ran to unload railway iron and sleepers, building materials and food supplies. Soon railway trains would be coming though. And more people. New buildings and tents were appearing daily, it seemed.

But what was this? Her attention was caught by a hoarding being nailed onto a rough shack. A large woman was shouting instructions below. SEDDON HOUSE TEMPERANCE HOTEL the hoarding read. Prop. Mrs A Kerr. At last a kindred spirit!

Amelia Grice smoothed her hair, took a deep breath. She threw the police report into a corner. It had been a week now. Perhaps nothing would be discovered. She opened the door and stood where Mrs Kerr might notice her.

Change of name

Gabriel Locke, preacher and, by necessity, supplier of cookhouse wood, was not, in the winter of 1907, overly pleased with his lot. He had come to this railway-building enterprise expecting growth, prosperity, an ever-expanding population — fertile ground for converts. The population was growing, true — over a thousand souls this side of Ohakune, they said, and the same south of that squalid little headquarters. But ready for conversion they were not. Several times he had considered moving on, but last year there had been a little trouble with the authorities in Napier, and again a few months later in Nelson. Gabriel Locke (a new name which he rather fancied) felt it better to keep clear of the authorities for the moment.

Gabriel, born Stanley Lamb of Grimsby, Yorkshire, was the son and grandson of successful itinerant preachers. He had grown up travelling with his father from town to town, listening to thundering sermons and collecting, with a sweet smile, the coins donated by the grateful and comforted congregation. His father was revered. Food and other gifts were donated when money was scarce. It seemed to young Stanley that a preacher's life was a profitable one, and that he was well suited to follow in his father's footsteps. Mr Lamb, however, had a different view.

'This life is not for you, son,' he said one Sunday over a good round of roast beef that Mrs Lamb had cooked to perfection. 'You have not the calling.'

Stanley was startled. Could his father see what went on in his head? 'How can you know that, Father? If the Lord calls me, then I am the one to say so.'

'I fear you see the benefits—' his father waved a fork at his slice of beef and silky gravy — 'rather than the comfort you can bring to lost souls; the guidance you can give to feet that have strayed.'

Stanley had argued; had pleaded with his father to let him try a sermon. His father had remained firm.

'A sermon is only part of it, son. There is the ministry. You are not cut out. That is my word on it.'

Mrs Lamb had taken Stanley's part. 'Why not give him a trial, Father, he's that keen.'

But Mr Lamb had instead taken on a young orphan lad, adopted into the family a year past, as apprentice preacher. 'I have arranged for you to train as a clerk with lawyer Grampian,' he told Stanley. 'It will do you good to sit with him and learn the ways of the law. You have a fine copperplate and will write up his notes well.'

An outrageous decree. Stanley raged; wept; appealed to his mother. He tormented the adopted lad mercilessly, snatching food from his plate, hiding his shoes, pinching his arm. When his father caught him at it, Stanley was beaten. He considered taking his father's life and his preaching circuit both, but could think of no satisfactory way to achieve either. In the end he opted to leave home with as much of the family savings as he could lay his hands on, and boarded a ship — assisted passage — to New Zealand.

On the voyage out a tall, striking man entertained the passengers with acts of mesmerism. Stanley was fascinated and attended every performance. The showman, 'Doctor Faustus', would call for a volunteer. Stanley was reluctant to step up for fear of ridicule — or worse, that some unpleasant trait of character might be revealed. The volunteer was then hypnotised, sometimes with a pocket watch swinging before his eyes, sometimes (in the case of women) with a stroking finger and soothing words. The resulting antics of the mesmerised person were often hilarious, sometimes shocking. Stanley tried the trick on a shipboard acquaintance — a suitably gullible lady. Under his stroking finger and deep gaze she fell into a trance. He was highly amused — and aroused — to find how suggestible she became, readily baring her breasts and murmuring suggestive endearments. That first time he found it difficult to snap her out of the state and was becoming panicked by her increasingly frantic approaches. When she finally regained her hold on the real world they were both sweating and dishevelled. The lady slapped his faced and threatened to call her husband. Stanley resolved to hone the skill. Perhaps mesmerism could be a useful tool in his future ministry.

It was easy enough, on arrival, to change his name (to Wesley Priestley) and avoid those who expected him to navvy on the railroad. He would show his father and become a famous preacher. A lady on the ship had extolled the delights of Napier. That's where he would settle. Armed with a forged set of glowing recommendations from his father's Wesleyan Mission (a better use of his fine copperplate than lawyer's drudge), he presented himself to the Methodist circuit and offered to travel wherever there was need. Wesley had a way with ladies, there was no doubting that, and an engaging flow from the pulpit. Sometimes he preached from the wool saleroom in the manner of the Methodists, but he was beholden to those more senior and was confronted too many times by recently arrived members of the congregation whose searching questions about his background in the Home Country irritated him.

One Sunday he experimented with what he called 'laying on of hands', using his newly learned technique on a young girl who had sat throughout the service drooping, pale and sickly. The girl fell into a trance readily enough, but when he murmured to her that she was now cured she jumped to her feet and shrieked that the devil was attacking her, that she was burning, that she was a sinner; finally falling into a deep and alarming faint. The mother scooped up her daughter and ran from the church, calling for a doctor.

There was no chance after that of further preaching work among the serious and hardworking Methodists. Stanley became disillusioned with the idea of preaching. He 'purchased' a fine thoroughbred from one of his flock — his promise to pay the next day accepted in good faith — and set out south, Sunday's collection jingling in his pocket, in search of more gullible souls.

Stanley Lamb (now Dankworth Fearnley) arrived in Nelson with a new career in mind, that of general medical practitioner. His mother had trained as a nurse and practised in a doctor's surgery back in Grimsby. He knew something about the business. Why not give it a go? Again the copperplate handwriting served him well. In Wellington he had visited a doctor's surgery complaining of congested lungs. In the waiting room he slipped a medical journal into his satchel. In the inner sanctum his quick eyes had studied the set-up, the citations on the wall, the manner of writing a script. He wheezed, coughed, invented more symptoms and, while the doctor was busily writing, strolled towards a tray of instruments and pocketed one or two.

He arrived in Nelson as Dr Dankworth Fearnley MD. He searched for an area a little out of town but with a growing population, and with no sign of a rival doctor's surgery. He rented a cottage, distributed leaflets advertising his qualifications, hung a notice above the door and waited for customers. They came. He bought a supply of blue bottles and mixed his own medications (main ingredients: sherry, camphor, cold tea, milk of magnesia and sugar syrup).

For a while he enjoyed charming (and sometimes hypnotising) the ladies, teasing the children and joking with the men. The income was pleasing. But the life didn't suit him. He was bored sitting in the same room every day listening to complaints. He missed the performance of preaching: the flow of words, the raised arms, the exhortations; the way a congregation could be roused to a fervour. Stanley Lamb was convinced a great future lay ahead for him. His father was wrong to say he was not cut out for preaching. He dreamed of founding a wealthy new church in New Zealand, news of which would confound and humble his father back home. Treating colicky babies and their peaky parents was not part of this dream.

One evening a burly man came back to the surgery just as he was leaving and confronted him in the street. 'That medicine you sold me nearly killed my wife!' he ranted. 'She's been throwing up for two days and it only stopped when I poured the damned stuff down the toilet. I want my money back!'

Dr Fearnley frowned. 'Your wife was ill. My valuable elixir would have cured her, you stupid man.'

The man was drunk. He took a swing at the doctor, a

blow that connected painfully with Lamb's ear. Enraged (he had always possessed a quick temper), the doctor rammed the drunken man's head against the doorpost and then, when he fell, kicked him savagely in the stomach. The fellow lay still. Fearing curious passers-by, the gasping doctor shoved open his surgery door and dragged the man inside. His head was bleeding profusely. Was he dead or simply unconscious? In either case, matters could soon become messy: police would be involved; his credentials checked. Stanley Lamb shrugged. He was tired of this particular venture anyway. Time to move on. He emptied his safe, retrieved his horse from the stables, shaved off his beard and moustache and headed away.

Preaching was his calling, he was sure of that. But for a time somewhere isolated might be a good idea.

Now, after another name change, he was stuck in Makatote. Perhaps his luck would change. He dumped another load of firewood beside the voracious stove and straightened his back. His good looks and fine bearing had no effect on Mrs Bright. He might as well be an ugly imbecile for all the extra tidbits he earned.

'I'll need another load — and a bigger one — before the hour's out, Gabriel,' she said. 'There's a new bunch of workers arriving for a meal. On their way to Raurimu. Must be more than a hundred working there now.'

Gabriel gave her one of his narrow-eyed looks — to no effect. There was no way to pierce her armour or to control her. It frustrated him. He could charm most people. Or strike fear.

'Off you go, Goldilocks,' she said, bending over the stove, her behind inviting a good kick. But the truth was, Gabriel Locke feared the cook. Her bulk, her forthright manner and her way with a cleaver did not invite confrontation of any kind.

He walked out humming what he hoped was a cheerful and defiant tune. Soon Billy would be back from work. Billy was another matter entirely. Billy was fertile ground. A lovely boy who would follow him anywhere. Several of the other workers would listen to his preaching and pay for the pleasure or comfort of his words. But Billy was the one. He must be separated from that half-caste friend who, like the cook, was definitely stony ground. With Billy as a fervent and unquestioning acolyte what mightn't they achieve together!

'Praise the Lord!' sang Gabriel Locke. And meant it.

A willing convert

Billy Cameron wiped the sweat out of his eyes and signalled across to Ruri. He shouted with pure pleasure to see the great column swing a little, drop, swing again as they hauled on their ropes. The last iron strut of the pier slotted into place. Now the valley was filled with the bang bang bang of the riveters' hammers. Tommy Tar, the new top man, untied the ropes from the girder. Down they fell, snaking past the lattice to fall on the rocks below. What a structure! And this pier was by no means the tallest. The middle piers would rise from the riverbed itself, two hundred and seventy feet or more, they said. Meantime, though, work on those giants was held up by difficult foundation work.

Billy longed to climb the girders, to handle the hot rivets or ride the Blondin as it winched its lofty way across on the wire rope. That would be something! He was nimble and surefooted. Ruri had no ambition in that direction — 'leave clambering to sailors and circus acrobats' — but Billy dreamed of being up among those airy girders, looking down on the world and up towards heaven. Gabriel said it was a noble desire and that the Lord would give him strength if his faith was sufficient.

Ruri whistled their secret signal. Billy whistled back. Shift over. They started scrambling down the slope to the riverbed, winding their ropes as they went. Long, heavy lengths; carrying them back up to the Workshop ready for tomorrow took all of Billy's strength. Ruri, bigger and taller, slung the coil over his shoulder and scrambled hand over hand, hardly puffing, while Billy's coil dragged and threatened to trip him on the treacherous slope. Ruri laughed to see his friend tangled in a heap. 'Wait there. I'll come back and help.' He headed on up though the scrub while Billy puffed and heaved at the maddening rope. Wet from the river, it was twice as heavy. He sat there in a messy heap until Ruri returned. Ruri had a way with rope — somehow it behaved under his fingers, formed into neat coils and stayed put. Together they dragged it up, deposited it ready for the next day, then raced across the slope and down to the village, looking forward to a hot drink and a good supper.

Billy paused at the cookhouse door. 'I'll just see if Gabriel is waiting back at the tent.'

'Come on, Billy, the preacher can walk over by himself.'

'He might be waiting, though. For me.'

'He's not your nanny, Billy. Let him be.'

'I'll just see though. Keep a place for us.'

Ruri went inside shaking his head, while Billy ran.

Gabriel *was* there, inside the tent, waiting. 'Billy! I knew you would come!' He slung an easy arm over Billy's shoulder. 'The Lord greets you.' He kissed Billy's cheek softly.

'The Lord greets you,' replied Billy, kissing Gabriel's hand, which was then placed in blessing on the boy's head. Billy loved this secret ritual. They stood face to face, hand to hand for a moment. Gabriel called this 'silent communion'. Gently he took the boy by the shoulders and turned him, then wrapped him in a warm embrace, pressing his whole body against Billy's back. It felt good.

'Now to eat! Praise the Lord!' sang Gabriel.

'Praise the Lord!' whispered Billy. Then in his ordinary voice, 'Come on. Ruri's saving us a place.'

'Oh, Ruri. He's not a believer, Billy.'

'But he's my friend. Come on! I'm starving.'

Gabriel held out his hand for one last touch, but Billy was off, running.

At the cookhouse door Billy stood, searching for Ruri. Gabriel, behind him, saw a space and was manoeuvring Billy in that direction when a great shout rang out.

'Billy! Billyboy Cameron! Come on over here!'

Billy's mouth dropped open. He stared, then whooped with joy. 'Freeman! Is that you?' He turned to the grinning workers. 'It's my brother! It's Freeman. Hey, Ruri, it's my brother!' Ruri rose from his seat, still chewing, and waved for them both to come and sit down. The three boys, laughing and back-slapping, sat together. They fell on the chops and mash, full of questions and news. By the time Billy remembered the preacher, Gabriel had disappeared.

An even greater surprise, which Freeman had kept to himself, came after tea when he led the way to the Scobie shack. There was Maggie, one child on her knee, the other sitting on the floor beside her while she told them some wild tale that had them both giggling. Rose and Brennan sat at the little table watching.

Billy stood in the doorway laughing. 'The Lord bless us!' (A favourite phrase of Gabriel's.) 'I knew Mrs Scobie would make it happen for Freeman, but I never thought Maggie, too! Hey, Ruri, this is my sister, Maggie.'

Ruri ducked his head. 'Good evening,' he said, his voice barely audible. He turned to leave, but Rose held out her hand.

'Come in, Ruri, I've seen you about and heard how you made a good stretcher when there was need. I'd like you to show me sometime.'

Ruri nodded.

'My sister,' said Billy, digging him in the ribs, 'is a pretty one, don't you think?'

Ruri nodded again.

Maggie flushed scarlet. Clear to see she liked the look of Ruri. 'Shut your mouth, Billy, you blather on too much. I thought man's work might change you. '

Ruri backed against the wall, then slid towards the corner. This happy family group was interesting, but he had no idea how to become part of it.

Billy remembered something. 'Maggie, I have a new friend, a grand preacher, and he's the one cured you back at the camp.'

Maggie jigged little Alice on her knee. 'He said that?'

'And he has cured others. Hasn't he, Ruri?'

Ruri remained silent.

Billy frowned. 'Ruri doesn't care for Gabriel, but I believe. And so do lots of people. You should come to his sermons. He can make things happen. Good things. And change the world—' Billy stopped. They were all listening too hard. He was talking too much. He flushed. 'Well, anyway.'

Freeman slapped him on the back. 'Billy Cameron, you'd believe you could fly if someone honey-tongued you into it. Have you room in your tent for one more? I am fair dropping and Mr Scobie is likely the same.'

Billy danced a jig that had the children laughing. 'We have room! Eh, Freeman, it's great to see you.'

'Maggie will sleep here,' said Rose Scobie, 'with the children. But you are free to come whenever you like, boys. Ruri, my Con is quick with his fingers, you might teach him some of your tricks.'

Ruri cleared his throat; his quick smile was for Maggie. He tilted his dark head in Rose's direction and was gone.

Amos Bread is comforted

Mrs Bright dumped a tray of warm loaves on the kitchen table and swatted at the flies with her tea towel. Someone was standing at the door looking in. A new face. Mrs Bright prided herself on recognising them all — her horde of hungry workers. In Mrs Bright's view it was her food that kept the whole vast enterprise going. That great pile of iron girders wouldn't be rising in the gully without her roasts and pies and mashed potatoes. The lad at the door looked peaky, something desperate about the way he stood so quiet.

'Cat got your tongue?' Mrs Bright was not one for easy banter. The boy stood there silent. She sighed. 'Are you new employed here? What's your name?'

He shook his head, whatever that might mean. 'Well, if you want a bite of food, fetch me a pile of wood from out the back. Then we'll see.'

He disappeared like a shot and was back just as quick — a sight more nippy than Preacher Goldie. Mrs Bright banged a plate of cold meat and a hunk of bread on the table, then poured him a mug of sweet tea.

'Thanks.' The boy set to. His fair hair was plastered with mud. Everything about the lad needed a good wash. Looked like he'd been living rough for some time. He gulped at the tea through a mouth stuffed with bread and almost choked.

Mrs Bright cut another round of meat for him. 'Steady on, lad. That's good meat. Don't waste it now.' There's a story here, she thought. That boy is afraid of something or someone. 'Where did you come from then?'

The boy swallowed and looked up at her. Clear to see he was making up a tale. 'Up north,' he said, his accent giving him away as a new feller off the boat. 'Looking for work.'

Mrs Bright guessed he had come from the south, was a recruit who'd found the navvying too tough and had run. She'd seen plenty before him who couldn't take it. But they were usually angry, growling about being trapped or tricked by the bosses or forced to work longer hours than was fair. This lad seemed different. Lost and frightened. Mrs Bright was not known for her soft spot, but the fellow touched her. She brought out another tray of loaves. He was still sitting there, head hanging, fingers scraping at the mud on his trousers. She could do with another hand in the kitchen.

'Want a job?'

His eyes brightened. A quick nod.

'We'll see what the boss says. What's your name then?'

Another pause, then, 'Amos.'

He'd made that up. 'Just Amos?'

He nodded.

'Need to have a surname if you're on the payroll, lad.' She waited. 'None of my business. You thought of Amos. Think of a last name.'

'Bread,' he said, and his eyes filled with tears.

Dear Lord, thought Mrs Bright, he's in a bad way. 'Well, Amos Bread, clear the long table and scrub it and I'll find you a tent. Ruri and Billy have a space. You'll like them. You can help that layabout Goldilocks with the stoves and lay out food at mealtime. But first get over to the pump and wash off that mud.'

I might regret this, she thought. The lad looks like he's in desperate need of a mother. And I'm too busy for that kind of carry-on. She smiled, though, as she scraped potatoes for the mash.

Billy and Gabriel were in the tent when Amos arrived with his stretcher and blanket. The two were sitting together, Gabriel reading out loud from the Bible. Amos swallowed. It looked so warm and safe in the candlelight. He cleared his throat. Gabriel noticed the newcomer but held up a finger to stay him.

' "I am the good shepherd; I know my sheep and they know me." ' Gabriel paused in his reading and nodded towards Amos; patted the bed beside him, then went on. ' "As the Father knoweth me, even so know I the Father: and I lay down my life for the sheep." So, Billy, Jesus laid down his life for us. We are his sheep.' Again he looked up at the new lad. 'And if we are called to lay down our life for the Lord that is an honour and cause for rejoicing.' He patted Billy's knee; closed the Bible. 'So, who is this new brother?'

'Amos.' It came out in a whisper. 'Amos Bread.'

Billy jumped up and shook his hand. 'Come in, brother. This is Gabriel Locke, a preacher and my friend. Are you to stay in our tent?'

Amos nodded.

Billy helped set up the stretcher, chattering about the viaduct, the layout of the village, the power of the words in the Bible. Amos listened, his eyes darting here and there as he unpacked his few possessions but remained silent. Gabriel Locke lay back on his stretcher, studying the new lad. He noted the careful way Amos laid his pack out of sight under the bed: something precious in there. Amos kept clasping his hands to stop them shaking: a deep fear or anxiety? Gabriel would soon ferret it out.

'Do you love the Lord?' said Gabriel Locke, his voice silky as water running over stone. 'Do you follow Him, Amos Bread?'

Amos cleared his throat. 'Eh? I went to church as a lad, sir. Not much chance recently.'

'I hear by your voice you are from the north of England like myself?'

For a moment Amos's face split into a smile, then just as quickly closed down. 'No, not really. I been in Australia.'

Clearly a lie. Gabriel left that line of enquiry for later. He kept his voice quiet and friendly. 'You're on your own?'

Amos nodded. He turned away, then slumped to the bed, tears pouring down. Great sobs shook him.

'Hey!' said Billy, looking to Gabriel in alarm. 'We're all friends here, Amos.'

Gabriel sat beside the howling boy. He held him in his arms and rocked him. 'The love of the Lord will comfort you in your anguish, Amos. You are the lost sheep who has returned. Blessed is he who returns to the Lord.' He talked on, intoning the words in a way that he knew would calm, perhaps mesmerise. Gabriel held the boy's head against his shoulder and stroked his back, still intoning. Billy sat on the other side and held his hand. Slowly the sobs receded, then ceased. Amos breathed steadily, slower and slower, his head still buried in Gabriel's embrace.

The preacher laid the boy down and covered him with his blanket. 'We have a new brother, Billy. Look, he has fallen asleep in the love of the Lord. Amos will be a true believer. He has a story to tell, I think, a troubled one. We will leave that until later.'

Billy took his friend's hand. 'How do you do that, Gabriel? You are so good at it.'

'It is a gift from God.' Gabriel opened his arms and pulled Billy into an embrace. 'But it is a difficult path, Brother Billy, and you are a comfort to me.'

The surveyor's son

As the evenings grew longer Ruri was often seen after work, or on a Sunday, outside the Scobie shack with Maggie and the two children, Alice and Con. Con was a serious boy, fair-headed like his mother but in temperament more like his quiet father. Alice was the tearaway. She loved this wild environment, loved to climb trees, explore the stream or wander off into the gully. 'I thought I saw a bear,' she might say when Maggie scolded her for running away. Or, 'There was a long thing in the river, I needed to poke it.' Maggie encouraged the little girl's imagination, but was glad when Ruri arrived and took one of the children under his wing. He showed Con how to make a pigeon trap, though when a bird was caught, Con cried and begged for it to be freed. Ruri winked at Maggie and carried the kereru around to the back of the house. Con was happy enough to eat his share later. Fresh meat, especially kereru, was a treat.

Ruri often brought a bunch of watercress or peppery leaves to the house 'for the pot', but wouldn't come inside or eat with them. He was happy enough to sit in the sun near to Maggie and watch the children. Maggie would chatter away to him or the children, pointing out a flowering tree or bird or some other bright thing, and then repeating the name Ruri gave it. Rose wanted the children to learn Ruri's language as well as their own.

Rose came and went, always busy with something. She helped out at the little school — singing and arithmetic were her favourite subjects — and was soon a great favourite with the handful of grubby children from all corners of the world. But the construction of the viaduct was her obsession. Always curious to discover new techniques, she marvelled at the inventiveness of the team in the Workshop. After a school day she could usually be found inside that noisy cavern, shouting questions or examining machinery.

Andrew Anderson, partner with his brother in the Christchurch engineering firm, had recently arrived with his wife and children to oversee the operation — the biggest viaduct anyone had attempted in the colony. Rose and Brennan were often invited to their fine cottage, where they contributed to musical evenings, Rose with her lovely singing and Brennan on trumpet.

One wet Sunday, Maggie was playing games with the children inside. Rose saw Ruri hovering outside. She opened the door and Ruri began to walk away.

'Come in, Ruri!' she called. 'Please do. I'd like to talk to you.'

Ruri looked alarmed. Rose was a rather terrifying woman. So tall, too full of life for a woman. But Maggie beckoned, too, reassuring him. Ruri came inside, head bent, eyes lowered. He gave Maggie a quick grin and joined the children on the floor.

Rose sat on a chair nearby. 'Thank you for teaching the children your language,' she said.

Ruri nodded.

'What does your own name mean?'

Ruri looked up at her, a certain pride in his face. 'Ruri is short for Kairuri. Kairuri is surveyor.'

'Surveyor! A fine occupation. And necessary if we wish to have railroads. Your parents wished you to become one?'

Ruri shrugged. 'Maybe. My mother maybe. I am named after the man who planned this railroad.'

Rose frowned. 'There were many surveyors—'

'Ae, but I am named after the man whose plan was chosen. My other name is Rokipoto. That is our way of saying Rochfort. My mother gave me that name.' Ruri looked to Maggie for support, anxious that he had spoken for too long.

He need have no worry on that score. Rose leaped to her feet, obviously delighted. 'John Rochfort! But I come from the Rochfort Plateau and Mount Rochfort, which is named after the same man! The one who discovered coal on Denniston! But tell me. Tell me the story. Why are you named after him?'

Again Ruri looked to Maggie, needing her reassurance.

'Tell us, Ruri.' She settled sleepy Alice on her stretcher and gave Con a wooden puzzle. 'Even I have heard of Rochfort. How are you named for him?'

Ruri stood. He nodded towards both women and then began to speak. His words were quiet but strangely formal, his eyes fixed on the trees beyond the window. 'I come from Papatupu which is not far from Ohakune. My river is the Maunganui o te Ao. I am of Maniapoto iwi. And also Ngati Rangi. Though my mother . . .' Here he paused and shrugged. 'Well, I will not give you my whole ancestry. It is not so simple to tell. Before I was born, Mr Rochfort was asked by Government to find a way for the railway through this —' he opened both arms wide —, 'this great wilderness. The Rohe Potae. It was forbidden by my tribe for white people to pass through. They may not cross the line.' Ruri drew an imaginary line across the room and little Con immediately jumped over it and then back, giggling.

Ruri laughed. 'Kao, kao, little one, you may not cross over. But John Rochfort, he *did* cross. You have heard of Major Kemp?'

Neither woman had heard the name.

'Te Keepa Te Rangihiwinui.' Ruri's mouth turned down. 'From down near Whanganui. A chief of a different tribe who helped the white soldiers against those of us further up the river. But that is another story. Major Kemp — Keepa — he said to Rochfort, "I have negotiated with the tribes. They wish to have a railway. You are safe to explore the Rohe Potae." So my father he come upriver with his chainman and his interpreter.'

'Your father?' said Rose. 'Rochfort is your father?'

Ruri stood tall. 'Ae. So my mother says. You can see my pale skin. But he is dead now, my father. He was already old when he came upriver.'

'This is surprising,' said Rose, 'I'm sure he had a wife and family in Nelson.'

Ruri grinned. 'Papatupu is a long way from Nelson. And Rochfort, so my mother says, was a man of strong appetites. When Rochfort came to Papatupu our elder was angry. He would not let Rochfort come any further. "Stop!" he ordered. "You may not cross the line." My father told him the Government and the tribes had agreed to allow him. "No one talked to me," said Koro, bravely. "This hapu says no railway and no crossing the line." He pointed his gun at my father's chest. "Go back!"'

Ruri was enjoying the story now and all in the room listened as he acted the parts. 'Rochfort he did this.' Ruri clutched his lapels and tore open his jacket. '"Shoot! Shoot me, then!" That's what my father cried. My mother she watched and she said

Rokipoto, my father, was very brave to say such a thing when a gun is pointed to his chest. The hapu admired this even though they did not want him to pass. And he spoke all his words in our tongue, te reo, so again he was admired. Even Koro was impressed. But he hated to have a railway or any white people taking our land so he locked up Rochfort in a whare. So!' Ruri wagged his head back and forth, his hands fluttering like birds flying. 'Much korero. Every night, arguments. Some want to kill him; some afraid of other Maniapoto, who agreed with the railway. Rochfort talk every night, too, in his whare, to whoever come past. My mother, her duty was to look after him. An important man, even a prisoner must be served with honour. My mother offer to comfort him. So she did this. Kept him company. And here am I after some months!' Ruri made a little bow.

'Take care,' said Rose, 'what you say in front of the children. Con understands more than you might think.' But her eyes were laughing. 'What happened then? What happened to the survey?' Rose as usual had to know all the details.

'Three days in the whare as prisoner and then our people take him back downriver to Whanganui — all the way down the river in many waka. They put his feet on Whanganui ground and say: "No more survey. Stay down among your Pakeha friends." But Rochfort my father he don't give up ever. Back he came. He could walk all day through the bush even better than our people. Without food for many days and still he can walk. This time he came with Government paper and Major Kemp and after more korero my hapu let him come through. My mother was very sorry to see him go on north.'

'Did you meet him? Your father?'

Ruri shook his head sadly. 'No, never. When my mother big with me she heard he was up north with the Maniapoto so she go to claim marriage in our own custom. She set off proud, even though some in our hapu laughed at her and some were mocking. They said she was making the whole story up. After many days she come back very quiet. She found out Mr Rochfort he already married in our custom with Ngahuia, a cousin of Rewi Maniapoto himself. She was much more powerful than my mother. Rewi Maniapoto would not believe her story. He said Ngahuia was the chosen wife, so he would not let my mother meet Ngahuia who also carried Rochfort's child. At any rate Mr Rochfort was away on more surveying. So.' Ruri sighed and they all fell silent.

'But,' said Rose, 'they accepted you, your hapu?'

'Not all. I am too pale. My mother maybe boast too much about my famous father. How great a man I will be. Soon she left the hapu and came to Ohakune. She grows vegetables there for the Pakeha on some land of her cousin.'

Rose leaned back in her chair. 'That is a wonderful story, Ruri. Your father was a very strong man. I wish I had met him. There was a great argument in the Government about which route the railway would take, did you know? Many powerful men wanted it to go through their own lands — east through Napier, or west through New Plymouth. There was so much argument that in the end they asked only the South Island Members of Parliament to decide. They chose your father's route — this one through the wild centre. In their view it was the best. Even though at that time Rochfort had no scheme for bringing the line down off the plateau, they accepted his plan. They took that leap of faith because of your father's fine reputation.'

'And here we all are!' said Maggie. 'My father and brothers and thousands of others. All here because of your father!'

Ruri's head was high now and he looked at them all with pride. 'So that is why I am named Kairuri Rokipoto, and why my mother has sent me to school and to work here on the railway.'

Con danced around the room. 'Ruri Rokipoto! You build the railway. I will drive the train.'

Ruri tossed the little boy in the air. 'Both of us, then, tamariki. Both of us railway men!'

RAILROADING

My great-uncle Freeman was a very tall and upright man even in old age, which was the only time, of course, that I knew him. I remember his great shock of white hair and his loud bellowing laugh. He always had some sweet or a coin in his pocket for us grandchildren. He never married. Gran said he was sweet on a woman back in the old days, but that she was 'not available'. I wonder now whether that woman was Rose, or one of the Anderson daughters and cousins who came to Makatote for the summer. Too late now to discover that thread of the story.

Uncle Freeman became an engineer with the railways. When he talked about those early days his stories were always happy ones. He often spoke as if he was still living the events. 'Here I am on top of the mountain,' he would boom. 'Magnificent view! Can see right to Mount Egmont!' Or 'Oho! The look on their faces! They're expecting a station and all they can see is wasteland!' Perhaps he was uncomfortable with, or was sheltering us from, harsh truths. More likely, I think, it was his nature. His outlook on life was generally optimistic. He remembered the good times, where Gran harboured dark memories. And I have to admit, too, that I may be biased: do I remember Gran's stories more vividly than Uncle Freeman's because of my interest in unravelling sad or shocking mysteries?

Once, when we were children and were waiting at Wellington railway station to catch the train back up home, Uncle Freeman was there with us. I suppose he was still working in the railways then. He must have come to say goodbye. The engine was puffing and hissing, raising steam for the journey. Uncle Freeman hoisted me up on his shoulders so I could shake hands with the stoker. He laughed when I cried and buried my head in his shoulder, overcome with the noise and size and blackness of the beast, breathing there in the dark night, wreathed in steam.

'Hey there, sweetheart,' said Uncle Freeman. 'That there is a thing of beauty. One of God's glories. It will work all night to carry you and a hundred others all the way home. A well-oiled marvel, that is. Nothing to be afraid of.'

But I was. And I still remember the fear. My brother clamoured to be lifted; to say hello to the engine driver and shake the grimy stoker's hand. He saw the thing of beauty.

When I was ten or eleven I lived for a time in Ohakune with Gran. Some unmentionable trouble at home. Uncle Freeman would stay with Gran when he was on one of his inspection trips.

'Do you remember,' he said one night, his long legs propped on a stool so that his feet were exactly in front of the coal fire, 'that wonderful Christmas when we climbed the volcano? What fun we had. Was it before the coach passenger service from Ohakune or after, do you remember?'

'After. And I wasn't with you. I had Christmas with Mam and Da like a good girl. You were mad. Stark staring. Could have died and who would have known?' But she smiled at that memory all the same.

'Yes, after, you're right. The railhead reached Ohakune earlier that year. I remember the first day an engine arrived here at Ohakune. You would have been at Makatote, Mags. A PWD engine, ex-Railways L class. A 2-4-0 tank locomotive.' (He often talked in riddles like that.) 'Sweet little lady; a lovely sight. Everyone gathered and cheered.'

'And that nice engineer fell and was killed,' said Gran. 'They were in too much of a hurry.'

'No, Mags, it was necessary. Government was demanding a return on their huge investment. All those thousands of pounds going out to workers every week. No passenger tickets sold. The Members of Parliament were asking questions.'

Gran wouldn't buy that argument. 'So they cut corners.'

Uncle Freeman wagged a finger at his sister. 'So you say. But there was no cutting corners on our coach road. Brennan Scobie and I and the workers. We made a top job of that. All those cobbles! Wonderful piece of work. I could have burst with pride the first day the coaches drove it.'

'Those cobbles,' said Gran, 'were a severe trial to many a lady's backside, mine included!' She plucked at a thread of loose wool on her jersey. Then came the sigh, the downcast eyes, the shake of the head. Was she remembering her father, perhaps? All Uncle Freeman's jollity ran off her back like water on oilskin. Yet there must have been happy times. She herself must have enjoyed life then. I wanted her to tell happy stories, like my great-uncle Freeman.

SPRING /
SUMMER 1907

The coach road

Brennan and Freeman leave their horses hitched a little distance away from the area that will later become the Ohakune railway station. Their horses, being wild-bred Kaimanawas and recently broken in, are still skittish around machinery and noise. The stolid coach horses, too, spook them: so many of them, their noses into feedbags, stoking up for the journey. The wild-bred horses seem to recognise their own and distrust all others. Freeman swings along beside Brennan, trying to look the nonchalant and experienced chainman. But his eyes are everywhere; once or twice he skips like a child. In the few months he's been at Makatote the railroad has arrived at Ohakune! But this is strange: the waiting coaches are here in the bush, several miles from the settlement.

'Why here?' he asks Brennan. 'The people of Ohakune won't be pleased.'

Brennan laughs. 'The railroad can't please every settlement. Not in this terrain. It's hard enough as it is, keeping the right gradient through these gullies and hills. But the passengers won't be pleased either.' He waves a hand towards the waiting coaches. 'No guesthouse in sight. No store. No restroom. I'll wager there'll be a few discreet trips into the bush before the coaches set out.'

Freeman points to two tents set a little distance away. 'They might be dunnies, don't you think?'

But Brennan has moved away to talk to Mr Furkert, who is standing among the wasteland of stacked timber, piles of rails and sleepers, heaps of stone ballast.

Mr Furkert keeps taking out his watch. Mr Hall-Jones himself is coming in on the train. It's important that everything goes smoothly. Not like the disaster last week when one of his best engineers fell from the work train as it rattled through the deviation. The engineer had been riding on the step and his foot was struck by a protruding rock. The poor fellow was dragged along and killed. Some of the men are muttering that the cutting for the deviation is too narrow, the ballasting insufficient. Not tales Mr Furkert wants his good friend the Minister to hear.

'The coach road,' reports Brennan to his boss, 'is in fine repair, sir. The ladies — will there be ladies? — will have a splendid ride through the bush.'

Furkert nods briskly, not really paying attention to Brennan. He fiddles with his watch again.

And here she comes! The little crowd cheers to hear the long whoo-oo of the whistle. Everyone looks down the track. Great clouds of smoke and steam rise through the bush; you'd think the whole district was on fire. The engine, when it appears, is almost an anticlimax. Freeman, who remembers the fine locomotive that brought them from Wellington to Marton, has been expecting something more imposing. This one looks back to front — driver's cab in front of the tank and smokestack, its flat front and two oval windows looking like a face with a cow-catcher for beard. More like something a sawmill might use, and ill-fitted to carry a rake of passenger carriages (only two today, and a horse-box). Nevertheless it whoo-hoos again and draws to a halt with an impressive release of steam. Mr Furkert hurries forward to welcome the Minister.

Brennan returns to Freeman. 'We'll lead the cavalcade,' he says, 'to make sure nothing goes amiss on this first trip. The coachmen are not used to this road. It's steeper in several places than the old long way.'

The deserted little clearing has come to bustling life. The coachmen turn the coaches to bring them side-on to the train. Passengers climb down stiffly and look around, obviously expecting something grander. Some hold tickets at the ready, but no one is there to collect them. Where is the stationmaster? Where, in fact, is the station? No one seems to be in charge. How can they be sure their luggage will be conveyed to the coach they occupy? Or must they do the sorting themselves?

Brennan chuckles. 'This is still a Public Works operation. These people left the security of the Railways Department and its endless rules and regulations way back in Taihape. Public Works trains are a much more relaxed affair.'

Freeman wants to stay watching the milling crowd. Everyone is shouting now. He sees that the tents he spotted earlier must indeed be dunnies: there are queues outside. Coachmen, eager to set out, are stacking cases behind and above, tossing mailbags and sacks of goods, while passengers ask unanswered questions. One man hastily removes his box from a coach: his journey is over here at Ohakune. But where is the settlement? And how can he get there? Freeman spots a man with a cart who might help, and then realises it's his own father.

'Da! Da!' he shouts, but man and cart have rattled past,

heading down the track to the settlement. His father is whipping the horse on, which is unusual; something must be amiss for him to treat Rusty like that. Freeman hops from foot to foot in frustration. What is his father doing up here on a work day? The big cutting won't be finished yet. But Brennan is at his side now, an arm at his elbow.

'Come on now, lad, time to mount. The first coach is ready and the other three will be right behind. We will lead the way.'

At the top of the first long rise, Brennan and Freeman rein in their horses and turn to watch the labouring coaches. The horses are hitched three and two. Twenty hooves, not to mention the iron-rimmed wheels of the coaches, would break up any dirt track in no time. Here's a test for their new road. Over the last months, stonemasons under Brennan's careful eye have split volcanic rock and laid cobbles, tightly packed across the whole width of the surface: this should give the horses purchase on the slope and protect the soft material beneath. Up comes the first coach, the horses thrusting forward against leather, hooves gripping the cobbles, coachmen calling for the heave. Some interested faces peer out; Freeman hears a woman shriek as her coach tilts and rocks. But the surface passes the test with flying colours. The horses snort and blow as coach after coach passes the riders. Now, for a mile or two, the journey alongside the unfinished railroad will be reasonably level.

Last to breast the rise are Furkert and the Minister on horseback, riding side by side, talking earnestly. Furkert introduces his engineers to the Minister, who leans across to shake their hands.

'A fine job,' says Mr Hall-Jones. 'The Prime Minister will be pleased to see passengers finally paying to travel the Main Trunk Line. Will the surface last, do you think?'

'It will, sir,' says Brennan.

'And will the line be open in time for a trip to see the Great White Fleet?'

Brennan and Freeman know of the wager. Mr Furkert has bet the Minister a silk topper that the line will be finished in time. And there's a rumour that the Minister has offered his chief engineer one thousand pounds if a Parliamentary Special train makes it through in August of next year.

'If anyone can make it happen, Mr Furkert will,' says Brennan diplomatically, though he thinks the possibility remote. There are still three unfinished viaducts and a half-excavated tunnel ahead of them, along the coach road.

'This co-op system,' says Mr Hall-Jones, frowning, 'is it holding up the work? Too many union johnnies making complaints?'

'My inspectors keep them on their toes. They know they'll lose their bonus if they fall behind.'

'They also know there's a strong taskmaster at the helm,' says the Minister, winking and nodding towards Furkert. Brennan and Freeman murmur their assent.

'Off you go, then,' says Furkert, a small twitch at the corner of his mouth betraying his pleasure at the praise. He pulls out his watch again. 'You are leading the cavalcade, are you not?'

Freeman chuckles when they are out of earshot. 'If it's not his slide rule, it's his watch. That man has to occupy his hands with detail every minute of the day!'

They overtake the coaches and ride ahead. Here the road is hard pumice; no need for cobbles. The day is fine and the bush sparkles. Riding is a pleasure. Apart from the quiet jingle of traces and the odd call of the coachmen, the bush is silent, hoofbeats muffled by fallen leaf litter.

Freeman recalls a matter he has been meaning to bring up with his boss. 'You remember the day you came to our work camp with two new recruits for Da?'

'And gained a promising chainman. I do.'

'Did you hear that they ran off?'

'I did not. A pity. I hope he gained New Zealand-born workers?'

'He did. But here's the thing. I think one of them has turned up at Makatote. In our tent. I can't be sure, I only saw him back then in the half-dark. Should I report it? I believe they ran off with some food and a shovel.'

Brenan rides on for a while, thinking. 'Is he fitting in?'

'He is, yes. In a quiet, sad kind of way. Works in the kitchen.'

'There were two of them. Brothers. Is he alone?'

'Very alone. My brother Billy and the preacher have befriended him.'

'I'd leave it lie, Freeman. The new boys off the boat often find it hard. And you might be wrong. I'd have said those brothers were thick as thieves. Not likely to part.'

Ahead they hear distant shouts and the sound of hammering — the bright harsh ring of metal on metal. They come to a clearing in the bush where the land falls away into a steep ravine. Felled trees lie in heaps; piles of ballasting stone and rails are ready for the platelayers. Here is the Taonui viaduct. It is an impressive sight. Almost finished, the girders now support trusses and sleepers, though the rails are not yet laid. Men carrying paint pots move easy as monkeys around the girders, high above ground.

Passengers are invited to climb down and walk across the structure rather than suffer the steep road down and up the other side (and to ease the horses' load on the upward slope). Many intrepid travellers accept the challenge and walk gingerly across.

Freeman's pony, newly broken in, dances and pulls. He's uneasy under those towering piers; wants to hurry ahead back into the bush. But Freeman loves the sight, and would linger. One day soon, an engine pulling carriages will cross. And he is part of this great enterprise!

A shallow grave

Jock draws up outside the police hut and jumps down. He's breathing hard and feels dizzy, which is not right. The horse is the one should be puffing. He pauses to let his feet steady themselves, then takes a careful step. But the door is padlocked. He checks the fenced paddock behind: only one horse is grazing there, which means that Sergeant Baker is out on the beat somewhere. Jock curses. He peers at a notice tacked to the wall, but it's only a poster announcing a meeting of the Anti-Asiatic League next Saturday. He turns to a pair of women who are also reading the notice.

'I'm after the sergeant, ladies. Any idea of his whereabouts?'

It's Mrs Grice who answers. 'He could well be on the Raetihi road.'

The other woman nods with some satisfaction. 'We have just reported a man who is most definitely drunk in charge of a horse and cart. Wandering all over the place.'

Jock, who has taken more than a dram of whisky before driving here, glares. 'I'll say goodbye, then.' He leaves them to their poster and sets out. Again he feels the world tilt and clutches the seat. What is happening? Surely a dram — or two — would not affect him this way? He slows Rusty to a walk. Up ahead he sees a mounted man coming towards him — or is he heading away? Jock curses again. He feels quite ill.

It is indeed Sergeant Baker. Jock hails him, relieved that he can report his news and return home.

'One of my gang has found a body in the bush, sergeant. Dead some time, I'd say. His dog unearthed it.'

Sergeant Baker takes out his notebook. 'Well, Jock?' This is more interesting than the unending parade of drunk-in-charge-of-horse and grog-shop complaints. He waits for more detail.

'Just off the road, buried in a shallow grave, north of our camp by about two mile, I'd say.' Jock wipes the sweat off his brow with a shaking hand. Has the dead body affected him so badly? 'He'd been shot, Sergeant, that much is clear, though the body is a nasty mess. Head wound.'

'I hope you haven't moved it?'

'No, no, it's left for you, but I'd be quick about it — wild pigs will be interested now it's unearthed. I've put one of my men on watch until you arrive, but we are pushed by the bloody boss to finish the cutting. I can't spare men to do your work.' Jock's usually genial manner has descended into belligerence. His voice rasps. He clears his throat and spits a yellow gob onto the road.

The policeman narrows his eyes and studies Jock. He returns the notebook to his breast pocket and takes up the reins. 'I'll get down directly. You don't look in great shape, Jock. Are you looking after yourself? Sarah keeping an eye?'

Jock shrugs. 'I get by. It's the bloody pressure. Dear God, I am more than ready to finish this blasted cutting and head out of the bush. It's gone on too long, man.'

'Look after yourself, even so.' The sergeant applies boot to flank and heads off at a fast canter.

Jock spits again, turns Rusty and follows. He has forgotten to name the dead man: Alec Hope, who now lacks any.

The news soon travels through the settlement. Trivial misdemeanours are common, but murder is rare — though this one seems disappointingly clear-cut: one brother dead, the other disappeared. A family fight most likely.

'Ask Mrs Grice,' suggests Sarah when the policeman calls. 'She was travelling up the road the day the boys ran off. She might have noticed something.' She also mentions — a little maliciously — the fact that Mrs Grice was in some sort of uniform and was carrying a gun. 'Why would those boys fight,' she adds, 'if they were running away together? They were always laughing and fooling. A right pair. I can't see it.'

But Sarah's mind is on other matters. Her good, solid husband is unravelling. She sees him sinking into himself night by night. And now coughing. He downs too much moonshine, goes grumpy to a troubled sleep and then wakes, still exhausted. Dirk has noticed, too.

'He doesn't lead the men properly, Mam. I have to do it, or Donal. We're covering for him. Some of the gang are beginning to complain.'

Sarah sighs. 'He used to be so strong.'

'Can you get him off the moonshine, Mam? It's rotting him.'

'It's more than the moonshine. Other things haunt him. The war. And now the pressure of this work . . . Be careful with him, son.'

Sarah mixes dough for the bread. She feeds the whole gang now so they can work longer hours. They come to the big tent for their breakfast and a hot drink, fill their lunch boxes from her table. By the time they come back for dinner it's already dark. They're rough and cheerful — all West Coast lads, tough as boots and proud of it. She enjoys their banter; likes to see them wolf down their food. If it's raining they sometimes just roll up in a blanket on the floor near the fire rather than find their way through the mud to their own tent.

As she shapes the loaves and places them in the iron box over the fire she thinks of the time when Jock went overseas. He was so proud then, setting out for Africa with his mates from Denniston. Fifteen of them on horseback, riding down to Westport and then travelling by steamer to Wellington. She had travelled with them — plenty of wives and sweethearts were there to see them off to the war. Jock had to provide his own horse and rifle, but they gave him kit and a uniform. Sarah had marvelled at the way all those horses — hundreds of them — were slung aboard, kicking and rolling their eyes. Half the ship must have been stables. It all seemed so noble, such a marvel that New Zealand lads should be needed over in Africa.

Then Jock came back two years later, alone. Not proud any more. All fourteen mates had died — of disease, not war wounds. He was ashamed, he said, of what they'd done; women and children, just like his own, made homeless and herded like cattle into compounds. Then they'd ordered him to shoot his own horse, beautiful Minty who'd borne him through all those terrible months. No room in the boat. The only friend he had left and he had to shoot him. Jock had wept when he told her that.

He had gone back down the mine but now the darkness spooked him. He felt shut in, he said. He kept seeing his mates lying in the heat, dying of dysentery or typhoid, calling for water; stink and flies everywhere. The dark walls of the mine were populated for Jock with these terrible pictures. So when, a couple of years later, they were recruiting for the railway Sarah suggested the change and Jock agreed — cheerful for the first time in months. Pick and shovel above ground and in the bush sounded like a good life. They came with the boys and some friends — a ready-made co-op gang.

'We'll make good money, Mother,' said Jock back then. 'Our lads are ready for work now. A couple of years on the railway, maybe three, and we'll be able to buy a bit of land on the Coast. Be our own boss. Build a house.'

We *are* making good money, thinks Sarah, cutting mutton for a stew, but will Jock be fit to enjoy it? She sees the crock of moonshine in the corner and is tempted to pour it away. But will that solve anything? Heaven forbid that she turns out like that stupid Mrs Grice with her black and white rules and her crusades. If Jock needs his drink, let him have it.

Rain drums on the canvas roof. She stokes the fire. A week ago it felt like spring and they were all smiling. Now winter has decided to cling on. The men will be cold.

Sergeant Baker finally tracks down Mrs Grice. She's sitting in the Seddon Temperance Hotel enjoying a cup of tea and a chat with Mrs Kerr.

'It's about that body, Mrs Grice, the boy who was shot.'

Amelia Grice sets down her cup. It clatters. She clasps her hands beneath the nice clean tablecloth. 'Oh yes?'

'I believe you were on the road the day the boys ran off.'

'The boys?'

'There were two of them. I'm sure you and Mrs Kerr will know all the gossip. It's the talk of the town.'

Mrs Kerr frowns. 'We are not common gossips, sergeant. We have more pressing duties, as you well know.'

Sergeant Baker lets a silence develop. Mrs Grice is uneasy, that's clear to see. He takes out his notebook, turns to a fresh page. 'Could you detail any people you saw on the road between Karioi and Ohakune?'

Amelia fiddles with her cup. 'Goodness. I don't know...'

The sergeant prompts her. 'You saw Mrs Cameron?'

'Yes, yes, of course I did! We had a chat. And before that some natives in a garden near the road. Have you spoken to them?'

'I have. They noticed you. They mentioned you were in uniform and carrying a gun.'

Mrs Kerr looks at Amelia in alarm. 'A gun? Surely not!'

'No no no.' Amelia's laugh lacks mirth.

The sergeant notes this in his notebook.

'No. How ridiculous. I do own a wooden replica. Part of my Khaki Corps uniform. Would you like to inspect it, sergeant?'

'I would.'

'Perhaps later?'

'I think now, if you will excuse us, Mrs Kerr.'

Sergeant Baker enjoys walking this busybody through the bustling settlement and hopes tongues are wagging. 'And why were you in uniform, Mrs Grice?' he asks. 'The war is well over.'

Amelia feels she might break down. The dead boy! The brother's fearful cry! 'Why? Oh. Never mind . . . It was a cold day. I don't know . . .'

'You saw no sign of the boys? Or a boy?'

'No.'

Her agitation is obvious. But the gun, when he sees it, is definitely wooden.

'I don't actually know how to shoot,' says Amelia Grice in a small voice. She slumps onto her bed in the little hut. And bursts into tears.

Healing hands

Now that warmer weather has arrived Gabriel Locke holds his services outside, which he feels best suits his open style of preaching. During winter he has been forced to hold his prayer meetings in the warm cookhouse where Mrs Bright's sceptical stance interferes with his inspirational flow. On this Sunday, however, an icy wind bringing flurries of sleet batters the settlement. Winter has returned. Work on the girders has been impossible for days and the men are restless. Fights have broken out over the two-up games; grumbles surface over work conditions and accommodation.

'Make sure you give a cheerful sermon, then,' says Mrs Bright. 'The men need uplifting. None of your hellfire and brimstone if you're wanting to use my cookhouse.'

Gabriel sighs. Trying to charm this flinty woman is futile. 'I preach hope and love, as you very well know, Mrs Bright. When have I ever mentioned the fires of hell?' Though privately, he is inclined to assign her to that baleful punishment.

Billy and Amos, clad in new black tunics with white sashes, are watching; Gabriel fears their admiration for him might be dented by the cook's attitude. He lays a hand on each lad's shoulder. The three stand together facing the men — and a few women — who have come in out of the cold into the cheery fug. Gabriel has encouraged the boys to let their hair grow; all three have a similar, unusual look — hair pulled tightly back, tied with a narrow white ribbon.

'Stand at the door, boys,' says the preacher. 'Welcome the good souls with a fervent "God bless". When I give the sign, lead the congregation in a "Praise the Lord!" as I've taught you. Then, during the last hymn, pass around your plates. Always happy, Amos. No down in the dumps on God's day. We are all uplifted by the sight of a cheerful believer.'

Billy smooths down his tunic, straightens the sash. Gabriel wears a full-length tunic and long white sash. Theirs are shorter — knee length — but Billy is proud to be noticed and welcomes everyone with a will. Amos struggles.

Gabriel is taken aback to see Rose and a group of her schoolchildren in the congregation. Do they expect him to run a wretched Sunday school? Billy's sister Maggie is there, too, with Rose's own children. They've never come before. For some reason Gabriel fears Rose: like Mrs Bright, she is impervious to his charm. The clear, questioning look she often directs towards him is unsettling; he becomes tongue-tied, incoherent. He would like to ask her to leave, but there is Billy, delighted to see his family, welcoming them with the broadest smile and a ringing 'God bless you all!'

Two latecomers slip in just as the preacher is about to announce the hymn: it's the supervisor himself, George Pascoe, and a pale, lanky fellow who coughs and wheezes as he sits. Pascoe looks worried, pats the man's back, wraps his own scarf around his companion's neck.

Rose and her family sit right at the front. Gabriel cannot fathom her expression. She's studying him as if he were some interesting botanical specimen; no hint of disapproval — or of greeting. What on earth is she thinking? Gabriel decides to look over her head and concentrate on Billy, who always responds to his words with a raised hand and a 'Praise the Lord!'

They start with a hymn. Rose's soprano soars above the rest. Gabriel, who likes to lead the singing with his own fine voice, cannot bring the congregation to heel. They are following Rose, who takes the verses at a cheerful gallop. At least she's enjoying the service.

'My text,' says Gabriel Locke, gazing warmly at Billy, 'is "With your faith you can move mountains", Matthew 17, verse 20.' Gabriel opens his Bible and reads, his voice high and ringing to battle with the storm outside. ' "And Jesus said unto them, Because of your unbelief: for verily I say unto you, If ye have faith as a grain of mustard seed, ye shall say unto this mountain, Remove hence to yonder place; and it shall remove; and nothing shall be impossible unto you." ' He closes his eyes and speaks extempore, urging his flock to believe; to attempt great deeds in the name of the Lord. He describes how Jesus calmed the waters with a word, coaxed the olive tree into bloom, cast out demons and cured the sick man. Gabriel feels the congregation's attention. They are with him. He warms to his topic, pleased to feel himself embroidering the text as he finds examples of faith overcoming great obstacles. He dares to glance in Rose's direction. A mistake. Quickly he looks back to Billy. The man at the back coughs mightily. Gabriel feels his flow faltering. He coughs himself, clasps his Bible. What is it in that woman's look that so unnerves him? But praise the Lord,

Billy's rapt face gives him strength to continue. He bestows his most joyful smile upon his flock and raises his arms for the final assurance. 'All things are possible if your faith is strong enough.'

As the last hymn is sung, the boys in their matching tunics pass around the plate. It's a larger crowd than normal and he has delivered an uplifting sermon. A goodly pile of coins is presented for his blessing.

'Will you do laying on of hands?' whispers Billy as he lays the plate on the table. Billy loves to see Gabriel lift the spirits of the sick or downcast with his healing hands.

But Gabriel only lays on hands when the mood is right. Today he's not sure. Best not to risk a failure.

'Preacher Locke,' Rose's clear voice carries easily to the back of the hut. 'I hear — we can all hear — that there is a sick man among us. Indeed, he is the very man who has designed this magnificent viaduct. Will your faith be strong enough to cure him?'

Billy turns, beaming, to Gabriel. The hope; the belief in those blue eyes cannot be resisted. Against his better judgement, Gabriel nods. 'Let the brother come forward,' he calls.

Peter Seton Hay — for it is indeed the designer of the viaduct, here on his first visit — comes forward, nodding to one or two of the men. He looks very ill. The breath rasps in his throat; bright rosy blotches on his cheeks contrast with the pallor of his skin.

'Kneel, brother,' says Gabriel quietly, 'and consider the Lord.' Rose steadies the man as he kneels, then stands watching as Gabriel lays his hands on the man's head and prays aloud.

The congregation waits in silence. Mr Pascoe stands to get a better view. Gabriel kneels. He lets his voice sink to a murmur that only the sick man can hear. The head under his hands is burning. He strokes the man's neck and cheeks, murmuring steadily.

But the moment is broken, shockingly, by a burst of desperate coughing. Mr Hay cannot catch his breath. He bends double, gasping. Gabriel, startled and at a loss, rises to his feet. George Pascoe hurries forward. Rose glances sternly at the preacher then lifts up Peter Hay, straightens his back, wipes his streaming face with a handkerchief.

Rose lays a soft hand on Gabriel's arm. He snatches it away. The look on her face is pitying! 'Perhaps this mountain,' she says, her clear voice carrying to the whole congregation, 'is too much even for your faith, which I am sure is well-meaning, to move. You've done your best, Mr Locke, but Peter Hay needs more than your laying on of hands.' She shrugs as if to make little of his endeavour. 'This poor sick man needs to lie down and get a hot drink into him. Good nursing can be a more effective form of faith than prayer. I will take care of this.'

Maggie giggles, and the schoolchildren follow suit. A ripple of stifled laughter runs around the room. Gabriel feels that his cheeks must be flushing as hotly as the sick man's. He tries to hide his fury, but his voice as he intones the benediction is harsh and his hand shakes as he signs the blessing.

Amos, as usual is looking at the floor; but Billy's eyes are full of questions.

The scent of roast beef fills the room. Mrs Bright has opened her oven door with a crash. The congregation rises and moves to the long tables, sermon and laying-on of hands forgotten. The Sunday roast is, of course, the main attraction.

Gabriel Locke turns away, collects the plate of money and leaves by the kitchen door.

In the tent that night Billy and Amos are alone with Gabriel. Freeman is away at Raurimu with Brennan, and Ruri is — who knows where; look for Maggie and Ruri will be close by.

Gabriel is still fuming, but manages a cool answer to Billy's question. 'I'm afraid that Mrs Rose Scobie is not a believer,' he says. 'She stood too close, Billy. It is hard for the Lord's healing power to come through my hands if an unbeliever is blocking the passage.'

Billy nods, but there is still a doubt lingering in his eyes. Gabriel decides to change the subject. He sits beside Amos, lays a hand on his knee. 'You have seen hardship, brother, I see it in your eyes. Why not share your story with me and Brother Billy?'

Amos shakes his head, turns away.

Gabriel takes the boy's head in his hands and tilts it until the downcast eyes are on a level with his own. He gazes searchingly into his eyes and talks quietly.

Billy coughs. He feels uncomfortable. Gabriel glances quickly — sharply — at Billy and then back to Amos.

Tears well up as they so often do when anyone speaks kindly to Amos. He shakes his head but then, after a silence, which Gabriel allows to linger, Amos begins to talk. He is a tall lad, but as usual he sits hunched; his lank hair, loosed now from its ribbon, falls over his eyes.

'I had a brother. Alec. He's dead. He was killed. Before I came here my brother and I —'

Amos stops. He frowns over at Billy, his narrow, spotty face suspicious. '*Your* brother, Freeman — has he said something to you?'

'Freeman? Something about you?' Billy frowns to see Gabriel's stroking hand. He's drawn unwillingly into the conversation.

'Freeman saw Alec and me, before. I thought he might recognise me.'

Gabriel continues to stroke; he enjoys seeing that Billy is jealous. He leans closer to Amos, his voice gentle, persuasive. 'Before what?'

Amos brushes a strand of hair out of his eyes and glares at the others. 'Before that terrible lady shot my brother. She killed him for no reason at all! She shot him and then drove on in her cart as if he was some stray animal lying there in the road.'

'She shot your brother. Yes.' Gabriel's fingers dig into the boy's thigh. He sits very still, holding back — treasuring — his excitement. His eyes glitter.

Billy recognises what has happened; he has seen this reaction in Gabriel before but doesn't understand it. Gabriel is breathing hard through his nose, lips pressed tightly together. Is he angry? Fearful? Billy watches the preacher — his friend — not sure how to react himself. He reaches out a tentative hand to touch Gabriel. The preacher's excitement is infectious.

Gabriel Locke groans. He leaps to his feet, his yellow hair flying. 'Wait boys! The Lord speaks!' His eyes close and he walks out into the rain.

'He's in a trance,' whispers Billy. 'He's done that before. He'll know what to do when he comes back to us.'

Indeed, Gabriel returns, dripping wet, hair plastered to his head, but calmer. The fierceness has disappeared; he speaks quietly. 'Now, Amos, tell it all from the beginning.'

Out it all tumbles: the blistered hands, the rough laughter of the men in the gang, the escape, the mad lady in the cart, the sudden explosion, Amos's despair and flight. By the end of the story, Billy is indignant. 'We have to go to the police, eh Gabriel? She shouldn't get away with that!'

Gabriel looks from one to the other, his eyes alight. He keeps his voice low but excitement underlies his words. He is confident he can draw them in. 'Wait, now. I think there is a better way. An adventure in the name of the Lord. Amos, you have been fearful that you will be blamed, have you not? A true and rightful fear. After all, you and your brother were runaways. You stole some articles, is that not so, Amos?'

Amos nods.

'Then you will be blamed. And if I am not mistaken, that is the very gun hidden in your bundle under your bed?'

Amos nods miserably. 'Aye. I shouldn't have taken it but I was afraid. And angry.'

'Indeed,' says Gabriel. 'Indeed. So, my friends. The Bible says an eye for an eye, a tooth for a tooth. I think our path is clear.'

'But,' cries Billy, his eyes round, freckles showing almost green in his pale face, 'you don't mean we should shoot her?'

Gabriel grins in a way that makes Billy uncomfortable. 'Not shoot, no, brother; we'll just give her a nasty fright, eh? A very nasty fright. Put the fear of Almighty God in her.'

'Good,' says Amos Bread. 'Give her a fright.' He straightens. For the first time since he's arrived, he looks almost happy.

Gabriel reaches out his arms and hauls the boys — one eager, the other hesitant — into a huddle. His laugh is joyous. 'Praise the Lord! He will aid us in our endeavour. Now to make a plan.'

Rumours and suspicions

Freeman dismounts in front of the Scobie hut. The sun is out today — the year finally accepting that summer might be allowed to arrive — and activity on the viaduct is roaring ahead. Even here in the village they can hear the shouts and clanging as a new column or girder is swung into place. Maggie is playing with Alice, pushing her on a rope swing that Ruri has made for her. Alice is screaming with excitement as she soars. What an active little thing! Freeman would rather spend his time on horseback in the bush or on foot, measuring distances and angles with Brennan.

Last week the two of them visited the Raurimu Spiral, which had just been completed. They sat on their horses outside the engineers' office at the settlement of Raurimu — now a bustling town with its own school and Post Office.

'You'll want to see this,' Brennan had said, pointing up at the escarpment covered in bush. 'Look and learn what can be achieved by an engineer's brilliance. Even the surveyor Rochfort couldn't work out how to do it.'

Freeman nodded. He knew now that even the largest locomotives couldn't haul a load up an incline steeper than one in fifty. The climb up onto the Plateau from Raurimu onto the Waimarino plain was four hundred and fifty-six feet in little more than a mile — seemingly hopeless.

'They could have done it with a great deviation that involved nine viaducts and miles of track,' said Brennan, 'and thousands more pounds' expense. But let's ride up the track and see what Holmes and his team dreamed up.'

The pair set out, riding first south, away from Raurimu and then doubling back in a tight horseshoe to arrive directly above the little township but eighty-eight feet above it.

'Now it gets interesting,' said Brennan. They approached a high embankment bridging a steep gully. The horses would not walk along so high and narrow a track so the men were forced to ride down into the valley and back up. Two more horseshoe curves and they were back again above Raurimu, though they had lost sight of the town.

Freeman shook his head in amazement. 'However did the surveyor plan this? How could he know the whole lie of the land? It's all hills and valleys and dense bush.'

Brennan nodded. 'They're a different breed, surveyors. They must somehow imagine the land from above, even when there is no vantage point. And here we burrow underground. Will your mount mind the dark? Mine is used to tunnels.'

It turned out Freeman's recently broken-in Kaimanawa *did* mind the dark. It snorted and laid back its ears and threatened to throw its rider. Brennan laughed. 'Well, we will use the service track. We can look back, up ahead. There are two tunnels here, one long and then a short one — part of a full circle which will take us up to the Plateau. An engineering masterpiece.'

When they joined the railway line again they were, for the third time, directly above Raurimu. This time they could look down to the town. And there, far below them, was a work train hauling a long rake of ballast wagons, climbing slowly up. The two riders hurried their mounts into a patch of open land so they could watch the train disappear into the tunnel and then emerge in a miraculous corkscrew until it seemed about to meet and swallow its own last wagon.

'Look and learn,' said Brennan. 'Our own Peter Keller, whom you met in Ohakune, pegged out the spiral.'

'Just like we pegged out the coach road!'

Brennan had chuckled. 'Well, ours was more straightforward. This clever spiral climb will become a tourist attraction, I'm thinking. They say it's a sight when a passenger train comes through — heads craning out of every window!'

Freeman has already boasted to his sister of the sight. But today, while he waits for his boss to saddle up, he has another matter on his mind.

'Maggie! Can you stop that screeching and listen, hen?'

Maggie leaves the swing to career on its own and comes over. She's nervous of his frisky horse and keeps her distance. 'Aye then, spit it out,' she says to Freeman. 'That girl will be off and away in a trice if I take my eye off her. Her mother's daughter, is Alice.'

Freeman tells her about Amos. He knows now that his suspicion was right: Amos is one of the brothers who were sent to replace him in Da's work gang.

'But here's the thing, Maggie. Billy let slip some kind of plan he and the preacher and Amos have. Seems like the other brother was shot. Billy wouldn't tell the whole story but he's worried, I think. Out of his depth. You know what Billy's like.'

'I know he's under the thumb of Mr Goldilocks.' Maggie screws up her face. 'That preacher gives me the creeps.'

'Aye, but Billy's besotted. He was ever like that, ready to follow any high ideal. He jumps in headlong, no questions asked.'

'Our Billy has a head on his shoulders, Free. He'll grow out of it soon enough.'

Freeman shrugs. 'I'm not so sure this time. He might do something silly. Keep an eye on him, will you?'

Brennan rides out from behind the cottage. He waves to Alice, who is now climbing the tree from which the rope swings. Maggie runs to the teetering child.

Freeman mounts and follows his boss. 'We'll be away a few days,' he shouts back to Maggie. 'Please?'

'I heard that,' says Rose, who is standing at the door, waving. 'Is Billy in trouble?'

Maggie hesitates. She fiddles with Alice's ribbon, which has come untied. 'Not really. Not in trouble.'

Rose lifts her head to the sun. Such a pleasure to feel it warming the skin. She decides, with no twinge of conscience, to leave schooling to the other teachers today. Over the past months she has petitioned the Education Board for slates and chalk for the children. She has fashioned a blackboard and persuaded some of the fathers to make desks and chairs, but now that the school is running smoothly she has lost some of her interest. What a strange, impermanent place this is! The children and their parents will all be — who knows where — next year. Or the year after. Will this be their last summer here in the bush? And hers? She's ready to return to the Hill but would like to see the great viaduct finished first.

She sits on the little bench Ruri has built them. Ruri and Maggie. One so quiet, the other a chatterer, but made for each other, anyone can see that. 'Maggie!' she calls, patting the seat beside her. 'Come and sit for a while. Alice, you come too and eat your apple!'

When they are all settled, Rose says, 'Your brother Billy — Freeman is worried. I have to admit I am, too.'

Maggie chuckles. Rose never beats about the bush: straight to the point, whether it is a detail of railway construction or a small thing like Billy's obsession.

'Your brother is a bright lad, Maggie, but easily led. He had some trouble at school on Denniston, do you remember?

'Aye. It was embarrassing. But he grew out of that.'

Rose takes an apple from her pocket, takes a large bite and then hands it over to Maggie. Little Alice giggles and makes a show of munching her own apple hugely.

'I do not trust the preacher,' says Rose. 'He is charming and knows how to please with his sermons, but there is something else; something darker. Do you feel it?'

'I don't like him,' says Maggie bluntly. 'But Billy seems to adore him.'

'Adore, yes.' Rose takes the apple from Maggie and bites again. 'Billy is inclined to adore, where you or I might simply like or dislike. Or do I make too much of it? I don't trust men who quote the Bible.'

'Surely there are some good ones?'

'Surely, yes. But I had a stepfather once who could quote pages and pages from the Bible. A very wicked man.'

'What happened to him?' Maggie has heard the rumours, the songs, but has never dared to ask.

'Oh, I killed him.' Rose frowns. 'In a way. I was very young.

I would call it self-defence.' She sighs. 'That was a different time. A different Billy. Billy Genesis is long gone and good riddance. It's your Billy we're discussing now — and a different man of God.'

Maggie wants to hear more, wants the whole story. Who else but this surprising woman, her teacher back on the Hill — who else would casually admit to killing a man and then move on to other matters?

'So,' says Rose, closing her eyes and tilting her face to the sun, 'I may be biased. But there is more, I think, to Mr Gabriel Locke, and I would like to know. The good-hearted preacher is something of a façade, I think.'

'Freeman is worried. He says Goldie and Amos and Billy are planning something.'

'Are they indeed?' Rose sits up sharply and regards her companion. 'Talk to him, Maggie. Don't let him forget his family. Remind him of family things.'

Alice is off again, disappearing into the bush. As Maggie gives chase, Rose calls after her, 'Why don't you bring Billy over for tea on his next day off?'

A confrontation

Billy is on painting duties whenever there's a fine day. Agile as a lizard, he scales the girders of the piers, high above the gully now. The mild steel that Andersons' Company uses is strong and forgiving but prone to rust. Several coats of paint must be applied as soon as possible. Billy waves a dripping brush up at Ruri, who is stronger and taller than his friend but has no head for heights. Ruri is driving the winch that operates the Blondin — a position he has lobbied for tirelessly and finally landed after Joker Potts allowed his attention to waver and let a section of lattice tilt and then fall into the river. Ruri nods in reply but keeps his eyes firmly on the task in hand — manoeuvring the first of the big trusses out from the bank to join piers one and two. The Blondin whines as the wheels run along the cable: this weight is heavy, much heavier than the single columns it's accustomed to.

Mr Anderson himself is standing on the north bank watching. In fact, there's quite a crowd. Billy sees Rose there, her purple scarf and yellow dress startling among the sombre colours of the men. Billy holds his breath as the truss inches out. All the painters pause in their work and take a firm grip: even these sturdy piers may move a little when the truss makes the connection.

In all the excitement no one — not even Billy, who has been expecting it — notices a lone cart making its way down the service road, across the bridge and up the opposite slope, Goldelocks driving and Amos Bread beside him. They breast the ridge and head off at a smart trot, into the bush and out of sight towards Ohakune.

Billy had assumed that he would be part of the 'act of revenge', as Gabriel put it. But when the preacher decreed that Amos needed to manage the task on his own — with Gabriel merely guiding him — Billy had to admit that he was relieved. Jealous that he would not be with the preacher, but relieved all the same. The lady was wicked to have done what she did, but he felt uneasy about the plan. Amos might be discovered, or denounced as a liar. He had not dared to say it out loud, but doubts kept surfacing. Amos was a different fellow these days. His eyes shone and he held his head up. There was a fierceness about the way he carried the wood or fed the fires. He seemed older — stronger. Gabriel noticed it, too.

'The Lord has made a man of you, Amos,' he had said (more than once, Billy noted with a twinge). 'You are ready to stand witness. You will take vengeance in the name of the Lord and be counted among His hosts.' And Amos's eyes would sharpen and his fists clench. These days Billy was a little afraid of him.

'You are known back in Ohakune,' Gabriel had said to Billy, ruffling the boy's blazing mop of hair, 'and easily noticed. Your time will come, Brother Billy.'

The top riggers — once skylarkers on sailing ships — are waiting at the top of the piers, unharnessed and nonchalant as sparrows on a wire. The long lattice of steel is lowered above their heads. This is easy work for them: the piers do not toss and weave like spars in a storm. Billy watches as the truss clangs into place. Now the skylarkers ram in the temporary bolts. The drilled holes match. Beautiful — miraculous — that it fits. Everyone on the bank above cheers. Ruri stands in his little cabin and raises his arms in triumph. Billy goes back to his painting and only then remembers that the others had planned to drive to Ohakune 'for supplies' this very day. He looks for any sign of the cart on the gully road. None. They will be gone by now.

Neither Amos nor Gabriel Locke wishes to be recognised. They have tucked their long hair into cloth caps and wound thick scarves around their necks. After they have bought flour and sugar, raisins and tea for Mrs Bright, they hitch the horse to a tree in a secluded part of the settlement and walk back into town. Gabriel is surprised to see how it has grown. New accommodation houses, half-tent and half-timber, have sprung up. There is a little school and a Post Office. Buildings in different stages of construction rise from the uneven, stump-covered land, like a giant mouthful of rotten teeth.

Gabriel suspects that the woman Amos has described may be the engineer's wife he met some months ago. If so, the engineers' quarters will be the place to find her. But it's still too light. The pair drift in the direction that everyone seems to be moving — a little hall close to the railway headquarters. 'We'll stay with the crowd for the moment,' whispers the preacher. 'Keep the rifle hidden, Amos.'

They linger outside the door of the hall, where some kind of meeting is getting underway. When speeches begin they slip inside and lean against the back wall, watching. The man at the front is speaking fervently, one finger pointing skywards to emphasise his words. Gabriel studies his delivery and finds it impressive. The fellow, dressed in a smart city suit, hair slicked back, watchchain gleaming across his generous stomach, is exhorting the meeting to drive out 'the chows who are heathen, unclean and are stealing the jobs of decent white workers — you and you!' He stabs his finger at the listening men. 'In this very town!'

Under cover of the groundswell of agreement, Gabriel points out a woman sitting a few rows ahead and off to the side. 'Is that her?'

Amos squints. It's too dark to see properly. He edges further forward, keeping to the side wall, and stares for a long time while the man rants on. When the woman cheers and claps, he nods. Yes, he's sure. Gabriel returns the nod and beckons him back.

'Join our movement!' thunders the man, 'Speak to your Member of Parliament! We must close the floodgates lest the Yellow Peril sweep into our beautiful country and defile it further.'

The crowd cheers. The man walks into the crowd. He hands out pamphlets and shakes a jingling box. Gabriel is interested to notice how readily people donate to the cause. Perhaps he might tap into this fervour himself.

'Shall I confront her now?' whispers Amos. 'Shame her in front of everyone?'

His excitement ignites Gabriel's own. The preacher would like to say yes, but knows they would quickly be overpowered here. He drags at Amos's arm and pulls him outside, where it has now grown dark.

'We'll follow her. Catch her on her own if we can.'

But Mrs Grice, when she appears, is accompanied by her

husband. Amos and Gabriel follow at a distance, drifting in and out of the dispersing crowd. At the door of their hut Mr Grice pats his wife on the arm and heads for the engineers' cookhouse. Gabriel winks at Amos. 'Perhaps a nightcap with his friends? Now is your chance, brother.'

Amos takes a breath. He nods. He draws the rifle out from under his coat, but then, suddenly uncertain, turns back to Gabriel.

'What if she—?'

Gabriel can feel the excitement building in his own body. It's a feeling he loves; cannot resist. 'Keep in your mind the great harm she has done you.'

Amos's eyes harden. 'Yes.'

'She must pay for that terrible injustice.'

'Yes.'

'Go now. Go! You are ready, brother.' Gabriel holds his groin where it is stiffening. 'Don't let her cry out. Show her the gun. Beat her a little; she should pay for what she has done to you. I'll be outside watching. Go with God's blessing.'

Amos opens the door silently and enters. Mrs Grice has just lit the lamp. She turns to see a man only a step away, pointing a gun at her face.

'Cry out and I'll shoot,' growls Amos. 'As you shot my brother.'

Amelia Grice's hands go to her mouth. She looks for a weapon but finds none. 'It was a mistake,' she whispers, 'a mistake.'

'And then you drove off like a coward.'

'I was shocked. It was a mistake. Please don't shoot.' She looks around wildly. 'I could give you some money.'

'Money! Do you think money can bring my brother back?' Amos swings the barrel of the gun fiercely. It catches her on the cheek and she cries out. Amos swings again and this time she is silenced. But Amos has lost control. 'This is for Alec!' He kicks at her as she lies sprawled on the bed. 'And this is for my own loss of my brother!' He holds a hand over her mouth and punches at whatever part of her body that he can reach. He stands in a fury and backs away. 'And this is for the Lord!'

The gunshot echoes in the little wooden room. Gabriel, who has been listening with mounting excitement, curses. The rifle was to be discharged only in an emergency. There is a shout, and then another. Someone comes running from the next hut. Gabriel finds a shadow, slips into the darkness, waits for a moment and then runs. As he ducks and weaves, stumbling over piles of rubbish, he hears a second shot.

Explanations

'We stayed for a meeting,' says Gabriel Locke to the policeman, 'A very interesting fellow from the Anti-Asiatic League.'

Sergeant Baker doesn't disguise his antipathy: his wife is Chinese. 'And then? Get on with it.'

'Then Amos said he would stay the night in Ohakune. He had a private matter to settle.'

'You weren't surprised?'

Gabriel spreads his hands, shakes his head sadly. 'I was, sergeant, I was. Alas. I should have pressed him further. But Mrs Bright needed her supplies. I left him to find his own way back.'

'Did he seem agitated?'

'Not at all. He is — was — a quiet lad. Withdrawn, I would venture to say. Ever since he arrived here at Makatote. I suspected a troubled past, sergeant.'

'He didn't confide in you? I believe he was one of your — flock?'

'He claimed that he was all alone in the world. When he arrived here Amos was very unhappy. I could tell by his accent that he was from the Home Country. But sergeant, he had seemed more settled recently. I believe my teachings and the love of the Lord were guiding him to a more sanguine view of life. He took part in our services with real pleasure. He was healing, I'm sure of it. Have you considered that he may have seen something — or someone — in town that tipped him over the edge?'

Sergeant Baker eyes the preacher sourly. He doesn't trust the silky words, the sad demeanour. This man knows more than he is admitting. He closes his notebook and sighs. 'No doubt I will need to talk to you further. Is there anyone else here who was close to him?'

'Mrs Bright at the cookhouse employed him. He had no friends, really. Tell me, sergeant, was he shot or did he shoot himself?'

'I am not at liberty to say at the present,' says the policeman with some satisfaction.

'And the lady? Did she survive?'

Baker frowns. 'What do you know of a lady?'

'News travels quickly even here in the bush, sergeant,' says Gabriel easily. 'We have heard a rumour that it was Mrs Grice, the temperance lady. Is that not so?'

Sergeant Baker purses his lips.

'But why,' asks the preacher, 'would Amos attack her?'

'Rumours can do damage, Mr Locke, and could well interfere with our investigation. Please keep them to yourself.'

Gabriel's laugh has an edge to it now. 'I'm afraid it's too late for that, sergeant. May I get back to my work now?' He turns and leaves anyway. He needs to talk to Billy before this unpleasant man can quiz him.

High on pier number three Billy paints the iron rivet with care. One hand holds both the pot and the girder, the other — his good right hand — paints. He tries to concentrate on his work but the thought of Amos lying dead, shot like his brother, confuses him terribly. How could it happen? Why didn't Gabriel stop it? There was no plan to have the gun loaded; he had been anxious on that point and Amos had reassured him: the idea was to scare her. Maybe force her into a confession. But Billy had seen the anger in Amos's eyes as he spoke. The eagerness for revenge. Gabriel would not have allowed Amos to lose control. The Lord loves all creatures great and small. Jesus believes in forgiveness. It all seems wrong.

Billy shifts his weight and moves along the girder, taking care to move always away from the wet paint as he's been taught. A falcon swoops past, startling him. He watches as it drops silently, lowers its legs, strikes and rises again in a single movement, some small bird dangling from its talons. Beautiful and deadly. Billy admires that freedom — such ease in the bright sky. He wishes his friend Gabriel could see it; Gabriel who so often talks of the beauty of the Lord's love — the freedom it brings. Oh! And now Amos is dead, they say. Shot. 'Gabriel!' Billy calls to the empty air, 'Gabriel!' He needs reassurance.

'Ah, Billy,' says Gabriel. 'I misjudged the anger burning in that poor boy's heart.'

'You said there would be no live ammunition. You promised.'

'I did, brother. I can only think that Amos had a different

plan from ours. He let us down, both of us.'

Gabriel sighs. It's important that Billy is won back. Is distanced from any doubt. 'He fooled us, I'm afraid. Worse, he used me to help him execute his wrongful deed. Now I am implicated. The police have questioned me.'

Billy's hands go to his mouth. 'Gabriel! Will they take you away?'

'Perhaps. They may question you, too, Billy. Best say nothing about the plan. The police would not understand.'

Billy is silent. Gabriel can see, in the low candlelight, the boy's confusion, his uncertainty. He shifts over to Billy's stretcher and takes his hand.

'Look at me, brother.'

Billy's eyes fix on the preacher, pleading for reassurance.

'You must trust me, Billy. I know the ways of the Lord, and sometimes they seem strange or difficult. Amos went too far, yes, but his desire for justice was righteous. It was a good cause and we must pray for Amos's soul. But what we know of the plan must remain between us two.' He strokes Billy's hand gently. The boy is softening, is opening to him. He smiles. 'God bless you, Billy. We will pray together, and think how we may have prevented this sad ending.'

Gabriel studies Billy. Is he mesmerised? Gabriel can't tell. The boy is so easily charmed! 'I don't want to leave you, brother. You are so precious.'

'And you!' Billy is crying now. 'I need you here, Gabriel. The police won't find out anything from me.'

Not mesmerised, no. Billy's emotion is his own and in this world. Gabriel finds it heart-warming. 'I know. I can trust you. Alas, I should not have trusted Amos. We are brothers together?'

'We are.' Billy squeezes the hand that grips his. 'We are, Gabriel.'

'Then let us continue on the path of the Lord.'

Amos is indeed dead, shot by his own gun in a scuffle with two engineers. Whether Amos intended to shoot himself or was killed accidentally is unclear. The Winchester has been identified as Mr Cox's, and Amos's body identified by Jock Cameron. He is Arthur Hope, brother of the dead and decomposed body found a few weeks ago. That much is clear. Mrs Grice's part in the drama has yet to be unravelled: she has been taken by riverboat to Wanganui Hospital but is still gravely ill; it's far too early to question her. Sergeant Baker has a theory which he keeps to himself.

Rose also has a theory.

Back at Makatote village, spring has established itself with good heart. For a whole week not a drop of rain. Men whistle and sometimes even sing a shanty or two, high on the piers. The Workshop clatters and roars day and night. In the bush, birds are riotous. But this morning Mrs Bright is definitely still lodged in winter; anything but Bright. As she sets loaves to rise and ladles porridge, a dark cloud seems to hover above her. She mutters; will not engage in her usual banter with the men. They recognise some outburst is on the way — have seen it before. They keep their heads down, spooning porridge, gulping hot, sweet tea, then stump out, grateful that they are not on the receiving end.

The last few men at breakfast witness it, though. As Gabriel Locke arrives with a fresh load of wood, Mrs Bright, floury arms akimbo, eyes blazing, blocks his passage to the stove. Gabriel, keeping his eyes down, tries to edge past, but Mrs Bright's usually ponderous body moves quickly to block again.

'Let me past,' mutters Gabriel, his usual jaunty manner entirely forsaking him. 'This load is heavy.'

Mrs Bright leans forward. She takes the whole bundle from his arms in one expert sweep. Flings the lot on the cookhouse floor where the logs rattle and roll, announcing doom. When Gabriel turns to leave, Mrs Bright grabs a handful of his shirt and holds him an inch or two from her nose. Gabriel is utterly powerless in her formidable clutches.

'My kitchen hand, Amos,' she thunders, 'was in your care, *Preacher*.' — she pronounces the word with scorn. 'He was also a close member — a *favoured* member — of your little flock. And yet you abandon him back down the line there. Abandon him! That poor lost boy. Would you care to explain?'

Mrs Bright is clearly not interested in explanations, she is merely pausing to take breath. 'And now he is dead, they say! Shot a woman, they say. Shot *himself*, they say! With a gun that came with him from Makatote, Mr Locke, while he was in your *Christian* care!'

Gabriel eyes spark at her sneer. He takes breath to answer, but she is away again, a steam engine of wrath, the bunch of his shirt still firmly in her grasp. 'Now, Mr Gabriel Locke, Amos Bread was a favoured member of *my* cookhouse. I cared for that poor boy. And I do not take kindly to the fact that you abandoned him. You are no man of God in my book and your preaching will no longer take place in my cookhouse. Nor will you soil my good clean firewood with your guilty hands. I do not trust you.' Mrs Bright waves at the little group of listening workers who are enjoying the drama but standing ready at the door lest her anger turn on them. 'Nor should these men here trust you.'

She releases his shirt with such violence that the preacher staggers and almost falls. 'Off you go,' she says, quieter now but even more deadly in her intent. 'You are no longer wanted in Makatote. Unless perhaps by the police. There is no place for you here. Pack your bags, Preacher Locke.'

Gabriel takes a step backward to be out of her reach. His face is pale; an anger almost equalling hers shows in his balled fists, his blazing eyes. 'You have no authority . . .' He turns to the men. 'She has no authority to send me away.'

Mrs Bright laughs, a short humourless bark. 'I provide food here, Mr Locke. I feed my flock rather than let them die alone, as you do. You will find that what I say is law in Makatote, believe me.' She turns her back on him, a final contemptuous insult that is not lost on all present. 'Now get out of my cookhouse.'

Gabriel Locke watches her back for a moment. 'This will not be the end of it,' he says in a low voice. 'The Lord looks after His own.'

But the men at the door are on their cook's side. One shouts, 'He didn't look after Amos Bread, did He?' Two of them pick up the spilt wood and take the logs to the stove; the rest leave. Mrs Bright clatters her pans.

Gabriel slips out the back door, ignored.

A warning

'This is not like you, Billy,' says Rose. 'Where's all your chatter gone?'

Billy doesn't answer but walks ahead. It is Sunday. There being no service today, Rose has suggested a walk in the bush with Billy and Ruri. They have followed the river up the gully, scrambling over boulders and sometimes wading where the banks are too steep to climb. Rose cares nothing for wet boots, and her hemline is always rather shockingly short. Ruri, who comes into his own in the bush, names the trees and bushes in his own language. He points out a fat kereru perched above them, plucking at new leaves and the fruit of the toi — the mountain cabbage tree. 'That would make a nice meal,' he says, drawing back an imaginary rubber and letting fly, 'but I left my slingshot behind.' The bird lets fly one of its own, which hits Rose. Ruri and Rose shout with laughter, but Billy is in a world of his own.

'Let's rest here,' says Rose. 'This is too beautiful. It begs to be admired.'

They have come to a small clearing in the bush. Low ferns, green and iridescent as a frog's back, make a soft carpet; a fallen log, moss-covered, is a ready-made seat, and beside them the river — only a stream now but fresh from yesterday's rain — chatters over rocks and gravel. Just visible above the towering trees is the tip of Ruapehu, its snow bright in the morning sun.

Rose sits, heedless of wet skirts. Ruri burrows into the bush, examining this and that. He has a feeling that Rose wants to speak to Billy, so will leave them alone. Rose signals her thanks with a wave.

Billy stands with his back to the clearing, staring down at the river.

'Come and sit with me, Billy.'

Billy comes reluctantly. He slumps down on the log and sighs.

'It's the preacher, isn't it?'

Billy eyes her fiercely. 'It's the Lord's day. We should be at service.'

Rose nods. 'You miss him very much?'

'They shouldn't send him away! He is a good man. The Lord's servant.'

Rose speaks gently. 'He has a wonderful way with words, Billy, but I wonder if he is indeed a good man.'

The boy's shoulders droop. He won't look at her. 'You just don't like him. Ruri doesn't like him either.'

'Well, perhaps it's true that I don't like him, Billy. I tried to. I was interested in his claim to cure people.'

'He does! He has healing hands.'

'You remember the sick engineer, Peter Hay? He died soon after your preacher laid hands on him.'

'It was your fault!' Billy is angry now. 'Gabriel said you stood too close. You're not a believer. He said you broke the bond.'

'Oh!' Rose laughs. 'I am a believer of sorts. I played piano at church back on Denniston. Don't you remember? The same church that your family went to?'

Billy is silent for a moment. 'Gabriel's church is different,' he mutters. 'More powerful. His is the Right Way.'

Rose regards him steadily. Billy shifts on the log. He wants to run off, but Rose reaches out to take his hand. He is close to tears, Rose can see.

'Billy, do you think I am a foolish woman?'

Billy shakes his head miserably.

'Well, perhaps there is a reason that I don't like Gabriel Locke.' She sighs. 'I know he has been a friend to you and you think him kind. But, dear Billy, I feel he is dangerous, and I worry that you will be hurt.'

'Dangerous!'

'This is a harsh thing to say, but you should hear it. I have a feeling that Gabriel Locke encouraged our Amos Bread into some kind of fury — may have egged him on to kill. I suspect that the preacher enjoys violence. That it excites him in an unpleasant way. There are men like that.'

Billy sits on the mossy log, his head hanging. He says nothing.

Rose sighs. She removes her hand. 'Think about it, Billy. Will you think about what I've said? I wouldn't speak if my words were not important. Maggie is worried. We all like you and don't want you to be hurt.'

Billy looks at her quickly. There is defiance in that glance, but uncertainty, too. Rose can only hope that she has sown a seed of doubt. That damn preacher's glib teachings have hooked Billy in too far. But perhaps the man has taken his ministry elsewhere and Billy will come to his senses.

Ruri returns with a bunch of tightly curled fern fronds. 'These will be good cooked with meat,' he says. 'Pity about that kereru.' He grins at the pair of them, so serious and silent. 'Are we taking root here then? I thought we were heading for the waterfall?'

'And so we are!' Rose jumps to her feet. She looks up at Ruapehu, distant and aloof in the sun. 'Could we climb that mountain from here, Ruri?'

'Aue, not me. He is tapu.'

'Can you not climb him in a respectful way, perhaps?'

'All those three mountains, Tongariro, Ngauruhoe, Ruapehu, all tapu, so the elders say. Even I with my father's exploring blood in my veins would not dare.' He laughs. 'Maybe your all-white blood might dare?'

Rose cocks a mischievous eye at him. 'It might.'

'I would dare,' says Billy, suddenly bright. 'The Lord would protect me. Gabriel says that with faith I can do anything. Move mountains. Fly, even.' He looks at Rose, defiance in his eyes.

Ruri laughs, pleased to see Billy cheerful again. 'I will run to that rock then and see if you can fly faster, e hoa.' And off they speed.

Rose walks after them. Two fine boys, she thinks, but Billy is so fragile. She fears deeply for him and is anxious that her words may have done more harm than good.

Climbing the mountain

The sky is clear and the air still that Christmas of 1907 — the last Christmas (please God, says Mr Furkert, who is still anxious about his schedule) on this monumental task of joining the railroads from north and south over the Volcanic Plateau.

'We may never get another chance,' says Andrew Anderson to Brennan and some of the other engineers. 'Shall we climb that damn mountain on our days off? Conquer the peak as we are conquering the gullies, eh?'

As Andrew is the overall boss, his word carries weight. A party is gathered. One of the Maori in a ballasting gang agrees, with some reluctance, to guide them across the desert, 'but not up the mountain, boss, not Ruapehu. I advise to not even try. The gods can be very angry.'

In the end, lacking a clearance from the local Tuwharetoa, they decide to tackle the smaller volcano, Ngauruhoe, which smoulders on Tongariro's flanks. Even so, the journey is frowned upon by several local Maori. Ruri shakes his head when Rose says she will join the party. 'Just pray that your gods are more powerful,' he warns.

Horses are readied, tents and food packed. They will head towards Waimarino along the good service road and then east across the scrubby desert by bridle track. There is a sense of excitement in Makatote village among the white workers; dire warnings from the natives. Rose is mounted ready, along with two of the Anderson nieces. After the months — years — of grinding work, all is silent at the Workshop. The generator is shut down; the winches and drills at rest. Rose had asked for a ride on the Blondin before it ground to a halt for the break, but even her formidable powers of persuasion were met with a flat refusal. What would it do for discipline if a lady were seen riding the wire, for pity's sake? All and sundry would be clamouring for a turn.

The workers have three days' holiday — the last before the final push to completion. Some are returning to neighbouring farms or kainga, others heading to Raetihi, Karioi or Raurimu, hoping to spend their wages on whatever these growing settlements might offer. Most, recruited from more distant places, will settle for the Christmas service held by the priest from Jerusalem and a few days' fishing in the river or simply sitting outside the tent, faces lifted to the blessed sun. A game of two-up as well, naturally.

The Anderson party sets out at dawn. On the service road they can ride three abreast and they do just that, chatting and laughing as the sun filters through the bush, warming body and spirit.

Rose rides alone, though, ahead of the bunch, her wild hair loose, singing some lively song and beating time with one hand. Brennan watches her — wants to ride up alongside but knows her well enough to realise that she treasures these moments of independence. He has been rather shocked that she would decide to join the climbing party rather than spend Christmas with the children; he had suggested that the four of them went camping somewhere out in the open, away from the bush. But Rose, alight with the idea of climbing a live volcano, had already arranged that Maggie, who wanted to visit her parents, would take the children with her. Brennan was interested to join the climbing party, too, so he agreed. He enjoys the engineering gossip, the camaraderie and the feeling that they are exploring the unknown.

Another unknown (to the engineers' party) is the little band of workers who have set out even earlier with the same destination in mind. Freeman and Billy are with them.

'We'll show 'em,' laughs Flipper Jacks, a wiry driller renowned for his skill at two-up. 'We'll be up there on top at our ease and give the bosses a surprise.' Flipper grew up in the area. His father was one of a surveying team working for Tuwharetoa tribal leaders and he knows the old surveying tracks.

No cart of supplies with these four stalwarts (Pinky Frost has joined them at the last minute). They double up on two horses and carry a sack containing whatever food they have managed to scavenge from Mrs Bright's cookhouse. Slim rations for a three-day adventure but never mind. They have matches and a rifle: rabbit stew would not go amiss.

Freeman and Billy (Free and Ginger to their mates) are atop Freeman's Kaimanawa, Olly. They have set out in the dark, giving the horses their heads along the service road, its pumice surface a ghostly white below the trees. Billy is silent. But he holds onto his brother, resting his head on Freeman's shoulder — a comfort to the older boy who has felt Billy slipping away into a different, alien world under the tutelage of the preacher.

'Mam won't be pleased with us,' says Freeman, chuckling, 'choosing an adventure over her Christmas dinner.'

'Mmm.'

Is Billy asleep or downcast? Freeman tries again. 'But Maggie will be there. And the little Scobies to take our places, eh? Mam will enjoy that. Like having grandchildren.'

Billy mumbles something that Freeman misses.

'Eh?'

'Ruri's going, too. He wants to marry our Maggie.'

The news is surprising to Freeman, who is often away with Brennan. 'Get on! Ruri! Whatever will Da think?'

'All Ruri thinks of these days is Maggie. He's not my friend anymore. Anyway, I don't care.'

Billy's voice is petulant, childish. He butts his head into his brother's back and then groans. Freeman is beginning to regret bringing Billy on the trip. 'Cheer up, grumpy. The others won't take kindly to a spoilsport.'

Billy sinks into silence again. The horses plod on as day breaks. Freeman's spirits rise. A beautiful day. Soon they will be out into open scrubland with a view of the mountains. He imagines riding a train along the nearly completed tracks beside them — ba-dum ba-dum, over the viaducts then out under clear sky. What a treat; what a view it will be! He hasn't seen the full spread of the three mountains yet — they seldom show their peaks — but today! Surely, yes. And then to look down from the peak. Will he be able to see the whole stretch of the line? The spiral? He grins to himself. Even Billy's bad mood won't ruin this trip.

By mid-morning they have reached Erua. Here they will turn off the service road on a small track that Flipper remembers.

'The Andersons are bound for Waimarino,' laughs Flipper. 'Much slower. Mind your head, Free, this track is pretty overgrown.'

Going is slow now, the horses picking their way along the

narrow path. Trails of barbed bush lawyer lean down to snag at them. The occasional fallen log needs skirting. Freeman wonders whether Flipper is right. This track is difficult.

'Nah, this is the way,' shouts Flipper over his shoulder, ducking his head yet again beneath a low branch. 'We're just coming round beneath Hauhungatahi. See the land rising there? Once we're over the stream we'll be clear.'

Their mounts snort and blow, unused to carrying two in difficult terrain. Billy, who has not ridden much before, grips his brother. 'Where on earth is Flipper leading us? This doesn't seem right.'

But an hour later they are in the open again, picking their way over the Whakapapaiti river — a gentle stream today and no problem to the surefooted wild-bred horses. And there are the mountains! All three in sight: Ruapehu still snowy, the other two stark and bare, a tiny wisp of steam rising from Ngauruhoe's crater. The four dismount. Men and horses drink from the clear water and while the horses nibble on the weeds by the river, the riders unwrap bread and bacon.

'Eh, this is the life,' says Pinky (who lost his little finger to a Makatote drill press a year ago). 'A bloody treat to hear silence, so it is.'

'You can't hear silence, it's silent!' says Billy and they all laugh. Billy grins. He scratches his mop of ginger hair, which is full of twigs. 'That volcano is smoking, look! Can we really get up there safely?'

'Get on, it always smokes.' Flipper cuffs the boy. 'My dad climbed it years ago. Tuwharetoa said he'd be cursed forever, but up he went and looked into the fiery vent and smelled the sulphur and came back none the worse.'

The boys munch their bacon butties and throw stones in the

river. They are in no hurry. The Anderson party plans to stay the night at Waimarino and hire a guide to take them up from that more distant direction.

'How about a night at the Haunted Whare?' says Flipper, grinning. 'We might see the ghost. They say she killed a shepherd and poked his eye out with a burning stick.'

Billy's eyes grow round at this news and the others tease him.

'Ginger would believe the world was flat if the preacher told him so.'

'Or ghosts existed.'

'Or the world will end tomorrow.'

Billy balls his fists. Squares up to Flipper, who is twice his weight. 'Preacher Locke knows more than you. You make fun of him and I'll knock your teeth in.'

Flipper throws up his hands in mock defeat. Everything in life is a joke to Flipper. 'Hey, Ginger-moptop, no offence. We're on holiday. Sun's shining. And these nags have had their rest. Let's move on.'

Freeman winks at his brother, but there's no response. The boy is so moody! Up one moment and in the dumps the next. Freeman shrugs and mounts, leaving Billy to scramble up behind without help.

At the Haunted Whare (which is no such thing, as Flipper knows but refrains from saying: the ghost inhabited an earlier hut nearby which has burnt down; this little slab whare has merely inherited the name) the boys light a fire, boil a billy and ration out what's left of the bread. It's a moonless night. The brothers sit outside marvelling at the brilliant sky. Back at Makatote village the crowding bush allows only a limited view of the heavens. Here, the Milky Way stretches — a bright convoluted mist — in a great arc above them. Behind the boys the dark bulk of Ruapehu masks the eastern sky, but the west is a miracle of pinpricks, some bright, others at the edge of vision.

'There's a sight,' says Freeman, hoping somehow to break the ice.

'Yes.' Billy's voice is quiet, almost a whisper. Then, 'Do you believe in God, Free?'

Freeman thinks. 'Yes. Course I do. Everyone does.'

'I don't mean just going to church. Really believe.'

'I suppose so. Don't think about it much.'

Billy turns to look at his brother. 'I'm different. I think about God a lot.'

'I know you do, Billy. Maybe too much.'

Billy sighs. 'You think that Gabriel — the preacher — is a bad influence, don't you?'

'Well . . . don't think about it that much to tell the truth. I'm busy in my job.'

'He's a good man, Free. I mean *really* good. I believe in him. He's a true leader, like Jesus was.'

Freeman shakes his head. 'Come on, Billy, that's going too far. He's not Jesus.'

'No, but, but, what I mean is—' Billy waves a hand at the night sky, 'All this. Gabriel understands it. He knows everything in the Bible. He can explain how true it all is. I believe in his way.'

'Billy boy, you've always gone overboard for new ideas, wild theories. Just ask a few more questions of this preacher, eh?'

'He doesn't mind questions! He's not a theory! Why is everyone so against him?' Billy looks down at this hands. 'He makes me feel so good. Like I can do anything. If I have faith.'

'Do you still feel so good, Billy, now that he's gone?'

'No. No, I don't. I wish he'd come back.'

'Sounds like it's the preacher you're missing. Just a friend. Where's your faith without him?'

'Oh!' Billy stands and walks away into the darkness. He mutters something that Freeman can't make out.

Freeman watches the slow movement of a planet in the western sky. He waits, then goes inside to join the others.

The boys are woken in the morning by a scrabbling in the corner. Billy is out of his blanket screaming and runs for the door.

'The ghost, the ghost! She's there with a poker in the corner!'

Freeman and Pinky are quick to follow, but Flipper just raises his head. 'It'll be rats. They're a bloody menace, my dad said.' He throws a boot and at least four big black rats scuttle away out the door. Billy shrieks as one races over his bare foot. The three of them dance on the frosty grass, their bare feet blue and fingers tingling.

'Eh then,' says Pinky, looking in at the still-reclining Flipper. 'If you knew about the rats, you great oaf, how come you didn't put our supplies away from them marauding beasties? Will you look at the mess!'

There in the corner, their bag of cake and biscuits lies torn to pieces, a small heap of crumbs all that remains.

Billy, still trembling, hastily pulls on his boots. Another pair of rats, hiding under the long bunk, make a dash for the door and they all jump.

Freeman takes a stick and bangs the wooden frame of the bunk. Another two run out. 'Dear God, I'd rather have a vengeful ghost,' he says. The others hastily gather their scattered clothes and hop around in the cold morning light.

'No breakfast then,' says Pinky, 'unless you fancy what the animals have left us. We'll be climbing on an empty stomach, boys.'

'Maybe we should go back to Waimarino?'

'Nah.' Flipper is back in charge and grinning. 'If we set out now we'll be up there before noon then back down to Waimarino or Erua for a slap-up dinner, eh?'

They fill their water bottle from the stream. The rats have even torn and scattered their twist of tea and sugar, so they don't bother with a fire. Billy, whose backside is sore from riding behind the saddle, suggests that it might be his turn to ride in front, but Freeman shakes his head. 'My horse, my saddle. Hop up behind.' Billy shrugs.

They're all out of sorts as they set out, hungry and cold. The sun has not yet come around the mountain; the stones sparkle with frost. But after half an hour the first rays strike Tongariro and they are cheered by the promise of a perfect day — warm and windless. The rough track skirts around a hill. Flipper waves a hand at it, laughing. 'That's Pukekaikiore, that is. The Maori knew a thing or two when they named that. They must have had a feed of rats here.'

'You making up stories, man?' Pinky, riding behind and sore like Billy, is still grumpy.

'That's what it means. Puke — hill; kai — food; kiore — rat. Perhaps we should have shot those bloody rats and roasted them.'

Pinky shifts his behind. 'When do we start walking, Flip? I'm losing sensation in me legs.'

Flipper points out a clearing up ahead, shining in the sun. It's an old surveying camp, a tumbledown hut and a few stumps,

deserted now, beside a small stream. Beyond that a gentle valley
stretches up towards the mountains. 'We'll leave the horses here
— grass and water for them. What do you say? Walk from here?'

They all cheer. This is what they've come for. Billy, on firm
ground now and more cheerful, watches the horses munching on
the grass. He pulls a handful of watercress from the stream and
follows suit. 'Delicious!' He grins at the others, a beard of cress
dripping down his chin. 'Much better than roast rat.'

Freeman laughs and claps his brother on the back. 'I'll just
drink the mountain air. It's a tonic, eh?'

They set off alongside the stream. To their right the perfect
cone of Ngauruhoe rises, bare of vegetation, its scree slopes
promising a difficult climb. The misshapen heap of Tongariro, who
blew his top millennia ago, is still in shadow. Up ahead blocking
the valley is a rampart of rock connecting the two mountains:
they must scale this before tackling the scree. Billy trots ahead,
jumping from rock to rock, nimble as a goat and happy now that
he's free to move at his own pace.

'Look at your Jesus brother go,' says Pinky admiringly as
Billy reaches the wall at the head of the valley and continues up
without pausing, 'You can tell he's been on the piers. All them
girder-monkeys are fit as fleas.'

The others save their breath for climbing.

Billy loves this. All his gloom has disappeared suddenly, unaccountably. He scales the rocky staircase, quick to find the best
footholds. At the top he dances along the rim of the escarpment,
waving at the other three as they labour up. The air is clear and
sharp, the sun on his head. 'Praise the Lord!' he shouts at the

top of his voice. He feels the closeness of his Lord and somehow Gabriel's presence, too. He looks up at the steep slopes of the volcano. Here is a fitting challenge. Gabriel said you can conquer anything if you have faith. He looks back, impatient to climb further, and sees figures way below. 'Here they are!' he shouts to his friends. Back near the camp the other party, riders and packhorses, are setting off up the valley. They must be going to ride all the way to the rock wall.

'Come on, slow coaches!' Billy looks for a track up Ngauruhoe but there is none. It'll be a scramble on the loose scree, but he's full of confidence, full of joy! He can't wait any longer and begins to climb. At first he tries to scramble straight up, hands and feet, but the loose scree makes it difficult; it's three steps up, two sliding back and his hands, tough as they are from work on the piers, are already bleeding. Now he tries travelling sideways. This is better; twenty steps in one direction and then zigzag back the other way. Loose stones still roll under his boots but he's making progress. The sheer delight of it, so high, so steep, above everyone in the world! He feels tears stinging his cheeks and would like to sing but saves his breath for the climb.

The other three are following his tracks, zigzagging upwards, where the stones have been settled a little under Billy's boots. 'I am leading my friends,' whispers Billy, 'upwards; up into the heavens. Look at me, Gabriel. Wherever you are, look.' He has never felt so happy.

Rose, tough and strong from a life spent on Denniston, climbs steadily. The Andersons are slower, stopping often to puff: the air here is thin, and lungs labour to suck in enough oxygen. Brennan climbs with Rose, stamping the scree to make steps for her.

'Look up, Bren.' Rose points out tiny figures standing on the rim of the crater and wonders who they could be. There was no mention, back at Waimarino, of another climbing party. 'Bother. I wanted to be first up there and alone.'

Brennan laughs at her, glad to stop and puff for a moment. 'Look around you, my dear Rose; there is plenty of room to be alone in this great empty landscape. Denniston is a pocket handkerchief compared to these mountains.'

Rose removes her scarf and tucks it in Brennan's pack; rakes her fingers through her wild hair. The sun is hot now and even her thick jacket feels too much.

'Keep going!' she urges. 'I want to be on top!'

The rim of the crater, when they reach it half an hour later, is a surprise. It's much wider than it looks from below. Two craters in fact: one wide and shallow and another, small and steep in the centre. 'Like an upside-down witch's hat,' says Rose. 'Smell the sulphur!'

She stands on the outer rim looking out to the grand vistas. Below are two lakes, blue as sky, and beyond them the peaks of Ruapehu still streaked with snow. She turns slowly, taking in the great ruined expanse of Tongariro. Near to them a huge flat-bottomed crater; beyond that a craggy rim and then, surprisingly, in the distance, another high blue lake. All, apart from the lakes, is dark and barren.

'We could be on the moon.' She shivers and takes Bren's arm. 'Oh, Bren, it's magnificent. Eerie. Can you feel it?'

He kisses her. 'Happy Christmas, Rose.'

She looks at him in surprise. 'Oh yes! I had forgotten. Oh dear.' She studies the ground for a moment then bends to pick up a stone — dark red and glittering — and wraps his fingers around it. 'Happy Christmas. Will he mind, do you think — Ngauruhoe — if we take a memento?'

He pockets the stone; looks around. 'But where is that other party? Have they gone down already?'

They scour the crater and Rose, seeing a telltale boot protruding from behind a heap of rocks, puts a finger to her lips and points. 'Are they hiding? Do we know them, do you think?'

Brennan, who knows of his chainman's venture, winks. 'They plan to surprise us. Let's not spoil the fun. Here come the Andersons.'

A little later, as the women spread a blanket and the men open tins of peaches and sardines, the party hear singing and lift their heads in surprise.

'We wish you a merry Christmas,
We wish you a merry Christmas,
We wish you a merry Christmas
And a happy New Year!'

Four boys burst out from behind the rocks, laughing, arms waving, galloping over the rocky scree. 'Happy Christmas, happy Christmas!'

They stop abruptly, eyes on the feast, shy in the face of such a spread, and their boss eating it.

Rose laughs and claps her hands. 'Billy! Freeman! What a surprise! Come and join us!'

Flipper looks uncertainly at Mr Anderson, who is perhaps also a little uncertain, but before he can say a word, his wife holds out a sandwich.

'Happy Christmas, boys! Plenty for all. Here is a feast we'll all remember.'

Billy dances a jig, grinning at Rose. 'We had cake but the rats ate it all.'

'Eh, we're that famished,' says Pinky. 'You are angels from heaven, sure you are.'

Rose is pleased to see how happy Billy is. He eats standing, cramming in the food, scooping fingers-full of sardines from his tin, letting the oil run down his chin. He can't stand still for a minute.

Suddenly he's off, leaping like a goat down towards the small inner crater.

'Hey Billy, watch yourself,' shouts Freeman.

But Billy is oblivious of danger — or doesn't care. Rose stands to watch, alarmed. Billy stands poised at the lip, arms stretched wide.

'Oh God, like Jesus on the flippin' cross,' says Flipper, straight-faced for once. 'The idiot.'

Brennan runs. He catches Billy's coat, just as the boy is about to launch himself. The two fall backward to land heavily on the rim. Billy shouts, struggles and the two start sliding down towards the vent.

Rose is running now, too, as man and boy disappear. 'Bren! Billy!'

But Brennan is the stronger. His boots dig into the treacherous rubble. One arm grips Billy and the other grabs at a rock that seems embedded. Their slide is stalled. Rose's face appears over the lip. Then their guide runs up with a rope which he tosses down.

Billy, lying spread-eagled on the scree, grins up at Brennan. 'I was fine,' he says. 'I could have run down a bit and up again.'

'You monkey,' growls Brennan. 'Climb up then, smartly. No!' As Billy struggles to his feet and starts sliding again. 'The rope, you idiot. And mind you don't kick me loose.'

Rose watches Billy as he climbs up. He's still grinning, on

some kind of high pitch of excitement that makes him impervious to the danger — or the trouble he has caused.

'See! I'm not hurt! I could have done it!'

Rose takes his shoulders; turns him to face the crater where a thin wisp of steam comes and goes through the crust. Brennan is hauling himself up on the rope, his boots scrabbling and slipping on the loose scree.

'Look down there, Billy. Look at the very centre. That crust of stones might be only inches thick. We don't know, do we? Beneath is a vent opening to the centre of the earth. Think of it as hell. Lose your footing and you — *or my husband!* — could have crashed through and burned to death.' She shakes the boy. 'Don't you ever take a risk like that again!'

'But I was safe! I *knew* I was safe! He was watching me.'

Rose looks into his blazing eyes. The boy is deep in some kind of ecstasy. '*He* expects you to take some responsibility for yourself, you ninny. Now get back up there while I help my husband.'

Rose has spoken to him as a teacher might to a young child. Billy responds at last. Calmer now, but still grinning, he goes to join the rest.

Rose shakes her head to see him go so lightly over the stones. What is she missing? What is the key?

GRANDFATHER RURI

'Oh he was a lovely man,' Gran would say. 'What a shame you never knew him. Lovely. And good at rugby. You would have got on well with him.' There's only one photo — a wedding picture of him and Gran — posed very formally in front of a tent. He looks rather serious. Much taller than Gran, who is smiling.

'The photographer told us not to smile,' Gran would say, 'but I couldn't see why. It was our wedding, for heaven's sake.'

Gran is wearing a simple white dress, full length; a white veil is attached to her head with a spray of flowers. Her bouquet is enormous. ('Ruri's mother grew those flowers.') Ruri wears a fine suit, the jacket buttoned high and then opening lower down to reveal a watchchain stretched over the waistcoat.

'That lovely watch! A wedding present from Brennan and Rose.'

'What did they give you?'

And Gran would go to her drawer, take out a silver box, flying birds etched onto the lid. Inside, on a bed of tissue, a pendant heart carved from Denniston coal. It is edged in gold and hangs from a gold chain. Gran would touch the little jewel, hold it up to the light. 'So like Rose to choose something from Denniston.'

I never saw her wear it though. Perhaps she was afraid it would mark her clothes.

Gran was always happy to talk about Grandad Ruri. Her disapproval and forthright views were saved for others. 'You should have heard him sing the old songs. A railway man, was my Ruri. He wanted to be a surveyor like his father, but in the end the railways got into his bloodstream.'

'Was he really Rochfort's son?'

Gran would laugh. 'Oh, who knows? His mother said so. Quite fierce on the matter. It's true that John Rochfort had a wandering way with women. He married twice in Nelson and had seven children there, they say. But then he came up north surveying for the Main Trunk Line, so I suppose he just lost contact with that family. Then much later he took a Maniapoto woman as wife. That part is true. He had daughters by Ngahuia. And he was always exploring, surveying — away for months. So maybe there are other Rochforts scattered around both islands.'

'And Grandad never met him?'

'No. He died when Ruri was a child. The sad thing was that he died with no one to claim him. A sudden heart attack while on a job up in the Waikato. No one knew at that time about any of his families. The authorities thought he was without kin of any kind.'

Gran paused in her tale and sighed. 'A famous man, but forgotten in the end.' She looked at me fiercely. 'Tell your mother that I will be buried in the cemetery here. Next to my father. Don't you forget!'

As if we would! She reminded everyone in the family. There had been a bit of an altercation over Grandad Ruri's burial place, which Gran had famously lost. In the end she came to accept that he should be buried next to his mother in tribal ground. But it had been a battle royal at the time.

A few years before Ruri died, he found out about Rochfort's grave and he and Gran had visited it. 'Hard to understand,' said Gran with heavy disapproval. 'Where was his family? Any of his families? They say two strangers witnessed his death and saw him buried. Sad. A man with landmarks named after him all over the place, yet he died alone. That upset Ruri.'

Gran lived most her life in Ohakune in a railway house at The Junction. Grandfather Ruri loved steam engines. After the railroad was built he got a job as a stoker and then engine driver. Like his famous father he was often away. But the railway workshop at Ohakune was the changeover stop for engine drivers so that's where Gran and he lived and where my mother was born.

'Mind you,' Gran would laugh, 'it was touch and go. If my father had had his way none of you would be here today.'

Once, when Gran was old and failing, she sighed and said to me. 'You've asked so many questions, my dear, and I must have told the same story a dozen times. Why don't you write it all down?'

I wish I had asked more questions about Ruri, though. He is still a shadowy figure to me. I will have to use my imagination.

SUMMER 1907–08

Christmas at the camp

How Rose managed to reserve seats on the coach from the north railhead was a mystery, but reserve them she did. 'Hone Coachman owes me a favour' was all she would say. So that Christmas Maggie and Ruri and the two children, Con and Alice, found that one of the crowded coaches arriving at Makatote on Christmas Eve had places for four travellers heading south. They heaved their luggage — mostly food — up on top, and the excited children clambered up with 'Hone Coachman', a cousin of sorts of Ruri's, as it turned out.

'Eh, cousin,' shouted Ruri, 'take good care of these two young mischief-makers.'

The coachman laughed. 'My life would be in danger if I let a hair of one of Rose's children be in danger. Ride in peace, brother.'

Ruri grinned as he climbed inside to sit with Maggie. 'Rose has tentacles like an octopus. I never knew myself that Hone was on this line.'

'Rose is curious about every single thing that comes her way.

188

I sometimes feel exhausted just watching her.' Maggie felt for his hand and held it, not bothering about the stares. Not many Maori rode the coaches, and few were dressed as smartly as Ruri. As the cavalcade of coaches headed down to the bridge Ruri, crammed between a large gentleman and Maggie, looked down at the floor while the other riders craned to see the tall piers of the viaduct beginning to march across the gully. Ruri was glad of Maggie's hand in his but felt uncomfortable to be so close — face to face — with strangers he had never met.

He cleared his throat, but couldn't spit in this crowded box. When Hone Coachman invited any able-bodied gentlemen to dismount on the upward climb and walk beside the coach, Ruri was quick to jump out. Outside, he ran ahead, waved to the children on the driver's seat, whistled like a bird.

'I know,' whispered Maggie when he climbed back on board, 'I feel it, too. We've become used to empty spaces and fresh mountain air. The smell in here!'

Ruri wrinkled his nose and winked. Maggie always made him feel better.

'That viaduct,' said a plump fellow, knee to knee with Maggie, 'will be the tallest on the whole of the Main Trunk Line.' He sounded as if he was used to being listened to with respect. 'Andersons of Christchurch are building it for a contract of fifty-three thousand pounds. Peter Seton Hay designed it.' The others nod, impressed with the detail.

Maggie felt the need to deflate the man. 'Peter Hay is dead; he died of pneumonia after visiting the Makatote.'

'I think you will find he is still alive, little missie. He is personally known to me.'

'He died, didn't he?' Maggie turned to Ruri who nodded, embarrassed by the attention.

'And my friend here,' continued Maggie, raising her voice so that all the passengers could hear, 'drives the winch for the construction. That viaduct couldn't go ahead without him.'

The big fellow regarded Ruri for several seconds. 'Well, perhaps he *helps* the winch driver.' This said in a tone so patronising, so secure in his own superior knowledge that Maggie was in danger of attacking him if Ruri had not intervened.

'I drive the winch which operates the Blondin, sir,' he said in a quiet voice. 'Mister George Pascoe, who runs the operation, will hire anyone who is good enough, sir, native or white.'

The fellow flushed at that and looked the other way. Another traveller — a young woman dressed all in black — laughed a little nervously. 'Well now, are we going to enjoy warm weather for our Christmas Day?'

When they changed horses at Horopito, Ruri asked Maggie if she would mind very much if he rode on the back plate with the bag man. Maggie smiled at him. 'I'd ride there too if there was room. What an ignorant fellow. So full of his own knowledge.'

'He thinks me a fool.'

'Well, he's the fool.'

But the exchange in the coach had dented Ruri's confidence. On the last leg of the trip, clinging on behind the rocking coach, he worried about his mother's reaction to Maggie and, even more uncertain, the Camerons' attitude to him.

At Ohakune a train was ready to take passengers on to Taihape. The engine was swathed in steam and whoo-hooing its intention to head south. Three passenger carriages were linked behind the mail car, a rake of flatbeds carrying timber and several trucks of ballast. Ruri and Maggie were surprised by the activity. Ohakune was growing. Fresh horses were being hitched to the coach they had climbed from. A crowd of travellers and their cases waited to board it and the other coaches in the cavalcade for the trip back to the north railhead at Oio. It seemed everyone was on the move this Christmas Eve.

Some of those who had just arrived by coach, the pompous gentleman included, paid a different coachman to drive them into the settlement. Ruri, Maggie and the children were happy to walk. A sack slung over Ruri's shoulder contained two cooked haunches of wild pork, one for his mother, the other for the Camerons. Maggie carried a basket holding a large cake crammed with raisins and currants, cooked under Mrs Bright's tutelage. The children each shouldered a small sack containing their overnight needs. But none of them complained of the weight of their load or the length of the road. The sun shone, though clouds were building over the mountain; the air was warm and this walk past open fields where animals grazed and vegetables flourished was a welcome novelty after the tall bush at Makatote.

Just before they reached the settlement, Ruri steered the little party down a side track. 'Tia, my mother, lives down here with her hapu. We'll stop for a while.'

Several women were bending in a field where carrots, potatoes, cabbage and onions were growing in neat rows. They straightened to watch the arrival, shielding their eyes against the afternoon sun.

'Tia!' called Ruri. 'Auntie!'

A large woman opened her arms in greeting. 'E Kairuri! Haere mai!'

The two women tramped down the rows, laughing and shouting. Young Con held back, overwhelmed by the exuberance of the greeting, but Alice ran forward, trying a few words in te reo herself and receiving an exuberant hug of approval for her pains.

Maggie's face ached with smiling as the greetings went on, wishing she had some words in the language. Ruri was obviously filling them in about her and the children. The explanation seemed to sober Tia; she stepped back a little and studied Maggie, then broke into English.

'I am Tia, Kairuri's mother. I come from downriver a way but live here with my sister. Welcome.'

'I am Maggie Cameron,' said Maggie. Ruri had explained that she should introduce herself properly. 'I come from the South Island, where I was born. My parents came here from Scotland.'

Tia nodded approvingly. 'These children are not your own?'

Conrad spoke solemnly. 'Ko Conrad ahau. Tena koe.'

'Ae! Tena koe! Ka pai, e tama!' Tia gave him a big hug and the ice was broken. As they walked towards the house, other children came running. They shouted with delight, pointing at Maggie's red curls and Con's blond hair. Ruri introduced Maggie to each person, child or adult, until she turned, laughing, to him.

'Ruri, I'll never remember all these names!'

'Just call the women auntie and the men uncle — that'll take care of the adults. Tamariki will do for the rest!' Ruri put his arm around her and squeezed.

Later, when the whole family were sitting around the long table eating a large meal of boiled mutton and vegetables, bread and butter and great mugs of tea, Ruri spoke to everyone in Maori. His speech was greeted with a thoughtful silence. One older uncle asked a question. Ruri replied. Tia herself frowned and asked another. Ruri's face fell. He turned to Maggie. 'I told them I wish to marry you and that I would ask your father tomorrow. Koro thinks that the Pakeha father will not be pleased to have his daughter marry me.'

Maggie turned to Tia. 'I will be proud to marry Ruri no matter what my father says. But I think he will be pleased to see so handsome and clever a son-in-law.'

Some of the family laughed and clapped, but Tia's manner seemed guarded.

'Would you be pleased, Tia?' Maggie was never one to beat about the bush. 'Would you welcome me into your family?'

Tia looked at Maggie and then at her son. She spoke to Ruri, who was obliged to translate.

'She says we should be prepared to wait. That I should gain more schooling; get my surveyor certificate; maybe university.' He hesitated. 'She thinks—'

Ruri spoke again to the whole group. This time he switched language back and forth so that Maggie could understand. He loved working on the railroad; loved operating the winch and was proud of what he could do with machines. It was his ambition to drive an 'atua whiowhio' and to understand how the great machine that was a railway locomotive worked.

'Survey work is uncertain these days.' He smiled at Maggie and placed a hand on her shoulder. 'And it takes you far away for months. I want to be close to my wife and family.'

Maggie's eyes filled with tears. She couldn't speak. The rest of the family, however, had plenty to say. Arguments went back and forth across the table. The younger ones spoke in English, but all understood the elders. Ruri whispered in Maggie's ear, 'They like you. Most of them think I'm right to want to drive engines. Some of them think a Maori wouldn't get such an important job. Tia still wants me to get further education, but I think she'll change her mind. Let's go for a walk and leave them to it.'

A river ran out of the bush and through the fields. Ruri and Maggie and a gaggle of children — Con and Alice included —

walked alongside the river and into the cool of the bush. The children waded in and threw stones. Ruri put his arm around Maggie. 'Today is the beginning of our life together. I can feel it. Can you?'

Maggie nodded. 'I love your family. They take it so seriously — our marriage. They all have a view.'

Ruri laughed, 'Ae. No lack of opinions.'

'But they listen to each other. There's a respect for other views.'

'Well of course. They're family.'

'I'm not sure my family will be the same. They'll all have opinions, but they might not say what they think. Da will say what *he* thinks and that will be that.'

Ruri threw a stone so that it skipped across the water of a dark pool. 'We'll cross that stream when we come to it, sweetheart.'

The first time he'd called her that.

Ruri spent some of his savings in Ohakune to hire a horse and cart.

'We can walk,' said Maggie stoutly. 'These children need to grow up strong.'

But Ruri wanted to make a good impression when they arrived at the camp. He spent more buying a side of bacon and some sweets, even though they were bringing food from Makatote.

Outside the store Ruri nudged Maggie. 'Look!' He pointed out a tall man assisting a woman across the road. 'Isn't that the preacher? I thought he'd left the Plateau weeks ago.'

Maggie narrowed her eyes. Yes, unmistakably Gabriel Locke; and the limping woman was Mrs Grice! 'Whatever is he up to?' she whispered. 'That's the woman Amos shot. I used to work for her.' She turned her face away. 'Don't greet him, Ruri, turn away. The greater the distance between him and Billy the better I'm pleased.'

Ruri was intrigued to see the two together. Billy's secretive hints had left him wondering about the preacher's involvement in the shooting, but surely Gabriel Locke would be avoiding Mrs Grice, if that were the case? Then Maggie tugged at his arm and he turned away.

Horse and cart set off for the bush camp, a short distance on an easy road. They should all have been at ease, but Maggie was nervous about the family visit and Ruri could feel it, which set him on edge too. The assurance he showed with his own family left him. He wanted to turn the horse and head back. His head drooped.

'They will welcome you,' Maggie reassured him. 'It's Christmas. They would invite even a stranger in.' But Ruri could see her face tighten with the effort of staying cheerful.

'When are we getting there?' Alice slapped her brother, who was fiddling with her hair. The children were tired and crotchety, perhaps feeling the tension in the adults.

Maggie tried to keep everyone's flagging spirits up. 'Round the next bend. See the smoke rising? See the tents among the trees? And the washing hanging out? Look for the biggest tent — that's ours. Mam will be sure to be watching out for us. There it is!'

Con stood up in the cart to see, just as Ruri flicked the reins and sent the horse into a smart trot. Down crashed Con, knocking into Alice, and the pair of them set up a wailing. This spooked the horse, which broke into a gallop. Ruri, who was not experienced with horses, lost control, and just as Mrs Cameron came to the door of the tent, the cart flew past, children roaring, Ruri cursing, Maggie torn between tears and laughter. By the time Ruri had managed to pull up the cart, Dirk was out on the road, a hand on the bridle, somehow turning and quieting the horse and leading them all back.

'Oh dear,' laughed Maggie, 'not the arrival we had in mind!'

Mrs Cameron hugged her daughter and lifted the children down. They immediately gave up on their tears and were happy to be led inside. Dirk unhitched the horse and led it away. Ruri could hear the questions and explanations rattling back and forth inside: Where were Freeman and Billy? Why were these children here? How could her boys find climbing a mountain more enticing than her Christmas dinner? He stood in the road, forgotten in all the busyness. He lifted the sacks of food from the cart and then waited at the door to be invited in. Was he welcome? Had Maggie even told them he was coming? Perhaps they thought he was just the carter. He cleared his throat, desperate for Maggie to come to his side, but it was Mrs Cameron who heard.

'Come in, come in, and Happy Christmas! Maggie, you wretch! You have left our guest standing at the door with no introduction, rude girl.' She took Ruri's hand in hers and drew him inside. 'I am Sarah Cameron, Maggie's mother. Her letters have been so full of you I feel I know you already. Here is Dirk, my eldest.'

Sarah exclaimed over the food they had brought, offered the children biscuits and lemonade, and fussed over the fire where a kettle was slow to boil.

Ruri watched her. Something was wrong. Sarah Cameron, for all her warm words, was on edge. He could hear Maggie's clear voice, but she was hidden behind the curtain that closed off the back room. Was the father in there, too? He needed Maggie by his side to explain what he should do. The tent was stiflingly hot. Why did they not cook outside as his mother did? Should he offer to help?

Outside, men were gathering. Ruri thought that maybe he should join them but there was a sombre, secretive rumble to their talk. He stood at the door looking out. Each man arrived with a tin mug which Dirk now filled from a flagon, but the expected Christmas jollity was absent. Ruri turned back to Sarah Cameron, who was listening to the children's chatter.

'Maggie?' he said. 'Shall I go in to her?'

Sarah shook her head. 'Not yet. I'm sorry Ruri. There has been trouble with the gang. And Jock is not well. Oh!' She ran desperate fingers through her hair. 'I want this to be a happy day. I want us to forget, but . . . Oh dear, I'm afraid we are not treating you well. Yes, perhaps go in. Maggie may need you. Wait though.' She turned this way and that, unsure what to do. Finally she sent the children outside with a tray of cold meat and bread for the men, then turned to Ruri. 'You may find Jock . . . out of sorts. Don't take too much notice. He may . . . Oh, Ruri, it's a bad time. Please understand. He's not himself.' She gave him a little push towards the back room. 'Go in, go in. I must see to the dinner.'

Unnerved by her outburst but eager to be with Maggie, Ruri lifted the curtain aside and stepped in quietly. The room was too warm. A milky light filtered through the canvas. Maggie stood beside a bed made from timber poles lashed together with rope, canvas stretched over the frame. The bedclothes were tossed aside, half of them dragging on the floor. Maggie's father shifted and groaned. His breath wheezed as he laboured to draw it in. There was a powerful smell of alcohol. Maggie was holding Jock's hand and speaking to him softly. She gave Ruri a quick, agonised smile and turned her attention back to her father.

'This is Ruri, Da. My sweetheart. He's come to ask you something.'

Ruri had not imagined it would be like this. A quiet speech

after a happy Christmas dinner was what he had rehearsed in his mind. This was too rushed. Maggie was dragging him forward. How could he ask for Maggie's hand when he hadn't even met the man?

'Who? Who is it then?' Mr Cameron heaved himself over in the rumpled bed and glared at Ruri. He drew in a long, rasping breath.

'Kairuri Rochfort, Mr Cameron.' Ruri felt it better to use the English form of his surname. 'I'm sorry you're not well.'

Jock didn't take the proffered hand, or perhaps he didn't notice it. 'Maggie,' he said, 'you didn't tell me he was a native, hen.' The words drawled out thick and slurred. 'We can't have this. We canna at all.'

'Da, will you just hear him out?' Maggie's cheeks were almost as flushed as her father's.

'Maybe we'll talk later,' Ruri murmured. 'He's not himself now.'

Jock pushed himself unsteadily into a sitting position. 'I heard that, young feller. I am drunk? Is that what you're saying? Cheeky monkey.'

'No sir. It's no concern of mine if you've taken liquor.'

'Damn right. It is not.'

Ruri floundered on. 'You are ill, Mr Cameron, that is clear. I'm sorry for that. Can we talk later maybe?'

'If by talk you mean ask permission to marry —' Jock wheezed and coughed mightily, almost choking —, 'then save your breath. My daughter will marry a white man.' (wheeze) 'Preferably a Scot. Preferably from the West Coast of New Zealand. With a steady job.' He slumped back onto the bed and turned his face away. 'Pass me my mug, Maggie.'

'I'll do no such thing, Da.' Maggie stood next to Ruri, shaking with rage — or despair.

Ruri took a deep breath of the fetid air. 'Mr Cameron, I love your daughter and wish to marry her. Half my blood is Ngati Rangi and I am proud of it. The other half is English through my father — not Scottish, but of good stock. John Rochfort. He spent much of his time surveying on the West Coast. I think you have worked on the plateau named after him. I have a steady job on the railroad and intend to make my life working for the railways. I will be a good husband to your daughter.'

'Born out of wedlock?'

'What?'

'You. A bastard child, I take it.'

'Oh Da!' Maggie stood over him, fists clenched, eyes on fire. 'Will you listen to yourself! What's happened to you?'

'I am sick, that's what. And sick of this damned nonsense.'

'You are drunk, Da. Shame on you. Where's our happy Christmas then? That Mam has set her heart on?'

Ruri took Maggie's arm. 'Leave him be, Maggie. There's no point.'

But Maggie had worked herself into a fine rage. 'Go and join the others, Ruri. This man is going to dress and wash and join his family for a Christmas dinner. Tell Mam we are coming shortly.'

'He's not well, sweetheart.' But Ruri could see by the set of her head that she would not be thwarted. She had made up her mind. Even so, he doubted she could shift this drunk and stubborn man. He left them to it.

The long plank table had been dragged outside and set up in the middle of the road — the only flat land available. Blessed sunshine filtered through the tall trees. Sarah had laid a white damask cloth — kept all these months in the bottom of her trunk — over the rough wood and decorated it with scarlet sprigs of native mistletoe. Dirk's black dog, Skipper, sat hopefully beside the table, his eyes fixed on the leg of pork that Ruri had brought. There were juicy venison steaks, cooked on an open fire by one of the gang, boiled mutton, a great pot of potatoes, and fresh peas from the market gardens at Ohakune. A feast.

Dirk was carving the meat into great chunks and Sarah ladling out gravy when Maggie emerged from the tent, supporting a white-faced Jock.

'Happy Christmas!' sang Maggie, the greeting louder than necessary as everyone had fallen silent. 'Here's Da to say grace for us!'

A sigh of relief went around the table.

Jock, still clinging to his daughter's arm, mumbled thanks to the Lord then sank onto his chair. He looked up at Sarah, whose eyes had filled with tears. 'Happy Christmas, Mother. You have done us proud. Happy Christmas all.' He could manage no more. His filled plate remained untouched, though Sarah managed to pop the odd tidbit into his mouth. Drunk he might be, but it was clear to all that there was a deeper sickness eating at him.

After the cake, Alice and Con sang *Away in a Manger* in their clear voices and everyone clapped. Jock looked imploringly at Maggie and she gave the nod. Sarah brought him his tot and joined him in raising a toast to the family. Ruri suggested a toast to the railway that had brought them all together, but Jock slammed his mug to the table and growled that he would not raise his voice to that cause.

There was an embarrassed silence. Maggie, unsmiling, put a hand on Jock's shoulder and faced the men. 'Right. Da's had enough. We'll let him go to his bed now. But I hope there's some cheerful entertainment that he'll hear through his dreaming?'

While she led the stumbling Jock back inside, Dusty and Sligo unwrapped fiddle and banjo and tuned them up. Ruri's eyes lit up at the sight. He loved nothing better than a sing. From a back pocket he produced a pair of flutes fashioned from the leg bone of a deer. He had drilled holes in the bone, and shaped the mouthpieces from totara wood. With a bow he presented them to Con and Alice, who shouted with delight and immediately set up a shrilling that threatened to overcome the music.

'Kao, tamariki,' laughed Ruri. 'Here. Listen.' He reached for the flutes and with both in his mouth played a tune, each flute harmonising with the other. Dusty and Sligo joined in and soon they were all singing.

'This is more like it,' said Sarah, hugging her daughter. 'Thank God you have come back. We need you, hen.'

'I can see that. Whatever has happened? The men's mood was darker than a dungeon earlier on.'

'We'll come to that later. Let's enjoy the singing. Shall we give them *The White Cockade?*'

Sarah and Maggie sang; then Con and Alice pleaded to sing their piece again, and Ruri gave them a couple of shanties he'd learned from the riggers. Bootleg flowed freely.

'Take your Da another tot,' said Sarah. 'Just one. He can't do without it these days.'

Maggie frowned. 'It does him no good, Mam.'

'You have not been living with him these last months to make judgements. It's Christmas Day.'

'All the same—' But Maggie went in to him with a small measure.

Later, when the children were tucked into their bedrolls and the gang had wandered into the night for a game of two-up, Sarah told them of the troubles.

'It's been one disaster after another these last months. Jock has not been able to pull the gang together. Now —' she held up a finger — 'don't you go blaming your father. It's the authorities, to my mind. And some of the toe-rags got foisted on Jock's gang.'

'But why, Mam? Why is Da like this? Why can't he pull the gang together? He used to be so strong. It's the drink, is it?'

Ruri saw the distress Maggie's forthright words caused Sarah. 'Let her have her say, Maggie. Listen to her. She's the one with the story.'

Maggie fiddled with her buttons. Her quick glance at Ruri showed surprise — then understanding. 'Sorry, Mam, sorry. It's been a shock. Tell us the troubles.'

Three months back, Sarah told them, when the weather was still wintery, George Gafferty, one of the leaders in the gang, a miner from Denniston and an old friend of Jock's, walked off the job. He hadn't brought his wife with him; the task had taken longer than he thought; the conditions were too punishing. 'I'm back to hewing coal, Jock,' was all he'd said before walking away. It hurt Jock badly — Jock had persuaded the gang to follow him from Denniston and he took it as a slight.

'It undermined Jock's status as foreman, or he felt it that way. Said the mood of the gang changed after that.'

The gang had been short of hands anyway after the two English recruits ran off. Without George, they couldn't operate properly. They were falling behind their targets. So Mr Furkert sent them two new fellers — older men who were handy enough with a shovel but lacking stamina.

'They would sit down for an hour with their lunch. Demanded half-hours morning and afternoon. The rest of the gang were used to a different rhythm — slow and steady all day with short breaks. There was tension. Jock came home exhausted as much from trying to keep the gang together as from the work. Then one of the old fellers messed up during a charge. He must've been deaf because Jock is so careful with the explosives — not like in some gangs. The charge was laid and the men all clear. Then while Jock was lighting the fuse this old fool wandered back to lean against the bank of the cutting. Down came a big rock and caught him on the side of his head. Mashed his head in. Not dead, but touch and go. He had to be loaded onto the train and sent to Taihape, his mate travelling with him, while Jock had to report to headquarters. Mr Furkert was not pleased, nor was his supervising engineer. It was unfair the way they blamed him. They were the ones who sent him poor workers. No doubt Jock was blunt about it, which did him no good with the boss.'

Two pink spots had appeared on Sarah's tired face. Ruri admired the way she defended her husband. He could see how angry she was on his behalf.

Jock had been told, Sarah explained, that if his gang couldn't improve their rate, keep to the timetable, they'd be pulled out and given less important duties — ballasting probably — while some other gang finished the cutting. Quite apart from the drop in wages, this threat enraged Jock. He was proud of the work they'd done; proud of the fact that they had one of the biggest hillsides to manage. He was determined to finish the job.

'He talked to the men. Got them fired up. Hired another worker himself, a good, steady man, and the gang got back into their rhythm again. Jock would drink every night — he always has, but he needed that relaxing tot or two. He *needed* it!' Sarah looked at Maggie fiercely. 'You should go and see what your father and his gang have done. You should be proud of your da, Maggie. All those tons and tons of rock and dirt! A whole high hill shifted with the strength of their muscles and the heave of their shovels.

But then—' Sarah shook her head. She was close to tears. 'Jock fell ill. Really ill. His health has never been the same since the South African wars. And this climate, not to mention living in a tent for two cold Plateau winters. We didn't reckon on that.'

Sarah told them Jock had been off work with a high fever for three weeks, almost four. Dirk and Donal had tried to keep the work on track, but without Jock it just couldn't be managed. Before the overseer and the engineer could note the slow progress, one of the gang had a 'bright' idea.

'It'd be funny if it wasn't so stupid,' said Sarah. 'Sligo's idea, silly chook. He's just a young lad, devoted to Jock and a hard worker, but short of a penny if you know what I mean. He knew that the overseer was coming to check the next day. One of the measurements they take is to note the level of the gunpowder in the barrel.'

'I remember that,' said Maggie. 'They were always pleased if they saw the level was low. Meant you'd been blasting away with a will.'

'Well, young Sligo knew that without Jock they'd not been blasting rock — Jock was the one for that. I suppose he thought that he was helping Jock with the bosses. Anyway, one night, after the others had left the cutting, he took a couple of good shovelfuls of gunpowder out of the barrel, put it in a kerosene tin, hid the tin in the bush and blew it up. Dear God! You could hear the explosion from here. Dirk and Donal drove down to the cutting fearing some disaster, which in a way it was. Did you notice Sligo's hair tonight?'

The others nodded. One side of Sligo's head was more or less bald, with the fresh hair growing tight and curled. Dirk had found the boy lying on the ground moaning and wisps of smoke drifting out of the bush. Sligo had expected a much smaller explosion and had stayed too close.

'He was playing banjo pretty well tonight.'

'Oh yes. He was singed all over and shocked but he came right. Trouble was, whatever Dirk and Donal tried they couldn't disguise the smell. That unmistakable stench lingered in the damp bush; no wind rose to clear the air. The overseer noticed when he came that morning and walked straight into the trees; found the evidence. His explosion was almost as loud as the gunpowder.'

'Well it wasn't Da's fault,' said Maggie. 'They couldn't blame him for that.'

'Oh yes they could. And did. Jock had heard the news that night from Dirk and struggled out of his bed in the morning. He had planned to be on deck for the bosses anyway so they could see his gang had a full muster. Trouble was they could see he was sick; they thought he must have ordered the gunpowder trick to cover the slow progress.'

'That's so unfair! Didn't Sligo confess?'

'He did. Profusely. Abjectly, poor lad. But Jock had lost control of his gang, they said. After the Christmas break they're putting in a new foreman. Some of the gang will stay in the new co-op but Jock will be on ballasting for the rest of the summer. Sligo, too. It's broken Jock's heart. And his health.'

Maggie and Ruri sat in silence. Down the road they could hear the shouts from the two-up school. A kiwi called in the bush. Inside the tent Jock coughed and then cried out in his sleep.

Maggie spoke at last. 'You should take him home, Mam.'

'What home? We were going to build one with the savings—'

'His chest is bad. And the drink doesn't help. You need to be somewhere else. Not here in the bush.'

'I know, hen, but you know how stubborn he is.' Sarah sighed. 'We'll see.'

Ruri looked into the embers of the fire. He knew what should be done but didn't want to say it. Feared losing Maggie. But it had to be said. And by him. 'Sweetheart, you should stay here to help your mother. She cooks for all the men. And your da needs nursing.'

Maggie nodded slowly. 'Aye, Ruri. I need to stay.' She reached for his hand. 'Never worry about me, though. I've made up my mind even if Da disapproves. He can't stop us marrying.'

Sarah snorted. 'Nor will he. Jock takes against people he doesn't understand, I don't know why. Maori, Chinese, he won't have them in the gang. Doesn't trust them. He'll learn.'

'He'll have to or lose out on family and grandchildren.'

Ruri beamed. He loved his fierce girl, her forthright ways. He needed that assurance. 'But what about Rose?' he said. 'She won't be pleased to lose your help.'

'Just till Da is back on his feet. She'll manage. Rose always manages.'

In the morning Ruri drove Maggie and the children down to have a look at the cutting. The much-used service road was smooth and the horse trotted along smartly, Ruri taking special care after yesterday's accident. All four were silenced by the sheer grandeur of the cutting. They dismounted and walked into the wide opening. The walls were finished here — sloping up and out to allow generous light in. The surface under their feet was smooth and hard, ready for the platelayers to lay sleepers and rails. Further in the walls narrowed; they had yet to be widened, though the hillside high above had been opened.

'It's as if a giant sliced it with a knife,' said Con, craning his head to see up. 'Did your da really do this, Maggie?'

'Da and his gang, yes, Con, with nothing but picks and shovels and the odd blast of dynamite.'

Ruri shook his head. 'Doesn't seem even possible, eh?'

They heard in the distance the scream of a steam whistle: a work engine travelling over the deviation — the temporary bypass, ordered by Mr Furkert, which brought the railhead to Ohakune. Soon trains would travel through this cutting — very soon, if Mr Furkert had his way — and then the deviation would be abandoned and left for the bush to reclaim. Abandoned, thought Ruri, like Jock.

'Look after your father,' he said to Maggie later as he kissed her goodbye. 'I'll have a word to Tia and the family. They will send fresh vegetables down.'

Maggie clung to him. 'Don't forget me, Ruri. Don't mind Da. Please.'

Jock had turned his head away when Ruri came to say goodbye; would say not one word. Sarah said he was ashamed of his behaviour yesterday, but it didn't seem that way to Ruri.

'Come back soon,' he said, and tickled Maggie's ear. 'E noho ra. Kia kaha.'

And off they rattled, the children waving, Maggie standing alone in the road until they were out of sight.

The stalker and his prey

It was indeed Gabriel Locke whom Maggie and Ruri had seen in Ohakune. And they had been right in supposing that the poor limping woman he was helping was Mrs Grice. Gabriel had been assisting her towards his new mission hall, the Glory Gospel Hall, in truth not a hall but canvas stretched over a wooden frame like many of the new establishments in the settlement. The hall had been endowed in large part by the generosity of Mrs Grice and her husband. On a Sunday the preacher extolled the love of the Lord, railed against the evils of alcohol (a crumb cast in the unfortunate Mrs Grice's direction), and consigned heathen Asiatics to eternal damnation — a mix of messages both popular and lucrative. Billy had thought that his friend the preacher was off in some distant town, but here he was, doing rather well, with a sizeable congregation of new settlers only a few hours' coach ride away. Gabriel was enjoying himself too much to worry about Billy. Perhaps soon he would send word. Meanwhile he played with Mrs Grice as a cat might taunt a mouse. Such fun.

After the cook's tirade Gabriel had recognised that the mood of the workers at Makatote had turned against him. At first he had thought of riding north to seek a new parish ready to welcome his talents. Preaching was his vocation, he was convinced of that now. But he was not yet finished with the railroad settlements — or with Mrs Bright, the cook, who should be punished. The night before he left Makatote, he had crept around to the back of the cookhouse where the great pile of wood was stacked under its roof of corrugated iron. He carried bucket after bucket of water from the tank and poured them carefully over the stack. That would slow down her baking in the morning. The men would complain about their breakfast and the cold cookhouse and Mrs Bright would know who the culprit was. Ha!

In the morning, early, he had blessed and kissed the downcast Billy, promised to return soon (though he had no intention of doing so) and set off back towards Ohakune. He knew he should stay away from Sergeant Baker and his suspicions, but he needed to know about Mrs Grice. Had she confessed to shooting Amos's brother? Was she recovering? Gabriel was sure she had not seen him; nor, he believed, had anyone else. Gabriel had felt that familiar excitement; that need to stir the pot just to see what might brew. He decided to pay Mrs Grice a visit.

'Praise the Lord!' he sang, stepping out on his fine thoroughbred, the contents of his congregation's generosity (not much but enough for a week or two) jingling in a small leather pouch at his belt. He waved a hand at the sharp lines of the viaduct just visible in the dawn light. Good riddance to the engineering marvel and its surly workforce.

Mrs Grice, it turned out, *was* recovering, but slowly. The bullet (Gabriel had learned from the garrulous — and easily charmed — Mrs Kerr of the Temperance Hotel) had entered her shoulder, and caused great loss of blood but no serious damage. Of more concern was her leg, which was badly broken when she fell, and her jaw, smashed by the butt of Amos's rifle. She had been patched up hastily and taken by dray ('an agonising ride for the poor dear and almost the end of her') down to Pipiriki where Mr Hattrick's steamboat had taken her downriver to the hospital in Wanganui.

'A lovely letter came from her only yesterday,' Mrs Kerr told him. She took it from her pocket, proud to show that she was the one chosen for such an honour. 'What a battler! She is able to write but is not yet on her pins. But she says the hospital is well appointed and modern with pleasant views to the north. She hopes to make the journey back here by Christmas. Are you acquainted then, Mr Locke?'

'We met briefly. I was able to bring her some solace on that occasion, I believe.' Gabriel finished his tea, and stood. 'The town is growing, I see.'

'You wouldn't believe! Since the railhead came, there's a new establishment every day.'

'And your own business is good?'

'Oh, I am run off my feet,' said the comfortably seated manageress, 'with the coach traffic and the overnight stays. The railway has brought us prosperity, God bless it.'

'And may He bless you, Mrs Kerr,' said Gabriel thoughtfully. Dare he stay here? He remembered the Anti-Asiatic League man and the generous donations from the crowd.

But now a visit to Wanganui Hospital.

Mrs Grice, seated in the grounds of the hospital under a leafy linden tree, gave Gabriel a crooked smile. 'I do indeed remember you, Mr Locke.' Her speech was slurred — perhaps the morphine, though missing teeth and a livid scar on one cheek may have contributed. Her leg, still in a plaster cast, was propped on a support attached to her wheelchair. The fighting spirit that Gabriel remembered from his previous encounter had entirely deserted her. This lady's shoulders drooped, her eyes were dull, her hand, when she offered it, shook. Gabriel took the hand and held it tenderly.

'God bless you, Mrs Grice, I am so sorry to hear of your misfortunes.'

'You heard about the attack?'

There was a touch of anxiety in the question, Gabriel noted, though self-pity also. Both might be exploited. 'I did indeed. From Sergeant Baker.'

That provoked a reaction. Amelia Grice's wan cheeks flushed. 'Oh! He has been to visit twice. I don't care for him at all.'

Gabriel stroked her hand. First he would charm her. 'He is certainly blunt in his line of questioning. I was subjected to some of that myself, Mrs Grice.'

'Oh, but why? Surely you had nothing to do with that . . . that horrible attack.' She closed her eyes and moaned.

'Well, in a way I did. But first tell me about yourself. Are you healing? Do they treat you well here? Is there any comfort I can bring you?'

Gabriel regarded her with great warmth. He held a glass of water to her lips. He rose politely when a maid brought them tea and scones and a chair for himself. For some minutes he let her talk on about her pain, her anguish, the sad fact that her husband was so busy on railroad business that he had only visited once. He nodded and made sympathetic noises and watched the colour return to her cheeks. Her eyes, so dull when he arrived, began to glow. Gabriel's own pleasure mounted; he could hardly hold back from taking the next, cruel step, yet still he listened and smiled as the sun began to drop behind trees and shadows on the grass lengthened.

Now is the right time, he decided. Did she not notice his anticipation? He wanted her to fear him. 'Ah, Mrs Grice,' he said, interrupting her flow. 'Alas, I knew the unfortunate boy who attacked you.'

Her hand jerked from her lap. Her mouth opened to no sound. All animation left her.

'Yes, Mrs Grice. That poor boy was a member of my congregation.'

Amelia Grice took a shuddering breath. 'Oh!' She searched his face but found no comfort.

Gabriel was grim now, his eyes sharp. His breath quickened. He could not for the life of him delay any further. This was the purest pleasure. 'He told me — in confidence you understand — everything. *I know that you shot his brother.*'

Gabriel sat back in his chair and watched her closely. He thought of himself as some handsome animal, a tiger perhaps, stalking prey. The way she crumpled, the animation draining from her face, was beautiful. Perfect.

Mrs Grice spoke at last. It was a croak really, hardly properly formed words. 'He . . . no . . . it was a mistake . . . you must see —' She subsided into silence.

Gabriel sat on, watching her. He felt so alive; felt his blood pounding. He wanted to sing. Her fear excited him profoundly. 'Well now,' he murmured, 'well now, Mrs Grice. We share a secret, do we not?' He had a sudden desire to bed her: that helpless, beholden fear — irresistible.

'You have not? . . . Sergeant Baker doesn't . . . Please believe me, it was a mistake.' Tears ran down her scarred face.

Gabriel would not let her off the hook; not yet. 'I believe Sergeant Baker suspects something. Yes, I believe so. But no, I have said nothing. For the moment it is our secret alone.' He beamed at her and was rewarded with a timid, hopeful smile.

'I thought the rifle was my own dummy one, you see? I had mistakenly taken the innkeeper's loaded rifle—'

Gabriel held up his hand, still affable, 'I am not interested in explanations. Not at all. No, Mrs Grice, I am interested in the future. How we may help each other.'

All hope died for Amelia Grice. 'Oh. You want to blackmail me. You want money. I am not a rich woman. My husband—'

The preacher stood. 'I feel the air is cooling. Time for you to go indoors. Shall I wheel you?' With the greatest solicitude he rolled her up the little path to the hospital. 'Now,' he said when he had politely delivered her into the hands of a nurse. 'A blessing.' He placed a gentle hand on her head. 'The Lord bless you, my dear, and bring you better health. Shall I come and visit tomorrow?'

'What a lovely man,' said the nurse, walking to the window to get a better view as he strode away towards the town. 'You're lucky to have such a handsome visitor, aren't you now? I'd take him off your hands any day.'

Amelia Grice closed her eyes.

Fire

For a few weeks, early that summer of 1908, Jock rallied. The warm weather, perhaps; his daughter's presence, certainly. Jock loved Maggie, and her presence lightened his mood and consequently his health. His coughing and wheezing subsided and, though he grumbled about the ballasting, he rode off, day after day, shovel strapped to Rusty's saddle, Sligo riding behind, to whatever section of new rails he was directed. They would find the place where a line of trucks full of stone ballast was waiting. It was a simple shovelling job; no skill needed, but plenty of strength. All day Jock stood in truck after truck, throwing shovelfuls of the heavy stone down between the rails until the sleepers were covered and settled. His arms ached, he could not find the old rhythm; he was exhausted by midday. And disheartened. Most evenings he had not the strength to see to Rusty but went directly inside, leaving Maggie to see to the horse, something that would have shamed him a year ago.

'It's poor man's work,' he grumbled, 'but I'm damned if my

family will go without because of me.' Maggie watched him set off each day and dreamed of returning to Ruri and Rose and the children. She imagined — hoped — that his strength was returning. Jock still drank heavily each night, but in truth the supply of bootleg was intermittent these days, so he was sometimes forced to go without. No bad thing in Maggie's eyes.

The days were hot and windy. The stream by the camp, usually running vigorously out of the bush, shrank to a sulky trickle. Maggie and Sarah were forced to walk for half an hour to find a pool where the water was clean and good for drinking — an extra chore and exhausting in the heat. Sweat poured off the women as they staggered out of the bush and onto the baking road, where they would leave the heavy cans for Dirk to bring home on the cart at the end of the day.

Dirk brought with him news of a fire at the new mill at Rangataua, a small settlement on the rail line. 'It's the train coming through,' he said as he unloaded the cans. 'You can see the sparks flying out of the stack, along with the smoke and steam. The bosses have asked us to carry wet sacks with us and to keep an eye on any fires.'

As they sat in the tent that night with the gang eating Sarah's good beef stew, all the conversation was over the fires: the mill at Rangataua was only one of many.

Jock nodded, happy to tell his news. 'A couple of settlers down our way were burning off ready for planting, the stupid buggers. A hot, dry wind blowing. Of course it got out of hand, but they're in a hurry to get seed in the ground and they took no notice of the direction. Lost their new-built whare and everything in it. Lucky not to lose wife and child.'

Sarah stopped her serving and turned to Jock. 'The fire was that quick?'

'It was. The women ran for the stream and sat in it.'

'Fat lot of use sitting in our stream would be.'

'Aye, but you should be safe enough here, Mother. The bush is green and we've burned all that we've cut. But out back a way it's open now. The loggers have cut for the mills and left the waste lying. Then the settlers move in and burn off as soon as it's dry. Recipe for disaster. There's several fires down on the Raetihi road, they say.'

The new foreman, who was generally quiet in the face of Jock's antagonism, joined in. 'And the trains make it worse. We put out three smouldering patches today and we're well away from the deviation. The sparks fly a good distance in the wind.'

Jock tipped the dregs of the crock into his mug and headed for bed. 'Dirk,' he called from the back room, 'wet some sacks for Mother before you settle. And keep one full can here inside the tent always. Just in case.'

Over the next days Sarah and Maggie could smell the smoke in the camp, even though the fires were distant. Then the air thickened and ash began to fall through the trees. Fires were everywhere, the men said. No one had enough water to put out the heart of the fires, which smouldered, crept along under the felled waste and then leaped to life again when the wind rose. Mills were particularly vulnerable. A cart full of tearful millworkers came up the road; the mill and their whares had been completely destroyed. They were heading for Rangataua, which they considered safer than Ohakune.

Sarah became fearful. Everything, even here in the bush, was so dry! She ran outside regularly to check whether sparks from the chimney might have set the dry leafy undergrowth alight. Once she noticed a little smouldering patch by the woodpile. Maggie found her sitting on the bench outside in tears; ash had drifted into her hair and smudged the washing.

'It's too dangerous. We should get out of here. What can two women do if the fires come? Look over there!'

Sarah pointed out behind the camp, to the west. When they had first arrived, two years ago, tall, dense forest had stretched away into the distance. Now only a narrow strip of trees lay between them and open land. On clear nights they could enjoy watching the light from the setting sun filtering through the leaves, but now, at midday, they could see the same rosy glow. 'Listen!' Sarah stood fearful, uncertain what to do. They stared into the trees. Both heard the small explosions as undergrowth caught fire, felt the hot wind driving flames their way.

Maggie picked up two of the wet sacks and dipped them in the water barrel. 'Leave it, Mam, it's too late for saving stuff. We have to run!' She grabbed at her mother, who was shoving her heirloom china into a sack. 'Leave it, leave it!' But Sarah, distraught, would not — until Maggie had snatched up all their good pieces and plunged them into the water barrel. 'They'll be safe there. Run, Mam!'

Holding the wet sacks over their heads, they ran away from the fire into the bush. Up past the sluggish stream they ran until they came to the deeper pool. Behind them the fire was roaring now, the heat of the flames bearing down on them. Out of breath, terrified, they waded in and sat in the cool dark water, only their sack-covered heads in the air.

'Put your head right under if it comes,' said Maggie. She scrabbled among the reeds to find a hollow stalk they might breathe through; tore at the tough, woody seed heads but could not break them off. 'Oh! I can't do it, the bloody things.'

Her mother's hand stilled her. 'Wait, hen, look: the wind's changing.'

Maggie peered out from under the sack. The flames, so purposeful and raging a few minutes ago, were wavering, softening. With no wind to drive the fire, the green bush stood a chance. And so did the women. They sat there in the blessed cool water, splashing their hot faces and, at last, daring to hope. The fire, tamer now, had turned south and was dying. Still they sat on, reluctant to walk back over the hot ash and discover what might have happened to the camp.

'We'll stay here till evening,' said Sarah, 'till the men come home — what's left of it. Oh Maggie, all our things!'

Sarah began to shiver. Maggie made her sit on the bank and rubbed her with fern fronds to bring the colour back to her waterlogged skin. Soon they would have to move. The bush was quiet, all the evening birdsong silenced. Had the birds escaped, Maggie wondered, or were the flames too quick for them, the smoke too choking?

Then the bush exploded in sound — a great crashing and shouting. 'Sarah! My darling! Maggie, hen! Sarah!' It was Jock. He burst out of the bush, slashing at it with his shovel. He stopped dead to see them both sitting there. 'Oh, thank God, thank God!' He came and knelt beside them, panting and wheezing, his face black, hair full of ash. 'Thank God.' He leaned over and spat a great gob of dark mucus. 'We thought we'd lost you — and then I thought of the pool.'

Jock reached a grimy arm around Sarah and another to hold his daughter tight. 'Ah!' He winced and withdrew one hand. Maggie saw the raw burn on his wrist. Carefully she bathed it in the clean water. It was badly blistered. Jock moaned as the pain bit.

There they all sat until Jock could breathe steadily again. Maggie wrapped the burned hand in a strip of her wet skirt then slowly, slowly, for Jock was near collapse, they walked back through ash and blackened trees to the ruined camp.

Dirk was there, and the rest of the gang, slapping wet sacks at patches where smoke still drifted. He set up a shout to see the three of them emerge from the bush, then ran to support his father who could stagger no further. Jock had left Rusty down the road and run through smoke and flames, fearing to find his women dead. Now he was retching, his smoke-damaged lungs threatening to finish him. Maggie scooped ash from the barrel and brought him a mug of clean water. He sat on a charred log, hands dangling, exhausted.

The fire had cut a narrow path; why here rather than a few chains away? Perhaps the road itself had given the flames room or air to build; or a wayward lick of wind. A small distance from the camp, on either side, the trees remained untouched, but the clearing was a smoking wasteland. Sarah's chimney still stood; two or three of the timber struts supporting the door, now stripped of their canvas, leaned crazily, charred and useless. All the tents had burned, along with their possessions and food. Sarah ran to the barrel and pulled out a piece of china, its blue and white pattern startling against the black ash. They all cheered: something was saved, at least.

Almost immediately work resumed. Fresh tents and blankets were allocated, supplies replaced. The camp was rebuilt on the same blackened spot. Nothing was allowed to slow down these last months before the railway gap was closed. The gang went off to the cutting; their job was almost finished, ready for the platelayers to move in with sleepers and rails. Jock was ordered back to ballasting.

'Give him a day or two,' pleaded Sarah, 'the smoke is still affecting his lungs.'

But Jock, grey-faced, shook his head. 'Leave it, Mother, I can manage. It's easy work.' He shouldered his shovel and headed up the road, but was back, more dead than alive, by midday. Sligo, whimpering with fear to see his boss so low, brought him home.

Air whistled in and out of Jock's ruined lungs. 'My tot, Mother,' he wheezed, 'Quick, in the name of God.' He fell, groaning, onto his bed, reached for his mug and turned his face away. 'No more. No more,' he whispered.

It was not the bootleg he meant.

The struggle to breathe

Maggie sat beside her father, listening to his laboured breath — a painful rasp in and then a slow rattle out. Again and again. She had propped him up on a high pillow made from a flour sack stuffed with sweet-smelling bracken. But nothing seemed to ease this dreadful battle for air.

Sarah would not deny him the bootleg. 'It eases his breathing, can't you see that, Maggie?'

Maggie suspected her father's addiction had grown partly from her mother's desire for a peaceful evening. Jock's rages were now a thing of the past, though. After the first few tots he became mellow — loving even — and then, a few drinks later, he slipped into a drowsy but restless sleep. Perhaps her mother, weary from cooking for the gang, welcomed the peace.

Maggie could see that she had no chance of changing matters. It was her duty now to collect the bootleg from Jock's hideout in the bush. When the gang paid Sarah what they owed for their week's meals, Maggie would take two empty jars, each jangling with hard-earned coins, to the secret spot in the bush known only to Jock (and now to Maggie as well). There she lifted the stone that marked the spot and left the jars and money in the hole beneath. The dropper who worked for suppliers in Karioi would slip through the bush at night on bridle tracks unknown to the authorities and locate all the cunningly marked dropper stations. In the morning Maggie would find that the empties had been replaced with full jars of bootleg. She longed to pour away the stuff, was convinced it was rotting Jock's stomach, sapping what strength he had. She would even have joined the Temperance Union if that would bring Jock back to health. But Sarah shook her head at any mention of unions or authorities. 'It's too late for that, hen. He would die without it.'

'He'll die because of it!' Maggie watered the bootleg whenever she had a chance, and tried spooning soup into Jock's slack mouth instead. But he was failing. He had no stomach for ballasting and refused to go again. Nor could he have managed a shovel. The overseer came and smelt the bootleg, blamed that rather than Jock's illness, and cut his pay.

'You can stay in the big tent,' he said to Sarah, 'if you continue cooking for the new gang. That's fair enough. Otherwise you should head out. We are not a charity.'

So Sarah cooked for the new foreman and the new gang — and for Dirk, who stayed on as a member. It was heartbreaking. Jock could hear the men laughing and discussing the day's work as they ate in *his* tent, food that *his* wife and daughter had prepared for them. Dirk was the only member of the gang who came into the back room of the tent and even he never spoke of the cutting. Or Jock never asked. Maggie tried giving him a bit of gossip one day, but Jock growled and coughed and told her to shut her mouth.

Once, at a mellow stage of his drunkenness, he reached for

Maggie's hand. 'It's a comfort to have you here. Don't mind my grumbling, hen. A comfort to Mother, too.'

'Oh Da, I'm pleased to be here.'

'You'll stay?'

'While I'm needed, I'll stay.'

'I'm dying, Maggie. My lungs are shot.' He coughed and spat and coughed again. 'I won't last much longer.'

'Don't say that, Da! You're young yet. It's just a fever. You'll get over it.'

'We both know that's nae the truth.' Jock sank back on his pillow, struggling for breath.

Maggie could see that he wanted to say more but couldn't manage. She stroked his hand. 'Rest, Da. Save your strength.'

Jock seemed to sleep, but then spoke again, his eyes closed and his voice distant as wind in the bush. 'Your feller. Maybe he would suit you after all.' A hint of a smile flickered and faded.

'I'll take that,' said Maggie with spirit, 'as permission to wed, Da. I'll hold you to that.'

But this night there was no talk, no response as she sat by him, wiping his hot face with a cold cloth; just the rattling, rasping fight for breath. Then she felt his breathing change. His eyes opened and fixed on her. The agony of that struggle to suck in air stretched every muscle in his face.

'Mam!' called Maggie, panicked by that stare, 'Mam, wake up!'

She heaved Jock into a sitting position, thumped his back. Still no breath.

Sarah rolled out of bed and rushed to hold his head, crying, 'Jock, Jock!' Then to Maggie, 'No, hen, leave your thumping, it does no good.' She whispered to her husband, 'Breathe my love. One more breath. Just one!'

Jock's hard, agonised stare fixed on her. His hand clutched

hers like a vice. But nothing the women did could bring air into those drowning lungs. His eyes glazed. All fight went out of his body. The weight of him dragged on their arms. He was gone, his heart overcome by the mighty battle to breathe.

Tears ran down Sarah's face. Maggie, still dry-eyed with the sudden shock of it, looked to her mother. Dirk, used to sleeping through Jock's rattling and wheezing, was now awake. He stood, pale and silent, in the doorway.

Sarah sighed. 'That's it then. Your father's gone.'

Dirk walked slowly to the bed, tears streaming down his face. He reached out one big calloused hand and, gently as a girl, brushed back a stray lock of his father's hair. He spoke no words.

They laid him back on the pillows. Dirk was sent outside while the women cleaned and stopped his body.

Sarah was calm, though the tears continued to run. 'We'll sleep now. The morning will come soon enough.' She hugged Maggie. 'Thank you.'

Nothing more needed saying.

'There's a newcomer,' said young Mr Lennox, the travelling missioner, 'who will try to persuade you to have the funeral in his *commodious hall*. Tent, I call it. And the Methodists have offered their pioneer church. But Mrs Cameron,' — and here he laid a hand on her shoulder — 'you will be at home I expect, among your own Presbyterians?'

Sarah had only once attended Mr Lennox's meetings, which he held up and down the line, in work camps or in the shearing sheds at Karioi. His message on that occasion was fiery, full of warnings of damnation, paying especial attention to the evils of drink. But she nodded now, thankful that someone would take charge. So the funeral was held in the billiard room of Mrs Kerr's Temperance Hotel. 'Ironic,' whispered Dirk to Maggie and they were comforted to share a quiet grin.

A small number of people sat against the walls in the billiard room. Two of the engineers and Mr Furkert were there. Poor Sligo, his sobs threatening to derail the proceedings, sat by the door, ready to run if the bosses so much as looked at him. Mrs Kerr had taken Sarah's arm as she arrived.

'Condolences, my dear. You've had a hard row to hoe. I heard it was the drink got to him. So sad.'

Sarah glared. 'You heard wrong. It was the railroad got him.'

Mrs Kerr shook her head and pursed her lips but said no more, taking her seat in a prominent position. Sarah could have hit the woman.

Maggie had sent word by Hone Coachman, who delivered Freeman and Billy the next day. The journey was fearsome. Fires were still burning between Makatote and Horopito and the coachman had to put the horses at a gallop through the billowing smoke. The passengers clung to the sides of the rocking coach, flames only yards away.

The boys ran down to Ohakune from the station, ash darkening their bright hair, their faces grimy. They arrived just in time for the funeral. Dishevelled and out of breath, they embraced their mother.

Maggie looked for Ruri, but he had not come. She wanted to quiz the boys about him, but their minds were on their father, the manner of his death, what would happen next to the family. Ruri's mother, though, had heard somehow, and arrived with a large bouquet of flowers from her garden which she laid on the coffin along with a small spray of green leaves. Sarah watched the woman embrace Maggie, and longed for a share of that warmth. She felt defeated. She had no answer when the boys asked what next. The children were all on their way, moving in different directions. Even Billy seemed taller, more serious. Her mind wandered as the chief missioner, Mr McKenzie from Raetihi, spoke the formal words of the funeral service. The coffin lay on the billiard table, which had been pushed to the wall. It seemed too high, too prominent, but there was no other space for it in the little room. Sarah was relieved when the prayers were over, the final hymn sung and the men carried Jock's body out to the waiting cart.

The family followed the coffin up to the little cemetery on the Raetihi road. Mr McKenzie and young Lennox rode with the coffin while Rusty, his mane tied with black ribbons, pulled the family in the work cart. Dirk's dog Skipper set up a howling all the way out of the settlement and up the hill towards the cemetery.

'He wants to ride with Da,' said Dirk.

Sarah smiled at last. 'Well let him, for goodness' sake, son. He'll drag us all into the depths with his moaning.'

Dirk released his hold and the dog bounded off the cart, caught up with the coffin and ran beside it, tail high and proud. It cheered them all to see it.

On the high, windy hill overlooking the lake, a group of Maori, Tia among them, was waiting. They sang as the coffin was lifted from the cart and carried to its resting place. After Jock was laid in the ground and the words had been spoken and the sods thrown, Tia walked to the mound and laid a bunch of leaves on it. Quietly she handed a bunch to Maggie. 'This is our way. The leaves of the kawakawa to honour the dead. Lay them for Ruri. He can't be with you but has sent a message.'

Maggie laid the leaves. 'How did you know? About Da?'

Tia shrugged. 'Oh, word travels among our people. Come

and visit me. And bring your mother when she feels up to it.'
She kissed Maggie then moved away with her group, leaving the
Camerons alone on the hill.

To the south, a distance away, a train whoo-whooed. They
listened, turning their heads to see, but the tracks were not
visible; only steam rising through the trees. Here and there were
blackened swathes where a mill or a settler's holding had burned.
Other luckier clearings were dotted with sheep or cows. A group of
ducks flew noisily over their heads to land, clattering and calling,
on the still water of the lake. None of the Camerons seemed able
to take the next step. Even Skipper sat quietly, looking at Dirk for
instructions.

It was Billy who broke the silence. 'Can I say some words,
Mam?'

Sarah looked at him in surprise. 'Of course you can, son.
Whatever is in your heart.'

Billy Cameron lifted one hand in salute. 'Praise the Lord,'
he said, his voice high and ringing (like Gabriel Locke's, thought
Maggie, frowning), 'for the life of Jock Cameron who worked on
the railroad here and in the mines on Denniston and was born
in Glasgow.' Billy now raised both arms and gazed skywards,
embarrassing his brothers. 'Heavenly Father, Lord of all, look after
my father's soul until we meet again in your embrace. Amen.'

Dirk, glowering, cuffed Billy on the shoulder. 'That's enough.
This is serious.'

Billy lowered his arms and turned on his brother. 'I *am*
serious! I'm giving Da a proper send-off. You're the eldest. You
should be praising the Lord and shouting Da's glory.'

Dirk snorted. 'Oh for heaven's sake Billy, what's got into you?'

Freeman stepped between the two. 'Shut it down, Dirk, leave
Billy to it if he wants. It's his way.'

Dirk turned his back on them and returned to the cart where he stood, his head bowed against Rusty's neck, Skipper a black shadow at his heels. Sarah, who had been as surprised as Dirk by the oration, put her arm around Billy. 'Thank you, son. That was well said. We'll go home now, shall we?'

As the cart wound its way down the hill in the sunshine, Freeman took a piece of paper from his pocket and handed it to Maggie. A note from Ruri.

They won't give me time off. I'm not family they say. My heart is with you. I wonder if your father said some kinder words about me before he died.

I have an idea. Maybe your mother would like to come to Makatote? They say the railhead is coming here in the next month and the coaches will stop for a meal. Mrs Bright cannot feed the men and the passengers both, she says, so would welcome help. Then we could all be together.

I am missing you sweetheart and hope you feel the same.

Kairuri

Maggie tucked the note into her bodice. Trust Ruri to think of a solution.

Clouds gathered as they headed back to the camp in the bush. Rain began to fall, at first light and fresh, then with a roar. The family murmured quietly at such a blessing; raised tired faces and drank in the sweetness. Even Rusty perked up and trotted along smartly.

Back at the camp, they and the remaining few of the old gang ate cold meat and raisin cake and drank bootleg in Jock's honour. The rain drummed on the new canvas of the tent. Dark rivers washed the road clean. The sour smell of wet ash rose from the bush. Sligo, who had hardly spoken since the mishap with the gunpowder, sang a sad Irish dirge and then, cheered by the rain, a more jaunty song with a chorus they all knew.

'The rain,' said Sarah as she and Maggie washed the good china. 'In the winter we curse it, but today—' She smiled. 'If I weren't so tired and heart-sore I'd go out and dance in it like a young girl.'

Maggie told her then of Ruri's idea, and watched the light come back into her mother's eyes.

'You would like Makatote, Mam. There's a proper stove and a cookhouse, and Mrs Bright and Rose and the Anderson women and—'

Sarah laughed and cuffed her daughter. 'And Ruri, you minx. But let us finish these dishes and keep our thoughts for Jock tonight, shall we?'

It wasn't until next day when Billy and Freeman spent an hour in Ohakune, picking up some supplies before they headed back to Makatote, that Billy spotted the Gospel hall tent. He wandered over to see. A smart noticeboard by the entrance announced, in fine copperplate, that the next prayer meeting would be held this Sunday at 11 a.m., signed Gabriel Locke, Gospel Missioner.

'Gabriel!' shouted Billy. And headed inside.

BILLY'S OBSESSION

'Of course I liked Billy,' said Gran. 'What a silly question. He was my brother.'

Gran was very strong on family obligations. She loved her children and grandchildren unreservedly and expected the same from us.

'But Billy sounds strange from the way you tell it,' I said, probing for a word or two of censure. 'Surely you were put off by his obsessions?'

'Billy was very likeable, don't you think otherwise.' Gran looked at me severely.

I waited. Often if I let a pause develop, Gran, who loved a 'good chat', might fill the silence with a less considered remark.

'Some possibly thought him a little odd,' she conceded. 'Perhaps today they might put a name to his oddness.'

'Bipolar?' I suggested.

'Whatever's that when it's at home?'

'They used to call it manic-depressive. Mood swings. Up and

down. You know, like Michael.' Michael is my brother, who needs medication to keep him level, as Gran very well knew. I have often wondered if it was hereditary in our family.

'There wasn't much down with Billy.' Gran chuckled, remembering something. 'It was all up with him.' She sighed. 'Well, sometimes he went quiet. Not often.'

In the last few years of her life, Gran moved into the cottage hospital on the hill at Raetihi. Two or three of her old friends were residents there, but she was by far the liveliest. And the oldest. The nurses loved her. In those days it was still a hospital where mothers gave birth and minor ailments were seen to. Also a small wing for the elderly. Gran was happy there. 'I've been cooking and cleaning all my life. Haven't I earned a year or two when someone does for me?'

It was a pleasure to visit her there on the sunny hill overlooking the dying town. The skiing industry hadn't brought fresh life yet, and many of the shops and homes were empty. Gran would tut-tut about the waste — 'perfectly good houses crumbling for want of a bit of care' — and shake her fist at the county offices as we drove past (an old dispute over unpaid rates), but she was happy enough and always ready to chat about old times.

'Billy,' she said firmly on this occasion, 'was a good boy. Just easily led.' She pointed to the wedding photo that hung above the dresser in her little room. Billy had been Grandfather Ruri's best man. 'How could anyone not like Billy?'

Gran had a point. The man standing next to my grandfather was a little shorter than him, slim and narrow-faced. And, like Gran herself, Billy was grinning. It looked as though he was trying to be solemn but just couldn't manage it. His eyes crinkled and his hair, combed back, revealed ears that stuck out almost at right-angles.

'That photographer had the hardest time to get Billy to stand still,' said Gran, 'He ruined two plates with his jiggling. The photographer nearly made him stand aside. But there he is, bless him.'

Gran took up her knitting again. 'Let's not talk about Billy. It's too sad.'

AUTUMN 1908

A plan backfires

Billy was almost sixteen in the autumn of 1908 and nearly as tall as his brother Freeman. Not as solid though. Billy, whippet-thin, agile as a monkey and seemingly without fear, was useful as a painter on the high girders of the Makatote viaduct. When he came to the settlement he had dreamed of being an engineer. That was before religion took his fancy. Now all he dreamed about was following in Gabriel's footsteps (or more precisely walking step in step, arm in arm with Gabriel) and proclaiming the word of the Lord.

There was something of fervour in the way Billy spoke and acted. He was noticeable — always had been, but now intensity had overridden the often aimless chatter of his boyhood. His blue eyes would fix on you. He would stand close, sometimes reach out and touch a complete stranger's arm in his effort to make a point. He had always been a boy for enthusiasms; now he was a young man with strong, compelling convictions. Or he hoped they were compelling.

He still wore his fiery hair long, tied back in a queue when on the girders, but falling loose to his shoulders after work. As he spoke he would run his fingers through the bright locks over and over again, as if teasing out a thought, and then wave his hand about in illustration. He was seldom at rest; his body seemed to need movement. He would dance a jig of frustration if his words fell on stony ground.

But for all his awkward intensity, people liked Billy. You couldn't help but warm to the innocence of that wide smile in his freckled face. He was never aggressive. Enthusiastic, yes, and sometimes unaccountably downhearted. But likeable. On the whole a good fellow.

Rose thought him bright. 'He can do better with his life than paint girders,' she said to Maggie. 'Work that challenges that brain of his might divert him.'

'Away from religion, yes,' said Maggie as she laid spoons on the table for the children's dinner. 'But I doubt even you can dent his fervour. Especially now that he's found that preacher again.'

Rose cocked her head at Maggie; fixed her with a bright eye. A challenge. 'Well, we'll see.' She opened the door to call the children in. The smell of smoke lay heavy on the air. Light ash drifted through the trees. 'Will these fires never end? It seems they just have one under control when another starts up. There is need for a fire service. We have one on Denniston. All volunteer. I'll have a word to the Andersons.'

Maggie thought that Rose had switched her enthusiasm from Billy to a much-needed fire service, but her employer had no trouble pursuing more than one issue. In the next week George Pascoe walked out over the trusses (he was almost as fearless as Billy) to where the lad was painting, hanging by one hand while he attacked the underside of the truss.

'Come up on top for a moment,' said the boss, smiling to see how quickly Billy swung up, keeping paint pot and brush from spilling or splattering. 'I hear you have an interest in engineering. Have we put you on the wrong job, then?'

Billy grinned. 'This suits me well enough, sir.'

'But would you be interested in learning to rivet? We are almost finished in the Workshop, but there is much construction still to be done in the next few months, so if you have an interest in steelwork, now would be a chance to learn.'

Billy balanced there, both feet on a girder no wider than a handspan, pot and brush hanging from his fingers, while he considered. He nodded slowly. 'Yes. Yes, I'd like that. I *am* interested in steelwork. But also—' He hesitated. 'Do you believe in the Lord, Mr Pascoe?'

George Pascoe frowned, then gave a snort of laughter. 'What an odd question! Here poised above the abyss! Yes, of course I do.'

'Because I have a need to travel to Ohakune of a Sunday. I'm a follower of the Gospel mission.'

George, who had not heard of the Gospel mission, nevertheless considered the problem. 'You would need to travel there on a Saturday afternoon? Then back Sunday evening?'

Billy nodded, his face alight. 'I would. But I can't work out how to do it.'

'Can you ride a horse? Do you own one?'

'I can ride, sir,' (not strictly true) 'but I don't own one.'

George cleared his throat. Perhaps the height above ground had become dizzying. 'Come and see me when you finish. I have an idea.' He smiled. 'You have a strong advocate in Rose Scobie, did you know that?'

'No, sir.'

'An extraordinary woman. Not a wise idea to cross her.' He

236

turned, one hand on the rail, and walked, very carefully, back to firm ground.

Billy whistled a hymn tune as he swung back underneath.

That evening when Rose came back from school, Maggie had Con and Alice washed and ready for bed. Rose kissed the children absently and chewed on a piece of mutton while walking around the room. She liked to do this: 'I think better on my feet,' she would say. When Brennan was away, meals were a casual event; Maggie would put food on the table, and Rose and she would graze from the dishes 'like a pair of wild cats' as Rose would say with evident delight.

'Well,' she laughed now, 'it is two steps forward and one back, I'm afraid. Billy has taken a job as a riveter and is keen to learn new skills. One step forward.'

Maggie waited.

'And I have persuaded the Andersons to use some of the workers who are no longer needed, as firemen. Partly paid and partly volunteer. Another step.'

'Oh, well done,' cried Maggie, who was heartily sick of the smoky air.

'But,' said Rose, 'my plan to wean Billy away from the preacher has backfired. That cunning brother of yours has volunteered to beat out smouldering patches on the coach road to Ohakune on a Saturday. So now he will be able to spend all Sunday in the Gospel Hall!' She spat a piece of gristle onto her hand and put it on the table. 'That boy is as wily as a Jesuit when it comes to his religion.'

Maggie, who was not sure in what way a Jesuit might be

wily, nodded. 'But the machinery will excite him. He will want to learn. It's a start.'

Rose sat down and took up one of her engineering manuals. 'I must be careful,' she said, frowning, 'that I don't become as obsessed as Billy. For some reason I want very much to bring that preacher down, to discredit him. Am I wrong, Maggie? Does he do some good? Any good at all?'

Maggie sighed. 'I agree, though I believe he has a good many followers. Can they all be deluded?'

'They can.' Rose was very definite on the matter. 'I'm afraid people are easily deluded, Maggie, easily persuaded — if someone tells them what they want to hear.' She bent to her manual. 'Well. We won't give up on Billy, will we?'

The Gospel flock

Billy held out his neatly folded tunic and sash as if requesting a blessing. 'Look, Gabriel, I've kept them ready. Can I be your server again?'

Gabriel Locke was a little unsettled by Billy's sudden intrusion into his new Gospel venture. He distrusted the young man's enthusiasms. Billy had known about the plan to frighten Mrs Grice and knew of Gabriel's involvement. He was also aware of Mrs Grice's murderous shooting. Gabriel feared that Billy's loose mouth might bring down the comfortable set-up he had forged in Ohakune. Mrs Grice, under Gabriel's careful grooming, had persuaded her husband to endow the Gospel Hall. Now that confused woman had become an ardent follower! Amelia Grice, much to Gabriel's amusement, was in love with him. Her face flushed with pleasure every time he called by. She would spend hours in the Gospel tent, ostensibly fixing flowers, but in reality waiting for a word or sign from her beloved. When he preached, Amelia would sit in the front row, glowing with ardour. She had embraced the Gospel style of crying out 'Hallelujah!' or 'Praise the Lord!' to show her agreement with his sentiments. It was all highly entertaining to Gabriel. From time to time he would mention the murdered brothers. Amelia would nod her head and moan and pray for forgiveness. She understood, now, that he liked her to grovel a little: it aroused him. She had come to believe her show of contrition was more play-acting than reality.

On these occasions Gabriel would touch her heaving breasts, sometimes pummel them. 'Oh!' she would moan. 'Oh, I am a sinner. Forgive me, forgive me!' It was Gabriel, not the Lord she entreated. Once Gabriel, unable to hold back, ripped at her underclothes and entered her with ferocity. Her moans were genuine then, for he hurt her, but she clung to him, begging for more.

By the time Billy arrived, these violent sessions had become a regular event; a necessary pleasure for both of them. 'Time for your atonement,' the preacher would say, his eyes aglitter and, pinching her arm painfully, he would lead her out of the Gospel tent and into the seclusion of the Grices' hut. Amelia still limped from the shooting but she would have run had not Gabriel gripped her firmly, nodding to this or that member of his congregation as they walked down the dusty street. Gabriel noticed with amusement that she no longer wore any undergarment beneath her petticoats.

Mr Grice noticed the change in her. He was pleased that she had recovered from her ordeal; her cheeks were pink and her eyes bright. The work kept him busy and often away. On a Sunday he would go with her to the Gospel meeting and would sometimes shake Gabriel's hand and compliment him on his sermon. 'You have certainly aided my wife's recovery,' he said. 'I hope she is an asset to your mission?'

'Indeed she is,' said Gabriel Locke, 'a fervent follower, praise the Lord.'

Now here was another fervent follower in the form of Billy Cameron. Gabriel was uneasy but found the lad's enthusiasm endearing. He placed a hand on Billy's flaming hair. 'Bless you, Brother Billy, and welcome to the Gospel mission.' His words lacked warmth, though, and Billy, sensitive to every sign from the preacher, noticed.

'I'm sorry I didn't come earlier, Gabriel, but I thought you had gone north.'

Gabriel sighed. 'It has been a busy time, with the fires. So many people burnt out of their homes and seeking comfort in the mission. I needed you but you didn't come.'

Tears glittered in Billy's eyes. 'I didn't know! You didn't call me! I would have run through hell!'

'Nevertheless, you didn't come. I expect more from my special followers.'

Billy reached out a tentative hand to touch the fine cloth of Gabriel's new suit.

'Sorry, sorry, Gabriel, I should have tried harder. I will. I promise.'

Gabriel allowed a small smile. He nodded. 'Would you like to hand round the collection box today?'

'I would, Brother Gabriel!'

'I am Preacher Gabriel now. We have a larger congregation and a new mission. I think we may need to find you a new tunic and sash, too.'

Billy's tears dried. He beamed. 'Set me tasks, Gabriel. I would do anything for you, anything!'

Gabriel warmed to the boy whose face glowed with such innocent joy. He'd missed the simple pleasure of Billy's hero-worship. He remembered their intimate times back in the tent at Makatote. 'I am blessed,' he said quietly, 'blessed in my mission.

Come into the tent and we will pray.'

Mrs Grice was inside, fussing over a new altar cloth. The preacher frowned. He'd forgotten she'd be there, waiting.

'This is one of our faithful — Amelia.' Gabriel sent her a warning signal. He hoped Billy would not recognise her name or her face. But the edge of danger pleased him. 'Billy, I have a private matter to attend to. Amelia is in great need. Will you come back in time for the service?'

Billy nodded — disappointed and curious but obedient — and left to wander the smoky settlement.

Gabriel winked at the radiant Mrs Grice. 'Time for your atonement, Sister Amelia?'

Mad Red

Ruri inched his levers forward and the Blondin carrying the steel column whined its way towards the centre of the steel rope. There was a sense of urgency everywhere now, pressure to finish, pressure to get the tall central pier up. The foundations for these giant piers had taken too long — difficult terrain and shortage of cement were to blame. Now the steel construction was behindhand. Latticework and support struts, drilled and formed, waited in piles on the bank. But Ruri knew that slow was best. If he moved this column — the last heavy thirty-two-foot column on the last pier — too quickly, it would swing and then the ropemen on the banks would take an age to get it lined up again. Good. The balance was perfect. The electric signal in his box indicated that he should begin to lower it. He shifted gear and the steel section began to descend. The foreman, standing at the top of the nearly-finished pier, signalled to the man sitting on a stump on the bank. He signalled to the ropemen far out in the gully. It swung ponderously; then lowered — a delicate operation for such a heavy piece of steel. Too wide a swing, too quick a descent and the foreman and his mate could be knocked off. Ruri could see Billy, proud of his new job, standing ready below the riggers, but waiting while the column was positioned. Now. On a signal from the foreman standing nonchalantly two hundred feet above the ground, everything paused for the photographer. Mr Pascoe hated these delays, and argued with his boss. 'My steelwork is rusting, waiting on the bank while you fool around with pictures.'

But Mr Anderson insisted. 'This is a masterpiece of engineering,' he said to his fuming Workshop manager. 'The people of New Zealand will marvel over this viaduct for years — centuries, George. There must be a record.'

Ruri pushed the button and his steam whistle whooped twice. Everyone stood still and proud while the Andersons' photographer clicked his shutter. For the count of twenty seconds the great steel column hung perpendicular and balanced, absolutely still above its anchor plate. All activity froze. Ruri wished he could stand outside and be photographed. He could see Billy, far below, riveting mallet raised in salute. The photographer raised his arm. All done. Ruri hit the whistle again and prepared to lower the last few inches.

For the photograph Billy was balanced on the corner plate of the second-to-top section. Beside him his blowtorch and bucket of hot rivets. Looped over the latticework support, an air hose. He had seen other photographs printed and hung on the walls of the cookhouse, so Billy knew you'd need a magnifier to see him and his equipment. Nevertheless he posed proudly, standing without support. Paddy Mathis, across from him, always clung to a column when a new one was being lowered. Not Billy. He liked to feel the shock beneath his feet and to move with it.

'You should be a bloody acrobat,' grumbled Paddy. 'You're a prize fool, at any rate.'

But Billy only laughed, and balanced on one foot as the column hit the plate and the bolt was rammed in.

'You bloody idiot!' screamed Paddy. 'You're making me giddy just watching. I'll report you!'

Billy shrugged, directed his torch to a rivet, then picked it out with his tongs; slid it through. He loved the way the holes on the lattice lined up with those on the columns. All measured and drilled in the Workshop. A marvel. I'll be an engineer one day, he thought, and make everyone proud. Especially Gabriel. He reached for the pneumatic hammer. Rat-a-tat-tat! Ra-a-tat-tat! The sound of his sharp blows echoed back and forth in the gully as the softened metal shaped into a dome and locked the lattice into the structure. Another riveter's blows joined in, and another. Billy's feet danced to the rhythm.

Paddy, manoeuvring a hot rivet, shot him a warning glance. Billy grinned. 'It's a test, see. I have been set tests.'

Paddy grunted; drove in his rivet. Billy passed him the handpiece and the rat-a-tat-tat rang out again.

'Who would set a mad test like that?'

'A private thing. To strengthen my faith.' Billy stood on one foot, both arms spread wide, facing the abyss.

Paddy's face paled. 'I'm not working with you anymore. What say you fall with the air hose in hand and pull me down with it? Eh? Have you thought of that? Bloody idiot.'

Billy sobered up, bent to his work again. 'Sorry, Paddy. Don't mean to scare you. Please don't report me.'

Paddy said nothing.

'It's just I like it up here. It gets to me. Don't you feel it?'

'Get on with the work, Mad Red. Here's what gets to me — finishing the work on time and home to bed.'

Other workers had noticed Billy's antics and were amused or angered, depending on their nature. Mad Red stuck as a nickname. At smoko Billy would stay on the piers, standing looking outward, balanced, often as not, on one foot, or clambering up and down the columns hand over hand like a monkey. 'Praise the Lord!' he would shout, raising his head to the sky above. Some of the men laid bets on how long before he fell.

Manly rapture

The canvas sides of the Gospel tent sucked in and out as the wind gusted. Rain spattered on the roof. The worshippers glanced around, not really paying attention to Gabriel's words. Some bent to shrug back into coats or wrap a scarf. Billy counted the number of the faithful. Only sixteen. Two weeks ago it had been eighty. The fires were over, and some settlers had returned to ruined farms or mills to repair or rebuild. But local followers were also drifting away. The Methodist mission on the other side of the settlement was drawing in worshippers grateful of the help offered during the fires. Also, the Methodists were building a solid — and warm — little wooden hall. The Baptists had just arrived and the Catholic mission on the Whanganui River had decided to place a priest at Raetihi, an energetic young man who held mass in Ohakune every Sunday. The worshippers lacked faith, thought Billy, to drift away to those old established churches. Preacher Locke told the Truth in the new, fresh way — none of the endless intoned prayers, the old ranting and condemnation.

Billy stood proudly at the front in his white tunic and sash, ready to pass around the shining new collection plate. He frowned to see a man — a newcomer — at the back of the hall slipping away before the last hymn and collection. Who was that? He knew all the faithful by name. He glanced quickly at Gabriel to see if he had noticed. Others shifted in their seats or looked sideways at the rattling canvas sides. Billy didn't want to admit that his own attention had drifted several times. In the front row, Mrs Grice was following every word of the sermon. Billy stared at her. He disliked the silly woman, the way she fawned on Gabriel, her cries of 'Hallelujah' in that deep, ringing voice. He looked at her again and then away.

Some memory tugged at the corner of his mind. Mrs Grice. Mrs Grice. Of course, that was it! Maggie had worked for her, and had been rude about her fetish for cleanliness, her fanatical temperance views.

As they sang the final hymn, Billy passed the plate. Mrs Grice cast several coins ostentatiously down so that they rang on the silver plate, but in the end it was a small collection that he handed up for blessing. Gabriel frowned to see the coins lying so sparse. His blessing lacked the usual warmth.

'A lovely sermon, beautiful words of comfort,' said Mrs Grice, who had waited outside the tent as was her habit. 'Will you come back for Sunday dinner? I have settled the matter with the cook.'

Billy, now divested of tunic and in his Sunday suit, touched Gabriel's arm to remind him. He turned to Mrs Grice. 'Preacher Locke and I will eat at Mrs Kerr's. I have arranged it and paid for both of us.'

Gabriel laid a familiar hand on each shoulder, beamed at them both. 'Well now, what riches! How to choose?'

'But it is arranged and paid for!' Billy could feel stupid tears rising. Money that should have gone to his mother had been paid over to Mrs Kerr for this treat. He had so much to tell Gabriel.

The preacher turned to Mrs Grice. 'Amelia, my dear, would you mind very much? Our new server here is an old friend.'

Mrs Grice looked at Billy with evident distaste. 'He is one of the Camerons, if I am not mistaken. My former maid's brother. Their father died a drunkard.'

'That's not true! My father died of an influenza.'

Mrs Grice shook her head, pursed her lips, a bit of her old spark returning. 'He brought his family down, took strong liquor illegally. I have proof of it.'

Billy stepped forward, his face close to hers. If she had been a man he would have hit her. 'That is a dreadful, cruel thing to say!' He looked to Gabriel for support, but the preacher was almost laughing. 'Gabriel! She's lying!'

Gabriel did laugh. 'Now now, my good friends. This is the Lord's day. Amelia, I will call on you later this afternoon. Brother Billy, shall we go to our dinner?' He hooked his arm in Billy's and led him away.

Mrs Kerr set their roast mutton dinner down with a bang. 'Billy Cameron. So this is your guest — the Gospel Hall preacher.'

Billy grinned. 'Yes, Mrs Kerr. I'm his server and good friend.'

Gabriel nodded a greeting, his mouth full of meat.

'I am surprised,' continued the proprietress, 'that you are not at my service here in the billiard room. Your father was buried a Presbyterian. Have you forgotten so quickly?' She looked through the properly glazed window of her solid establishment and pointed with some satisfaction. 'Your Gospel tent will not survive long in this wind. There's a timber loose.' She poured gravy. Three other guests were already eating and none requiring service. Mrs Kerr was inclined to continue the conversation. 'Poor Mrs Grice, now, she was Presbyterian, too, before her nasty attack.'

'She has seen the Light,' said Gabriel, frowning. 'Thank you, Mrs Kerr.'

But the woman would not move on. 'That wretched boy who shot her. He came from your way, didn't he, Billy? From Makatote?'

Billy looked at Gabriel in shock. 'Mrs Grice? She was the one?'

'Oh yes, indeed.' Mrs Kerr poured them each a glass of temperance ginger wine. 'This will warm your blood on a chilly day. Local brewed at Horopito. We are all partial to it here at the Temperance Hotel.' She drew up a chair and sat.

Billy sipped; coughed. 'Very gingery, Mrs Kerr.' He was pleased to see Gabriel draining his glass. The Sunday dinner was proving a success.

Mrs Kerr refilled Gabriel's proffered glass. 'I ask myself what would make a lad attack Amelia in cold blood like that. They say he was crazed. Bill Mathews across the way said he was screaming and shouting at her, poor woman. Did you know the boy, Billy?'

Billy looked from her to Gabriel and back again. Gabriel fiddled with his glass; tapped a warning finger on the table.

'I did meet him,' said Billy slowly. 'Amos seemed a nice enough fellow. Quiet. He was unhappy, Mrs Kerr.'

Gabriel cleared his throat. 'Well now, this is a sad conversation for a Sunday. Did I hear talk of a roly-poly for dessert?'

'Oh Lord, yes; where is that girl? She is that slow, it'll be Monday before she's out of her daze and dishing the portions. Excuse me.'

Gabriel reached for the temperance ginger wine, but Mrs Kerr, definitely speedier than her kitchen hand, whipped it from under his fingers.

Billy waited, wide-eyed, for Gabriel's explanation. Why was the woman who shot Amos's brother a favoured member of Gabriel's congregation? He opened his mouth, but before a word was out Gabriel raised a warning finger.

'No, Brother Billy, we will not speak of this. Not again. Not ever.'

Billy was shocked by the sharp edge to this warning. 'But Gabriel—'

'No. Trust me. You do trust me, don't you?' The voice softer, spoken with an intensity that both thrilled and disturbed Billy.

'Of course I do. With my life, Gabriel. But that woman —'

'She has repented. I am working to bring her back to the Lord. You must leave this in my hands.' Gabriel reached out to brush his fingers against Billy's cheek. 'My faithful server.'

Billy swallowed. His eyes filled. He would have embraced his friend had the situation allowed.

The kitchen hand arrived with the steaming roly-poly pudding, jam rosy in the centre and hot custard silky over all. Mrs Kerr's speciality.

'Would there be more of that temperance wine to go with this masterpiece?' asked Gabriel.

The girl shook her head. 'You are too late, sir, it is all consumed.' She giggled. 'Temperance my eye.'

Gabriel sighed. 'Well.' He spooned in the lovely sweet pudding. 'This is better than Mrs Grice's Sunday lunch. Thank you, Billy. A treat. Bless you.' He leaned back, watching the boy eat. For several moments he looked deeply into Billy's eyes, nodding slowly, smiling all the time.

Billy could not have looked away if his life depended on it. He could hardly breathe.

'Now,' said Gabriel softly, 'tell me about your tasks. Is your faith strengthening?'

'Oh Gabriel, yes.' Billy could feel light pouring out of him. If he did not have a grip on the table he felt that he might rise — float above these ordinary people eating their Sunday dinner. He had never felt this way before, not even on the piers high above the gully. An exultation. 'I am blessed indeed,' he whispered. 'I am with the Lord.' He reached towards Gabriel with both hands. 'Let us go to the Lord together! Hold me, brother!'

Other diners turned to look. A child in the corner laughed and pointed. Gabriel turned to the room. He raised his hands in blessing. 'My friend here is in a rapture,' he said in his richest preaching voice. 'The Lord has visited him and filled him with glory. Let us be joyful and embrace this gift bestowed upon him.' He paused; sketched a sweeping sign of the cross. 'Bless you all. My Gospel mission is open to all who seek the Light.' He turned to Billy, whose arms still reached towards him, whose eyes seemed blind to all around him. 'Come, Brother Billy, time to go. We will walk together.'

Billy's legs shook. He clung to Gabriel as they left. A gust of wind blew dust in his face, but he noticed nothing. Gabriel steered him towards the bush at the edge of the settlement. There under the trees, out of sight, he took Billy in his arms, kissed him tenderly, pressed him close.

'Oh!' Billy felt himself harden and swell. 'Oh, Gabriel! Praise the Lord!' he gasped as his world exploded with light.

Slowly he came back to reality: the trees above, the wind tossing showers of tiny leaves around like clouds of insects, Gabriel holding him; the gradual knowledge of what had happened. 'Oh!'

He looked to his friend for reassurance. 'Sorry. I was overcome.'

Gabriel relaxed his hold on the boy; felt Billy sag and then take his own weight. The preacher's smile was amused, distant. Billy's infatuation did not arouse him — the sessions with Mrs Grice were more to his taste — but the boy's fervent love was a new sensation to him: a little puzzling, not unpleasant. Gabriel suspected that temperance ginger wine, rather than love of the Lord, had caused the outburst. But what to do about this passion? How to use it? Billy's performance in the dining room had been impressive. Palpably genuine. At a church service it could attract new worshippers. A thought. His congregation here was dwindling . . .

Billy stood there anxious, uncomfortable. 'Sorry Gabriel. I didn't mean—'

'The Lord moved you. You felt the Lord through me. We call this a manly rapture. Don't be ashamed.'

Billy nodded, swallowed. He stuffed a pocket handkerchief into his trousers.

'Now I have matters to attend to. Keep working at your faith, Billy. Will we see you next week?'

'I will try, Gabriel. Now that the fires are over, Mr Pascoe might not release me.'

'Faith, Billy. Faith that can move mountains. You will find a way.'

Jealousy

Riding back towards Makatote on his borrowed pony, Billy came to Horopito. He remembered the temperance wine, how delicious it was. Mrs Kerr had said it came from Horopito. Maybe he could buy some for his mother, to make up for the loss of a share of his pay. He turned aside and rode into the tiny settlement. At any rate he was curious. Ruri had told him that sections were up for tender and he hoped to buy one. Some of Ruri's family worked in this construction camp. They had said the land was good — fertile and flat, once you cleared it. Billy looked around. No streets, the tents and rough whares placed haphazardly, smoke pluming, the air still and dank. Billy didn't like the feel of the place.

One very large tent stood in the middle of this collection like a mother surrounded by unruly children. This tent possessed a wooden gabled front and a tin chimney — a hostel or cookhouse. Maybe someone there would know of the temperance wine. From inside the big tent came raucous laughter and shouts. A man lurched out and vomited right in front of the pony, which shied and almost threw Billy. Two older fellows appeared at an opening of the big tent. They waved their hats and shouted abuse at the vomiting man, who now lay prone in the dust.

Billy decided against the wine and headed back onto the road. He would advise Ruri against Horopito.

The coach road was easy riding — wide, cobbled on the steep inclines, a little rutted where iron-clad wheels had cut the hard pumice surface, but comfortable for a horse and rider, even as shadows lengthened and ruru began to call.

Billy's mind kept returning to Mrs Grice. He remembered an occasion, two Sundays past, when she had almost dragged Gabriel away from him, simpering about her need for absolution, but bright-eyed and eager as a young woman. He frowned. Mrs Grice must be at least forty! Somehow she had managed to ensnare Gabriel. She was an evil woman of course, a murderer. Maybe she had some kind of hold on Gabriel. Maybe she had lent him money for the Gospel Hall and now that the followers were fewer, Gabriel couldn't pay her back. Gabriel was too good-natured, Billy decided. He might let a woman like that — who should be behind bars — walk free in the hope that he could save her soul. Billy resolved to warn Gabriel about her. He trotted on, eager for home, warmed by the memory of his — what had Gabriel called it? — his rapture.

'I am called,' he whispered. 'Gabriel says I am called to great deeds. I am ready, Lord.'

The man who stopped Gabriel in the street was in policeman's uniform — not Sergeant Baker, though. Could be the man who had left the Gospel service before the collection plate was passed around. Something familiar about him.

'May I have a word, Reverend?'

Gabriel stopped. Always wary where police were concerned, he inclined his head politely and waited.

'I believe you dined at the Seddon Temperance Hotel yesterday? With a young man from Makatote?'

'One of my flock, yes.' Spoken with easy charm, but Gabriel's eyes sharpened. Where could this be leading?

The new policeman nodded, notebook out. 'You partook of the temperance ginger wine?'

Gabriel relaxed. Something to do with liquor licensing no doubt. 'I did. Very refreshing.'

'You noticed nothing unusual?'

Gabriel grinned broadly. 'Now sergeant — are you a sergeant?'

'Sergeant McLeod, sent from Headquarters in Wellington to see to the situation in Horopito. And you are Mr Gabriel Locke?'

The emphasis the policeman put on his name — the doubt in his voice — had Gabriel on edge again. But the questioning was simply about the wine. Did he notice an alcoholic content? Did it seem stronger than he might expect? and so on. Gabriel joked his way easily through the interview, making much play on the fact that, as a preacher, he was inexperienced in such matters.

McLeod nodded, made notes and was about to leave, but then hesitated. 'Locke, you say? Your face is familiar. Where were you before here, may I ask?'

'Oh, all over. Gospel preaching is an itinerant profession, sergeant. Up north mainly.'

The fellow shut his notebook, nodded and took his leave. Gabriel watched him, frowning. What was it that McLeod couldn't remember? The incident in Nelson must be old news by now. Marked unsolved. Laid to rest. But still, he would be ready to move on if the signs were worrying.

Sergeant Baker, emerging onto the coach road after a sweep of the bush camps north of the settlement, found Billy Cameron on foot and running. He reined in for a word.

'How is your mother, Billy? She has found work at Makatote?'

Billy, puffing and red-faced, nodded. 'She is cooking for the coach passengers. They have a meal at Makatote now.'

'You in a hurry, lad?'

Billy looked up hopefully. 'I need to get to the Gospel mission for tomorrow's service. Couldn't borrow a horse.'

'Good lad.' The policeman liked a fellow who showed spirit. 'Hop up behind then. Old Duffer here can manage us both.' He nudged his big half-draught towards a tree stump. 'Mind my samples now.'

Billy jumped up nimbly, delighted at his good luck. As they set off, he asked, 'What are your samples, sir?'

'Hop beer. There have been complaints of drunkenness in the camps. In town, too, for that matter. You don't get drunk on three per cent alcohol — or not easily — so we have taken samples.'

Billy thought of his father and his bootleg. Sergeant Baker had seemed to turn a blind eye then. 'Maybe the men need a bit of fun? It's a hard life in the bush.'

The policeman chuckled. 'Well, I'm inclined to agree, but don't tell that to Mrs Grice and her cohorts.'

'Mrs Grice complained?'

'Aye, she did. And there's a new policeman at Horopito, sharp-eyed as a ferret. From Wellington, sent to inspect. Mrs Grice must have influential friends.'

Billy snorted. 'That's rich, sir, coming from her.'

Here was something worth probing. Sergeant Baker rode on for a while, then said, 'You don't like Mrs Grice? She's one of your Gospel stalwarts.'

'She's a fraud, sergeant. I think she has some kind of a hold on Gab— on Preacher Locke.'

'A fraud, son? Strong words. She sets herself up as a pillar of society. I'd say she and Locke were the closest of friends.'

'No, sergeant, they couldn't be.' Billy's words came tumbling out. 'Couldn't. He knows what she did. We both do.'

'Do you now?' Sergeant Baker kept his voice even and quiet. He sensed the lad's passion. Some revelation was on the way.

'She's a murderer, really. She shot that boy — Amos's brother — in cold blood.'

'And how do you know that, son?'

'Amos told us. Told me and Gabriel back in Makatote. Amos was dreadfully upset.'

'And you believed him? Amos?'

'Oh yes. You would have too, sergeant. He saw his own brother shot.'

Sergeant Baker wanted to keep the boy talking. Perhaps the fact that he was riding behind, not facing his questioner, helped him unburden himself. But what had prompted this confession — did the boy even realise it was a confession — so many months after the shooting?

'Billy, if this is true—'

'It *is* true! It is! She is a murderer! Why haven't you arrested her?'

'Why haven't *you* reported it, son? That's the question I'm asking myself.'

'You wouldn't have believed Amos. That's what Gabriel said. Amos had the gun, you see. She threw it away and Amos picked it up and ran—'

Billy abruptly stopped talking. They rode on in silence, both thinking about what had been said — Baker grimly aware that this was the missing piece of the puzzle; Billy suddenly fearful, remembering Gabriel's warning.

'Why don't you ask her?' he said finally, quieter now.

'Oh I have, I have. She denies having anything to do with it, Billy. Her gun is a dummy.'

Billy exploded. 'That's just what Gabriel said. That you wouldn't believe Amos. You'd say he shot his own brother.'

'So you took the law into your own hands?'

Billy chose his words more carefully. 'No, sir, no. Amos did. He just wanted to scare her into confessing. He didn't mean to hurt her. The gun wasn't supposed to be loaded.'

'The preacher knew about this plan?'

Billy touched his mouth with a finger. Held it there. He mustn't keep talking, but the words wanted to burst out. Gabriel needed to be rescued, not accused. His head swam; his heart pounded.

'Billy? The preacher knew?'

Billy threw one leg over and slid to the ground. 'Thanks. I'll walk from here.'

The policeman looked down at him. 'This is important information, Billy, if it's true. Think about what you've said. I'll want to talk to you again in town.' He touched his cap with his crop and rode on, leaving Billy standing looking down at the dust.

During the Sunday service Billy sat where he could watch Mrs Grice. She was in the front row as usual, her husband at her side, her eyes fixed on Gabriel. Once he saw her lick her lips as if tasting something delicious. Often she raised one hand and shouted praise to the Lord. During the sermon Gabriel turned three times and bestowed a warm glance in her direction, as if what he said was especially for her.

Billy hated her with a passion. It was obvious he was right. She had some kind of hold on Gabriel. He resolved to speak to his friend, warn him to keep away from the woman.

Again the congregation had dwindled. But Gabriel stood outside the tent in the morning sun, genial as always. A greeting and a handshake to all. Especially, Billy noted, to the Grices, who invited the preacher to the engineers' cookhouse for Sunday dinner. Billy couldn't bear Gabriel's pleasure as he accepted, Mrs Grice's familiar touch to his arm. He joined the group and reached out his own hand to grip the preacher.

'Gabriel, could I have a word?' He kept his voice low and private. 'It's important.'

Gabriel excused himself from the Grices and walked back towards the tent with Billy. 'Billy? Are you well? You look pale.'

Billy's heart pounded. 'That woman . . . Mrs Grice—'

'Well, Billy?' Gabriel led the boy into the tent, closed the new wooden door.

'Is she threatening you? I want to protect you!' Billy couldn't keep his voice down. 'She's evil! A murderer!'

Gabriel's grip tightened. 'Now, Billy—'

'What kind of hold does she have? Can't you see she is playing with you?'

Gabriel turned Billy to face him. 'Keep your voice down, for heaven's sake. Didn't we agree—?'

But Billy was wailing now, his words blurred by great heaving sobs that he had no way of controlling. 'She killed our Amos's

260

brother! She should be in jail! She shouldn't be part of the mission. Don't you see? Oh, Gabriel!'

The preacher pulled Billy's head roughly against his chest, stifling the cries. Billy relaxed in this embrace, thinking it loving, but when he finally looked up he saw fury and quailed.

'Billy Cameron,' said the preacher, his voice icy, 'you must never speak of this matter again. Never. You are endangering me. *Do you understand?*'

'But Gabriel, why do you . . . Why give in to her?' Billy was frightened now. What had he said? Why was Gabriel angry? 'She is a bad woman. You said so yourself. You said she needed punishment—'

Gabriel raised his hand and slapped the boy hard across his face. 'I said nothing. Nothing. Do you understand, Billy? You stupid boy.'

Billy's mouth opened in shock. He raised a finger to his reddening cheek. Stared in disbelief at his friend, who glared back.

'*Do you understand?*'

Billy shook his head. 'No. No, I don't, Gabriel.'

'Then let me make it clear as crystal. I work with Mrs Grice because I *choose* to. She has no hold on me. I am working to save her soul. That is my purpose, Billy. To save her. But if you run around like a silly child blabbing about murder you will get me, and her *and yourself* in deep trouble. Deep, deep trouble. Surely you can see that?'

Billy trembled to hear the anger in those words; the scorn. His face stung. All he felt and heard was Gabriel's rejection of him; the rest was meaningless. He nodded dumbly.

Gabriel turned him to face the door. 'Now. Go back to Makatote. Go away. Don't come back to the mission until you have reflected upon what I have said. And understood. And repented your rash words.'

Billy would not go. Could not. He stood rooted, his poor sore head hanging.

Gabriel sighed. At last he spoke calmly. 'Brother Billy, you have tested me sorely. But go now with my blessing.' He rested a hand on the boy's red hair. Then he opened the door, ushered Billy out, turned and went back inside.

Billy blinked in the bright sunlight. He saw Mrs Grice standing close to the tent, waiting. Had she heard? Billy stared at her. She stared back.

How could that woman's soul be worth saving?

Shame

Amelia Grice had indeed heard Billy's outburst inside the mission tent. Heard every word. The shock was almost as if *she* had received the slap. Murderer. Behind bars. An evil woman. When the trembling boy was pushed out of the tent, when he stared at her, she felt the hairs on her arms rising. She shivered. On that bright sunny morning she felt an icy breeze and looked to see where it came from. She walked away from the tent. Didn't want to see Gabriel or eat dinner with him. Especially didn't want to indulge in 'atonement'. She saw Mrs Kerr standing at the door of her establishment: her old friend whom she had avoided recently. Saw a pair of young engineers laughing together as they walked towards the cookhouse. A group of children played in the dust, drawing pictures with sticks. Two half-built houses, their interiors open for all to see, stood next to the bootmaker's shop. She hadn't noticed them before. Amelia rubbed a shaking hand across her eyes. She felt as if she had just woken from a long sleep to find everything different. Her legs trembled. She needed to sit down.

Mrs Kerr was walking towards her, concern showing in the way she hurried, the hand she waved. Amelia turned away, pulled her Sunday bonnet lower over her eyes and stumbled in the opposite direction. She wanted desperately to hide.

Safely in her own bedroom, she closed the door, pulled the curtains and sat on her little chair. In the half-dark she faced away from the bed. She couldn't bear to look at it; to remember what she and the preacher had . . . Oh! What madness had possessed her? Her nightrobe hanging from a peg on the back of the door looked like a sad, empty image of herself. She took it down, wrapped it around herself, stroked the shiny stuff. Soon her husband would come looking for her. How could she face him? Her good, sensible John who had supported her in all her crusades. Stumbling a little, she searched for pencil and paper then sat to write.

John Grice, coming to see why she hadn't appeared at the midday meal, found her lying asleep and, thinking she must have felt unwell, left her in peace. He didn't see the note.

Later that afternoon Gabriel knocked on the door and, finding it open, went in. For several minutes he stood watching her as she lay. Carefully he twitched a curtain aside and looked out. The road seemed deserted. Then quickly, silently, he removed the note and left, closing the door behind him.

Gabriel had a room in one of the many 'boarding houses' (in fact these were tents on timber frames). He shared his room with a coach driver who was often away. Now Gabriel sat on his proper sprung bed — a luxury — and read Amelia Grice's letter. It was written in a firm hand, and rational in its content. Gabriel had expected something more demented. He was surprised and disappointed to see that it was not addressed to himself.

My dear John,

I have been a foolish, weak woman. I hope you can forgive me. It was I who shot the boy on the Karioi road. I had thought the rifle was my dummy one, but I must have inadvertently picked up the innkeeper's real one. My dear, it was an honest mistake, but then I weakly hid the truth. The brother was rightfully angry that I drove on, though he should have told the police rather than attack me.

I have been rather out of my mind since, but now have come to my senses. I know I should confess to the police but find I cannot face the shame. Not so much the shooting but the fact that I hid the truth. I hope you can forgive me. Let it be known that I have taken my own life in deep remorse.

Your loving wife, Amelia

Gabriel sat staring at the letter. In a fury he crumpled the single sheet and hurled it across the room. No mention of him. Not a single word of his ministry or the Gospel mission. It was as if he didn't exist in her life. He picked up the ball of paper and smoothed it again. Could he replace it? Nothing in what that stupid woman had written could implicate him. But the paper was obviously ruined and the envelope torn. He walked back and forth in the tiny room, cursing; then lit a match and burnt the damned thing. But now? In the absence of a suicide note might they suspect him? Her infatuation would have been noted in this nosy little settlement. He paused in his pacing as a thought struck him. Perhaps her infatuation could be used. She was ashamed of her hopeless love for him? That might work.

Gabriel Locke walked out for his evening constitutional in a better frame of mind.

Mrs Kerr found Amelia Grice dead. Worried by her friend's odd demeanour in the street earlier, she had called in and found her in bed, cold and lifeless. Breathless, her own heart threatening to give way, she found John Grice and told him the news. Soon it was all over the settlement: Amelia Grice had taken an overdose of her medicine. Her husband was at pains to point out that his wife had not been well recently and, in her weakened state, had mistaken the dose.

Sergeant Baker, remembering Billy Cameron's outburst, was not so sure. But the blood sample that was sent to the Government analyst confirmed death by overdose of Bayer's heroin and laudanum taken together.

The results of the sergeant's liquor samples, on the other hand, were of note:

> *Temperance ginger wine — 11.63% absolute alcohol or 22.3 proof spirit.*
> *All hop beer samples over-proof.*
> *Horopito medicated health wine — 10.01% absolute alcohol or 21.95 proof spirit.*

The sergeant sighed. The new policeman would be triumphantly demanding arrests, and Mr Furkert would be fuming if he lost workers in these last months of track-laying.

THE GREAT WHITE FLEET

'The Great White Fleet?' I asked Gran, 'It sounds like some monster from the deep.'

Gran laughed and put down her knitting, eager to talk. 'In a way, yes, a big showy monster, but not down in the deep. On the surface of the ocean, in full view, inviting admiration.'

Gran liked to see me with my notebook out. She said it made her feel like someone important. 'Write it down, write it down,' she would say, 'while I've still got my marbles.' She would put aside whatever she was doing and concentrate on her memories. 'Did you get that spelling? F-U-R-K-E-R-T.'

She never lost her marbles, even in her last few weeks when a stroke had robbed her of movement and speech. I would read her a sentence and she would say 'yes' (the only word able to navigate a pathway from brain to mouth) or shake her head, if she thought it incorrect. Then, to discover my mistake, we would launch into a sort of 'twenty questions' game: me phrasing all my queries so that her answer could be either yes or a head shake. We had some laughs over that. And tears. Back then I had thought of writing a memoir. Gran preferred biographies and memoirs to novels.

But she talked about the Great White Fleet before she had the stroke. 'Oh, that Great White Fleet visit. It meant nothing to us — the workers. But the bosses on the railway were forever on about it. America's fleet, it was. The American military wanted to show off to the whole wide world how great and mighty they were.'

I found an old newspaper photograph of the fleet and showed Gran. I said it must have been an impressive sight, but Gran would have none of that.

'It was a waste.' (One of Gran's favourite criticisms.) 'Every ship in the whole United States fleet, so they said, all painted white for effect, steaming around the Pacific and then around the world stopping everywhere and expecting loud hurrahs and parties ashore. Right around the world! Can you imagine how much fuel that took! My Ruri said they had spent thousands of dollars — millions, perhaps — building this big fleet, but then there were no wars so they dreamed up a lovely jaunt. To me they were like children — or prize fighters flexing their pumped-up muscles: Look at us! A young country — so wealthy, so strong. We're the best! Best navy in the world!'

Gran was fierce on the subject because of the effect on the railway construction; on her family.

'All those Members of Parliament down in Wellington, of course they wanted to be in on the party. The fleet was to arrive in Auckland, you see, eighth of August 1908. A big party was arranged and entertainments ashore for the sailors. Everyone who was anyone wanted to be there. Normally those big-wigs would have had to go by train to New Plymouth then by steamer to Onehunga on the Manukau Harbour, then coach or train into Auckland. Three days. By coaching between the railheads it still took three. But Mr Furkert, try as he may, could not find enough coaches in the whole of the Plateau to get the members and their wives across the gap.'

'There was a secret wager involved?'

'Oh, it wasn't secret. We all knew about it. The Minister of Works promised Mr Furkert some sum — and a silk topper was involved — if he could have the railroad finished. Mr Furkert was not a man to shy at a challenge — or a nice little bonus. They shook hands on it: the train would go through and that was that. Never mind workers like my da being trampled in the rush.'

My great-uncle Freeman had a more sanguine view of the wager: 'Don't mind your Gran, you know what she's like. It was great fun. We all had a bet on it. The engineers would egg on the gangs and the rivalry was pretty fierce, as I remember. Mind you —' He frowned, remembering, — 'it could have been a complete disaster. All the nation's leaders in one train on that Horopito section — an unfinished, unballasted fifteen miles of track. Tricky.'

'It *was* a complete disaster, of course it was,' said Gran sharply. 'Whatever is Free talking about? Has he forgotten Billy?'

WINTER 1908

A trip to the railhead

On a blustery May morning in 1908, the Honourable William Hall-Jones boarded the Wellington and Manawatu Railway Company train at Thorndon station in Wellington — his third trip north in as many months. Naturally he sat in a first-class seat, his briefcase on his knee. He nodded to the lady traveller beside him.

'You are a through passenger, madam?'

Young Mrs Singleton, newly wed, was indeed a through passenger. She told him her father had paid the fifty-eight shillings so that she might travel to Auckland and meet her husband when he arrived back from a tour of duty. 'He's a naval officer, sir.'

The woman was as pretty as a picture in her flowery hat and lace-trimmed jacket. Hall-Jones knew she would not be so spruce when her journey was over, but he smiled and bent to his papers. As the engine chuffed its way laboriously up the incline to Johnsonville the young lady was, however, ready for conversation.

'You are someone important, then, by the way the station-master treated you?'

He nodded, put aside his columns of figures and turned to her. 'Minister for Railways. And for Public Works.'

She clapped her gloved hands. 'Oh, then you own this very train we are riding in! How extraordinary to meet you!'

Hall-Jones felt the need to correct her. 'Indeed no. This train is bound for New Plymouth and is privately owned. Although—' He looked out the window as the train slowed — 'the Government will soon take it over if I have my way.'

'But I am going to Auckland!' Mrs Singleton laid her pretty hand on his sleeve. 'Have I boarded the wrong train?'

Hall-Jones reassured her, explaining that they would change trains at Marton. He then rose and went to find the ticket collector. 'I need to have a quiet seat; can you find me something?' The fellow was quick to accommodate him.

Hall-Jones settled in a corner seat and sighed with pleasure. The pile of papers were not really of concern. He liked to study the line they travelled, the sidings, the activity at stations, the watering of the engines, the mailbags dropped off and collected. He loved the whole important *business* of the railway. And the knowledge that he was in charge. When the Wellington and Manawatu Company was bought by the Government, he decided, there would be a separate carriage for businessmen and Government officials.

At Marton, those remaining on board would continue west to Wanganui and New Plymouth. Hall-Jones, standing on the platform, watched with satisfaction as two passenger cars containing thirty travellers (the chatty Mrs Singleton among them) were uncoupled and joined with a Railways Department train waiting on the siding. He wandered over to inspect what was being loaded. He couldn't help totting up in his head the revenue. Two horses (eight shillings and eight pence plus extra mileage), several dogs (sixpence each) and a sack of squealing piglets (parcel rate) were coaxed into the livestock and horse-box car. A wagon (ten shillings for the first ten miles) — presumably to be hauled later by the horses — was secured to a flatbed along with several crates of vegetables (not big earners).

Finally, when all passengers were embarked and the animals secure, Hall-Jones removed his hat as a coffin was carried by a group of mourners and handed with care to the station staff on the luggage car (twenty-one shillings to Hunterville or Mangaweka, twenty-five to Taihape). The minister corrected himself as he climbed aboard. The coffin was small; a child's corpse was half-price (minimum ten shillings).

The stationmaster rang the bell and raised his flag. The guard blew his whistle and the big engine moved slowly towards the interior: a moment that never failed to thrill Hall-Jones. This was new territory, newly opened up by the singular effort of the Public Works Department. A massive — and expensive — undertaking, but one which would bring wealth and prosperity to the whole colony. Again he corrected himself: the whole *Dominion*; he must not slip back into old ways of thinking.

The most thrilling moment on the next leg up to Taihape, in the Minister's opinion, was when the engine slowed almost to a walking pace and crossed the Makohine viaduct. Only six years old, it was the tallest viaduct in the country, but soon to be topped by the one being built at Makatote. Though passengers were advised to keep to their seats, Hall-Jones pulled rank and stood on the open platform and leaned out, clinging with one hand to the railing, to see, far below, the cart road snaking through dense bush — and there, yes! Several clearings. Progress! The dense forest of the interior was being readied for productive farming. Inside the car he heard cries of amazement and one or two feminine screams as the train seemingly ran over thin air: the magnificent structure of the viaduct was completely invisible from inside the car.

Two and a half hours after leaving Marton (a slight delay at Ohingaiti station while an extra flatbed car piled with timber sleepers was added to the train), Taihape was reached. Hall-Jones pulled out his pocket watch. Half-past five: very creditable. He nodded to the young wife who was standing on the platform, looking uncertain.

'But where—?' She waved at the row of unprepossessing shacks lining the station. 'Surely we are not to stay in one of these?'

'The station staff will direct you to your quarters,' he said. 'You will be very comfortable.' He strode off before she could complain further. The accommodation was perhaps not ideal as yet. He himself would spend the night in the solid and warm stationmaster's house.

Next morning passengers were no sooner in their seats and settling to their morning newspapers than they were out of them again. The jurisdiction of the Railways Department ended at Mataroa, only six miles north of Taihape. The Hon. Mr Hall-Jones now metaphorically doffed his Railways cap and donned his grander Public Works topper. The engine that was to carry them onward was much smaller, however: *Josephine*, his favourite little double-shooter, was waiting, steam pluming, on the siding. The track that lay ahead was not yet finished to Railways standard, nor were the stations equipped with signalling and tablet communications. From now on it was up to the vigilance of the driver and guard to see them safely to Ohakune. Two small passenger cars and five goods and luggage wagons were hooked up ready.

Joe Vickers, the guard, was pacing around the cases as they

were loaded, bending to poke a bag or rattle a case. No liquor of any sort might be smuggled aboard when he was on duty. A legend in these parts, was Joe, for smelling out liquor; his wife, a temperance stalwart, boasted of his prowess to all who might listen. Joe now nudged one gentleman's case with his toe, hefted it by its handle, motioned to the stationmaster. The two of them lifted the bag onto a pallet and opened it. Aha! Joe's face said it all. Three pint bottles of a golden liquid were removed and taken into the stationmaster's office.

Joe addressed the red-faced owner. 'Ye can collect them on your way back.'

'But I'm not coming back this way. Have a heart, Joe. I'll not open one of them until I'm clear of this damned dry section.'

'Sorry, sir. Those are the rules and ye knew it afore ye came.' Joe climbed up into the guard's van. 'All aboard now!'

The Minister gallantly steadied Mrs Singleton as she stepped over rails and cables to mount this new conveyance. 'There are adventures ahead,' he promised. 'You are in for a most interesting day.'

She was looking a little wan. 'I do hope the next accommodation is of a higher standard. I was kept up all night with singing and laughing. The walls of my room were as thin as paper.'

Quite likely they *were* paper, thought Hall-Jones, or at best canvas. 'Never fear, my dear, the hostel at Taumarunui is well established. But sit back now and enjoy the magnificent views. Once we disembark at Ohakune you will have a fine coach ride to Waimarino, including lunch at Makatote, and then a train adventure down the Raurimu Spiral to your hostel.' He beamed. 'A day to treasure and recount to your grandchildren.'

He walked forward to the front passenger car. His journey would end at Ohakune. He had important matters to discuss with Furkert.

Ohakune railway station had not altered much since the Minister's last visit: 'A rowdy shambles,' he had described it in the House, 'set too far from the township; but it moves passengers and goods with surprising efficiency.' Carters rattled up alongside the flatbeds and unloaded railway sleepers directly onto their carts. Millhands filled the now empty wagons with building timber southbound. Coachmen shouted encouragement to the through passengers: 'Hup! Hup! All aboard for Horopito, Makatote, Waimarino! All aboard!' The five coachmen, each with five-in-hand, were highly competitive: to arrive first at Makatote meant their passengers ate lunch first and would be first away to the northern railhead at Waimarino. They knew they would be out of a job when the railheads met. 'Make hay while the sun shines,' Hone Coachman would say with a grin. 'Tomorrow we'll be back watching cabbages grow.' Eighteen miles now to cover between railheads — a three-and-a-half-hour coach ride that included lunch: an easy day's work for men and horses.

Gabriel Locke, mounted on his big thoroughbred, watched the activity. His case was strapped behind, his bedroll over the horse's withers. He studied the travellers closely. When he saw pretty Mrs Singleton struggling with her bag, he jumped down to help. 'Now what is a lovely lady like you doing travelling alone?'

'Well now,' said Betty Singleton as Gabriel stowed her case and handed her into the coach; here was a more genial travelling companion than that abrupt Mr Hall-Jones. 'Where shall I start? I was born, you see, in Wellington . . . Oh! You are not travelling with us?'

'Alas, no. But travelling north nevertheless. Perhaps we will meet up again soon?' He elicited her name and destination, then tipped his hat. 'Why, I am a Singleton, too! Adrian Anthony. Who knows, we may be related!' He took her hand, kissed it 'like a well-bred gentleman' (she would later say) and returned to his horse.

Mr Furkert and two of his engineers had gathered at the station to greet the Minister. As usual Furkert was in a hurry. He pulled out his watch. 'Welcome, William. We have tea prepared in the tent and then we'll mount up and inspect the progress, shall we?'

'Progress. That's a word I like to hear, Frederick. How is the deadline looking? Does our wager still stand?'

Hall-Jones noted that although Furkert was full of confidence, the engineer Keller looked somewhat less sanguine. 'You have doubts, Peter?'

Peter Keller puffed at his pipe for a moment before answering. Furkert fixed his fierce blue eyes on his employee. 'Of course he has doubts. He's a perfectionist. But I say we'll get your train through by August. It might not be a pretty ride in some places—'

'Keller?' The Minister was determined to hear all views.

Peter Keller removed his pipe and pointed north to where the coaches were now raising dust. 'I think the viaducts will squeak through in time, sir. But there's a stretch just north of Horopito—' He put his pipe back in and drew deeply. 'The formation gangs are having a tough go of it. It's a swamp, sir, and we don't have suitable fill to hand—'

Furkert interrupted. 'As I say, William,' (he was proud of being on first-name terms and dropped the name in as often as possible, not realising that the Minister's close friends all called him Bill) 'my engineer here is a stickler for detail. As I am myself, of course. Trust me, this is no blind leap of faith. I have planned down to the last detail. We might have to cut corners — a temporary measure — but we'll get your guests through. Twenty-four hours is the wager. We'll do it in less.'

Keller looked into the distance. Narrowed his eyes. 'How many guests have you invited, sir?'

Hall-Jones cleared his throat. 'I can't get it down below two hundred. All the members are keen. And their wives. And then of course there are our important business colleagues . . . No, I can't pare it down further.'

Even Furkert blanched at this. 'The Prime Minister included?'

Keller removed his pipe again to whistle. 'Two hundred? That's eleven of the new long cars. That means a heavy locomotive. No, sir, we can't get such a weight over the Horopito swamp by August.'

Furkert frowned. 'It's up to me to say what can and can't be done, Peter. There will be a way, and I'll find it. A temporary deviation perhaps . . . Ah. Here are our horses!'

He led Hall-Jones away, eager to get out of Keller's earshot. 'Trust me. You can count on it. My engineers are brilliant men but they tend to lack drive. Make your plans, William. I absolutely guarantee that all your important guests will get through.' He chuckled. 'But save a seat for me. I hear there will be great celebrations when the fleet arrives.'

Lunch stop at Makatote

As he rode towards Makatote, Gabriel's thoughts turned to Billy Cameron. Thinking about the lad put him in a surprisingly good mood, considering the boy had been instrumental in this need to move on. Billy's hero-worship stimulated him; was unexpectedly pleasurable. A strange young lad. Gabriel could not quite fathom what drove Billy. Was the boy a genuine believer? Someone like those monks who spent their entire lives in contemplation of the Lord? Or had Billy confused a love for Gabriel with religious fervour? The puzzle of it amused the preacher — and irked him. Most likely, he decided, the boy was no saint but a simple lad, easily led.

Gabriel had sensed yesterday that it was time for him to move on. The mission was no longer popular. The Horopito policeman was sniffing around. And there had been questions about the death of Amelia Grice. Mrs Kerr, damn the woman, had reported seeing him coming out of the dead woman's hut. He had cause to rue taking the suicide note. Now Sergeant Baker had a whole new raft of questions which included the loss of certain pieces of jewellery (now concealed in the lining of his case). Yes, time to move on.

And yet the thought of Billy still piqued him. Gabriel resolved to break his journey north at Makatote, but to keep his eyes peeled for trouble. He was not eager to cross paths with that termagant of a cook again.

Having ridden ahead of the coach cavalcade, he hitched his thoroughbred to a secluded tree and waited, hat pulled low and collar up, to mingle with the travellers. As the coachman reined in the horses and the coach rocked to a halt, he opened the door for Betty Singleton. 'Well, here we are again. But this is my destination. Let me help you down.' He offered her his hand (deftly removing a delicate gold bracelet) and pointed her in the direction of the cookhouse. Before she had time to take breath, he was gone, case swinging from one hand (always best to travel light), heading down towards the men's quarters. He would have to lie low until work finished.

Sarah Cameron, standing at the door of the cookhouse to welcome the travellers, saw him disappear. She nudged Rose Scobie, who often came to help at these times. 'Look who's washed up here. It's that preacher, Locke.'

Rose frowned. 'Are you sure? He's not welcome here. Not at all.'

'Our Billy would say different. Billy is a follower.' Sarah found his fervour quaint, but not a worry. His serious study of the Bible could only be commendable. At his age he could be up to much worse. No doubt it would all blow over, and if it didn't? — No shame in having a preacher in the family.

Rose forked meat onto plates, quick and neat as she was in all her endeavours. 'That preacher was mixed up in something shady earlier on,' she said, 'Your Maggie has no time for him either.'

'Well, we'll see then.' Sarah moved down the line of customers, smiling and ladling, too busy to continue the conversation. Billy had come back from Ohakune downhearted a week or two ago. Now he was working well, determined to do his bit for Mr Pascoe and the Andersons. Sarah had no time to worry about Billy: plans for Maggie's wedding invaded every spare moment of her life.

One of the travellers, a pretty young woman, was casting around in search of something. 'My bracelet! Oh my pretty bracelet! I've lost it. Oh, do help me!'

Rose, who had finished serving the meat, went to her. 'You had it when you came in? Are you sure? Think when you last saw it.'

'I had it when I stepped off the coach, because I showed it to that nice man. I had it then. It is a present from my husband. Oh where—' She rose from her meal and ran to the door, searching the floor.

Rose, watching her, suspected 'that nice man'. She went into the kitchen for a word with Mrs Bright. 'Keep an eye out. Your favourite preacher is back in town.'

Mrs Bright raised her ladle threateningly, then went on with her stirring.

Rose hurried to the back door and looked out. No sign of him. Perhaps Sarah had been mistaken? Why on earth would Locke return after his humiliation at Mrs Bright's hands — and at hers, for that matter? She picked up a tray of sliced cake and returned to the rowdy cookhouse.

Out front, fresh horses were being hitched for the short afternoon run to Waimarino Station where a Public Works locomotive would already be working up pressure. Nothing — not even a lost bracelet — waited for the three-day railway excursion to Auckland.

Zeal

From a vantage point, hidden among a remaining stand of bush, Gabriel spotted Billy Cameron. There he was, balanced high on one of the piers, bending and straightening, working with his hands. From the trees, Billy looked tiny against the giant pillars. Others were working, too, but Billy was unmistakable. There was a lightness about him — so quick and nimble — that almost defied gravity. Once, the boy looked out and Gabriel felt those bright eyes searching. For him? For the Lord? What was Billy thinking? He needed to know. He held his breath to see the boy run up a diagonal strut, hand over hand like a monkey, then stand on the top platform silhouetted against the sky and raise his arms. Was that a shout? Was Billy singing? Calling him? The possibility pleased him.

He settled on his cushion of moss. He would find Billy when darkness fell.

In the days following Gabriel's slap, since his banishment from the Gospel mission, Billy's world turned dark. He lay on his stretcher looking up at the grubby canvas but seeing nothing. His mother, thinking him ill, brought him soup and warm blankets. On the third day the Bible that Billy was clutching grew warm against his chest. It seemed to glow. A sign. Billy let the pages fall open. He read: *Because of your little faith. For truly, I say to you, if you have faith like a grain of mustard seed, you will say to this mountain, 'Move from here to there,' and it will move, and nothing will be impossible for you.* Another sign. This was the very passage that Gabriel had preached from on his first service at Makatote!

He sat up, staring at the precious words. Jesus was sending him a message. Or perhaps it was Gabriel himself. His faith must be too little. He knelt beside his bed and prayed. 'Lord, give me strength to move mountains. Let my faith grow even as a mustard seed grows to a healthy plant. Let me be worthy of Gabriel your servant.' He felt a great excitement building and hurried into his work clothes. He was chosen for something great. He felt sure that Gabriel would send a message; would call him back to the fold.

Every day, morning and night, he read his Bible and prayed. On the great viaduct he tested his strength and his daring; he accepted tasks that others found unnerving. Once, when a guide rope had become tangled with a girder as it was being lowered, he scrambled to the top of the pier and, under the astonished eyes of the foreman, climbed onto the swinging girder itself, freed the rope and jumped back down to the platform. That earned him a cheer — and a few shaken heads. Such madness! Often he sang hymns as he worked. 'Holy Billy' was his new nickname these days. Billy grinned. He loved it when they called him that, and wished Gabriel could hear.

Gabriel had returned to Makatote on a Saturday. With pressure mounting to finish the viaduct, night shifts and weekend shifts operated. Electric floodlights shone eerily on the latticework of iron girders; hammer blows and the grinding of machinery echoed in the gully. But back in the camp all was dark and quiet. Ruri was not in the tent. Gabriel waited outside until he was sure Billy's friend would not return, then slipped in quietly. Billy knelt praying.

Gabriel laid a gentle hand on the lad's curls. 'The Lord be with you, Brother Billy.'

'Oh!' Billy shot to his feet, his eyes shining. 'I *knew* you would come. I prayed that you would send word for me to return.'

'And your prayer has been answered.'

Billy held the preacher's hand, drew him down to sit on the bed.

'Now,' said Gabriel quietly, 'tell me what you have been doing. I saw you today on the girders.'

'You watched me!' Billy squeezed the preacher's hand. 'I wish I had known.'

'Why? What would you have done?' Then, as Billy was about to speak, Gabriel held up his hand. 'Wait. I want to see you.' He bent, struck a match on his shoe and lit the stub of candle beside the bed. As the tiny glow grew and shadows began to flicker against the canvas, Gabriel leaned back and studied Billy. 'There. Now tell me.'

'I am growing my faith like a mustard seed. Soon I will be able to do anything!'

Gabriel smiled at the boy's zeal. 'Truly? Anything?'

'Truly,' said Billy, a bright candle-flame mirrored in each eye. 'I will move mountains!'

'Good. Yes. If your faith is strong.'

'It is, it is! I will walk on water like Jesus!'

Gabriel chuckled. 'Walk on water, I would like to see that.'

'I could stop a train even! A big one.'

Gabriel sighed. 'That would be a hard task, brother.'

'But if my faith was strong? A train is not as big as a mountain.'

Gabriel nodded. 'A train, indeed! If you believe, brother.'

'I do Gabriel! I believe! If the Lord wished it.' In the faint light reflected on the canvas Gabriel saw Billy's two hands rise, palms thrust forward as if pushing against a great force. 'Yes. I could. A mountain! A train!'

'That would be a sight, my friend. That would show the power of the Lord — and of you and me, his servants together.'

Suddenly, shockingly, Billy leaped to his feet. His voice rang out — a shout of great joy. 'You and me his servants together! Oh Gabriel!' He flung his arms wide and would have shouted again if Gabriel hadn't leaped up too and taken him in a fierce grip, one hand stopping the tumbling words.

'This is between you and the Lord,' he whispered into the boy's ear. 'If you feel that He has a mission for you, then you must pray that your strength will prevail.'

Billy struggled against the constriction. He needed to shout, to dance, to sing! Gabriel held him sternly until the exultation faded, and the boy, staring into Gabriel's eyes, relaxed.

'I have a plan, Gabriel,' he said, 'The Lord has put it into my head. I have been practising.'

Gabriel nodded. 'Yes. Go on.'

'I will do a miraculous feat on the day that the Parliamentary train comes through.'

'Good. Very good Billy.'

'All those people will witness the power of the Lord.'

'They will, yes. And I will, too.'

'You will be proud of me, Gabriel.' Billy was almost asleep now, his head drooping, his breathing slow.

'I will.' Gabriel looked over to the empty beds. 'Is Ruri not coming in tonight?'

'No, he's with his family this weekend, arranging the wedding.'

'I will sleep and pray with you tonight then.'

Gabriel bent to pinch the candle-flame. What an extraordinary young man! So easy to plant a seed. He rolled himself into Ruri's blanket and closed his eyes. A public display in front of the country's most influential — that would be something. He was almost tempted to stay. For a moment the thought of Billy's fervour caused him discomfort; guilt, even. Not for long though. He had played with Billy long enough. Time to move on. At any rate, whatever antic Billy was planning would be performed without the preacher's blessing.

Billy lay in the darkness, his eyes wide, his heart bursting. 'Thank you Gabriel. Thank you Lord,' he whispered.

Outside the tent Rose stood silent and unmoving. She shivered — not only from the cold that for some time had been seeping through her shawl. The distant hammer blows of the night shift now sounded dire: Rat-a-tat-tat! Danger! Rat-a-tat-tat! Had she heard aright? She waited until there were no sounds from inside then, using a fresh burst of hammering to cover her footsteps, she returned home.

Pressure

'July will be too late,' said Furkert, standing on the deck of the viaduct, looking out at the gap still to be closed. 'You forget that the approaches north and south are not yet begun. Cannot be started until these damn gantries are dismantled.' He fiddled with his slide rule as if the little tool might supply an answer. 'Can you not put on extra shifts?'

Andrew Anderson shrugged. 'George already has them working double shifts. You don't want us to cut corners?' The head of Andersons, familiar with the building of viaducts and bridges all over the country, was not going to be rushed by a civil servant. 'It was your delay in building access roads that held us up.'

The little group of men walked back to solid ground. Towering above them was the north gantry, a tapering structure which supported one end of the great wire cable spanning the gully. At that moment the Blondin was travelling along the cable, a worker standing in the bucket, ready to be lowered. From the top of the gantry a series of wire ropes stretched behind the group of engineers, anchoring the structure deep in a solid block of concrete. Another gantry, mounted on the viaduct itself, raised the level of the cable even higher, counteracting the thirty-foot sag at the centre of the cable: the twenty-ton steel trusses joining the middle piers had proved too heavy for a single gantry at each end.

Furkert slapped at a leg of the gantry as if he could make it disappear. It stood in the path of what would eventually be the approach to the viaduct. He frowned. 'The approaches will take three months. Our formation gangs need to start on them now.' He pulled out his pocket watch and tapped it. 'Next week at the latest.'

George Pascoe shook his head. 'The gantries must stay for another month. Obviously! Look at what they are doing.' He waved to the operator of the winch, who grinned back cheerfully, both hands fully occupied in a delicate manoeuvre. 'Good man, that Ruri. I'd have him back in Christchurch but he says his home is here. Getting married next week. That'll be a good party. First marriage in Makatote.'

Furkert spoke sharply. 'You're not giving him time off, surely? Tell him to save the celebrations until after Parliamentary Special goes through.'

Anderson shook his head. 'Everyone has their day off under our watch. In these conditions you'd lose the men if you worked them too hard. Our men don't work under the co-op system. Oh, well done, Billy!'

Billy Cameron, the man in the Blondin, had freed some kind of obstruction in a wire rope attached to the forward end of a great truss. Now the whole structure inched out into space, sliding over an already completed section. A brilliant, grinding, miraculous feat in Pascoe's and Anderson's opinion.

Furkert turned to Peter Keller. 'Can we do the approaches in less than three months?'

Keller looked across the gully, shook his head. 'There is a good deal of material to be shifted on this side. I can't see it.'

'Think of a way, Peter. You're our ideas man.'

Keller sighed. Pointed with the stem of his pipe at the offending gantry. 'What say—' He studied the gantry anchors set deep in the ground. He paced back along a line then walked towards the little group, counting his steps. 'What say our formation fellows start by digging a tunnel under the anchor blocks? That way we can get rid of some of the material straight away.'

George Pascoe raised a hand in alarm. 'For heaven's sake, Peter, look at the weight that gantry supports. You undermine my anchors and it could be a disaster! Lives lost! Let alone a truss dropped into the gully.' He stabbed a finger at Furkert. 'And your Parliamentary Special plan scuppered.'

Furkert paid little attention to this argument. He patted his engineer on the shoulder. 'Good idea, Peter, draw up a plan. See if you can convince these Andersons.' He winked at the grim-faced Pascoe. 'I am not inclined to indulge in lost causes, George. That train will go through on August eighth. Make sure you do your bit.'

A white wedding

'White? Of course white. Look at this.' Ruri's mother, Tia, produced a magazine which up to now had been hidden in her kete and laid it with a flourish on the table: *The New Zealand Graphic and Ladies' Journal.* Maggie watched in surprise: copies of this were as rare — and as coveted — as good whisky on the Plateau.

They had been discussing wedding costumes. Tia was full of exuberance; Sarah tired and pale. Maggie sighed. Perhaps she, too, lacked the energy to fulfil Tia's hopes and plans.

They were gathered in Rose's little room, the only space suitable for the women to meet. Sarah slept in a room off the cookhouse which could scarcely fit one body. Maggie looked out to see Ruri — banished outside for this 'women's talk' — playing with the children. She wanted to be out there, too, in the sun. She and Ruri had so little time together these days. He worked long hours on the winch and she was often called to help her mother cook for the travellers. Soon, she thought, soon we'll have our own tent, our own private space. It seemed such a luxury.

Tia had arrived that morning, her plentiful kete bulging with fresh carrots, a cabbage, ten apples and two jars of Jerusalem cherry jam. 'Good idea,' she had said when Rose suggested opening the jam that moment to go with Sarah's fresh scones. 'If you like the flavour we will have cherry jam tarts for the feast. And one of my pigs.'

Feast! Maggie tried not to show her dismay. She and Ruri wanted a quiet, simple wedding. Anyway, he was busy at work and would not be able to take more than a day off until the viaduct was finished. She looked at the magazine, which Tia now opened at a photographic display.

'Oh dear, no,' said Sarah, staring at the picture. She brushed her straggling hair back off her face. 'No no, Tia, what are you thinking?' Her look of defeat tugged at Maggie's heart.

Rose laughed and slapped Tia on the shoulder. 'Good enough for the Prime Minister, good enough for your son, eh?'

Tia laughed, too, a lovely rich gurgle, and gave Sarah a hug. 'No, dear, I am not so bold — or not quite. But the dresses. Look at the women. Every single one in white.' She stabbed a finger at a bridesmaid standing in the foreground. 'Here we have the latest fashion. We can copy that at least.'

The photograph was of a vast crowd solemnly arranged for a photograph. *Wedding of Cyril and Elinor Ward and Silver Wedding of the Rt Hon Joseph Ward and Lady Ward,* read the caption. There would have been a hundred well-dressed guests standing on a hillside in rows, men all in suits and top hats, women tightly corseted, ruffs at the neck, voluminous hats. Lady Ward's hat outshone them all. 'You could hide a nest of kittens in there and no one would know,' said Rose. She snatched up a scarf and wound it around Maggie's head, fluffing it into an outrageous concoction.

Maggie stared at the photograph. Could Tia really be thinking of such a celebration? 'Ruri and I are not the son and daughter of prime ministers, Tia. We live in a makeshift camp in the wilderness. I thought to wear a nice new dress and coat in green that would be useful later on.'

Tia spread her hands; looked sternly at Maggie, and then at Sarah. 'My son is not good enough? Not good for a white wedding?' She wagged a finger at them. 'The son of John Rochfort himself?'

Rose broke the tension by laughing. 'Now Tia, you rogue, that's unfair. I suspect Maggie would love a white dress in the latest fashion, but money is scarce in her family—' She held up a hand to stay Maggie's threatened outburst. 'Here's a suggestion: the Andersons have a splendid sewing machine. I would like to provide good silk for a dress — white or cream or green, as you wish. Sarah can sew it with my help over at the Andersons'. Tia, you provide a fine suit for your son.' She cocked her head at Tia. 'Eh? Ka pai?'

Maggie felt tears rising. She stood abruptly. 'Oh you've got it all organised! Why don't you just get on with it, then? Never mind that it's *my* wedding. Just leave me out of it!'

Sarah heaved herself up and hugged her daughter. 'No need for tantrums, hen, you're just on edge, that's to be understood. But my dear, in fact it's not just your wedding; we're all involved.' She looked over to Tia, who was chuckling.

'Ae. All the whanau. But Sarah, I like your daughter's spirit; she will make a good wife to my son. Good and fierce.'

Maggie looked at them all, tears running down. 'And no top hat for Ruri, or I won't marry him!'

Ruri must have been watching through the window; now he burst in, Alice and Con trailing behind. 'What's up, Maggie? Has my mother said something?' He gathered her in protectively and glared at Tia. 'What did you say to her?'

He looked so fierce standing there, the solemn, bemused children flanking him, that everyone had to laugh.

'We are simply discussing a wedding dress.' Rose indicated the photograph.

Ruri glanced at it, then looked closer. 'Maggie is much prettier than her.' He ran a finger over the image. 'I like the veil, though. With flowers. That would suit my Maggie.' He flicked away her tears; touched a curl of red hair above her ear. 'Do you fancy a veil, Maggie?'

Maggie gave in. She smiled at him. 'A veil. A white dress. But no top hat.'

'Don't be ridiculous, Maggie, whoever suggested a top hat? Something wrong with my hair?' Ruri hoisted Alice up high so that she could inspect his thatch. She squealed and ruffled it into spikes, then demanded to be let down to taste the cherry jam.

Thank goodness for my Ruri, thought Maggie. We will manage this.

The wedding was, in fact, a grand affair. Grand, but in a very different manner from the picture of the prime ministerial celebration. Several cartloads of Tia's whanau arrived, laden with supplies. Andrew Anderson decreed that there would be no Saturday shift that day so that all the workers could join in. All of *his* workers. The formation co-ops tunnelling their way under the gantries worked on — they were under Public Works jurisdiction. Brennan Scobie had pleaded for a day's dispensation but Furkert was adamant: the only celebration in his diary was the Parliamentary Special on August the eighth. Nothing even Rose could say or devise would budge that ruling.

'I'll hold the fort for the moment,' said Brennan to his chainman, Freeman. 'There is no way you are going to miss your sister's wedding.' He winked. 'Keep it under your hat though. If the gangs get wind of a party they might all invent ailments. I'll slip away in time for the ceremony.'

Freeman clapped his boss on the shoulder and ran to join the party.

What a day it was! As Ruri noted afterwards, the white and native gods had united for once to provide clear, sunny weather, and a light, warm breeze from the north had died away by mid-morning. At this time of year you could expect worse. The bush sparkled; smoke from chimneys rose straight up. Ruapehu — also dressed magnificently in white — presided from above. Of course the ground between the huts and tents was muddy, but planks had been laid between the Scobie cottage and the cookhouse so that the wedding party could keep their skirts clean.

The ceremony took place in the cookhouse. Mr McKenzie, the Presbyterian missioner, arrived somewhat dishevelled to find the cookhouse crowded.

Ruri, tall and handsome in his new suit, head bare as Maggie had decreed, stood quietly in front of the makeshift altar waiting for Maggie, a grinning Billy beside him. Billy as usual couldn't keep still; he fidgeted with the wedding band, dropped it, retrieved it, danced back and forth.

Tia's whanau filled one side of the room — every single one resplendent, from baby to old kuia. Large hats and high, lacy collars, white skirts for the women; even some gleaming silk toppers among the elders. Freeman whispered to Dirk — who had also contracted a mysterious last-minute ailment and slipped away from his gang — that the natives were much better kitted out than the railway men, who wore Sunday suits at best; cloth caps and collarless shirts for many. Brennan, who had run over from the earthworks, took a deep breath to still his beating heart, put his cornet to his lips and blew a fanfare — a magnificent arpeggio that had all the dogs in the yard joining in.

And there was Maggie, in creamy silk, tightly corseted, lacy ruffles at her neck, a veil secured to her head with a spray of white roses and jasmine from Tia's garden, radiantly happy to see Ruri waiting for her. In the absence of a father, Sarah, in a new silk dress, led her daughter in, while Brennan played Mendelssohn's *Wedding March* — a miraculous rendition considering the lack of orchestra or organ. The crowd stood; someone started to clap and soon they were all applauding. Billy laughed out loud and punched the air, then remembered his manners and stood by the groom, bursts of excited giggles erupting as the bride advanced. Con and Alice, both in white, solemnly carried the trailing veil. Oh it was a sight never before seen in Makatote; possibly not in any of the new railway settlements.

Ruri took her hand; they made their vows and were wed.

At the end of the ceremony an elder of Ruri's hapu came forward, his carved stick marking time with his footsteps. Ruri tensed, for this was the uncle who had not favoured the marriage. Certainly the old man looked fierce enough to do some damage. But he raised his stick, shook it at the heavens and, in ringing tones, called down a blessing on the couple: a lengthy blessing, which was finally brought to a close by Ruri taking Maggie in his arms and kissing her roundly. The koro nodded, grinned and followed suit. Soon everyone was lining up to kiss the bride.

The feast would follow in the afternoon; but first there was the excursion and the rugby match. A patch of more-or-less flat ground had been located at Dunwoodie's Mill. The wedding party were to be conveyed there on the tramway that usually carried logs and timber, an exciting journey through the bush. Rough plank seats had been fitted onto the flatbeds of three open bogies. The ladies sat, the men stood, the children dangled their legs over the edge and the little locomotive chuffed away, pulling all of them up through cleared land and then beautiful bush, across a rickety bridge, a clear stream flowing beneath, to the 'sports field', which was in fact bare, lumpy earth mixed with sawdust, cleared of stumps but stony enough to trip up the unwary. Now the forms were lifted down from the flatbeds and placed around the field for the spectators. Dunwoodie himself, who was related to Tia and Ruri (who wasn't?), had made two millhand cottages available as changing rooms for the players.

The match was between Ruri's hapu and the Makatote viaduct men. Freeman and Dirk, though strictly Public Works, were allowed to play on account of being family — and because they were strong runners with a ball. Impossible to find an impartial referee — the missioner had no idea of the rules — so Dunwoodie was given the whistle while George Pascoe kept a strict eye on him. What a sight it was! All the wedding finery, skirts now a little muddy at the hem, arranged around this clearing in the wilderness. Piles of totara logs edged the space, the mill smoking in the background, and beyond that in all directions the dense and towering bush.

Up and down the lumpy field the men pounded, Ruri captaining his team and Freeman the opposition. A wilder game you would never see. Kicking the ball away was dangerous as it either skittered through the sawdust or bounced unpredictably, so it was a matter of running and tackling. Soon the players were covered in mud and sawdust, the coloured sashes — red for Ruri's team, green for Makatote — rendered indistinguishable. Maggie shouted for both teams, and screamed approval when Ruri wrestled the ball over an imaginary line for a try. Dunwoodie allowed it, though there were plenty of protests, and then allowed another by fleet-footed Billy to equal the score and the game.

'Don't come near me until you have changed!' screamed Maggie when Ruri came trotting over for a kiss. Sarah loved seeing them both so happy. If only Jock had been alive for this day. There was something to be learned from it, too — her own prejudices had been exposed and erased.

Tia, whose hat would not have been out of place at the Prime Minister's wedding, nudged Sarah. 'Your youngest makes a good footballer. Almost could be a Maori.'

Sarah laughed. 'Not with that red hair.'

'Oh, there are plenty red-headed ones in our tribe.' Tia winked. 'Soon maybe some more, eh?' She linked arms easily with Sarah as they walked back to the tramway. 'Will you stay here when the railway is finished, to be with your daughter?'

Sarah had thought about this. Ruri intended to find railway work in Ohakune. 'I don't know, Tia. Jock and I had planned to build on the West Coast. I have friends there, and a brother in the mines. I feel that is my place. Dirk, my eldest, will return to Denniston. Maybe Freeman, too. I don't feel comfortable away from the sea.'

Tia nodded. 'You were born near the sea?'

'I was, yes. In Scotland. In the north.'

'Why did you leave? I can't imagine leaving my birthplace —' Tia gestured —, 'my mountain, my river.'

'We were crofters. They were taking our land. Building fences—' Sarah sighed. 'There was no living anymore.'

'Aue.' Tia patted her arm. 'Same old story eh? . . . Whoops!' The wagon lurched on the uneven rails. Several of the standing men lost their balance and fell off; a couple of children, too. Sarah looked for Maggie and Ruri, but they were safe. Tia laughed to see members of her whanau dumped so unceremoniously into the mud. 'Big washday tomorrow!'

The engine driver, unaware, chuffed slowly on. Billy, quick as a flash, jumped down and sped past the wagons. He ran ahead until he was well clear then turned to face the engine; raised his two hands in an imperious gesture and shouted, 'Stop!'

With a sigh of escaping steam the little locomotive obeyed; slowed, came to a halt inches from Billy's raised hands. Those seated on the first wagon cheered and laughed. They saw it as a piece of theatre — a joke. But Billy, his eyes shining, walked quietly back to his place on the last wagon, looking neither left nor right, acknowledging no one.

'In a world of his own, your Billy,' said Tia. 'Good of him, though, to stop the train.'

The feast was a triumph, as Rose remarked, of both cultures. Members of Tia's hapu had dug a hangi behind the cookhouse a day earlier. All morning the fire had been heating river boulders carted in from near Erua. While the excursion party watched the match, wire racks of food had been steaming away under fragrant leaves, wet sacks holding in the moisture: the jointed carcases of a pig and two sheep, a sack of potatoes and one of kumara, a rack of smoked eel and a large bag of mussels brought up by riverboat from Wanganui and then carted in from Pipiriki. Mrs Bright had roasted three long rounds of beef and made her famous steamed raisin pudding; Tia's five luscious cherry tarts gleamed on the table and above them all, in pride of place, a two-layered wedding cake, bursting with raisins and currants, iced by Mrs Anderson herself with little sugar roses.

They ate and sang and danced until evening. No one questioned the alcoholic content of the local hop beer. If Mr Anderson produced a bottle of champagne to toast his winch operator, there was no policeman present to comment.

'Do you think we can go now?' whispered Ruri to his wife. 'I would like to be alone.'

Maggie reached up to kiss him. 'With me, I hope!'

Holding hands, applauded by all, they left the party and headed to their own tent. Ruri had built a wooden floor, a bed and a fireplace; Maggie had filled sacks with sweet fern fronds and laid new blankets — gifted by Rose and Brennan — over them. Sarah had slipped away earlier and lit a fire. Gleaming beside it stood two silver candlesticks — Sarah's mother's — ready to light.

'Our own place,' whispered Maggie. They lit the candles and sat by the fire for a while, reliving the day. Then Ruri pinched the candles, took her hand and together, man and wife, they climbed into bed.

Back at the cookhouse only a few of the wedding party remained. Tia's mob had climbed aboard the carts and drays and headed home. It would be dawn before they arrived. Andersons' men had staggered off to their quarters. In the kitchen Mrs Bright set bread to rise for the morning. Billy, yawning, swept the floor while his mother and Rose wiped down the tables. Brennan, standing propped against a window, raised his cornet and played a quiet old favourite — *Rose of Tralee* — to settle the day.

'That was a dangerous act,' said Rose quietly to Billy, 'stopping the engine.'

Billy, more asleep than awake, shrugged. 'It was going slowly. I was practising.'

'For what?'

Billy shrugged again. 'It's a secret. To do with my faith.'

Rose laid a hand on Billy's shoulder to stay his sweeping. 'Billy, my friend, please listen. Don't try that on a full-sized locomotive. They cannot stop quickly. Your mother would not like to lose another.'

Billy grinned. 'Oh ye of little faith. That's what Jesus said.'

'He was speaking a metaphor. Do you remember what a metaphor is?'

Billy nodded, not really paying attention.

'Jesus didn't mean you could actually move a mountain. He meant a mountain of self-doubt maybe, or a mountain of prejudice.'

Billy frowned. 'You don't know that. He said mountain.'

Rose could see she was not making her point well. Billy was too tired. She was tired herself. 'Trains were not invented in Jesus' time. Think about that.'

'I know that, Rose,' said Billy, sure of himself, of his belief. 'I'm not stupid.'

The first time, she thought, that he had called her Rose. It had always been Mrs Scobie. Was that a dangerous sign or a good one? 'Well, Billy, we are both too tired for religious discussions. Let's talk again soon, shall we?'

But Billy was already moving away, sweeping the debris steadily out the door into the dark night.

The join

Ruri saw the last girder being winched into place. Not on his shift, alas, but he was there nevertheless, along with any others not working. June the third it was, two months before the Parliamentary Special was due.

'Alright, alright,' growled Andrew Anderson to the waiting demolition crew. 'We'll take one last photograph, if you don't mind.'

Then down came the gantries, the great wire rope and the Blondin — all in a day. The concrete supports took longer but the Public Works gangs were at it day and night, north and south, to work on the approaches, open out the tunnels and build an embankment on the south side. Bets were laid over whose approach would be finished first. Brennan's teams on the north had the easier task, but no one could relax. Everyone felt the pressure. Riveters were still at it, Billy among them, and every last hand was pressed into applying two final coats of paint to the steel. Meanwhile the deck and rails were laid over the great Makatote.

But time was running out. Furkert rode up to the viaduct every day or two, egging on his sweating gangs. Andrew Anderson, however, could relax, confident that his work would meet the deadline. A month after the gantries had come down, he stood on the deck of his viaduct and shook the chief engineer's hand. Ahead of them the rails stretched, shining, a magnificent span across the gully.

'We're done here, Fred. Good luck with the rest. Will you win your wager?'

For once Furkert looked worried. Exactly one month to go: the approaches only half finished and the platelayers still several miles from joining. 'We'll make it, no doubt about it.' But there were lines under his eyes. He was losing sleep, that was plain. He managed a wry smile. 'You're not done until the viaduct is tested, Andrew. When is the emergency brake test to be? Not that I would care for that to fail. God forbid.'

Anderson laughed. 'It won't fail. All in hand. Come and watch.'

On the third of August, five days before the Special would come through, Furkert heard the news he wanted to hear most in the world. The north and south platelayers were about to shake hands near Horopito.

'We'll have a photograph of that,' he said. He was in high good temper. Five days was cutting it fine and the track would be unballasted, but the rails were laid! Auckland and Wellington were now connected by two parallel lines of steel running over some of the most difficult terrain in the world.

Freeman and Brennan, who had been working on the Makatote approaches, rode in from the north, just to be part of the photograph. Picking his way down past the track, Brennan shook his head. 'He won't make it, Free. Not a chance. Look at the state of the formation. It won't take the weight, not of a big locomotive.'

Furkert, just arrived from Ohakune, heard the comment. He chuckled. 'Wait and see.' Nothing seemed to undermine his good spirits. 'This is a temporary solution, true, and a firm foundation will follow over the next six months. But we'll get those Wellington fellows through on the eighth.'

Brennan, when he was safely out of earshot, muttered to his chainman, 'How can he be so sanguine? What if they derail at the swamp? If lives were lost? His head would roll.'

Freeman kicked at wet ponga logs underpinning the sleepers. 'True — if there was anyone left to give the order.'

A little crowd of workers was waiting, hands on hips and grinning, in the middle of — well, nowhere much. But there were the rails. An almost perfect join after years of slow advance over unbelievably broken landscape. Furkert congratulated the cheering men and stood in their midst while the photographer lined them up.

'Eh, boss,' said a tough young cockney who'd come out two years earlier from London and was now a hardened railway man, 'cut us a ribbon, why not?'

He and a friend stretched a string across the tracks and, with a flourish, presented Furkert with a knife.

Furkert shook his head. 'I won't invite bad luck, lads. Let the Prime Minister do that job when we've finished the task. Plenty more to do.'

The fellow laughed. 'That's a true word, sir. God only knows how we'll get these tracks up to scratch.'

'Well, they'll be tested this very night, so I'd be grateful if you stay on the job late to guide us through this patch.'

Freeman nudged Brennan. 'Tell me he's joking.'

'Furkert doesn't joke. Goodness knows what he's up to.' He pointed to a bundle of wet manuka branches. 'This section is no better than Dunwoodie's bush railway.'

The notorious Horopito swamp — five waterlogged miles of it — stretched north. A temporary corduroy of ponga logs and manuka fascines had been laid down over the roughly cleared swamp; over the corduroy, longitudinal planks were laid; and over that the sleepers and tracks. Something sturdier would be needed by August eighth. Five days hence! The Parliamentary Special pulling two hundred dignitaries would be no light weight.

But Furkert seemed undaunted. 'Want to join the adventure? I could do with all available hands tonight.'

Freeman and Brennan, curious, rode back with the boss to Ohakune. There stood a rake of shining carriages — the new long design, made in Wellington and bound, so they heard, for Taumarunui. The Railways Department expected heavy traffic north of Taumarunui: everyone wanted to get to Auckland for the Great White Fleet spectacular.

'We'll take these through tonight,' said Furkert, 'while the weather holds. Bring a crowbar or shovel.'

Brennan and Freeman boarded the new carriages, along with several other engineers. The lightest twenty-ton locomotive pulled them. To start with it was a picnic, the men lounging in the brand new seats, pretending to be famous dignitaries. As dusk fell they cheered as the carriages crossed safely over the Hapuawhenua and Taonui viaducts.

Then trouble struck. With a lurch, the first carriage rocked and then stuck hard. The cuttings weren't finished: their batters were almost vertical, and the carriages — much longer than the little Public Works ones — couldn't manage the tight curve.

'All out!' shouted Furkert.

'He'll have a plan,' grinned Brennan. 'He always does.'

The men stood in the dark as the locomotive chuffed and steamed and backed the carriages up.

'Crowbars at the ready!' Furkert was enjoying himself. He stood, lit by the locomotive headlamp, and waved his own long bar. 'Forward!' he roared. This time the train inched forward and the men levered the cumbersome carriage around the curve. Forward and back, forward and back, they edged the whole rake through the cutting, beavering away under the harsh headlamp. The process was repeated whenever an obstruction was encountered — backing up while the silhouetted men worked to smooth the rough patch.

'It's worse than a sea trip,' groaned Freeman, as they rocked and lurched over the swamp. His stomach was churning. 'Thank goodness we won't have to do the return trip.'

Brennan laughed. 'Those parliamentarians might get more than they bargained for. Imagine being stuck in the Horopito swamp awaiting rescue! At any rate, Free, they might think they are the first to travel the Main Trunk, but we've pipped them!'

Easy and smooth, travelling now over hard pumice, the engine pulled them up to the great Makatote viaduct and over, the men hardly aware, in the dark, of that maiden voyage through the air.

One last rocking, lurching passage over the not-quite-completed northern approach to the viaduct, and the carriages were safely delivered to a handsome Wf locomotive, smoking eerily in the station lights, ready to take them on to Taumarunui.

'So, my dear,' said Brennan, as he warmed his icy feet on Rose's sleepy body, 'I have ridden the first passenger train from Ohakune to Makatote. You missed an adventure.'

Rose sat up abruptly. 'There were no mishaps?'

Brennan chuckled. 'A hundred mishaps but none fatal. That Furkert is a driven man, but he gets away with his temporary this and shortcut that every time. It was fun!'

'Billy wasn't with you?'

'Billy Cameron? No, why would he be?'

'He is dangerous around trains. Driven, too, in a way, by religious fervour or puppy-love — I can't make out which. Perhaps both. That preacher is playing with him like a cat with a bird, Bren. We need to watch over him.'

Brennan mumbled something, sighed and turned over. He was already asleep.

Police work

Sergeant Baker leaned back in his chair, his feet propped in front of the potbelly stove. The weather had turned bad again — snow flurries driven by a biting wind. He was glad to catch up on paperwork. *'Drunk in charge of a dray,'* he wrote, then *'Found on premises ten quarts of over-proof hop beer, hidden under floorboards. Suspect claimed brew was for his own consumption not for sale.'* He counted the entries for the month. Twenty-five were for illegal brewing or illegal sales of alcohol. Only one for drunkenness. A single theft: jewellery taken from the Grice hut. If liquor was made legal, he thought, I'd be out of a job.

Through the window of the police station — a tiny hut but at least solid and warm, with a proper lock-up next door — he saw Charlie McLeod ride up. The Horopito sergeant dismounted, waved cheerfully then set about rubbing down his horse, blanketing and feeding it. When the big bay had been released to join Baker's two in the windswept police paddock, McLeod shook his oilskin coat outside, removed his boots and stumped in. A careful young man. And ambitious. He wouldn't be long at Horopito.

Stew Baker lifted the kettle from the potbelly, poured black tea into two mugs and added condensed milk. 'Well, Charlie?'

McLeod stood by the stove. Crystals of ice still decorated his dark hair; the hands that he held to the warmth were blue. His nose dripped. 'They should bloody close down construction till summer, then we could all go north like migrating birds. I don't know how the men in tents survive.'

Baker nodded. 'Some don't. Get that tea down you. Trouble up your way?'

'No. Well, nothing new.' McLeod drew up a stool and sat as close to the stove as he could without catching fire. 'It's another matter. That preacher of yours: something about him has kept nagging at me. I sent away for information and it's just arrived by post.' He took from an inner pocket a folded piece of paper, spread it out on his knee and handed it to Baker. 'I knew I'd seen him before. I was a junior in Nelson last year. Your preacher is a wanted man, Stew.'

'Not my preacher, not by a long chalk.' Baker looked at the poster.

WANTED FOR MURDER
DOCTOR DANKWORTH FEARNLEY

The man depicted is a bogus man of medicine who arrived in the country as Stanley Lamb. Wanted for theft in Napier. Yellow hair; blue eyes; six feet tall.

Any information will be treated in confidence.

8th December 1906 Nelson Police Station.

'You sure it's our fellow? This drawing could be anyone.'

'Sure enough. I took a friend of mine to him with a chest cough. Must say he took me in completely.' Charlie snorted. 'Very solicitous, he was. Very ready to sell us some of his snake oil. Those eyes though — bright blue, a little wary. They were familiar — memorable. And his height. He had a moustache in those days, and short hair, but it's him alright.'

Sergeant Baker rocked back in his chair. 'Well well well. I am very pleased to hear this, Charlie. I've had my eye on Gabriel Locke for some time, but he is slippery as an eel. Murder, you say?'

'He attacked a man outside his own rooms. Fellow had come to complain about medicine given to his wife. The body was found dumped in the rooms. No sign of the "doctor". Hasn't been seen since.'

Sergeant Baker tapped the piece of paper. 'Date would be about right. He turned up at Makatote a few months after that. Makes sense. Hiding himself away in this wilderness.'

They discussed Baker's own suspicions: the boy killed; Mrs Grice's death. 'The preacher was involved, no doubt about it,' said Baker. 'I suspect he was blackmailing Amelia Grice. I think he could have done her in, too. If it was suicide, why didn't she leave a note? Some jewellery disappeared at the time, and he was spotted at the scene. But we can't prove it wasn't an accidental overdose.'

McLeod whistled. 'Trail of destruction. Sounds like a thoroughly rotten bastard.'

Baker nodded. 'But clever. A manipulator I'd say. I suspect he played poor Mrs Grice like a fish on a hook. A con man who can charm the ladies. And the lads. There's a boy up at Makatote besotted with him. I'd say that preacher is one of these twisted folk you see sometimes — black hole where the heart should be.

But you can't arrest someone *in possession of a black heart.*'

'You can for murder, though.'

'True, Charlie, but can you catch him?' Baker sighed. 'He skipped town the day after Mrs Grice died. As I said, slippery. I don't suppose he's washed up in Horopito?'

McLeod shook his head. They sipped their tea in silence. A fresh burst of hail rattled the window.

Sergeant Baker cleared his throat. 'My guess is he's long gone and changed his name again. But we can send in a report.'

McLeod put down his mug. 'That boy at Makatote.'

'Billy Cameron.'

'That one. It's just a hunch, but our man may still have his hooks in Billy. If he's a manipulator as you say, he may not be able to resist playing on Billy's adulation.'

Baker grinned. 'That's fancy reasoning. You been studying those foreign psychiatric fellows?'

'No, but it's worth a shot, eh, Stew? A feather in both our caps if we got him.'

Baker looked doubtful. 'Long way to go in this weather.'

This was just the chance the Horopito policeman was waiting for. Makatote was under Baker's wider jurisdiction, but if he got the nod . . . 'I'm heading north anyway. What say I have a nosey round? Ask a few questions? Report back to you?'

Baker stood up and looked out the window where the three horses were sheltering under one of the few remaining trees in the settlement. He would be glad to stay inside. 'Alright, alright, Charlie,' he said, 'I get the picture. Your case! But gently, gently with the boy. He's a good kid. Good worker, I hear — just besotted, as I say. Left alone he'll get over it, is my guess.'

McLeod nodded, shook his senior's hand, shrugged into his wet coat and headed out.

A lame horse

Gabriel Locke had ridden north from Makatote but was, in fact, not far away. A lonely widow in the tiny settlement of Erua had welcomed him into her cottage — and then her bed — in return for a little wood chopped and cheerful conversation by the fire of an evening. For a few weeks Gabriel, now Michael Lorde (another archangel) enjoyed this idle life, but questions and raised eyebrows from inquisitive neighbours prompted him to move on. Promising to return with supplies, he set out with the widow's savings in his pocket and headed north. A short distance past Waimarino his horse became fidgety, pulling at the reins and finally refusing to budge. Gabriel swore and whacked at the beast's flanks, but the big thoroughbred lowered her head and stayed put. Gabriel dismounted in a foul mood. The weather was turning: grey clouds bulked up over the mountain; drops of sleety rain began to fall.

For Gabriel this was the last straw. If he hadn't needed his horse he would have beaten her severely. Instead he dragged at the reins, pulling her along until they found shelter under a large mountain beech. Now what? Gabriel was not used to managing on his own. His skills lay in persuading other people to supply his needs. He stood under the tree in a black rage. This cursed cold Plateau; the tough, thankless inhabitants; his failed Gospel mission which had begun with so much promise. He looked at the shining new railway tracks heading into empty wilderness north and south. He needed a fresh start. A more civilised population of gullible women with well-heeled husbands.

The cold began to creep under his coat. Tears threatened to fall. He felt abandoned, lonely. No one would know if he died of cold here. No one would say, 'Oh I miss that lovely man. Where is he?' No one. Well — Billy would. But he angrily put the lad out of his mind. Billy's outburst had been the cause of Amelia Grice's suicide, he felt sure of that.

He gathered his bedroll around his shoulders. Was he about to die of cold? The horse came close and nuzzled him. Gabriel felt the warmth of that solid flank. He gave in, laid his head on her flank and cried bitterly. He cursed his stupid parents who had refused to recognise his preaching talents; now they had no idea — didn't care — whether he prospered or died. He cursed every misguided fool who had brought his various clever enterprises to a ruinous end, no matter how well he'd planned. He clung to the horse's neck and howled. Oh! Would no one come?

As dark approached, the wind dropped and snow began to fall. Gabriel, half asleep, clinging to the warmth of his mount, heard sounds at last. A horse and cart, heading north, rattled along the road, the carter roaring out a drunken song. Gabriel ran from the sheltering tree out into the road, waving his arms madly.

'Whoa there! Whoa, my darling!' cried the carter. 'What have we here then? A ghost, is it? A taniwha come to haunt me?'

'My horse is gone lame. Oh please, I need help!' Gabriel was ashamed of the abject pleas but had no control over his desperation.

The carter dismounted rather unsteadily. 'Well now, let us see. Can't have a good nag like that in pain.' Gabriel's saviour seemed more concerned about the animal than her freezing owner. Drunk though he was, he was easily able to handle the big thoroughbred. He raised each foreleg, felt for damage and then, to Gabriel's chagrin, found a stone in the left hind hoof. The horse kicked and nearly upended the carter who, unfazed, roared with laughter. 'Hey there, my sweetheart, give over. Steady . . . steady.' He reached for his knife, peered drunkenly at the hoof and then, with an amazingly sure hand, flicked out the stone.

'There you are, sir. Your beast will carry you now.' He thrust a wavering finger under Gabriel's nose. 'In these parts a fellow must know how to care for his nag.'

Gabriel felt a flash of anger. He could scarcely restrain his frozen hands from striking the oaf. 'Thank you,' he said through gritted teeth. 'Do you happen to know of accommodation in these parts?'

The carter climbed up and settled himself. 'There's Raurimu, five mile ahead. Boarding houses aplenty now the railroad's finished. Then back a way at Waimarino, two mile at most. Take your pick.' And off he rolled, 'Hup! Hup!' into the dark, leaving Gabriel to fend for himself.

'Ill-bred, mannerless clod,' grumbled Gabriel. He had difficulty mounting, his legs were so frozen. 'He might have offered a bite to eat. He might have offered to guide me.' Shuddering with cold, snow drifting into his face and sliding down inside his collar, he turned back towards Waimarino. He had noticed a boarding establishment there; perhaps with a warm and comforting proprietress?

A week later he was still in the little settlement. It had until recently been the bustling railhead, but was now a quiet backwater. Tourists sometimes paid for a ride up to the volcanoes in summer, but at this time of year the place was almost deserted. For Gabriel it was lacking in any interest. A dump of snow had blocked the road for five days. Gabriel sat before the fire in Mrs Abernethy's billiard room and tried to charm her with fanciful stories of his life to date. She was hard work, a no-nonsense widow who laboured all day and demanded payment in advance. Gabriel felt that he was gaining no traction. But her food was excellent and the cottage warm.

During those quiet, snow-bound days, Gabriel (who had introduced himself as Michael Lorde) found himself thinking more and more often of Billy Cameron. His thoughts were mixed: anger at Billy's innocent — or jealous — outbursts; but also the boy's genuine (or so it seemed) and undemanding love. Gabriel missed that — in fact, he had never before experienced such a love. Now that he had no congregation of worshippers to echo his views and admire his oratory, he felt somehow bereft. Naked almost. A strange restless feeling. He should move on as soon as the road cleared, but the itch that was Billy wouldn't go away.

He thought about his last meeting with Billy, the boy's almost mystical belief. At the time Gabriel had been playing with him — a punishment rather than any real intent. Now he had a sudden change of heart. What if Billy was the key, the missing link to his successful future? Yes! Gabriel ticked off the advantages Billy would bring: the boy was a genuine believer. He always brought a positive enthusiasm to the service. He loved not only the Lord but Gabriel himself. Billy was also fearless and easily mesmerised.

He began to plan a new Gospel mission, somewhere further north. With Billy as accomplice they would gain fresh converts. He dreamed of a crowded mission tent where not only his own sermons uplifted, but miraculous acts were performed.

The black-clad bulk that was Mrs Abernethy stood in front of him, blocking the fire's warmth, broom in one hand, duster in the other and her face stern. 'What is it that you do, sir, to earn your crust, if you're not a railway man? We all work hard in these parts.'

Gabriel smiled. 'I am a preacher, Mrs Abernethy.'

Her stern exterior melted a little. 'Well for heaven's sake, why did you not mention it earlier? We have had no preacher of any persuasion for the past four months. Are you Church of England by any chance?'

'I am not.'

'Well, no matter. I am very partial to a good sermon. Would you preach here in my billiard room on Sunday? I guarantee you would have a goodly number.' Her face clouded, 'Well, not so many as might . . . At least ten. Maybe fifteen. And I would put on a special luncheon after. What do you say?'

Gabriel, who had been happy to lie low, was nevertheless tempted. He accepted graciously after Mrs Abernethy promised to give him free board for that Sunday.

On an impulse he gave a carter who was heading for Makatote a note for Billy.

I am preaching at Waimarino this Sunday. I would like you to be my server if you can find a way to be here. We will also discuss the display of your faith at Makatote. If all goes well we may travel north together.

Not a word to your friends though, Billy.

He did not sign the note. Billy would know.

Plans for the future

Every day now at Makatote the sound of hammering and the shouts of men signalled both creation and destruction. Furkert's gangs were still blasting and shovelling, levelling the approaches, all day and all night. But George Pascoe was busy overseeing the dismantling of the great Workshop that had been his and his workers' pride. Everything that was salvageable — the great drills, the winches and pulleys, the generating engines — would be sent by rail and sea back to Christchurch.

At the village, the railway huts, cookhouse, wooden-floored tents, even the Andersons' cottage — all would have to go. Other railway construction settlements — Ohakune, Rangataua, Waimarino — would now become busy milling towns, but Makatote was on the edge of the newly gazetted National Park. No milling. No farming. Makatote would soon disappear and the bush would take over.

'What'll you do, Mam?' asked Maggie, 'Would you not stay with me and Ruri?'

But Sarah would not. She looked out at the snow, lying these last few days and now turning to grubby mush. 'I need to warm my bones again, hen. And hear the sea roar of a morning. A little cottage on the Coast with a cow and a few chooks, that's my dream. My good, solid Dirk says he'll build it for me. He's as keen as me to return. Did you know he has a sweetheart waiting back on Denniston?'

'Dirk has? He never said!'

'You know Dirk. Tom Gently's girl: she's as staunch as he is. She'll be waiting.'

Maggie knew her mother would not stay, and it grieved her. But nothing could dent her joy each morning as she woke next to her husband, felt his steady warmth, relived their love-making in the night. Even her lightest touch would wake him and he would yawn and reach for her again: 'Shall we make another great surveyor? Or maybe a railway man?'

And she would laugh and open her arms and draw him in.

Tia's whanau had given them a piece of land in Ohakune: their own place. Ruri would build a house and she would grow vegetables and babies and — who knows? — maybe teach children at the school. Rose said she had a talent with children.

Freeman would stay on with the Railways Department. He'd found his niche and would train as an engineer. But Billy? What about Billy? Ask him what he planned and he'd turn dreamy eyes on you and grin and shrug. Maybe dance a little jig of pure joy. 'You'll see,' he'd say. 'Wait a bit.'

Billy was a worry.

Emergency brakes

Before the Parliamentary Special came through, the viaduct must be tested. A train must brake to an emergency stop on it: that was in the contract. Andrew Anderson said it would be even more spectacular than the Parliamentary. 'You can't leave until you've seen that.' Rose was almost as excited as Andrew. She made her own calculations of weight and tonnage and whistled.

'Where will you find the rolling stock? Can you be sure the viaduct will hold?' Rose, her eyes alight, showed her sheet of figures to Andrew. 'You say three hundred and fifty tons? The train would have to reach twice the length of the viaduct! Three times!'

Andrew laughed. 'More, even. No, we'll do it with locomotives. We're bringing in a big new X class 4-8-2 engine from Taumarunui, plus an A class 4-6-2 and two Wfs. That's four locomotives, plus two wagons loaded with timber, a passenger car, and a guard's van. That should do it.'

Rose shook her head. 'You'll never get that weight over the

Horopito swamp. Have you seen the track there?'

'I have. No, we'll come from the north. You can get up a good head of steam along the Waimarino plain. We'll build to thirty miles an hour and then brake to an emergency stop in the middle of the viaduct.'

Rose clapped her hands. 'Oh, I hope Brennan is back for it. What a sight.'

'Everyone will be here. All the top brass from Railways. Hall-Jones of course — he wouldn't miss a sight like this.'

Rose decided that the little school would close for the day. Maggie and the older children would supervise the handful of younger ones. 'See if Ruri and Billy can come, too,' said Rose. 'Especially Billy. We'll watch from the south side. Take a picnic.'

Never mind that it's a cold winter day with a threat of sleet, thought Maggie. Rose would never be deterred by such details. She made sure the children were all wrapped up in hats and coats and, if they had no mittens, then a pair of socks for their cold fingers. The little party set out, walking down the coach road and into the gully. The clouds hung low, but everyone was excited. At the bridge they stopped and looked up at the great viaduct stretching in all its completed glory at the head of the gully. Rose had them count the number of piers. 'We know that without counting,' said one bright lad, 'Ten! Our das built them!' Amazing to think that three years ago there had been nothing but bushclad slopes and a rushing river. Up they marched, up the other side, keeping in step with a ditty Rose had them sing, warm now and eager to find a good spot. A coach full of dignitaries passed them, the horses snorting as they pushed against their traces, steam rising from their backs. The children cheered them, and the dignitaries waved back.

On a little rise above the south approach to the viaduct, they settled to eat their lunch. Billy climbed a rock and stood on one foot, balancing with his arms waving like a windmill to make the children laugh. Then they all wanted a turn and fell about, running and climbing and generally keeping warm.

Rose watched Billy closely. He seemed in good spirits — *high* spirits — but that was normal for him. She called to him. 'Billy, bring the children over here now. The train is coming.'

In the distance, on the other side of Makatote viaduct, they could see a great cloud of steam and smoke approaching. Most of the workers were watching on that north bank but there was a good crowd on this side too. Whoo! . . . Whoo! . . . Whoo! They all cheered to hear the lead locomotive's whistle. Then they fell silent: those two-tone blasts sounded like a warning. The train thundered towards the viaduct. Would the structure hold? Would it sway? Would there be some part that had not been riveted or bolted properly that might give way? Would Peter Seton Hay's radical light design be strong enough?

Maggie held Ruri's hand. 'Are you proud?'

'Ask me in a few moments. At this moment I'm bloody nervous.'

'What must the drivers be feeling?'

Ruri, whose poor head for heights was legendary, nodded. 'They must be sweating! It's a long way to the bottom.'

Rose clamped a hand on Billy's arm. She spoke quietly into his ear. 'Watch, Billy. There's three hundred and fifty tons pounding down the tracks there, at thirty miles an hour. Watch how long it takes to stop.'

A short whoop came from the leading X class engine as it roared onto the approach. Rose held her breath. Nothing seemed to be happening. Then suddenly, showers of sparks flew from every set of wheels, spraying out into the void. The children cried out. The train slowed, then slowed again. As brake blocks clamped down on wheels, and wheels skidded on rails, an eerie singing moan echoed up the gorge. Lost souls in hell would not have cried so sadly. Young Con Scobie stood white-faced, hands clamped over his ears. Still the train slowed. Would it never stop?

Rose felt Billy tense. She tightened her grip. Billy was humming — a high, keening whine like wind through taut wires. Surely Billy didn't think he was managing the stop?

With a billowing of released steam, the train came to a halt — past the midway mark, almost up to the concrete end-piers, but the whole length entirely on the viaduct. Rose realised she had been holding her breath; they all had. Everyone was gulping air. Four locomotives, two loaded wagons, a passenger car and a guard's van, all motionless, steaming, held high above the gully by the great Makatote viaduct that they had built! All that weight and pressure on Hay's airy structure and not a waver, not a crack, no sign of weakness. The train sat there panting like a pleased dog waiting for a pat. Then slowly, at a signal from Mr Furkert, it backed off, chuff, chuff, towards Makatote village as if nothing out of the ordinary had happened.

Rose felt Billy relax under her hand. 'What a marvel.' she said quietly. 'What power. A single person — no matter how strong his belief — could never stop a train. I know you have been thinking about it, Billy. This is not something your God would ask of you. Your God is kind. Think how dreadful for a driver who could not stop in time; who ran you down before his very eyes. Or before the eyes of your mother. There are other ways to show your faith. Not this. Believe me, Billy.'

Billy turned to her, his eyes bright. 'Yes. I know that. There are other ways.'

Rose wanted to shake him, to wake him into the real world. What was going through his mind? His detachment disturbed her.

'Gabriel was only testing me,' he said. 'My faith. He didn't want me to stop a train, of course not. But we will perform other marvels. Together we will praise the Lord.'

Rose looked at him sharply. Why was Billy not surprised that she knew? And where, for heaven's sake, was the preacher? She had told the police that he had headed north; that it was unlikely he would show his face again in these parts. Yet Billy said they would act together. Was she wrong? Or was Billy dreaming a private hope?

'Have you seen Gabriel Locke, Billy? The police would like to talk to him. They say he killed a man.'

Billy looked out at the viaduct; that distant, disconnected smile again. 'They're wrong. Gabriel couldn't kill. He's a man of God.'

Rose took his shoulders and turned him to face her. She shook him hard. 'Wake up, Billy! Your precious man of God is a fraud. He's dangerous. He can hurt you.'

For a moment it seemed as if she had broken through. Billy's eyes widened; he looked at her in shock. 'You hurt me!' he said. But then he shrugged off her hands and walked away.

Rose watched him go in dismay. Had she been foolish? Pushed this fragile boy too far?

'Rose!' called Brennan. 'Come and join the congratulations. Everyone is delighted.'

Rose ran over to join the group of men. Mr Furkert was shaking Andrew Anderson's hand. 'Very impressive, Andrew, can't fault it. Safe as houses.'

Andrew, grinning like a schoolboy, gave George Pascoe a great slap on the back. 'This is the man you should praise. An amazing feat. Three years from wilderness to modern marvel. And on budget.' He sobered for a moment. 'Hope Peter Seton Hay is watching from Paradise.'

George Pascoe scratched an ear. He said nothing, but the glow of pride could have warmed a room. All around them workers and bosses and gang foremen were lighting pipes and cigarettes — a sure sign that the tension of the past hour was released. Rose laughed out loud. 'Here is another puffing engine! Look at your cloud of smoke rising!' The men grinned, shifted feet and patted pockets, embarrassed by this woman's odd outburst.

Rose turned to Furkert. 'And will your Parliamentary Special be as successful? You have no one to blame now if you don't get it through.'

Furkert regarded her coolly. Why was she not standing quietly with the other Makatote women on the north bank? 'I have no need to lay blame, lady, I rely on good planning and hard work.' He turned to his engineers. 'Speaking of which—' Out came his pocket watch. One of the engineers guffawed; another silenced him with an elbow to the ribs. But the little group followed smartly enough towards their waiting horses.

Rose looked around. Maggie and Ruri were already shepherding the chattering children back down the road.

No sign of Billy, though.

The Parliamentary Special

Freeman Cameron:

You should have seen those poor blue faces peering out! Dawn at Ohakune on a freezing August morning, you could expect no better, but had they thought of that, those parliamentary blokes and their wives? They set off, you see, at night — 10 pm — and travelled through the night, all two hundred of them in carriages that were not yet equipped with proper heating. That came the year after, if I remember right. They had the copper foot-warmers, of course; those were handed out in Wellington — you wouldn't remember them. But that's all they did — warm the feet; noses and fingers turned to ice. And anyway, by Ohakune the sodium acetate inside them would be losing its heat. How they worked was interesting: the copper tubes with the sodium acetate crystals sealed inside were heated in a great vat of boiling water for an hour or so, and then given to each passenger, along with a pillow. You had to bring your own blankets. After about seven or eight hours, if you shook your foot-warmer or tipped it on end, some kind of crystallisation occurred and the heat prolonged and . . . well, don't get me started on chemistry. What I'm saying is that by the time they drew into Ohakune icicles were forming on the ceilings of the cars and frost crazed the windows.

Brennan was there on the station, and me and Peter Keller — and Furkert, naturally. I'll say this for the PM — he looked spruce enough after a rough night and a change of locomotives; Lady Ward, too, her hat huge and immaculate; how she did it I can't imagine. Where did she or any of the ladies keep their hats? There wouldn't be room in the overhead. But out she came — she and Sir Joseph — not onto the station but on the platform of the carriage in the full icy blast of morning to receive a wee bunch of flowers from little Mary Kerr. No speeches, mind. Furkert had his pocket watch out the whole time the train stopped. He had to get the train to Auckland inside twenty-four hours. That was the wager. A Wf locomotive was pulling it then — 501, if I remember right. Or was it 502? Anyway, the Public Works' finest.

So. Off we set towards Horopito. Furkert had us fellows — five or six of us — ride in the guard's van for the tricky section coming up. In case of emergencies. If he was to lose his wager anywhere, it would be in the Horopito swamp.

Clever. Furkert was a clever man, no doubting that. He might have pushed things a bit — railroaded us, you might say, ha! — but he had thought it all through. That swampy section was still unballasted; still laid on ponga corduroy, some of it. Could never stand the weight of a Wf. Yet he needed that sort of grunt to pull eleven cars and two hundred corpulent adults and their luggage. So at Horopito we stop. Furkert has three of our lightest locomotives, two Ds and an L, all under twenty ton, pressure up and billowing, ready to go, waiting on the siding. Like a military operation it was!

Drop off the Wf. The three small locos marshalled into the train, spreading the weight, you see. Us engineers ready to jump off and crowbar any wheel that threatened to come adrift. And a gang of platelayers on the track keeping pace with us. Walking pace, the whole five mile. Carriages rocking and pitching. There would have been a green tinge to plenty of those cold blue parliamentary faces, I'll be bound.

It was damn risky. My boss, Brennan Scobie, looked pretty shaky. You could hear the sleepers cracking. Unballasted totara will split. One after the other we heard those sleepers go. Crack! And then a lurch. Crack! A shudder. But she kept on rolling. Over a hundred broken or damaged sleepers, they said, needing replacement after the Special went through. But there's politics for you. Make a statement. Show off how New Zealand is just as progressive as the Yanks with their Great White Fleet. Two hundred of the country's best and most influential transported the length of the North Island — or a good part of it — in under twenty-four hours. The Main Trunk Line: in my book just as remarkable as the Great White Fleet. A triumph of modern engineering.

We stopped on the Makatote viaduct for a photograph. Right on it! Train stretched from end to end across the void. Another heart-stopper for those brave souls who run our country. There was cloud that day, no view of the mountain, but peaceful after the Horopito swamp. The gentlemen taking a sip of whisky to steady their nerves and the ladies daring to nibble at their cold breakfast sandwiches. Then a triple toot from the three little locomotives and off we rolled, on to Makatote village. Job over for the small fry: another big Wf was hooked up for the trip down the Raurimu Spiral and out to Taumarunui. Our job over, too. Plain sailing — or steaming I should say — from then on up to Auckland.

They made it to Auckland in twenty hours and thirty minutes. Wager met as far as Furkert was concerned. Did he collect his wager? I never heard. But the fellow sported a new topper next time I saw him. The passengers were not so lucky. They missed that night's panto, *Mother Goose*. The ladies had set their hearts on seeing it. Maybe they saw it later, but not the gala night. Evidently it was a wonderful lavish production that had the Yankee seamen laughing and cheering.

I was busy watching the marshalling of engines at Makatote. Never saw Billy.

Maggie Rochfort:

Rose was fidgety those last few days before the Parliamentary Special came through. At first I thought it was just all the packing and her looking forward to getting back home. But it was Billy and the preacher on her mind.

'Something's up with that boy,' she said to me as we parcelled up the blankets and linen and found a box for the children's little treasures. 'Where in God's name has he got to?'

Billy had disappeared a day or two earlier. He'd told no one. Mam was not really worried. 'He's a grown man,' she told me, 'he'll have his reasons. You know what Billy's like. He'll be thinking what next, what new adventure now the viaduct is built? Maybe he'll get work at Andersons.' I think Mam was hoping he'd go back to the South Island to be near her.

But Rose had this fixation with the preacher. She thought him evil, and was afraid Billy had been entirely won over; had gone to join him. To be honest I thought she was more determined to see the preacher put down or locked up than any thought of saving

Billy. Maybe that's harsh. It's true she had a soft spot for Billy, her pupil. Well, we were all her pupils, weren't we? But she saw something in the preacher that we didn't. Something she wanted to crush. When she talked about him her hands would clench and her mouth draw into a thin line. I didn't like Gabriel Locke, but I suppose at that time he seemed harmless. He could be charming if he tried, which was often enough.

I think Rose hated him. Feared him. 'He will always slip out from under,' she said, 'after he has enjoyed destroying someone else's life.' The way she spoke, it was personal. She needed to bring him down. Perhaps it was something in her own past.

At any rate, she wrote a note to that Horopito policeman who'd been sniffing around earlier. Told him she thought the preacher was still in the vicinity. 'Think, Maggie, think,' she said to me. 'Where could he be hiding?' She wrapped the crockery in old newspaper and banged the plates into the box as if they were the preacher's head she was attacking. I put out a hand to stop her before she broke the lot. 'I'll do this, Rose. You go and search, if you're so worried.'

She shook herself like a dog with fleas, gave me an apologetic grin and walked out into the day.

Later I thought of a deserted whare downriver on the south bank of the gully. Not Rochfort's — Rose had already searched that — but another surveying one. My Ruri told me about it.

'Ruri knows where it is?' asked Rose.

I nodded. Ruri told me he used to go there when he was young; liked to sit in the abandoned whare looking out at the wilderness of bush and river and think about his father.

Off trotted Rose, on the scent now, to find Ruri. She must have telegraphed the policeman too, because he came up our way the next day — the day of the Parliamentary Special.

We were all excited. All the village gathered by the half-demolished Workshop to see it come through and to wave the little flags that Mr Furkert had distributed. Not Rose, though; she was on a different mission, tramping up and down, looking this way and that, peering into the bush, taking no notice of the viaduct or the train or the rest of us. I had my hands full, watching Con and Alice, who would disappear in the blink of an eye.

Sergeant Charlie McLeod:

On the morning of 8th August, acting on information received, I approached a whare south of Makatote village. The man known as Gabriel Locke alias Dankworth Fearnley, real name Stanley Lamb, a wanted man, was outside the whare, beside his horse, apparently about to mount.

The young man Billy Cameron, construction worker on the viaduct, was standing beside him. His garb was unusual — a white tunic and dark sash — ritualistic in some manner perhaps. The wanted man had recently run a Gospel mission in Ohakune.

I warned the suspect, using his real name, that he was under arrest. Suspect whispered some message to the boy, then mounted swiftly. I presented my rifle and ordered him to dismount immediately. I was on foot, having led my mount down the steep bridle track.

The young man, Billy Cameron, then ran towards me crying out for me to desist. He dragged at my arm.

While I was engaged in disentangling from the boy, suspect rode away.

I fired a shot which did not reach its target, mounted and set off in pursuit.

The track was narrow and not easily traversed. By the time we reached the main road, suspect was well ahead, riding north. My mount, being a sturdy half-draught, was no match for his thoroughbred. (It is respectfully suggested that mounts of a speedier disposition — the Kaimanawa for instance — might be issued in future to police in these parts.)

On the north bank of the Makatote viaduct a large crowd was gathered to view the Parliamentary Special cross. They had not seen the suspect ride past. A local woman, Mrs B. Scobie, my original informant, suggested that he may have ridden through the village and on north. She led me to the telegraph office where I rang ahead to Waimarino. I rode on in pursuit.

At Waimarino, the Parliamentary Special overtook me and steamed on. There had been no sign of the suspect. I assumed he was hiding further back and headed south again.

Suspect had been apprehended and was held at Makatote until I arrived. I charged him with murder, possible murder, theft (and subsequently, incitement to a dangerous act). Suspect did not come willingly. He had already hurt one man and badly bruised Mrs B. Scobie in his attempt to break free. I was forced not only to handcuff him but tie his legs. Once restrained he became extremely disconsolate, crying and howling in a most unmanly manner. He was confined in an empty railway wagon and thus transported next day to Taumarunui. His thoroughbred is held at the Ohakune station and remains there until further instructions.

Sergeant Baker of Ohakune has asked me to include a warning, thus: the arrested man, if convicted of the charges, will likely hang, but authorities should be aware that he can be most plausible and is bound to spin a believable fabrication of lies. Solid witnesses to the Nelson murder will be essential, in Baker's opinion.

Kairuri Rokipoto (also known as Ruri Rochfort):

My good friend Billy worked with me, shared a tent and was best man at my wedding to his sister. In his head he was different. But a good, true man.

Mrs Rose Scobie had sent me to search the old whare. She feared for Billy, who was under the influence of the preacher. As I walked down the track, first the preacher rode past and then a policeman. Not Sergeant Baker. I had to jump aside or they would have trampled me.

When the preacher rode off I thought Billy would be upset — to be left like that, in his tunic and sash as if they were about to hold a service there in the bush. I put my arm across his shoulder. 'Never mind,' I said, 'I'm here, e hoa.' Speaking gently, as is best with Billy, who can get very excited.

Billy looked at me in a strange way. Distant. But not upset. I thought then that maybe he and the preacher had been drinking. Though I had never seen Billy take liquor.

'He will wait,' Billy said. 'He will watch me. He promised.'

We walked up though the bush. I offered my friend my coat, but he shook his head. It was a cold morning, the mist lying heavy in the tree tops, but he seemed in good spirits. This was very strange to me. His good spirits.

'We will proclaim the Truth together,' he said, 'Gabriel and me. We will perform miraculous deeds in the name of the Lord.'

I said nothing. But we walked together.

'We will bring lost souls into the Light,' he said. I thought maybe he was in some kind of trance.

Then we heard the train whistle up ahead. That would be the famous Parliamentary Special. Heard it rattle onto the viaduct. Heard the singing of metal on metal as it slowed. I was glad we would miss that sight. Mrs Rose Scobie had feared Billy was fired up to do something foolish.

My friend quickened his pace, but no more than I could keep up with. Still that strange lightness about him. His white tunic against the dark of the bush.

We came out onto the road. The place where the viaduct goes across the gully and the coach road snakes away down to the bridge far below. We saw the guard's van moving slowly about halfway across the viaduct, and the pluming of many stacks — it seemed like three locomotives — in the cold morning air as that train headed away.

Together we stood and looked at the viaduct. 'We helped to build that,' I said. My heart was swelling with pride.

Billy smiled. 'Gabriel is watching me. I know he is. Will you watch, too?'

'My friend,' I said, 'I will always watch over you.'

Then Billy ran. He ran faster than I could keep up, straight onto the viaduct. There is a handrail each side of the bridge and a narrow space to walk. That handrail is a light thing compared to the solid sleepers and track — a thin metal bar, the thickness of my wrist, supported every few yards by another bar connecting it to the viaduct. Only the very confident would walk the footbridge. But Billy ignored the walkway. He touched the handrail on the upstream side then swung up onto it, crouching, his feet bare, which I had not noticed before. Then stood, balanced! I cried out to see him balance there on that flimsy rail. And walked! He walked that bar. His arms spread wide, step after easy step, balanced on that small strip of metal that was the handrail. It would have been an admirable sight if it were not so fearful.

I swallowed to keep down the vomit. Because I knew I must follow. There might be black ice. Even Billy could not keep his footing where there is black ice. He might lose his balance, agile as he was, and need a friend's hand. But I had never crossed the great Makatote. Most other workers had dared to walk over, for the joy and pride of it, but not me. I cannot.

Yet I followed, clinging to the rail, not daring to close my eyes in case I was needed. 'For pity's sake, Billy,' I whispered, 'wait for me. Let us walk on the footbridge together.' But Billy continued, steady and confident, his head high, not even watching his feet or the abyss below.

The train had gone, thank goodness, and the rumbling under my feet ceased. I could hear those on the other bank shouting. They must have noticed Billy by now. I think I was crying or moaning, my eyes fixed on my friend, who walked that slim rail quickly, secure as if he were on a good road. I thought perhaps he had not noticed me — was not aware that I was there watching over him as I had promised.

But then, about halfway across, he *turned*. Without losing balance he turned to face me and smiled. He was breathing quickly, his eyes wide. That smile! There was pure joy in it. I speak truly: pure joy. Me clinging to the rail in pure misery. 'Have a heart Billy,' I said. 'Come down.'

Then he turned to face the mountain — my mountain — which was hidden by cloud. Billy bent his knees and leaped. Before I had a chance to guess his intent, he leaped straight outward, arms wide, legs wide, head up as if flying. For a moment he did seem to fly — to move upwards. And then fell.

Then I heard a great cry echoing in the gully. 'No! No, Billy!' It was the preacher. I saw him burst out of the bush on the far side, his arms waving, then fall to his knees. I saw Mrs Rose Scobie, her skirts flying, jump at him like a tiger and push him down into the ground. Then my eyes turned back to the crumpled body that had been Billy.

This remains in my memory and comforts me: All that terrible long way down he remained stretched as if in flight, the white tunic, the flaming hair bright against the wreckage and rubble of the gully. Even when he hit he did not crumple but met the ground with wings out, like a bird coming in to land.

I cannot understand why he jumped. Perhaps he also did not know. But I am sure of this: it was not from despair.

I clung there, high above him. I was the one in despair.

My Maggie came running then, flying over the bridge as if it were firm ground, calling for me to wait, to wait. No need for her call. I could not move. She took me in her arms and we wept together.

Then she guided me, my wife, step by trembling step, back to the land.

LOOKING BACK

When Gran turned eighty we had a small party for her. She was still living in her little cottage in Ohakune, an old railway house that she and Grandad Ruri had bought from the Railways. It sat on a rise up near The Junction. 'I like to hear the trains in the night,' she had said when we suggested she move closer in to town.

I wrote to Rose, inviting her to join the family for the celebration — a slim hope as Rose was a good eight or nine years older than Gran and famous for staying put on the Hill when so many had left. I knew she was still alive, because when they closed the Incline on Denniston she had been featured in the papers — a photograph of her standing tall and elegant in front of the last wagon to go down. Gran cut out the picture and put it in her scrapbook. She showed it to me more than once.

Well, there was no reply to my letter and I left it at that. We had our little family lunch and a few locals called in. Gran enjoyed it all. I was glad my invitation to Rose was never mentioned.

A couple of days later I called in to bring Gran her groceries and there was Rose! Sitting in Gran's kitchen as if she belonged. As if she had visited many times, which she had not. I must have stood there with my mouth hanging open because those two old ladies laughed out loud.

'Hello there,' said Rose. 'Thank you for the invitation.'

'But however did you get here?' I asked. In my letter I had offered to arrange transport; mentioned buses.

'She came by train, of course,' said Gran, 'and walked from the station. Would you put the kettle on, dear?'

'No, wait.' Rose produced a bottle of champagne from her carrybag and handed it to me. 'Why not open this?'

Gran gave me a hug when I brought out her best glasses and poured for the three of us. 'Thank you, dear. The best present.'

I think Gran was always a little in love with Rose. She wouldn't be the only one, I imagine. Rose was eighty-nine but looked younger than Gran, her red woollen dress immaculate, a scarf embroidered with birds and flowers draped over her shoulders. Gran had obviously been surprised in her old black work dress.

'Come on, Gran,' I said. 'Let's dress you up for this party.'

So while Rose walked outside and admired the mountain and the views down to the town, I helped Gran into her new green silk dress that had been a present from Mark and me, and her green patent-leather shoes with a little heel.

'Aha!' cried Rose as we made our entrance from the bedroom. 'There's my Maggie! Do you remember how you wanted green silk for your wedding dress?'

They laughed and reminisced like a pair of youngsters. Stories that I had never heard before came to light: the wedding dress; the rugby match after the wedding.

'No.' Rose lifted her hand — an imperious gesture — as I prepared to refill her glass. 'We'll finish that later. I see you have a car outside. Would you take us to see the great Makatote?'

No thought about what else I might be needing to do. She was worse than Gran who, goodness knows, was demanding enough. I looked sharply at Gran. A trip to the viaduct was bound to encourage less happy recollections.

'And what is that look for, miss?' Gran was already out of her seat. 'If Rose would like to visit Makatote, then we shall go. Or shall I ring George?'

George was a notoriously bad driver who lived next door — always eager to ferry her into town. Gran knew I hated and feared her trips with George.

So we drove out, the three of us, Gran leaning forward from the back seat to shout in Rose's ear some piece of information, or to point out landmarks that they both remembered.

Rose looked out at the lush pastures; the sheep and cattle grazing. 'It's all so different! That beautiful bush! The ferns! All gone. Do you know,' she said, turning to me, 'the bush is returning to Denniston now that the houses have gone. Could you not have saved the bush here?'

Gran laughed. 'You and your crusades, Rose.'

She was so happy that day. All her fierce contradictions and pronouncements mellowed. Even when we drew into the carpark by the viaduct, her mood was reflective; the usual recriminations softened by the presence of her friend.

We walked to the railing. From this distance the great girders looked airy: a spider's web against the sky, seemingly incapable of taking weight.

'Oh, what luck!' cried Rose, clapping her hands like a child, 'Look!'

We heard the two-tone blast of a goods train, and there it was, crossing over, nonchalant, matter-of-fact, rattle rattle —

an endless succession of wagons and flatbeds — and then gone, rumbling into the distance.

The silence settled. A bird somewhere sang. I leaned against the car in the sun and watched them — one tall, the other shorter, both white-haired, their bright finery incongruous in the scruffy carpark.

'That damn preacher,' said Gran.

I thought, here we go.

Rose nodded, still watching the viaduct. 'A twisted soul, yes. They'd call him a con-man now, I suppose. Or worse. But I doubt he caused Billy's death.'

This was news to me. Gran always blamed the preacher.

'He corrupted my brother, Rose. You can't deny that. At the time you were just as worried as I was. More so.'

Rose nodded; turned and linked arms with Gran as if they were everyday friends. As far as I knew they hadn't seen each other for a good ten years. 'Let's get in the car. It's too cold for our old bones.'

But, once settled, Rose was ready to talk again. 'I've thought about it, Maggie. Often over the years; worried at it. Those were headlong times. The pressure to finish the railroad — to advance the nation. And poor Mrs Grice with her crusading zeal. Perhaps the preacher recognised that general fervour and harnessed it.' Rose flicked at a lock of hair as if worried by some thought. 'Am I being fanciful? Who knows, Maggie. Could I have prevented it? Billy's jump? Could any of us? The preacher tried to corrupt Billy, true. That's what gave him pleasure — having power over vulnerable people. But I believe that he failed with Billy.' Rose raised a forefinger to make her point. 'Billy was different. We all recognised that. Another person possessing Billy's fervour and excesses could have become a dangerous fanatic. Not Billy. He was somehow incorruptible. And I believe it irked the preacher like a sore tooth. He couldn't let it be.'

She and Gran were both sitting in the back seat, arm in arm, Gran's soft old cheeks pink with the pleasure of it.

'Billy loved him.' Gran spoke without her usual sour anger. It was a simple, if puzzled, statement of fact.

'Yes.'

I watched them through the rear-vision mirror; listened with great interest. It seemed an important conversation for both of them. Possibly that was the time when the seed was sown. To write about it.

Rose gazed up to the viaduct. 'I think Billy wanted to show off to the preacher. And to all of us. There was religious zeal in the mix too, of course. But he knew he could walk that handrail. He was not in danger.' She turned to me. 'Have you ever been tempted to jump?'

The question startled me. 'Jump, like Billy did? No.' And then I thought of standing on the bridge over the Mangawhero River, mesmerised by the flow of water in flood. 'Well, tempted, maybe.'

'Yes. The feeling is common enough. I was seduced once by the idea of falling. Brennan saved me. Perhaps it was that with Billy? The height and the freedom seduced him?'

We all fell silent.

Then Gran shook her head. 'No, no, no, Rose. I disagree. Without the religious fervour, without the preacher's mumbo-jumbo, Billy wouldn't have jumped. Being tempted is different from jumping. I still blame the preacher.'

'Oh, blame,' said Rose. 'Possibly we all failed Billy one way or another. Blame is a waste of energy. Let's go and finish that champagne.'

NOTES

Events in 1907/08 relating to the construction of the Main Trunk Line and building the Makatote viaduct are as accurate as a fiction writer can — or should — make them.

The rest is fiction.

The co-op system

Richard Seddon, as Minister of Public Works, promoted and developed the co-operative system of undertaking large Government projects. Instead of contracting out work to established businesses, the Government engineers employed and supervised gangs of men. The Government believed this system would save money, favour local workers and be more efficient. Others believed the system gave the workers too much power. Most of the work joining the North Island Main Trunk Line over the period of this novel was achieved using the co-op system. However, as time was pressing and lines of supply were considered problematic, the design and construction of the Makatote viaduct was contracted to the experienced Anderson brothers of Christchurch.

The Parliamentary Special

The train carrying two hundred Members of Parliament and their associates travelled the North Island Main Trunk Line on 7–8 August 1908, as described. Six months later, on 13 February 1909, the final section from Waiouru to Erua was handed over to the Railways Department, and even then a large workforce was still employed in completing the line.

In 2008, a century later, an excursion re-creating the Parliamentary Special journey set out from Wellington. The cover photograph is taken from that re-enactment — thankfully a safer journey than the original.

Historical characters in this novel

- *John Rochfort,* surveyor, whose rail route through the Volcanic Plateau was accepted as the best of three options. He married twice in Nelson and left a large family there, then had two children with Ngahuia, of Maniapoto lineage. (There is no evidence of other children.)
- *F W Furkert,* Public Works engineer-in-charge at Ohakune headquarters.
- *Peter Keller,* Public Works engineer.
- *Peter Seton Hay,* designing engineer, Makatote viaduct (died of pneumonia before it was completed).
- *Hon. William Hall-Jones,* Minister for Public Works and Railways.

- *Andrew Anderson,* partner in Christchurch engineering business Andersons, and his family.
- *George Pascoe,* employee of Andersons, in charge of Makatote viaduct construction.
- *Clarkin Brothers* of Paeroa, cartage business.
- *Mrs Bright,* cook, Makatote.
- *Mr Stone,* pay clerk.
- *Rt. Hon. Joseph Ward,* Prime Minister, and *Lady Ward.*
- *Mrs Kerr,* proprietor, Seddon Temperance Hotel, Ohakune.
- *Mr Cox,* proprietor, boarding house at Karioi.
- *Mr McKenzie,* Presbyterian missioner, Raetihi, and *Mr Lennox,* his assistant.
- *Dunwoodie,* mill owner, Makatote.
- *Joe Vickers,* railway guardsman, Taihape — Ohakune.

The Cameron family, Gabriel Locke, the Scobies, Ruri and Mrs Grice are fictional characters. Rose, of course, has a life of her own.

ACKNOWLEDGMENTS

Merrilyn George, historian, Ohakune: her book on the history of the area and her help in ferreting out little-known information has been invaluable.

KiwiRail for their generosity in providing travel and in making available their excellent on-board commentary for the KiwiRail Northern Explorer.

Railway Museum, Ohakune: a little gem beside the railway station at The Junction.

Article in *New Zealand Railfan*, 'Constructing the Great Makatote Viaduct 1905-1908' by Graeme Jupp.

Bill Pierre's book *North Island Main Trunk* is a treasure trove of detail.

Peter Keller's handwritten memoir, held in the National Library, provided insight into daily life during the construction.

Ross Manderson for test-braking information.

Vicky Ellis for early NZR Scale of Charges.

The *Papers Past* website, paperspast.natlib.govt.nz, provides a wealth of information of the era, as do *Te Ara — The Encyclopedia of New Zealand*, (teara.govt.nz) and the Alexander Turnbull Library.

Thanks also to Gillian Tewsley and Harriet Allan for their sensitive editing.

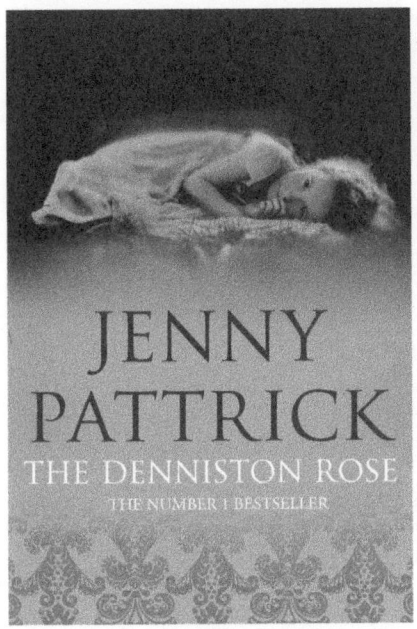

The bleak coal-mining settlement of Denniston, isolated high on a plateau above New Zealand's West Coast, is a place that makes or breaks those who live there. *The Denniston Rose* is about isolation and survival. It is the story of a spirited child, who, in appalling conditions, remains a survivor.

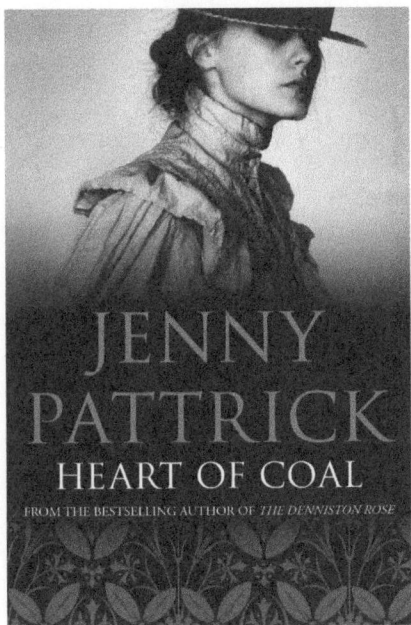

Eighteen years have passed since the child Rose first arrived in Denniston. She has grown into a young woman, intelligent and talented, with an outrageous zest for life … and love.

This is the tale of Con the Brake. A talented and impetuous Faroeman, he finds he cannot escape his past. The novel is set in the Faroe Islands, Denmark and in New Zealand during the land wars.

The lives of the people scattered along the edges of the Whanganui River come together in this vivid and moving story of a stunningly unique place.

After a short stint in prison on trumped-up charges, the loveable simpleton Donny Mac returns to the house left to him by his grandfather. When an accident threatens to put Donny back into prison, he and the Virgin Tracey come up with a solution to cover it up. But can the secret remain hidden?

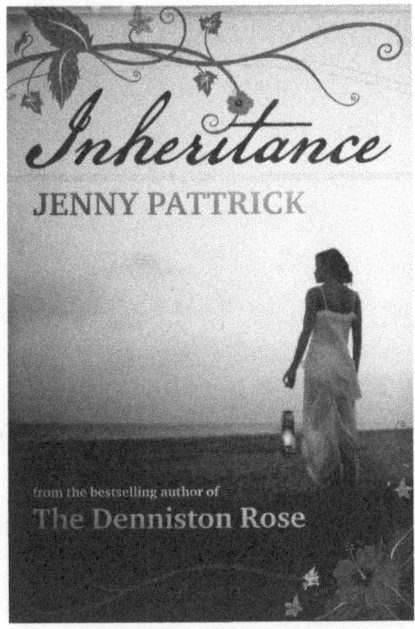

Elena glimpses her friend Jeanie in a New Zealand art gallery twenty-three years since she disappeared in Samoa. What are the secrets she is hiding?

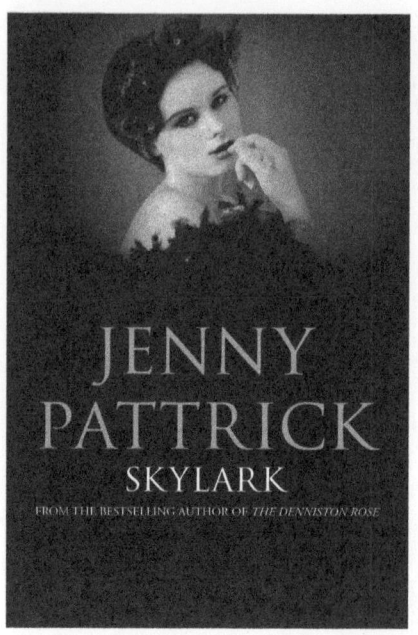

For the little French girl, Lily Alouette, performing became a way of life. A life that those who love her must be prepared to share.

A tender and amusing novel set in the nineties, with the Springbok Tour still a recent memory.